Bowl Off!

By Daniel Landes

Elemar Publishing

Elemar Publishing

profdanl@yahoo.com

Print ISBN: 978-1-956912-23-4
e-Book ISBN: 978-1-956912-11-1

Cover Design by Daniel Landes, Martha Landes,
and Tahomina Mitu

First Edition

Also by Daniel Landes

Hang the Innocent (2022)
www.hangtheinnocent.com

DEDICATION

To my wife, Martha Kemm Landes, for her endless help editing, formatting, and overall production of this book.

To my son, Jeremy Landes, for his editorial feedback and overall storyline suggestions that were spot on.

To my friends, Matthew Toronto, a Los Angeles film director and writer, and his brother, Aaron Toronto, an actor, musician, and writer from Brookings, South Dakota. Your contributions to the story and your continuous efforts to get it made into a film are deeply appreciated.

And finally, to all the bowlers in the world who love the sound of the ball hitting the headpin.

PREFACE

Bowl Off! was originally written as a screenplay set in present-day small-town America. It chronicles the lives of four good friends, who love to bowl and drink beer but struggle to find their way in the adult world.

After several revisions, I decided to write a prequel, which I titled *Gutter Ball.* This origin story takes place ten years earlier when AJ Bowers and his best buds are high school seniors.

So, the novel you are about to read is a compilation of the two screenplays, an expansion of the overall plot, and the addition of several of the characters' backstories.

INTRODUCTION

Several years ago, the Associated Press ran an article about a California couple who, while walking their dog one day, stumbled on a treasure trove of rare coins valued at millions of dollars and buried in the shadow of an old tree. For some reason, this incident resonated with me, and I began to think about how such an unlikely discovery would change a person's life. Based on that premise alone, I began to write *Bowl Off!*

Having grown up in a small Midwestern city, I chose to have my story take place in the fictitious town of Greenvale, Wisconsin, where people's favorite pastime is bowling and the sleepy community's identity comes from the fact that it has a bowling manufacturing company, where almost everyone in town works. Once I established the setting, the story evolved into a tale about lasting friendship and the consequences of the main character putting his dreams on hold. Langston Hughes perhaps says it best in his poem, *A Dream Deferred*:

"What happens to a dream deferred?
Does it dry up
Like a raisin in the sun?
Or fester like a sore—
And then run?
Does it stink like rotten meat?
Or crust and sugar over—
like a syrupy sweet?
Maybe it just sags
Like a heavy load.
Or does it explode?"

PART ONE

High School and Friends

"The bowling alley is the poor man's country club."

Sanford Hansell

Chapter 1

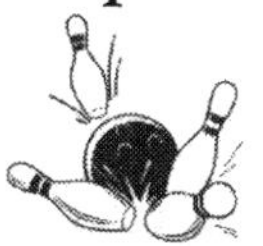

Greenvale High School

A LIME GREEN 1978 FORD PINTO in need of a new muffler but equipped with oversized studded snow tires, roars past a brightly lit sign: *GREENVALE, WISCONSIN – Home of the United States Bowling Corporation and the Tenpin Capital of the World - Pop. 12,209.*

The car slides cattywampus around a corner and speeds down Greenvale's snow-covered Main Street, interrupting the small town's tranquility and rattling several storefront windows. His radio blaring George Thorogood's oldie, *Bad to the Bone*, AJ Bowers sings along as he beats his right hand on the dashboard. "Bad to the bone…"

The Pinto backfires, emits a cloud of black smoke, coughs again, and the car slows to a stop. The dark-haired driver rolls down his window and waves at two middle school boys walking down the street. The teens hesitate and trudge over to the rusty-fendered Pinto, knowing full well what the driver wants them to do. AJ hands them each a dollar bill and the thirteen-year-olds, clad in matching blue hooded parkas, handmade woolen mittens, Green Bay Packer stocking caps, and black rubber high-top overshoes, make their way to the back of the car.

AJ leans out the window and yells, "When I say go, give me all ya got!" The boys shoulder the trunk of his car and push as hard as they can, but the vehicle only moves a few feet. They try again; nothing.

Frustrated, the high school senior jumps out of his Pinto and joins the two boys. With his help, the three manage to get the vehicle moving a little faster. As the underweight boys continue to push, AJ rushes back to his car and hops inside. He pops the clutch, the car sputters, lurches forward, and the motor engages. As the Pinto picks up speed, AJ checks his mirror and sees the boys hunkered down behind his car, hanging on the back bumper for dear life. When AJ rounds a corner, the blond thirteen-year-olds go flying into a snowbank. He checks his rear-view mirror and laughs when he sees them climb out of the snow, brush off their parkas, and refit their frost-covered tuques.

Two blocks down the road, the car backfires again, frightening an elderly couple who are tottering down the street with their tethered Basset Hound. The dog howls and AJ laughs.

When he arrives at school, he can't find a place to park, so he slides his Pinto into the assistant principal's spot, the only remaining space in the parking lot.

The gangly, but strikingly handsome seventeen-year-old, waits as his car shimmies for a few seconds, wheezes, and dies. AJ grabs his custom key ring, fitted with two miniature bowling balls, and vaults out of his Pinto.

Dressed in a green and gold letterman's jacket that has a bowling ball and two white pins with red stripes on the back of it, AJ balances his four books in one hand and his ball bag in the other.

Slipping and sliding, he jogs his way to the three-story brick building, passing a sign: "GREENVALE HIGH SCHOOL - GOOD LUCK WOODCHUCKS AT THE WISCONSIN STATE CHAMPIONSHIPS ON SATURDAY!"

AJ squeezes his way through the front door and enters the senior wing, where he sees a couple making out in front of a locker. The lovebirds separate when they hear AJ approaching, and wipe their mouths. A green-sweatered senior, Dwight Barstow, who is trying to grow a mustache, steps away from his red-headed and his girlfriend, Melissa Springer, who towers over him. "Hey, Bowers, good luck Saturday."

"Yeah, thanks, man. What's your name again?"

"Dwight. We were in the same biology class. You called me Doofus."

"Yeah, right. Doofus. Sorry, I can't chat. Late for class."

Melissa tugs her braided ponytail hanging down from her green stocking cap and smirks. "Bowl on, AJ. Bet ya got some big balls in that bag."

AJ grins. "Yeah, just the one."

Dwight pulls his girlfriend's cap down over her eyes and punches her arm. Melissa yanks up her cap, jabs him back, and scolds, "Oooh! Ya abuser. I was just trying to be nice."

As Dwight gently rubs Melissa's arm, he shifts back to AJ hurrying down the hallway. "Hey, my folks got a cabin in the UP if you ever wanna hang out."

"Yeah…maybe after rolling season's over."

"Fer sure." Dwight grins. "Tell yer folks I said hi."

Melissa slaps her boyfriend on the back. "You don't know his folks...Doofus."

AJ rounds a corner and slides his bowling ball bag down the hallway. He waits for it to come to a stop and tosses his hands in the air like he just threw a strike. He walks over, scoops up his bag, opens the classroom door a smidge, and peeks inside.

Forty-something English teacher and assistant principal, Harold Swenson, finishes writing on a whiteboard: "I am sick when I do look at thee." Act 2, Scene 1, Line 212.

Before his teacher turns back to the class, AJ sneaks through the door and plants himself front and center in the last empty desk in the front row. Several girls giggle as the latecomer slouches down and tries to make himself small.

Mr. Swenson ignores the distraction as he points at the whiteboard and addresses the class. "In *A Midsummer Night's Dream*, why did Demetrius say this to Helena?" A few hands pop up as Swenson turns and spots AJ. "You're late again, Bowers."

"Mr. S., yah know how it is? Had to stop by the little boy's room. Ate some badass pizza last night." A few students begin to laugh, so Mr. Swenson holds up his hand, and they hush.

"Spare us the details. We'll talk after class."

"Gotcha. I'm your monkey."

Mr. Swenson squints, straightens his black-framed glasses, and points to the quotation on the board again. "Back to my question; why did Demetrius tell Helena, 'I am sick when I do look at thee'?"

Buster Shetty, whose East Indian brown skin and jet-black hair make him stand out amongst his mostly Scandinavian- rooted peers, shouts, "Cuz she's a Disney poser and isn't in the same league as him."

"Let me guess, Mr. Shetty, you being a member of the bowling team, I assume your use of the word 'league' is in reference to a bowling league?"

"Yeah, the Demetrius guy probably averages two hundred plus, the Helena chick, not even a hundred."

Marcy Phillips, a short-haired blond with a feisty attitude, pipes up. "Buster's analysis is sexist mansplaining!"

"I ain't sexist, but if I was, I'd have you fetch me my slippers and fix me a sandwich, ya man-rib."

Everyone laughs except for Marcy, who opens the palm of her hand to Mr. Swenson and says, "See there. He a chauvinist rhino-pig!"

Buster gripes. "Keep your eggs in your ovaries, Marcy, and shut the hell up." Several boys celebrate Buster's point of view by tossing wads of paper in Marcy's general direction.

Marcy pivots and takes one last jab. "Maury Povich guests!"

Shane Peterson, a jock wearing his own football jersey, interrupts from the back row. "Hey, Shitty, why don't you shut the hell up!"

Buster yells to the back of the room. "The name's Shetty… number twenty-three!"

"Well, bowler boy, I pronounce it shitty."

"Like I haven't heard that before." Buster hides his middle finger behind his left hand, points it at Shane, and everyone laughs.

Mr. Swenson raps his desk with his pen. "Knock it off, you two. Save the foul language for the football field…and the bowling alley. Now, back to the question? Someone who's actually read the play."

Sam Hill, another one of AJ's close friends and a bowling teammate, raises his hand. Sam is wearing a military green shirt and camo pants. His long blond hair is in a ponytail that reaches the center of his back. Mr. Swenson reluctantly points to Sam, who stands up and salutes his teacher. "Sit down, Mr. Hill." Sam salutes again and takes a seat as Mr. Swenson shakes his head. "Okay, what do you have to say?"

"Yeah, so, here's the thing. H is good lookin' and all, and this D fella can have her if he wants. But D, he don't wanna be a battery-operated boyfriend. Knockin' boots with H would be like stealin' cake from a baby. You see, he doesn't wanna put all his chicks in one basket, but this H gal puts some hot moves on him anyway. Ya know, she thinks the squeaky wheel's gonna get the worm."

Marcy scowls. "So sexist."

Sam wags his head. "Come on Marcy; not that kind of worm. Get your head out of the toilet."

Mr. Swenson smirks. "Mr. Hill, I have to say, you are the king of the mixed metaphor."

"Yeah, I'm a master debater."

Sam laughs at his own joke as Marcy grimaces and says, "Oh my God!"

Mr. Swenson points at a bright-eyed young man with horned-rimmed glasses in the front row. Theodore Ennis, dressed in a white shirt and tie, is destined to be the class valedictorian. "Theodore, can you help a poor English teacher out here?"

The socially awkward nerd sits up in his desk and straightens his glasses. "Of course, Mr. Swenson. You see, Billy Wigglestick..."

"Whoa, whoa, whoa. Did you just say, Billy Wigglestick?"

"It's a pun, sir, in honor of the world's greatest punster. As a tribute to the bard, I shortened his name to Billy and revamped his surname of Shakespeare to wiggle stick."

The class erupts with boos and catcalls as Theodore bows and continues. "But in answer to your question, the subtext here is that Demetrius, in a previous conversation, had rebuked Helena for trying to tempt him with her womanly ways. The specific line you're referencing is an additional reproach in which Demetrius informs Helena he can't possibly hate her any more than he already does. He reiterates this point by telling her that whenever he sees her, it makes him sick."

Mr. Swenson raises his eyebrows. "Excellent textual analysis, Mr. Ennis."

From the back of the room, two t-shirted boys chant, "Anus, anus."

Other students boo and catcall, so Theodore bows again. "Thank you. Thank you very much. I'll be here all day."

AJ raises his hand. "Hey, Teach. "I'm pretty sure that's what Sam already said, only with words we can understand."

Buster pats Sam on the back. "Way to go, Sameo."

Sam throws a real alley shaker and raises his hand in the air. "Boom! Nailed it."

The bell rings signaling the end of class, so Mr. Swenson tosses his pen on his desk. "Don't forget your personal essays are due Monday." He lowers his head and whispers to himself, "And try not to breed any children."

AJ starts to sneak away, but Mr. Swenson waves him over. "You were late again and you bathroom lied to me. You do know I'm the assistant principal in charge of detention?"

"Yeah, the thing is my car stalled on me again."

"That's the third time this week. Hope you don't have any plans for Saturday." AJ avoids eye contact as his teacher continues. "A state bowling tournament perhaps?"

"Cut me some slack, Mr. S. It's my last year."

"Oh, so now I should bend the rules because you're a senior?"

AJ smirks. "Want I should wash yer car?"

"Mr. Bowers, bribery is the lowest form of corruption."

"Well, then, I got nothin'."

Swenson softens. "I'll let it go on one condition. You need to read all of Shakespeare's *A Midsummer Night's Dream* before class on Monday."

"Come on, man. You know I don't understand all his shit talk."

"Language, Mr. Bowers, language."

"Yeah, sorry." AJ thinks long and hard. "Hey, how about we compromise and I read the *Cliff Notes*?"

"Or maybe you can read the entire play during our Saturday morning breakfast club."

"All right, already. Pile it on. Haven't even started my personal essay yet."

"Not my problem. I assigned it two weeks ago. Going to quiz you on the play Monday morning. Now, go...before I change my mind."

SEATED AT A school cafeteria table, AJ is eating lunch with his three best friends and bowling teammates, Buster Shetty, Sam Hill, and Natalie Jones, whom everyone calls Possum. The petite seventeen-year-old, who was born in China, is small in stature but can hold her own with just about anyone. Despite her reputation for being fearless, she hides behind Buster when she sees Theodore coming her way. Theo, a close talker, spots her anyway and leans over his miniature classmate. "So nice to see you, Natalie. Your appearance is exceptionally pulchritudinous, today."

Everyone at the table leans back and chuckles as Possum's face turns beet red. AJ flattens himself back in his chair and says, "Pulch...what?"

Theodore tightens his face. "Not that it's any of your business, but pulchritudinous is a Latin word that means beautiful."

"Then say beautiful," AJ snorts. "Possum ain't Latin."

Theodore shifts his attention back to his crush. "Natalie, I hope you didn't think I was trying to objectify you?"

She scowls. "Go away, you dweeb."

Theodore slumps away as Buster scoots his chair next to Possum. "Hey, is Theo your main squeeze? You two doing the bounce?"

Possum's face sours as she grumbles, "Oh, please. Gag me with a spoonful of tapioca pudding."

Sam pipes up. "Yeah, the guy's a regular walking Mary Webster dictionary."

AJ corrects him. "Merriam, Sam. It's Merriam."

"Don't buzz me with the facts, Leroy. Theodore is an egghead."

"Come on," AJ counters. "Be nice. Theo's our teammate."

Possum doesn't let up. "He's a nerd and a geek. He needed to list a sport to enhance his resume for college"

Buster flips his head. "And why do you think he joined our bowling team?"

In unison, AJ and Sam point at Possum and tease, "Ahh!"

She gives them the finger as Buster changes the subject and says, "Hey, only two days until State."

Sam lifts his hand in the air and Buster yells, "Bowl on!"

They high-five one another and chant. "Uh, uh, uh…Go Woodchucks!"

As everyone at the table leaves, AJ taps Possum on the shoulder. "Hey, you still have the Cliff Notes for *A Midsummer Night's Dream?"*

"No, but the girl with the locker next to mine has them. Want I should borrow them? She has the hots for you."

"Oh, yeah. Who's that?"

"Marcy Phillips."

"You know what? I'll buy my own copy, but how about I pay you to write my personal essay?"

"Hell no. I don't know anything about your creepy shit past."

The bell rings and everyone heads for their fourth-period classes. In the hallway, Harold Swenson exits his room reading a student essay as a bowling ball rolls past, just missing his shoe. He doesn't notice and walks the other way.

FRONT AND CENTER in her classroom, history teacher and bowling coach, Barb Dwyer sorts through her lecture notes. The fifty-something woman is dressed in a white polo shirt and red plaid slacks. Her long blond hair is pulled back in a ponytail, and she's not wearing any makeup.

AJ, Sam, and Buster are slouched in their desks at the back of the room. Possum is sitting in the front row next to a new student, Claudia Giovanni, who is staring straight ahead, trying to avoid any eye contact with anyone near her. She's a pretty girl with shoulder-length black hair, dark brown eyes, and long slender legs. Her V-neck blue sweater and designer jeans accentuate her slim body and suggest she might come from a family with money. As AJ continues to gawk at her, his only thought is that this tan-skinned girl is probably a sun worshiper, the kind who eats shredded wheat and skim milk for breakfast, if she eats breakfast at all.

Mrs. Dwyer clears her throat, undoes the top button of her shirt, steps to her lectern, and addresses her class of twenty seniors. "Before we get started, I want to introduce a new student, who recently moved here from Milwaukee. This is Claudia Giovanni." Several people clap and a few boys, including Buster and Sam, whistle. Claudia's face pales as she stares straight ahead.

AJ scolds Buster and Sam. "Jeeze you two. Flatten out."

Ignoring him, Buster hollers, "Oh, baby!"

Several students laugh as Mrs. Dwyer taps her pencil on her podium and raises her voice. "That's enough. I'm sorry, Claudia. As you can see, we have a few barbarians in this class."

Sam waves his hand. "Hey, Mrs. D. What time we supposed to meet at the bus in the morning?

"Sam, I'm your history teacher right now. But to answer your question, seven am. And don't be late for practice this afternoon. We have a lot of things we need to work on."

Sam salutes. "All right. Semper Fi."

Mrs. Dwyer nods at Claudia. "In case you are wondering, I'm the bowling coach and we have our state tournament on Saturday."

Several students break out in a chant, led by AJ, Sam, and Buster. "Bowl On! Bowl On! Bowl On! Bowl On!"

Mrs. D raises her hands in the air like she's a choir teacher. The class settles down as Claudia squirms in her chair. "All right everyone, turn in your books to page 371. Today, we're going to examine the mysterious diseases of Western Europe."

Two students in the back of the room yell, "Boo!"

Buster, trying to be clever, yells out, "Sick!"

Sam raises his hand but he doesn't wait for Mrs. Dwyer to call on him. "Hey Teach, can we get extra credit if we puke?"

"Very funny, Mr. Hill. Now who can tell me the name of the devastating disease that arrived in Western Europe in 1348?"

No one answers, so Claudia slowly raises her hand. Mrs. Dwyer points at her, and Claudia answers in a low-pitched voice.

"I know I'm new here, but it was the bubonic plague, which people referred to as the Black Death. It's estimated that anywhere from 75 to 200 million people died because of it."

From the back of the room, a boy in a black hoodie, whispers loud enough for everyone to hear, "Suck up."

A few people near her giggle as Claudia adds, "Sorry, I read about it last week in some random book my father gave me."

"No need to apologize, Claudia. I wish all my students would read a random book once in a while."

AJ whispers to himself. "Shit, she's too smart for me."

Chapter 2

Final Practice

THE MARQUEE IN FRONT of the Strike and Spare bowling alley reads: "GOOD LUCK TO THE GREENVALE KEGLERS! BRING US HOME A STATE CHAMPIONSHIP!"

Inside the brown-stucco building, Barb Dwyer watches her three squads practice, each one made up of four Greenvale H.S. bowlers. Front and center is the number one seeded foursome in the state, AJ, Buster, Possum, and Sam.

In the aisle next to them is another four-person squad, as well as Theodore Ennis. Theodore winds up and throws a ball that knocks down one pin. AJ wags his head and says, "Not bad. Only nine left."

The three squads continue to bowl as Barb Dwyer oversees practice. Wearing a bowling shirt with a wolverine on the back, the stoic woman fits a whistle, blows it hard, and lets it fall from her mouth. "Come on people! First ball strikes! Spares are not gonna cut it."

AJ throws a strike on cue as his weather-faced coach beams. "Thatta boy."

Next up, Theodore throws a gutter ball and Mrs. Dwyer shakes her head. "Theodore. Lower your back, arm straight, tighten your wrist, and spin the ball. Good God! How many times do I have to tell you?"

Theodore gives it his best effort, but he ends up looking like a pretzel after he releases the ball. "I know what I'm supposed to do, Mrs. Dwyer. I just can't do it. Sorry."

"Don't be sorry. Do the best you can." Barb blows the whistle again and all thirteen bowlers circle around her. "Okay. Tomorrow's our big day. Get some rest, eat right, and don't put your fingers where they're not supposed to be." Several boys laugh until Barb gives her whistle a quick blast. "We're short-handed this year, so we need all three of our squads to perform well…and for God's sake, don't get sick. No offense, Theodore, but you're our only alternate."

Several of his teammates groan as Theodore forces a smile. "No offense taken, Mrs. Dwyer. I know I suck.

She blows her whistle one more time. "All right. See everyone tomorrow in the parking lot at 7 a.m. sharp. Remember, if you're on time, you're late."

AJ catches up with Mrs. D as she's leaving. "Hey, coach. Can me and my team practice a little longer? We wanna work on a few things."

"Suit yourself, but save something for Saturday."

Coach Dwyer and the other bowlers head for the door as AJ moves over to his three friends. He waits patiently for the rest of the team to exit the building and for the bowling alley manager to disappear in his office. Then he gives a thumbs up and Buster and Sam lay down in the middle of one of the lanes, two feet apart. AJ yells, "We all live and die!" He sizes up his shot and throws a ball between B and S for a strike. They cheer and high-five one another as Buster picks up his ball.

Not to be outdone, Buster spins full circle three times and throws his twelve-pounder down the lane for a strike.

Next, Possum faces the opposite direction, bends over, and throws a ball between her legs. Her ball knocks down all the pins for another strike.

AJ puts a chair twenty feet down the middle of the lane. He steps back, lofts the ball over the chair and down the alley, and his ball knocks down eight pins.

Next up, Possum puts a ball down and shoves it with her foot. The ball slowly travels down the bowling lane and knocks all the pins down. Possum throws up her hands. AJ, Sam, and Buster yell in unison, "Boo ya! Boo ya!"

Sam grabs two balls. The first one he throws has a slow back-spinning action. He tosses the second ball, and it passes the first one and knocks down nine pins. The first ball arrives and completes the spare by tapping down the final pin. They all hoot and holler as AJ slaps Sam on the back.

An hour later, the foursome exits the bowling alley and say their goodbyes as a Dodge minivan pulls up. Buster gawks at the driver, Vanessa Hill, Sam's attractive forty-year-old blond-haired mother. "Ooh, la, la. Sam, yer sister's a real Victoria Secret."

"That's my mother, ya spoon head."

Vanessa peers out the window and winks. Buster blushes and turns to Sam. "Tell your mom I said hi."

"Yeah. Whatever." Sam gets in the car and mother and son drive off.

Buster shifts his attention to Possum. "Hey, is Sam an only child?"

"He's got a younger sister, but she lives with their father in Milwaukee."

"His mom...she's single?"

Possum slugs Buster. "Ick. You perv."

"So, what. I'm mom curious. Shoot me."

AJ moves over. "You shouldn't be thinking about your friend's mother like that, Buster."

"Why not? I'm not hurting anyone."

"Bull shit! It makes Sam feel weird and you know it."

"Does not."

AJ keeps pushing. "Does too."

Buster slaps his bowling bag. "You think you're right and I think I'm right. So what?"

"Let's let our balls decide," AJ growls.

"What?"

"Let's have a bowl off."

Buster raises up. "What the hell is a bowl off?"

AJ has lined up twenty empty beer bottles he found in a trash bin. There are two separate ten-bottle bowling formations sixty feet from where Buster, Possum, and AJ are standing.

AJ and Buster hold their respective balls as AJ explains the rules. "Each of us gets up to two rolls. High scorer wins the argument and the results are final. Buster, you're first up."

"Why am I first?"

"Because I'm the one who came up with this."

Buster swings his arm as he tries to loosen up. Finally, he takes aim and lets it rip. He knocks down nine bottles. Disappointed, he chases down his ball and prepares for his second attempt. He throws a second time and smashes the remaining bottle for a spare.

AJ steps up. "Not bad, not bad." He eyes the beer bottles and lets it fly. His ball curves, hits the head-bottle sweet spot, and they all shatter. AJ walks away as Buster snarls, "Bowl off, my ass."

AJ grins. "I win. Now, don't be lusting after Sam's mother."

Chapter 3

Homework

AJ IS SEATED AT HIS DESK staring at the blank screen of his outdated laptop, trying to write the first sentence of his personal essay. Scattered on the floor are piles of bowling magazines, three bowling bags, two multi-colored bowling balls, and several worn-out pairs of bowling shoes. His bookshelf is lined with championship photos, junior bowling trophies, and blue and red ribbons. He lets out a sigh, cracks his knuckles, and starts to type:

So, here's the scoop. My folks told me I got my start on Valentine's Day, when they got all frisky after finishing off a bottle of Two Buck Chuck. They named me Augustus Julius Bowers, which is a real mouthful, so I go by AJ. It's all kind of confusing, because my dad's name is Augustus too. Why he named me after himself seems pretty narcissistic, if you ask me. Everyone calls him Augie though, so that helps. Hey, Mr. Swenson, do I get extra credit for using the word narcissistic? Anyway, the Julius part of my name comes from my Uncle Julius, my dad's older brother, who lives in our basement. My friend Possum once called him a misanthrope, so I looked the word up and it pretty much describes UJ to a T.

I asked Dad why his folks named them Augustus and Julius and he said his parents fell in love with the names when they were studying the Greeks in high school. Dad and Julius are pretty close. Sometimes, they even share the same bedroom that they call the Snorer's Room because they get to snoring so loud that Mom can't sleep.

My mother's name is Marge, but I never bothered to ask how her parents came up with that name. The only other Marge I know is Marge Simpson, but

Mom was way before her. I don't know, maybe I'll get around to asking her about it sometime.

My folks claim to be Lutherans, but they don't attend church, so I don't go either. If that means I'm going to hell, the way I figure it, I won't be alone. I know that's a crappy attitude to have, so maybe one day I'll get tired of being a sinner and check out a church somewhere.

Dad works in the warehouse at USBC, where he loads bowling balls, pins, and pinsetter machine parts. Hell, half the town works there, including my mother, who is a secretary in the vice president's office. Uncle Julius use to work there, but he got shit canned two years. I've never why, because I don't wanna embarrass anyone.

Dad and Mom still bowl, and even Uncle Julius bowls, although he seems kind of angry at the game after losing his job at USBC. In a rag town like Greenvale, bowling isn't just a sport, it's a way of life. The old-timers around here still call it tenpins. I don't know why. I guess I need to ask.

I've been rolling for a long time. The way Dad tells it, they took me to a bowling tournament when I was four. Between games they let me roll my first ball down the aisle and I scored my first baby with company, a 2-7-8 split.

In grade school, I wore a bowling glove to class every day until my non-bowling principal threatened to expel me if I didn't take it off. I even wore a Brown Bomber junior bowling jersey to bed and dreamt of bowling a perfect game almost every night. When I turned twelve, Mom made me throw the ratty-assed shirt away. I didn't speak to her for three days.

I love everything about the game: the bright lights, the smell of leather shoes and gloves, the shine of varnished lanes, and even the feel of my reactive resin bowling ball as it grips my thumb and fingers.

Whenever I visit a new alley, I check the floorboard oil patterns, look for any cheesecake lanes that might help my score, and try to avoid playing on any graveyard low-scoring lanes. I'm pretty much obsessed with the game. When I turned fourteen, I had one of my friends videotape my approach and shot, so I could study the number of revolutions my ball took from the foul line until it hit the head pin. My arm is getting stronger. I'm what they call a right-handed cranker and my ball hooks to the left.

You probably know this, Mr. S., but this year I was named captain of the Greenvale Woodchucks bowling team and I anchor the best four-person high school squad in Wisconsin. Oh, and I have a 238 average, the highest high school average in the state.

When I'm not reading Shakespeare shit (I know language), my bowling magazines, or checking out the latest bowling ball equipment, I work on my game. Most people, who aren't my friends, think I'm a bowling junkie, but since I might turn professional after I graduate, I need to practice, right? I know this essay is kind of short Mr. S., but that's all the time I've got because I still have to read the play you're making me read.

AJ opens his backpack and removes the Cliffs Notes for *A Midsummer Night's Dream* that he bought on his way home from school.

Later that night, AJ's father, "Augie," and his Uncle Julius are seated at the dining room table ready for dinner. Augie is slender and handsome, whereas his older brother is a shorter and stockier version of himself. Julius, who wears a Milwaukee Brewers baseball cap to cover his balding pate, is a deadbeat who does little to earn his keep.

Both brothers sit up in their chairs when they hear AJ's car backfire in the driveway. Julius centers his cap, stares out the window, and grumbles. "For Christ's sake, Augie, get the boy a new car."

Augie forks his salad. "Why should I? It gets him where he wants to go."

In the kitchen, Marge Bowers, who looks to be in her early 40's, smooths her skirt over her slim frame and walks into the dining room with a platter of meatloaf just as AJ enters the house toting his bowling bag. "You're late, young man."

AJ apologizes by kissing his mother on the cheek. "Long practice. State tournament coming up. You coming UJ?"

"Like I got something better to do."

AJ studies the table. "Yay, meatloaf. I need some ketchup."

He heads for the kitchen as his mother yells, "Wash your hands! You've been handling those grimy balls."

Augie and Julius chuckle and shift in their seats as Marge gives each of them a large helping of meatloaf. "You two get your minds out of the gutter."

With their backs to Marge, the brothers look down at their plates and stare. Augie turns back to his wife and grins. "Looks good, Babe." He nods at Julius. "Any word on the skating rink job?"

"Nah. Probably want someone younger."

Augie adds. "...Or someone who can skate."

Marge tries to soften Augie's comment. "It's a security guard position. You won't actually be on skates, will you, Julius?"

"Hell, I don't know," Julius says. "They say fights break out on the ice sometimes."

Augie chortles. "I'd pay to see you on skates."

Julius stabs his meatloaf. "I use ta could skate."

Augie reacts. "Not true."

"You just don't remember? I played Pee Wee hockey that one year."

"Yeah, goalie. You fell down so much we had to let you wear rubber-soled shoes on the ice."

"Still."

Marge gives her husband the evil eye. "Be nice. Something will come up, Julius."

"Well, If I don't find a job soon, I'm headed back to Mexico.

Augie takes a moment and finally says, "So you know, I'm not going down there again to save your ass."

"Never asked ya to in the first place."

"Yeah, well…you'd still be rotting in that rat-infested jail if I hadn't."

AJ enters from the kitchen carrying a bottle of ketchup and a large pickle jar. His mother spots the half-gallon container and frowns. "AJ, you are not going to put your hand in that jar while we're having dinner. Why do you do that anyway?"

Augie gives his son a stern look. "You heard your mother, not while we're eating."

AJ puts the jar on the floor next to his chair as everyone shakes their heads. AJ explains. "So, here's the dealio. Nolan Ryan soaked his hand in pickle juice between games. It rehydrates and toughens the skin."

Julius begins to pray, so AJ, Marge, and Augie lay down their forks and close their eyes. "Lord, bless this food we're about to eat and thank you for a sister-in-law who is willing to cook for three unruly but grateful men." Julius opens his eyes and winks at Marge.

Augie closes his eyes again and adds to his brother's prayer. "…And Lord, help my brother Julius here find a job. It's been too long. I mean, we're tired of him sponging off us." He opens his eyes and laughs.

Marge wags her finger at her husband. "Augie, stop. That's not funny. Julius, you know you're always welcome in our home."

Augie clenches his teeth, makes sure AJ and Marge aren't watching, and gives his brother the finger. Augie closes his eyes again. "P.S., Lord, you know I'm only kidding about my brother. Now as far as AJ here, please help him on Saturday to bowl as well as I did at his age, or at least as well as his uncle or mom. Amen."

AJ throws a biscuit at his father. Julius winds up to throw his, but thinks better of it and takes a bite out of it instead.

Augie and Julius are still sitting at the dining room table, but now they're smoking matching meerschaum pipes. AJ, who has a smaller cherrywood pipe in his mouth, is seated on the floor across from them soaking his right hand in the large pickle jar.

Julius nods. "Doesn't that make your hand stink?"

"Yeah, pretty much."

Marge comes in from the kitchen and sees her son with his hand the jar. "Can't believe you soak your hand in pickle juice."

"I told ya, it gives me a better finger grip and a faster thumb release. It works."

"Pickle juice?" Marge puckers her lips and goes back in the kitchen.

Julius lowers his pipe. "Maybe if ya don't wash your hand, you'll throw off the other team." Augie laughs as AJ's uncle asks, "Hey, you gonna play baseball in the spring?"

AJ blows a ring of smoke. "I can curve a bowling ball, but I can't hit a curveball. Think I'm gonna stick to bowling."

Julius pontificates. "Yeah, that's one thing 'bout bowling; it's you, the ball, and ten pins. That's it. Knock them down, beers all around. Leave them standing, ya got no one to blame but yourself."

AJ's father turns serious. "Bowling's all well and good, but ya need to pick yourself a college, graduate, and find you a good job."

"I wanna be a professional bowler."

Julius adds, "Being a professional bowler is a real long shot."

"But I really don't think I'm cut out for college."

Marge walks in from the kitchen again and sits down as Augie continues. "You don't get it, son. No one's cut out to do anything. That's why you go to college…to find your way."

"You never went to college."

"And look at me. I work at a bowling factory for God's sake."

Marge chimes in. "You sell a life insurance policy…once in a while."

"I haven't sold one in six months."

She pats her husband on the leg. "We do all right, Augie."

"Marge, you sell Tupperware and Avon so's we can make our house payment."

AJ squirms in his chair. "So where would I even get the money to pay for college?"

Augie stands up, slams his pipe down on the table, and hustles into the kitchen. "How the hell do I know?"

AJ changes the subject. "The tournament starts at eleven in the AM, tomorrow morning."

Augie comes out of the kitchen and grumbles as he opens a can of beer. "Yeah, we'll be there!"

Chapter 4

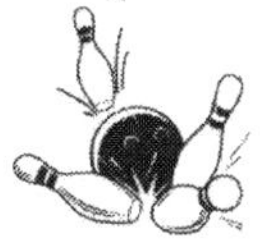

AJ Speaks His Mind

BUSTER, SAM, POSSUM, AND I MET in Mrs. Hazel Service's first-grade classroom at Lombardi Elementary. The four of us were put in the lowest-level reading group, and Mrs. Service allowed us to come up with our own name, so we called ourselves "The Butterballs." I guess it was because we all liked turkey. Anyway, we were terrible readers; Buster stuttered so much, we would all say his words before he could finish; Sam, he'd freeze up when he didn't know a word and stop reading altogether. Possum, who we called Possum back then, spoke so softly that no one could hear what she was saying. Our teacher would pester her to speak louder, but the more she badgered her, the softer Natalie's voice got.

Mrs. Service would always say, "Natalie, a little bit louder."

Natalie would simply lower her voice even more and whisper something like, "The duck walked into the pond and began to swim."

Mrs. Service would lean forward and say, "We still can't hear you, dear."

After a few more do-overs, all we could see were Possum's lips moving and hear her take an occasional breath. I don't know if reading in front of people traumatized her or if she was just stubborn, but Mrs. S would finally throw up her hands and move on to the next reader, which was usually me.

I didn't understand it at the time, but my problem was decoding words. I'd read from right to left instead of left to right and say, "deb" when the word was "bed." Sometimes, I'd get so frustrated that I'd make up words that weren't even there. Instead of saying, "The duck liked to swim in a lake," I'd say, "The duck jumped in the lake and got bit by a snake."

Later, when I got to middle school, some specialist told my mom I had dyslexia. Funny thing is, once I found out there was a reason for me not being able to read very well, I got better at it. The problem is, by the time I got to high school, I hardly read anything, other than the shit my teachers forced me to read.

I've never been very interested in school unless you count gym class, where I got to move around, and the occasional art class, where I got to dip my hands in finger paint, roll out some clay, and sniff Elmer's glue.

Always the class clown, I spoke out of turn and poked and prodded my classmates. One time, I even pulled the fire alarm to see what would happen. Mrs. Service accused me of doing it, but I never turned myself in.

Whenever Mrs. S got tired of putting up with my shenanigans, she'd move my desk away from the other kids and put me in a corner by myself, not far from her. A few weeks would pass, and she'd allow me to move back into the regular formation, but I always ended up back in my corner by the end of the day.

A few years later, after I took an interest in bowling, everything changed. My parents and teachers suddenly had a bargaining tool. The principal and my folks got together and told me that if I didn't behave myself in school, I wouldn't be allowed to bowl. Although I still maintained my reputation as the class clown, I only acted out when my teachers weren't looking and used my two friends to do a lot of the dirty work I could no longer do myself.

For example, in the fifth grade, I talked Sam and Buster into pulling a prank on our teacher, Mrs. Watson. The way I remember it is this: We were on our way home from school, and I tossed a snowball and hit Buster in the shoulder. I said, "You still got that rat?

He wiped the snow off his coat and said, "Yeah. Why?"

"I wanna pull a trick on old lady Watson."

"I ain't putting Felix in no danger."

"Don't be a chickenshit," I said. "He'll be fine. I got it all worked out."

Sam chimed in. "The last time you worked something out, my parents grounded me for a week."

"Me too, and you got nothing," Buster added.

"That's cuz I was smart enough to keep my mouth shut." After a few more tries, I finally convinced Buster to bring Felix to school. When the class emptied for recess and after Mrs. Watson shooed everyone outside, we hung back and hid Felix in her top desk drawer. Then, we waited all day for her to open it.

A few minutes later, just before the final bell, she finally heard Felix scratching. She slowly opened her desk drawer, peeked inside, and screamed like a banshee. "Ahh! Everyone out of the classroom.! Go now! Go home!" Happy to get out of school early, we all ran out of the room giggling and laughing, Mrs. Watson a step behind us. After everyone cleared out, the three of us doubled back into the classroom, where Buster opened Mrs. Watson's desk drawer, scooped up Felix, and hid him down the front of his pants.

As we tiptoed out the door, we saw Mrs. Watson and our principal, Mr. Todd, headed our way. Mr. Todd spotted us and pointed. "You three…back in the classroom…now!"

We stood back with Mrs. Watson as Mr. Todd slowly opened the desk drawer, only to find that it was filled with pencils, paper clips, and other odds and ends.

He shook the drawer as our teacher stepped forward. "I don't see anything, Katherine."

Mrs. Watson scrunched up her face. "It was right there. I saw it chewing that eraser."

Mr. Todd removed the pink eraser and looked it over like it was a diamond ring. "Could be. Seems to be a small piece missing."

"It was big and white and had a long tail."

Our principal put the eraser back in the drawer and turned and glared at us. "All right….boys? Where's the rat?"

I looked at Sam and Buster and said, "What rat?"

Mr. Todd stuck out his lower lip and growled. "Follow me."

We spent the next thirty minutes in Mr. Todd's office denying everything as Buster tried his best to control the movement in his crotch. I got kind of cocky and even suggested that Mrs. Watson was probably having a bad day. After all, she was the only one who claimed to have seen a rat. Having no evidence, Mr. Todd finally let us go home.

When we were a safe distance from school, Buster fished Felix out of his pants and started rubbing his junk. "I think he ate a hole in my underwear."

Sam and I laughed, and I said, "You're lucky he didn't chew off one of your balls."

That same school year, the three of us were walking down a side street on a snowy day in December, just before Christmas break. It was a Saturday, so we had the whole day to ourselves. For some reason, we had dressed in similar clothes: blue denim jeans and the long-sleeved hooded blue sweatshirts we had gotten for playing junior league touch football. From a distance, we probably looked like triplets.

Bored out of our minds, we decided to stand on a street corner and chuck snowballs at passing cars. Our plan was always the same. If one of our snowballs hit a car, the driver would usually slow down, roll down his or her window, and cuss at us. A few times after we tossed a snowball at what we called a 'repeat customer', the driver, almost always a man, would get out of his car and chase us down the street. He'd follow us for half a block or so, huffing and puffing, and slipping and sliding in leather loafers. Then he'd stop, bend over, suck in freezing air, and cough like he had lung cancer. Sometimes in one final fit of rage, he'd flip us the bird or call us assholes as we disappeared in the distance.

When the occasional "in shape" driver would chase us further than half a block, the game got that much more exciting, cuz we had the opportunity to show off our running and hiding skills. We would always gauge the speed of our chaser and teasingly weave our way in and out of the evergreens that lined the streets. Our winter game of "throw and go" was really just another version of hide and go seek.

After spending an uneventful hour heaving snowballs at unsuspecting motorists, our arms got tired, so we decided to go home. At the last moment, a black Chevy pickup crept around the corner, so Sam took careful aim and fired one last ball. He aimed it at the driver's side window as usual. The window of the truck was open, and the snowball missed the driver. However, the snowball traveled through the interior of the truck and smashed up against the passenger side window. I gawked at Sam and Buster as if to say, "We're in big trouble now."

The driver swerved and pulled his vehicle to the side of the road. Next, in what seemed like slow motion, he reached his left arm out of his window and placed a red flashing light on the roof of his truck. We all froze until I broke the silence and yelled, "He's a cop!"

We ran off in three directions, all of us desperate to find a place to hide. Headed for home, I ran down an alley, where I saw the Hellerman's garage. I opened the side door, slipped inside, and hid behind a snowblower. Just as I was getting comfortable, I heard the crunching of snow on the other side of the door. I curled into a ball and tried to make myself small as Sam and Buster stumbled inside. Sam spotted me behind the blower and whined, "He's after us."

I uncurled myself and sat up. "Who is?"

“The cop; he’s right behind us," Sam moaned.

I panicked. "We’re all going to jail!" Sam stared blankly at me as if he didn’t know the answer to a test question. I’ll never forget watching his skin turn pale, like the *Cream of Wheat* my grandmother used to make me eat whenever I went to visit her.

Desperate, I broke out of my trance and made a mad dash for the door. As I made my exit, my heart in my throat, I caught a glimpse of the plain-clothed off-duty policeman making his way down the alley and coming my direction. No more than thirty feet away, a tall cop was following the tracks Sam and Buster left in the fresh snow. When he looked up, he gave me this toothy grin like he had mistakenly walked into someone’s bedroom. He narrowed his eyes and pointed his right hand at me. “Stop right there, mister! You’re in deep doo-doo!”

I turned, ran five steps, and leaped head-first over a three-foot barbed wire fence that circled the garden behind old lady Goodman’s house. I landed softly in the snow and somersaulted to my feet. Then, I ran through the garden and rolled over the barbed wire fence a second time. As I climbed over the concrete wall separating the Goodmans’ front yard from the back, I heard the cop breathing hard behind me. As I was about to jump to the ground, I spotted my pursuer straddling the wire fence that I had managed to jump over earlier. Too scared to laugh, I watched as he tried to free his pants from the wire. When he finally looked up, he spotted me. As I ran off, I heard him scream, “You’d better run, you little shit!”

Once I reached the Goodmans’ front yard, I made a right turn and ran directly down Eleventh Street past the spot where Sam had launched his perfect snowball. With the cop nowhere in sight, I wondered if the Goodmans had seen me, but then I remembered they had gone to Arizona for the winter.

After I stopped breathing hard, I crossed the street and hid behind some raspberry bushes in the back alley of Old Lady

Cooperman's house. A few minutes passed, and I saw the cop's black pickup, red lights flashing, making its way slowly down the alley. As I peered through the thin branches of the bushes, I saw the policeman lean out his passenger-side window surveying both sides of the alley. As he drove past, he turned and stared at the bush where I was hunkered down. I made myself even smaller and held my breath until he was a safe distance away.

A few seconds later, I climbed out of the bushes and dusted off the snow that had caked itself on my pants and sweatshirt. With the truck nowhere in sight, I circled back to the Hellerman's garage. I started to open the side door, but I hesitated as I imagined Sam and Buster still in the garage, wearing handcuffs, as the policeman stood next to them.

Instead of going inside, I circled the garage carefully, still fearful that the pickup might come roaring down the alley. I made my way to the window at the rear of the garage. What I hoped to see was my friends hidden in a corner somewhere, but the garage was empty. I panicked again as I pictured them under a bright light in a smoke-filled detective's office, naming me as their accomplice. In my head, I heard two distinct voices, "All right, Mr. Hill, did you throw that snowball or was it AJ Bowers?"

Next, I imagined Sam saying, "Yeah, Bowers threw it, and I know where he lives."

When I got home, I was pretty sure I was gonna find a pissed-off cop in torn pants, sitting in the living room in my father's La-Z-Boy. Not hearing anyone upstairs, I crept down the steps to Uncle Julius's bedroom, where I hung out for what seemed like an hour. Finally, I heard my parents and UJ walking around upstairs, so I figured they probably had just got home from one of those farm auctions they like to go to. Anyway, I stayed put a while longer, waiting for UJ to come downstairs.

Ten minutes later, the upstairs phone rang. I listened hard, but all I could hear was the faint murmur of my mother's soft voice. Finally, the door leading to the stairs opened and my mom yelled, "AJ! Are you down there? Buster is on the phone; he wants to talk to you."

Relieved it wasn't the police, I hollered, "Okay, I'll be right up!"

I shuffled up the stairs and into the kitchen and my mother gave me this curious look like she knew I had done something wrong. I picked up the phone resting on the counter and waited for Mom to leave the room. When she finally did, I whispered. "Hello."

Buster spoke just loud enough for me to hear him. "AJ, where did ya go?"

Still trying not to raise my voice, I said, "That cop almost snagged me. What happened to you two?"

"We waited for you in the garage, got bored, and went home."

"You idiots stole my hiding spot!" I slammed the phone down as my mother walked back in the room. She raised her eyebrows, probably surprised by what she heard, but didn't say a word.

It wasn't until I saw Buster and Sam the next day that I figured out that the policeman who chased us probably got confused by our look-alike clothing. The way I figured it, he must have seen Buster and Sam enter Hellerman's garage after I had gone inside. Then as he was closing in on my goofball friends, I had come rushing out wearing the same-colored blue sweatshirt and jeans Buster and Sam had on. For some reason, the cop must have decided to chase me instead of going into the garage where Buster and Sam were holed up. My buds had simply waited for a few minutes and walked away from the garage without a hitch.

The three of us have had several other encounters with danger over the years, but we always managed to escape the scene of our crimes undetected. I hate to admit it, but we even threw Mrs. Smith's three-legged calico cat named Winston in a hornet's nest just to see how fast he could run on three legs. We thought it was hilarious when Winston leaped from the hornet's nest screeching and snarling. In a furious hobble, the cat made three laps around a woodshed with hundreds of hornets in direct pursuit.

I know that was a cruel thing to do, but we were idiots back then. The three of us really love animals. I guess that's why I donate fifty bucks to the Greenvale dog and cat shelter every year…to ease my guilt over what I did to poor Winston.

We were also fruit and veggie thieves. We stole raspberries, crab apples, carrots, and rhubarb out of our neighbors' yards. Actually, stealing crab apples from old man Hedges' trees was quite risky, considering the rumor that he owned a shotgun loaded with salt pellets and that he wasn't afraid to use it.

All winter long, when the roads were good and icy, we enjoyed "hooking" cars, which is the suicidal practice of grabbing an automobile's back bumper and crouching down out of the view of the driver. When the car would drive off, we would hang on for dear life. We would slide along, like skiers with no skis, all the way across town or as far as we wanted to go. Quite often, the three of us would hitch ourselves onto the same car. Our joyride would almost always end when we would hit a dry patch in the road, which would send us head over heels across the pavement.

Somehow, we survived and even learned to control our behavior enough so our parents and even a lot of our teachers thought we were normal kids. Truth is, I don't really want to be normal. Anytime I hear the word, I always think of the doofus, Igor, from the movie, *Young Frankenstein,* who brought the doctor a damaged brain he found in a jar labeled, "Abnormal", claiming it must have belonged to some woman named, Abby Normal.

The thing is, we had a common goal. We wanted to be great bowlers. So, we polished our balls and our skills and now that we are seniors, we are three-quarters of the best high school bowling foursome in the state of Wisconsin. Oh, and that first-grade quiet reader, Natalie Jones? She's our fourth. Sometime along the way, she started calling herself Possum. None of us knew why at the time, but we went with it.

Chapter 5

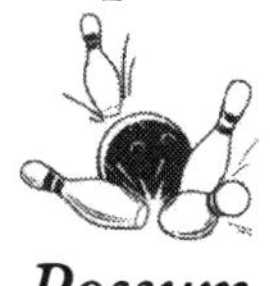

Possum

NATALIE LOUISE JONES IS THE NAME on my birth certificate, and I pretty much hate it. Most people call me Possum. I'll tell you why later.

I'm a shortie. As a matter of fact, I'm real short. I've been called a munchkin, Tater Tot, half-pint, little bit, and even a hobbit. I stopped growing in the fourth grade. I kept measuring myself, but it always turned out the same, five foot even; four eleven in my bare feet. I'm what you might call a woman in progress, a real unicorn. The truth is, I didn't join the Blood of the Month club until my junior year. Not your typical Wisconsinite for sure, because when I was a baby, my so-called parents adopted me straight out of China. Don't know why they picked me, but to be honest, I think they would have sent me back if they could have.

So, here's the thing. I live in this crappy single-wide in a rundown trailer park with my mom, who drives her boyfriend's rusted-out Honda Civic that only runs half the time. My so-called life has been chaotic from day one, and I don't really have a stable of friends, except for my bowling buddies, AJ, Sam, and Buster. I don't care much for girls and spend a lot of time wishing I wasn't one. I have a lot of glitches in my life and for a long time, I thought life wasn't fair, but as my friend Sam always says, "A fair is where even a pig gets a blue ribbon." Kind of makes sense if you think about it.

If you were to ask my classmates, they would probably label me anal, because I like to finish my work right away. I figure that makes me a ducks-in-a-row kind of gal, not one of those so-called multi-taskers who end up taking longer to finish their work than I do. I get plenty of sleep, but I'm a real night owl and love to read murder mysteries in the middle of the night.

This might sound like a brag, but I'm in the gifted program and am a real whiz at math and science. I know what you're thinking: a real Asian stereotype. I'm not interested in any of the macho sports, but I do love to bowl. Our high school team has a good chance of winning State this year, and I'm kind of proud, because I have the highest average of any of the high school girl bowlers in Wisconsin, and it's only twenty points lower than AJ Bowers' average. I know I'm bragging again, but we live in a scorecard world.

Another thing about me is I'm a half-time cynic and a fifty percent romantic. The romance part of me is pretty much dormant, which is just as well, because I don't want no guys sniffing around me. And of course, there's Theodore Ennis. He's got a real thing for me, but all he does is annoy the hell out of me. Whenever the ostentatious creep walks into a room, he acts like he's some kind of big deal. He's so pretentious that no one likes him…including me. He's all the time flaunting his intelligence…like last week he called me a stoic. I hate to admit it, but he's kind of got me pegged right on that one. I really am someone who suffers more in my mind than in reality, but I sure don't want it from some pompous dweeb.

Theodore and I do share one thing in common though: we're real logophiles. Go ahead and look it up. It's not as bad as it sounds. Anyway, I'll never tell Theodore any of this shit. He already thinks he's God's gift to the world.

That kind of tells you why I hang out with Sam and Buster. Most of the time they're pretty stupid and don't care what I think. Best thing is they tolerate me, because I can get pretty overheated.

Whenever I get home from bowling practice, I pretty much always find my mom's 40-year-old boyfriend, Troy, laying on our green sofa watching some Monster Truck show and drinking cheap beer. He's usually wearing a wife-beater shirt, dirty jeans, and a filthy "Old Milwaukee Beer" cap. A few months ago, I began writing an anthropological study on him for my biology class but I ran out of things to say in the first paragraph.

Anyway, it's Friday, the night before our state bowling tournament, and when I walk through the door of what my mom calls our manufactured home, I find Troy laying on the couch. But this time he's watching some lame soap opera. When he hears me, he sticks out his beer belly like he's proud of it, belches, and crumples his beer can. He tosses it on our orange shag carpet and grumbles, "Hey, mini-mouse, fetch me a brewski out of the fridge, will ya?" I give the scumbag the evil eye, but he doesn't give up. "All right, princess, would you please, pretty please, get me a beer."

I ignore him, plop down in our worn-out red La-Z-Boy, and open my book bag. "You don't have the bubonic plague, get it yourself."

"What the hell? Bubonic plague? Come on. I've had a bad day."

"You have no job. How bad can it be?" The thing is, I will dance with anyone on any subject, except with Troy, because he's a pompous ass and constantly irritates me.

Troy scratches his stomach and snarls, "Smart ass!" He gets up and wobbles to the refrigerator. He pops the tab of his beer can, staggers back to the couch, and drops back down. "Got it myself!"

"Aerobic activity! Glad to help!"

Troy whispers loud enough for me to hear. "Bitch." Then

what does the idiot do? He lifts his arm in the air and sniffs his armpit. I grimace as he removes his cap, and runs his hand through his greasy hair. He takes a moment, rubs both armpits with his oily fingers, and takes another drink.

Disgusted by what I just saw, I head to my room at the back of the trailer. I plop down on my twin-sized bed with the Star Wars bedspread that I've had since the third grade and grab a book out of my backpack. Bored to death, I start reading yet another Agatha Christie, "whodunit" novel. My motto is if you want a new idea, read an old book. Anyway, my mind drifts off as I think about going to the bowling championship in Milwaukee in the morning. Like I said, we got ourselves a championship team.

AJ, Buster, Sam, and I have been bowling together since the fourth grade. At first, they weren't too happy having a girl on their team, but they got over it when I started knocking down more pins than both Sam and Buster. Like I said, AJ is our best bowler for sure, and to tell you the truth I kind of have a crush on him. Always have, since the first grade on. But he doesn't know it. Nobody knows but me. To quote Chuck Berry, "He's a brown eyed handsome man." I guess that's one of the only things I like about being human...having a few secrets. Even though he treats me like one of the guys, he always protects me from any yahoos who try to give me the business about being a shorty with slanted eyes. I know he never thinks about me like I'm some kind of girly girl, but that's okay, because having those kinds of feelings would probably ruin our friendship and both our bowling averages.

The real key to opening my crypt is a sense of humor and AJ has plenty of that to spare. One last thing that's kind of weird. I have this recurring dream, where I'm dressed like a black-and-white nun and AJ is dying. He recovers fast, tries to cop a feel, and that's when I always wake up in a sweat. I catch myself thinking about it again, so I try to concentrate on my book. But here's the sitch. Usually by the fifth chapter, I figure out who the killer is. This time it's the third chapter, so I toss it aside, and start for the kitchen to get-who knows-what to eat.

When I pass Troy, still parked on the couch, he stops snoring like maybe he just died. As if I could be so lucky. Anyway, I watch him for a few seconds until he snorts back up again. He rolls over on his back, fondles his crotch, and groans. Grossed out, I change my mind about eating something, grab my backpack, and head back to my room.

A few minutes later, I hear the toilet flush and the sound of Troy's clunking feet coming my way. There's a rap on my door, so I reach down, remove my ten-pound Brunswick from its bag and put it in bed next to me. I close my eyes and wait. A few seconds later, I hear the door open and Troy whisper, "Ya playing possum, Possum?"

Yeah, so that's how I got the name Possum. It started when I was a little girl, just after I started school. Whenever I felt like I was in any kind of danger, I'd pretend I was asleep…kind of like one of those fainting goats. I guess it's a survival thing or something. Years ago, when my so-called dad would slap my mom around, I'd close my eyes and not open them until they stopped screaming.

That was about the same time that Frankie Tyson and his younger brother, Jerry, used to constantly bully me after school. One time, I improvised and dropped to the ground and shut my eyes like I was dead. It must have scared them because when I opened my eyes, they were long gone.

So back to creepy Troy, who standing at my door. I watch as he takes a step forward. I panic, reach under my covers, and slide my three fingers into my bowling ball. Saved by the bell, we both hear the front door open and my mom holler, "Where's everybody?"

Troy does a quick one-eighty and trots down the hall, while I take a deep breath and push my ball aside. From the living room, I hear Mom say, "What's going on back there?"

I exit my room, sneak halfway down the hallway, and listen as Troy tries to explain himself. "Nothin'. Lookin' in on Possum is all."

"Why you checking on my daughter?"

"Hell, I don't know. Makin' sure she's still alive, I guess. Get a lot of tips, did you?"

I hear what is probably my mother kicking an empty beer can across the room. "Not enough to pay for all the damn beer you've been drinking!"

"Wow! You're in a bitchy mood."

"Been on my feet all day. How about you? You look for a job today?"

"Maybe."

"Maybe?"

There's a moment of silence until I hear Troy's voice get all snarky. "Or maybe not."

Still hidden in the hallway, I can almost see my mom giving Troy the middle finger. "So, you've just been lying around all day drinking my beer?"

"Don't be bustin' my chops."

The next thing I hear is Mom walking into the kitchen, opening the refrigerator, and slamming it shut. "Would it have killed you to leave me one?"

"It was a long day."

I walk into the living room, just in time to see my bleach-blond mom in a pink restaurant uniform, pull a twenty out of her pocket and toss it to Troy. "Go buy some more."

Troy tosses it back. "Buy it yourself, Amber. I ain't yer friggin' boy toy."

My mother, who all the time smells like fried food, gives Troy the finger and growls, "Watch yer mouth, Mister. This is my place you're slumming at. And for your information, you're about as far from being a boy toy as you can get."

She looks more tired than usual, as she kicks another beer can across the room, grabs her coat, and starts for the door. Having not even acknowledged my presence, she flips around and sneers at me like she wishes I'd take a hike and never come back. "Warm up that stew I made yesterday. I'll be back in twenty minutes."

She slams the front door behind her, but Troy quickly opens it, steps out on the porch, and yells, "Amber!" Mom doesn't answer, so Troy tries again. "Get some smokes and badger lottery tickets, them scratch-off kind."

I glare out the kitchen window and watch as my mom gives Troy the finger again as she approaches the Honda.

"You wish. Hey, nice ass."

Mom wiggles her butt as she strides off. She crawls in her car, parked next to Troy's pickup, and struggles to get it started as usual. The engine finally turns over and she drives off, blue smoke coming from the tailpipe.

I move away from the kitchen window and watch as Troy steps back in the trailer, slogs his way back in the living room, and plunks his butt down on the couch. I turn on the stove, remove a bowl of beef stew from the fridge, put it in a cake pan, and shove it in the oven. I head back to my room, but stop when I get to Troy. "Tell Mom I'm not hungry and going to bed early."

Troy grabs my arm and gives me a weird grin. "Need for me to tell you a bedtime story?"

"Gross!" I yank my arm free and give him a dirty look. "Don't touch me, you perv. I got a weapon in my room, and I'm not afraid to use it."

"You do not."

"Open my door again and you'll find out.

Technically, I was lying about having a weapon, but when I got to my room, I laid down on my bed again and put my bowling ball under the covers.

The next morning, I put on my team bowling jersey and my stretchy black pants. I exit my room dressed in my blue team parka, carrying my bowling ball bag all fancy like I'm off to Europe. I soft step my way down the hallway and sneak past Troy, asleep on the couch.

When I reach the kitchen, I'm kind of surprised to see my mom. She's dressed in her raggedy-ass pink robe and sitting at our small kitchen table. I watch as she takes a drag from her cigarette and sucks up the last of her beer.

She knows I'm standing there, but she doesn't bother to look up, so I pour myself a cup of coffee. She finally raises her head and I notice her cheek is black and blue. She puts her hand to her face and grumbles, "Where ya going? It's Saturday."

"State bowling tournament in Milwaukee. I told you."

"When you be home?"

"When it's over."

"Don't be a smart ass."

"Probably late tonight." I open the refrigerator, but all I see is beer. "There's no food in here?"

"I get paid Monday. Have a beer."

I nod at Troy. "So, when's that asshole gonna contribute?" I put a can of beer in my pocket and wait for Mom's reaction.

"Watch yer mouth. He's been looking for a job."

"Kinda hard to find one laying in a prone position all day. Is he looking for a sleep study job?"

"You don't like Troy, do you?"

"What's there to like?"

"Well, he's all I got. I know he has a mean streak, but he can be a lot of fun too. Truth is, I wish he'd find a middle ground."

"You're not Goldilocks, Mom. He's never gonna be just right."

"What are you talking about?"

After my failed attempt at a literary allusion, I touch my mother's cheek, and she brushes my hand away. "He do that?" She doesn't answer. "He really is an asshole, Mom."

She jumps up and yells, "I don't need you shit-talking my man!"

I don't back off. "Your Rip Van Winkle boyfriend is sleeping here, and I don't even know his last name?" She doesn't say anything, so I wait.

"It's Hanky…Troy Hanky. Now, go on! Get the hell out of here!"

"Before I do, I have a question. Why did you adopt me?"

As my so-called mom lights another cigarette, she says, "It was your father's idea, not mine. I never wanted kids. It's not my fault he ran off with big ass Sheila Klitsky."

"Why didn't he take me with him?"

"You really wanna know?"

"Yeah, I think I deserve to know."

"You don't deserve shit." She sits back down, takes a gulp of beer, and matter-of-factly says, "Y'know at Christmas when someone gets a new puppy and it's all cute and cuddly? The thing is, ya gotta feed it, clean up all its shit, and it chews up all yer shoes?"

"Let me get this straight. Are you comparing me to a dog?"

"What I'm trying to say is you're lucky your so-called father didn't take ya. Knowing Bill, he probably would have left you on the side of the road somewhere."

"Yeah, well thanks. I got it. My self-esteem is much better now. Hope my rabies shots are up to date."

"What?"

I remove the can of beer from my pocket, and pop it open. When I reach the door, I raise the can in the air, and holler, "Thanks, for the swell breakfast, Mommy dearest."

I slam the door shut, but from inside the trailer I hear her yell, "It ain't easy bein' yer mother, Possum!"

Chapter 6

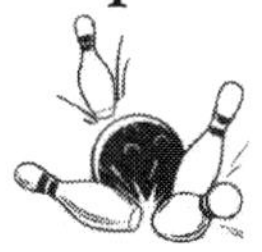

More Than Bowling

ON A FRIGID SATURDAY MORNING thirteen members of Greenvale High's bowling team huddle together in the school parking lot. They are all wearing matching blue parkas and white beanies, clutching their ball bags, and waiting for Coach Dwyer and the team bus.

Theodore approaches Possum smiling, gets a little too close, and she hops back like she just spotted a snake. Undeterred, he pontificates, "December in Wisconsin is the worst. An Arctic front moved in last night and the high today is only supposed to reach eight degrees. With the wind chill, we might see twenty-five below zero."

"You know, Theo," Possum says, "I'm really not in the mood for one of your shitty weather reports."

Theodore lifts his head, makes an abrupt pivot, and trots away as AJ slides over next to Possum. "You okay?"

"Oh, my God. I hate my life."

"Why? Cuz Theodore thinks he's a meteorologist?"

"No, because I'm nothing but black-top white trash."

"What? You are not."

"Here are the facts. I live in a tin can with my redneck mother and her Neanderthal boyfriend."

"At least you don't have their DNA. What'd they do this time?"

"Nothing. That's the problem. All they do is sit around all night and argue, drink beer, and smoke cigarettes."

"Speaking of beer, I kinda smell it on your breath?"

"Yeah, breakfast of champions."

Coach Dwyer finally arrives in a white mini-bus and everyone scrambles on board. As AJ and Possum walk down the aisle, two sophomore boys begin to chant, "Bowl on! Bowl on!"

Possum growls, "Knock it off, you idiots." The boys scoot back in their seats, afraid she might hit them.

While AJ, Possum, Sam, and Buster make their way to the back of the bus, Theodore takes a seat across from Coach Dwyer, who scowls at him, suggesting he doesn't belong there. "Don't you dare tell me how to drive, Theodore."

"Oh no, ma'am. I only got my learner's permit last week."

Theodore can't help himself as he spies on Possum. She catches him gawking her way and growls, "What are you staring at shit face?"

He spins around as Mrs. Dwyer adjusts her mirror and yells, "Language, Possum!"

Theodore looks at his coach for sympathy. There's no response, so he says, "Though she be but little, she is fierce."

Mrs. D starts the bus's engine and says, "Did you make that up, Theodore?"

"No, AMND."

"AMND?"

"*A Midsummer Night's Dream.* Case you haven't noticed, Possum and I aren't exactly a mashup."

"A little advice, Theo. Intellectual humility goes a long way."

Theodore reaches in his bowling ball bag and removes a large baggie. "Perhaps you would like a lemon bar, Mrs. Dwyer? My mom made them last night. It's an ideal snack…nutritious, inexpensive, and portable."

"No thanks, I'm good."

As Coach Dwyer steers the bus out of the parking lot, AJ opens his bowling bag, removes a book, and starts to read. Possum gives him a half-smile. "What you got there?"

"*A Midsummer Night's Dream*, the shit play Swenson's making me read."

"I thought you were going with the Cliffs Notes."

"Yeah, I've got them as a backup, but I'm gonna try to work my way through the first few pages and see if I can figure out what's going on."

Possum nods. "It's deep, but kind of a good read." Not waiting for a response, she gazes out the window a moment and yells to the front of the bus. "Sorry for crappin' on ya, Theodore!"

Possum's crush swings around. "Apology accepted, Natalie. Perhaps you would like to join me up here. The view is spectacular."

"Don't push it, Theodore."

Theodore faces the front of the bus again. "As you wish." Several people behind him laugh.

AUGIE BOWERS WATCHES as his wife Marge, tosses her makeup bag in the backseat of their white Ford Taurus. She scans both directions of the street and says, "We're gonna be late, Augie."

Augie pounds the roof of his car. "Julius isn't here yet."

"Maybe we should go without him. If he got the job, he might already be working."

"All right. Damn it Julius." Augie checks his watch one last time and motions Marge to get in the car.

JULIUS BOWERS SITS at a small table in The Watering Hole drinking a sixteen-ounce beer. His body language suggests he's still jobless. A young blond barmaid, Judith Miller, approaches him to ask if he wants another beer, and he waves her off.

A few minutes later, the Bowers' car speeds down the highway headed for Milwaukee. There's an awkward moment of silence as Augie adjusts the sun visor. Finally, he turns to his wife and frowns. "I hate to admit it, but AJ's already better than I am."

Marge turns to her husband. "Augie, you're a wonderful bowler."

Augie furrows his eyebrows. "I'm not just talking about bowling. He's got a great future ahead of him." He takes a deep breath. "You know Marge, I've always wanted to give you the moon, but I don't have what it takes."

"I don't want the moon. I have everything I need, and I'm very happy sharing my life with you."

"Well, I think AJ is going to accomplish something very special. I don't know what or when, but I know it's gonna happen. I understand that every father says that, but I can see it in his eyes." Augie reaches over and takes his wife's hand. When he looks up, he sees a red pickup truck approaching in the distance.

"Where we gonna eat after AJ's done bowling?"

"Let's live it up. How 'bout that steakhouse AJ likes so much?"

"*Steakarama*? Sounds good to me."

As the speeding red pickup nears the Taurus, it swerves onto their side of the highway. Marge braces herself on the dashboard and screams, "Augie, watch out!"

Augie tries to avoid the truck, but the pickup side-swipes their car and sends it spinning sideways. The car flips over twice as the red truck continues in the opposite direction.

When the Bowers' car comes to a stop, it is upside down and steam is coming from the radiator. An approaching SUV, stops on the side of the road, and the driver dials 911.

TWO WISCONSIN HIGHWAY patrolmen, clad in steel gray uniforms, stand next to the Bower's heavily damaged car as a red and white ambulance with flashing lights drives off, siren blaring. The oldest patrolman writes something on his notepad and nods at his younger colleague. "So, you knew them, did you?"

"They work at USBC, where my wife works. We saw Augie in the bowling alley last week."

The older patrolman examines the side panel of the car and sees a red streak. "Something's not right here. See this red paint? I think their car was sideswiped by another vehicle."

"Could be, skid marks suggest what you're saying. Might be another vehicle over-corrected and slid their way."

"Put it in the report. We need to contact their next of kin and call the Greenvale police, so they can be on the lookout for a damaged red vehicle…and have them monitor the body shops."

THE GREENVALE BUS arrives at a Milwaukee bowling alley parking lot, filled with several cars, trucks, and yellow school buses. Coach Dwyer parks under a sign that reads: WELCOME TO THE WISCONSIN STATE HIGH SCHOOL BOWLING CHAMPIONSHIP. Everyone on the team evacs the bus, and then push their way inside the 1960's style brick building.

Thirty minutes later, the twenty-four-lane bowling alley is filled with dozens of high school teens with uniquely colored jerseys. A dozen coaches, including Coach Dwyer, stand and chatter amongst themselves as they watch their bowlers warming up.

In front of the twelfth lane, Buster, Sam, and Possum stretch their arms and watch AJ as he throws a strike. Buster points. "Hey bud, save some of that for the real deal."

As the foursome wipe off their balls, the tournament director and a Milwaukee police officer appear. They move over to Coach Dwyer, and the policeman whispers something in her ear. Mrs. Dwyer lowers her head, pauses a moment, and shuffles over to AJ and his teammates. "AJ, can I have a word with you?"

"Yeah, what's up, Coach?"

She pulls him aside, puts her hand on his shoulder, and whispers, "AJ, I'm afraid I have some bad news."

"That detention thingy? Simpson gave me another chance."

"It's not that. There's been an accident." AJ's eyes grow as Coach Dwyer continues, "We need to go." She takes AJ by the arm and points at Possum, Sam, and Buster. "You three need to coach the team…until I get back. AJ and I have to leave."

Possum steps forward. "What's going on?"

"I'll explain it to you later." Coach Dwyer waves Theodore over. "You're filling in for AJ. Warmup."

Possum shakes her head and glares at Theo. The other team members watch as their coach, the officer, and AJ start for the door. Coach Dwyer talks quietly to her star bowler as he hangs his head.

The Woodchucks resume their warm-up, including Theodore, who finishes by rolling a gutter ball. Then Sam, Buster, Possum, and Theodore circle up and end their practice with their traditional fist bump explosion. As they go their separate ways, Buster gives Possum a look of concern.

TWO MOHAGANY CASKETS rest on burial lifts next to adjoining holes in the Greenvale cemetery. The cold wind is blowing hard as three dozen mourners dressed in black, including AJ, Julius, Barb Dwyer, Mr. Swenson, and AJ's three best friends huddle together. Finally, the silver-haired Lutheran minister closes his Bible.

After the mourners walk away, AJ and his uncle hang back. The new orphan puts one hand on each coffin as Julius puts his hand on his nephew's shoulder and says, "It's you and me now. You and me." AJ drops to his knees and sobs as Julius looks up at the sky.

IN THE KITCHEN of the Bowers' house, Julius and his nephew sit in silence until UJ finally speaks. "So, here's the deal. You know your father sold life insurance, right?"

"Yeah, I heard Dad say car accidents pay double the policy amount. So, we're gonna be good, right?"

Julius sighs. "No, your father let his own policy lapse. Nothing times two is nothing."

"Well, at least the car insurance company already gave us emergency money to replace Mom and Dad's Taurus. And we've got the house."

"So, about that. The Ford Escort I bought is a piece of junk."

"Why don't you take it back?"

"The guy skipped town." Julius takes a deep breath. "Your folk's will puts me in in charge of the house and mortgage until you turn twenty-one. "Bad thing is your father refinanced the house two years ago to pay off some bills, so there's no collateral. Plus, I had to get one of those fast cash loans to pay their funeral expenses. We're in deep shit. I have to pay it pack in a couple of weeks and the mortgage was due last week.

"How we gonna have enough money to buy all the other shit we need?"

"Well, that's the thing. I still gotta find me a job."

"What about USBC? Maybe they'll hire you back."

"Not gonna happen. Stole one of their precious bowling balls."

"Why'd you do that? We got plenty of balls."

"Cuz when USBC got a shipment of the latest design in balls, I decided to borrow one…for a few days. Anyway, there was this big tournament in Milwaukee. One of the big wigs spotted me with it, and that was all she wrote. Now, I can't get a job at a skating rink."

"So now what?"

"Well, I get my last unemployment check tomorrow. We'll go from there. One more thing. The police think your folks might have been hit by someone, who forced them off the road."

"Why do they think that?"

"I don't know. Something about finding red paint on the side of your folks' car."

BACK AT SCHOOL after a week's absence, AJ passes several students in the hallway, but he doesn't make eye contact with anyone of them. When he reaches his World History class, he finds Barb Dwyer standing outside the door. Barb takes a deep breath and gives him a big hug. The embrace goes on a little too long, so AJ steps back and shyly moves into the classroom. His teacher follows a few steps behind with tears in her eyes as several students stare at them. Instead of sitting in the back of the room with Sam and Buster, AJ takes a seat front and center next to Claudia.

AJ STANDS AT the rental shoe counter with the owner and manager of the Strike and Spare bowling alley, Monty Owens. Monty, who is dressed in black slacks and a Wolverine team bowling jersey, puts money in the register and says, "You can start tomorrow. Again, I'm sorry about yer folks. Tough break. But listen, this ain't no charity job I'm giving you. Any funny business and yer ass is grass. Want clean toilets, clean floors, clean balls, and clean behavior."

"Got it. Everything clean."

Monty points at the shoe rack. "See those shoes? You need to powder them every time someone brings a pair back. People got nasty feet…and change the shoelaces when they need changing."

"Got it."

"Hey, I heard your team got third at state without you."

"Yeah, our team alternate bowled a 185."

"Hey, that's not bad."

"That was for three games."

"Damn. Was he blind?"

"No, but he set a tournament record for gutter balls."

Monty shakes his head. "Bummer. See you tomorrow."

Chapter 7

Uncle Julius

IN THE BACK ROOM OF THE WATERING HOLE, seven local men, including Julius Bowers, are gathered around a repurposed pool table playing no-limit Texas Hold'em. Vince Anderson, a local banker, deals everyone two-hole cards and five of the seven men check their cards and fold. Vince deals three cards face up in the middle of the table, a deuce of spades, a Jack of diamonds, and five of clubs.

Across from Julius is a thirty-something sharply-dressed and handsome lawyer, Gil Williams, who is new in town. Already having a reputation for being a megalomaniac, Gil pushes in most of his chips. Julius studies his cards, takes too long, and Gil growls, "Come on, Pops. Lay 'em or play 'em?"

Julius matches Gil's bet and the two remaining players check each other when they see the turn card is another deuce. When Vince flips the river card, an ace, Julius gulps down a shot of whiskey, pulls his remaining chips out of the side pocket in front of him, and pushes them to the middle of the table. "All in."

Gil chuckles, counts his chips, and matches UJ's bet. "You're done old man...done."

Julius anticipates a win with his eyes as he carefully lays his two aces on the green felt table, matching the flop card, the ace of diamonds. "Beat that, ya smartass. Full house…aces and twos."

"Be happy to, Gramps." Gil lays down two deuces, matching

the two deuces on the table. "Quads…four of a kind." Everyone at the table lets out a collective sigh as Gil pulls in his winnings and gloats. "When I kill, I kill all the way." Julius quietly stands up and puts on his coat and stocking cap. When he reaches the door, Gil snorts, "Come back when you learn not to overplay your hand…What a donkey fish."

AJ POLISHES A bowling ball at the east end of the Strike and Spare. He is not terribly engaged in his work when he sees Buster and Sam coming his way. He tries to make himself small, but his friends see him anyway. When they arrive, Sam furls his eyebrows. "What's goin' on?"

Buster chimes in. "Yeah, why ya rubbin' down house balls?"

"I'm not rubbing them; I'm cleaning them."

"Someone paying you to do that?" Sam says politely.

"No, I'm doing this for the hell of it. I work here, doofus. I need the money."

Buster removes the ball from his bag and offers it to AJ. "Mine could use a shine."

"Aren't you funny? Shit, here comes the boss. Go away."

Monty Owens, carrying a bucket and mop, places them in front of AJ. "I don't pay you to talk, Bowers. There's shit and piss all over the men's bathroom. Toilets and urinals need to be spotless. Check the women's too."

After Monty walks off, Buster takes a bow and signals Sam. "Come on. We mustn't bother the king. He has a lot of thrones to clean."

AJ gives Buster and Sam the finger as they walk away laughing. AJ racks the bowling ball, grabs the scrub bucket and mop, and starts for the men's room.

When he gets inside, he finds three middle school boys standing next to each other having a peeing contest, shooting their streams across the room. They see AJ and quickly put away their weapons.

AJ drops his bucket, grabs the mop, and swings it at them. "Get the hell out of here, you little assholes!" The boys run out of the bathroom as AJ trails behind them still swinging his mop. As they scamper off, he sees Mr. Owens glaring his way. AJ waves, gives his boss a sheepish grin, and walks back in the bathroom. He reviews the mess and groans, "Why me?"

THE NEXT MORNING in senior English, Mr. Swenson is writing on the whiteboard when he hears AJ snoring in the front row. Claudia, who is seated next to him, taps him on the shoulder. Several students laugh as Mr. Swenson clears his throat and stares blankly at the snoring culprit. AJ finally sits up, gawks at his teacher, and clears his head. "Mr. Bowers, are you having a midsummer's daydream?"

Theodore laughs. "Very good, sir. Your wordplay would be even funnier if we were in summer school."

"Theodore, if I need an assessment of my humor, I'll ask for it." Mr. Swenson shifts his eyes back to AJ. "Am I boring you?"

AJ sneaks a peek at Claudia. "Nah. I'm all into the spirit of the play." AJ's eyes brighten. "Truth is, I peeked over at Claudia here, closed my eyes, and it was kinda like Puck cast a spell on me." Everyone around him hoots and hollers as Claudia blushes.

"Sure, you weren't just sleeping?"

"No sir, I'm all into this play. In fact, I have a question."

"Related to the play?"

"Yeah, why do you think Shakespeare called Puck… Puck?"

"Anyone care to answer Mr. Bowers' question?"

Buster raises up like an exclamation mark. "Did they play hockey back then?" No one laughs, except Buster.

"No, but you do bring up an interesting point. Shakespeare's use of the name Puck is a play on the word poke."

Sam gives his input. "So, if you poke someone, you might actually be pucking them?"

Everyone laughs except for Marcy Phillips who groans, "Oh my God!"

Theodore pipes up. "Good one, Sam…double entendre."

Mr. Swenson rolls his eyes and continues. "As I was about to say, the Scottish Gaelic word puc means to punch or deliver a blow."

AJ, who now seems genuinely interested in the topic, says, "So maybe, just maybe, Shakespeare gave him that name because Puck is so good at delivering a blow, ya know, like pranking people or pulling practical jokes."

Mr. Swenson says, "Hate to admit it, AJ, but that's one of the best interpretations of Puck's name that I've heard." Everyone claps and AJ stands up and bows. As he takes a seat, he smartasses Mr. Swenson one last time. "If it's all right, I'm gonna finish my nap now."

On cue, the bell rings, ending class. AJ gathers his books and heads for the door followed closely by Claudia. In the hallway, she taps AJ the on shoulder. He swings around, almost knocking her off her feet. He apologizes with his eyes as he reaches out and grabs her arm to steady her. "Oh, it's you."

Claudia steps back. "Yeah, ahh. That was pretty funny…I mean the whole Puck thing."

"Yeah, I guess it helps when you've actually read the play."

Claudia shifts her mood. "I wanted to say how sorry I am about your parents."

"Thanks. Probably shouldn't be crackin' jokes already. Sometimes, I act like a smart-ass to cover up how I really feel. Truth is, I'm a real mess."

Claudia softens her voice. "It's okay. Everyone mourns

differently." There is an awkward moment of silence until Claudia says, "Hey, if ya ever wanna hang out sometime?

AJ's face lights up. "Mean like you and me...on a date?"

Claudia smiles. "Well...yeah, sure."

"You like pizza, right?"

"Sure, I can eat that."

"How about Friday night at the bowling alley?

"They have pizza in the bowling alley?"

"Yeah, there's a place inside called Big Cheese. It's the best. I'll meet you there at seven."

"Wait, we're going to meet there?"

"Sorry. My car's low on gas and I'm kinda short on cash with what's been going on."

"Okay, yeah, sure. I can pay for the pizza if you want."

"Oh, no. I got it covered. You're in my budget...weekly entertainment."

"Ah, so I'm entertainment?"

"Yeah…nah, you know what I mean."

She gives AJ a gentle shove. "I'm kidding. See you Friday night…and I'm paying."

They walk their separate ways as AJ pumps his fist. He makes sure no one is watching, opens his bowling bag, pulls out his ball and rolls it down the hallway. A tall blond cheerleader, who is about to exit the school, sees the ball coming her way and opens the front door. "Hey, don't your balls get scratched up when you do that?"

"What did you say?"

The girl blushes and her mouth falls open, revealing her braces. "Sorry, I didn't mean..."

"No worries. It's my practice ball."

The ball rolls out the door, down the steps, and onto the street. A crossing guard raises a stop sign as the black orb travels along within the confines of the crosswalk. AJ rushes to the other side of the street, picks it up, salutes the guard, and starts for home.

SAM HILL ARRIVES at his house in an upper-middle-class neighborhood. He stops in his tracks when he sees an old blue Dodge pickup parked in the driveway filled with pool supplies. When he reaches the front steps, he glances back at the rusted-out junker and opens the front door.

Inside the living room, Sam checks the upstairs landing and sees Skip Rawlings tiptoeing out of his mother's second-floor bedroom. The former high school football star bounds down the stairs two steps at a time, pulls down his shirt, and winks at Sam. "Sammo, it's been a while. What, you a senior now?"

"Yeah. What are you doing here?"

"Uh. you know…working. I'm a pool man."

"We don't have a pool, and it's January."

"Yeah, well, your mom says she wants to buy one."

"So, you don't just service pools, you sell them too?"

"Listen, I should go. Hey, maybe we can meet up and tell some lies." Sam narrows his eyes. Skip chuckles and runs out the door.

As Sam makes his way up the stairs, he hears the squeal of tires as Skip peels out of the driveway. When he reaches the second-floor landing, his mother marches out of her bedroom dressed in a pink bathrobe. Her hair is disheveled, but she has a big smile on her face. "Hey, Sweetie."

Sam rolls his eyes. "Can this get any weirder, Mom? If dad were here, he'd be turning over in his grave."

"Okay, first off, your dad's not dead, so there's that. The second thing is… we're divorced. Now, why are you upset?"

"Cuz we don't have a pool."

"No, but as long as your father keeps paying child support, I can at least afford a pool boy."

"Stop! You're grossing me out. Skip is only two years older than me."

"What? That rascal told me he was almost thirty."

As Sam hustles down the stairs, he grumbles, "Yeah, in ten years."

Vanessa Hill strolls back to her room, but pauses when she hears Sam slam the door of his main floor bedroom below.

When she enters her sanctuary, she stares at the posters of the half-naked men that cover all four walls, plops down on her bed, looks up at the ceiling, and begins to cry.

She takes a moment, picks up her bedside phone, and dials a number. A woman on the other side of the call matter-of-factly says, "Sexaholics Anonymous Hotline. How may I help you?" Vanessa doesn't say anything. "Hello. Anyone there? Vanessa is that you? I recognize your number. Are you okay?"

Vanessa gently hangs up the phone and walks over and sits down at her makeup table. She peers into the mirror and frowns at her reflection as she applies bright red lipstick on her silicone enhanced lips. Not satisfied, she lifts her breasts with both hands and stands up. She sashays around the room, studies her butt, grabs the phone, and dials another number.

A man with a heavy Hispanic accent, answers. "This is Manuel. How may I be of service to you?"

"Manny? It's me, Vanessa."

"Hey, girlfriend. How's my favorite señorita? You ready to get busy?"

Vanessa pulls a credit card out of the pocket of her robe and reads "4200, 3889..."

Manuel interrupts. "4001... got it, baby. So, are you horny? You want for me to churn your butter?"

Vanessa switches the phone to her other ear. "No, I need

someone to talk to."

"Girlfriend talk or sexy man talk?"

"Girlfriend talk." Vanessa lays on the bed, phone to her ear.

On the other side of the line, in a one-bedroom apartment in Manhattan, Manuel Hernandez, a hefty seventy-year-old Hispanic male with a bad wig, sits on a toilet with his pants down around his knees and a cell phone to his ear. Vanessa drones on and on as Manuel checks his watch and yawns. "That ungrateful child...after all you've done for him."

Manuel stands up, covers the phone with one hand, and flushes the toilet with the other. He lifts himself up to his walker equipped with an old-style bicycle horn and pulls up his pants. Next, he shuffles over to the bathroom sink and lays down the phone as Vanessa continues to chatter away. Manuel checks himself out in the mirror, removes his wig, adjusts it, puts it back on, and picks up his phone. "Relax yourself, sweetheart; you have too much drama. Time for sexy talk."

Her ear still to the phone, Vanessa hears two blasts from Manuel's bicycle horn. Confused, she whispers into the phone. "Manuel, are you all right?"

Outside his mother's bedroom door, Sam is about to knock when he hears his mother's high-pitched voice. He puts his ear to the door and listens. "Oh yes! Yes! No! Yes! In Spanish, say it in Spanish!"

Sam rushes down the stairs with his hands over his ears and hollers, "Oh my God!"

Chapter 8

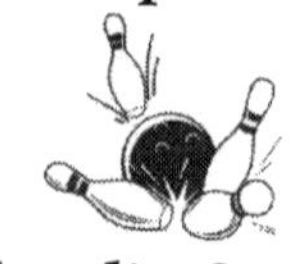

Claudia Speaks

I'VE NEVER REALLY LIKED BOWLING, but AJ wanted to meet at this bowling alley, so I'm going with the flow. While I sit in the parking lot in my dad's Volvo, I watch for him, because I don't want to go in that nasty building by myself and take the chance on some lowlife hitting on me. I won't tell AJ, but I hate the stench of bowling alleys and the sound of rednecks hooting and hollering all because they knocked down a few pins.

When I check my watch, I see I'm twenty minutes early, so I take out some polish and start painting my nails. I kind of like AJ, but I'm not sure why. Maybe it's because I feel sorry for him about losing his parents in a car accident. I know it's horrible, but I almost wish it would have happened to me. I love my folks, but they're just so annoying…always wanting to tell me what to do or how I should feel.

Anyway, I'm not ready for any kind of serious relationship, because what I learned in Milwaukee was that most of the guys I dated just wanted to see me naked.

I know I'm a phony, and sometimes I dress kind of skanky to get boys' attention. But the thing is when they come on too strong, I push them away like I'm someone special. It doesn't make a lot of sense I know, but when I like a guy and he starts to like me back, I start to think he's not worthy.

Look at me, I'm wearing a short denim skirt, a white see-through blouse, and some of my mom's expensive perfume. I don't have big daddies, but they are pretty perky. I know that's real sexist. Poor AJ.

So, there you have it. I'm a total bitch, who hides it well. I blame a lot of it on the fact that I'm an only child, but I know that's a lame excuse. A lot of people think I'm a real Mother Theresa, but I do a lot of raggin' and swearing in my head. I think I get that from my mom, who constantly complains about people, but only behind their backs. My dad thinks that sort of thing will serve me well if I ever want to be a lawyer, which I do.

Speaking of parents, mine are headed for divorce court. They didn't even bother to tell me about it until I was snooping around one day and found the divorce papers on my dad's desk. When we moved here, I thought they had a chance to maybe work things out, but my mom's all set to go back to Milwaukee. She told me she's waiting until I graduate, so she doesn't interrupt my life any more than she has to. Oh my God. Are you kidding? Interrupt my life? Divorce sucks! I don't ever wanna get married.

AJ doesn't show up, so I go in the bowling alley and wait for five minutes. Finally, I see the sign for the Big Cheese, figure he might be waiting for me in there, so I go inside.

I sit down in a booth and a waitress brings a glass of water and a pizza-stained menu. When I look out the window and into the bowling alley, I'm kind of shocked, cuz I see AJ bowling all by himself. I must have walked right by him.

Kind of pissed, I strut out of the Big Cheese and over to AJ. He's about to roll his ball, when he sees me out of the corner of his eye. He swings around and grins at me like I'm some kind of movie star. "Hey, I've been killing time until you got here. Wanna turn?"

"No thanks, I'm not a bowler."

I watch as AJ places his ball in his bag and removes his

gloves. I look down at his shoes, the kind a circus clown might wear, and I smirk. He sees me staring and says, "Oh, yeah."

He acts all embarrassed as he removes them and slips on his sneakers. He kind of surprises me when he hops to his feet and offers me his arm. I take it and he escorts me into the pizza joint like we're going to the prom.

Now seated in a corner booth, I watch as AJ takes a large bite of pizza and sneaks a peek at my see-through blouse. I pretend not to notice as I flirt with my eyes. "You certainly enjoy your pizza."

"Yeah, it's like there's a party going on in my mouth."

I laugh and wait for AJ to stop chewing. "So how long have you been friends with Sam, Buster, and… Possum?"

"Since the first grade."

"I'm curious. Why does Sam always dress in camo?

"His grandpa was a decorated Marine who served in Vietnam."

"Is his father a Marine, too?"

"No, he sells insurance. Well, he did until he ran off with his business partner, Chuck Henderson."

I blink. "Oh dear."

"Yeah, kind of strange, but not because he turned out to be gay. People change. Shit happens. The strange part was him leaving Sammy the way he did. No explanation, nothing. One day he was there and the next day he was gone. They started seeing each other again last year. Sam's sister lives with him, so he goes to visit them in Milwaukee once a month."

"And you live in your folks' house with your uncle."

"Yeah. It's not worth much, and Julius had to borrow even more money to pay for my folk's funerals."

"Can you afford all the expenses?"

"We can't. Julius doesn't have a job, and I'm working part-time at this bowling alley… for minimum wage."

"You work here?"

"Yeah, I practically live here anyway."

"Wow. You really do like bowling."

"Hell to the yeah."

"School, work, a house to take care of…you're busy."

"Yeah, sometimes I feel like I'm a pigeon chained to a Mack truck, and someone's making me pull it."

"I've never heard anyone put it that way." I touch AJ's hand kind of feeling sorry for him again. "I sure hope things get better for you."

He gives me the biggest smile. "I think they just did." I don't want him to get the wrong idea, so I remove my hand and he changes the subject. "Hey, how was it living in Milwaukee?"

"It was all right. There are a lot of things to do there."

"So, why'd your folks move to Greenvale?"

"My dad wanted to. He grew up here."

"How's that working out?"

"Not so good, my mom hates small towns and moved back to Milwaukee last week."

"So, are they headed for the big D?"

"Yeah, I think they are."

"I'm sorry. All my friends' parents are divorced. Possum's, Buster's, Sam's..."

I tighten my lips. "Pretty soon all of your friends are going to have something in common."

AJ's eyes light up. "So, we're friends?"

I try to calm him down. "Yes, but that's all we can be…friends."

"You seem awfully sure about that. Guess we can talk about an upgrade later."

"No, I already know. We're only going to be friends."

"Okay…already…friends. Are you moving back to Milwaukee with your mom?"

"There are only a few weeks of school left, so I'm staying with my dad until I leave for college.

"Bummer. So, friends for the summer?" AJ toasts me with his glass of coke.

I clank my glass against his. "To friends and good pizza."

We stand up and AJ helps me with my coat. He winks at me and says, "Maybe next time you'll let me pay."

I grin. "Don't worry. You'll have plenty of chances to pay."

Chapter 9

Texas Hold'em

THE GREENVALE STREETS ARE VACANT except for an older couple walking past The Watering Hole. They are dressed for the season, wearing hooded parkas, stocking caps, and large leather mittens.

Inside the bar, in the backroom, Julius, Gil Williams, Vince Anderson, and four local gamblers are drinking beer, smoking cigars, and playing their usual game of Texas Hold'em.

Gil gloats as he pulls in his winnings, adding to his large stack of chips. "Thanks, boys. Check out this shit." The young lawyer lays his two bluff cards on the table and chuckles.

Vince Anderson reshuffles the cards, deals out two-hole cards to everyone, and three flop cards to the middle of the table. Everyone folds except for Gil and Julius, who check one another as Vince reveals the turn and river cards. It's Julius's final chance to bet. The other men grow restless as the oldest man at the table takes his time. Finally, Julius shoves in his remaining chips. "I'm all in."

Gil studies Julius's chip stack. "How much you got there."

Julius counts his chips. "Five thousand, two hundred."

The lawyer sits up. "Come on, Pops. I've got ten thousand here. Let's make it a real bet."

"That's all I got. That's why I'm all in, ya jackass."

Gil surveys the other men at the table. "Listen to this feisty bastard." Gil glares at Julius. "You got a house, right?"

Vince interrupts. "He has a house with no equity. Not to mention, he hasn't made a payment in four months."

Gil snarks, "How you keep track of all that shit, Vince?"

"Cuz, that's what a good loan officer does."

Gil rolls two chips between his fingers. "So, chicken shit, what you got that's not on the table?"

Julius studies his cards. "I got a house full of furniture."

The young lawyer gives Julius a sarcastic grin. "Working appliances and TVs?"

Julius tightens the grip on his cards. "Yeah, that too."

Vince clears his throat. "Don't do it, Julius."

"Come on, old man. Now's your chance to get all your money back."

Julius grits his teeth. "All right. All my chips, the shit in the house, against your ten thousand. You're bluffing."

Gil nods at the other players. "Anyone got a piece of paper?" Bob Wilson, a Main Street paint store owner, pulls out his wallet and fishes out a laundromat coupon. He hands it to the lawyer, who flips it over and slides it over to Julius. "Write your bet on the back and sign it." Gil scans the room. "You're all my witnesses."

Vince points at Julius. "Sure, you wanna do this? You're down to nothing already. I'm ready to repossess your house."

"Ten thousand will end that. Give me a pen."

Vince hands him a souvenir pen from his bank. "I hope you understand, this is binding. I got a notary stamper in my pocket."

Julius prints the amount of his bet on the back of the promissory note, signs his name, and shoves it over to Vince. The banker examines it, signs the note himself, pulls an embosser out of his pocket, and squeezes a seal on the back of it. His patience running thin, Julius grabs the note out of Vince's hand and tosses it to the middle of the table.

Gil instantly pushes in all his chips. "All in."

Julius takes a breath and proudly displays his two Jacks. "Full house. Jacks high."

Gil flips his cards over. "How sad. So close. Full house. Kings high."

Julius looks like a deer in the headlights as Gil pulls in his winnings, holds up the note Julius signed, and gloats. "I'll have a moving truck at your place on Saturday morning."

Vince grimaces. "Gil, don't be a prick."

"What? You don't think he would have taken my ten thousand dollars?"

Julius quietly slips away as the pompous winner addresses the room. "You know, I almost feel sorry for him. Almost."

JULIUS, WHOSE SHOULDERS are drooped, sits across from AJ sipping a glass of whiskey and watching TV. Seated cross-legged on the floor, AJ scoops out the remaining ravioli from a tin can and sets it on the coffee table. "I sorta miss mom's meatloaf."

"Yeah, she wasn't a great cook, but tried really hard…Her spaghetti was pretty good."

"Her spaghetti was the best."

"Know it's not been easy losing your folks. Augie and Marge were good to me. They took me in when I had no place to go. How's school going?"

"I graduate in three weeks. You'll be there, right?"

"Wouldn't miss it. What comes next?"

"Been thinking about college."

"Thought you weren't cut out for it?"

"Dad really wanted me to go. Maybe I'll ease my way into it; go to a JC."

"Yeah, that might be good."

"Hey, I didn't see the Escort out front when I got home."

Julius takes a moment. "It's still downtown. Got to drinking and didn't dare drive it home."

"Guess it'll be okay until morning unless you want me to get it now?"

"Nah, I'll take care of it."

AJ stands up and yawns. "I'm going to bed."

Uncle Julius takes another drink of whiskey. "Yeah, I'm gonna stay up for a while."

AJ is sound asleep in his bedroom, when he hears a car backfire outside his window. He sits up, gathers himself, and groans, "Shit!" He jumps out of bed and runs into the living room. He looks through the picture window and watches as someone in his green Pinto backs out of the driveway.

Still half asleep, AJ stumbles to his uncle's room and opens his door. "Hey, UJ! Someone stole my car!" He scans the room again and sees that his uncle's bed is empty. He flips on the light and notices that some of his uncle's belongings are missing and that a lot of his clothes are scattered on the floor. "What the hell?"

Chapter 10

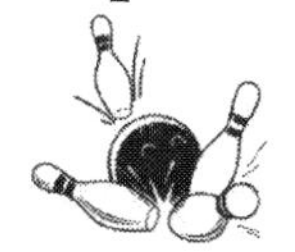

It's My Problem

I'M IN THE SCHOOL CAFETERIA AT OUR USUAL table chewing on a lunch lady-baked brownie, when Possum says to me, "So, he up and left in the middle of the night?"

"Yeah, rode off in my Pinto and never came back."

Buster tosses me his tab of butter, cuz he knows I freakin' love it so much and says, "Maybe he'll come back with an explanation."

I paste the yellow grease on my brownie, stuff it in my mouth, and mumble, "I don't think so. This morning I went downtown looking for our Ford Escort and it wasn't there either."

Possum reacts to AJ's butter wolfing. "Dude, That's nasty."

"The butter makes it moist."

Possum's eyes widen. "Gross."

Sam slides his chair over. "He can't drive two cars."

I down the rest of my brownie, smile at Possum, and burp. Grossed out, she slides over to the end of the table.

"I hope UJ comes back soon," I grumble. "I can't afford to make a house payment."

Buster scrunches his milk carton. "Maybe, he's on vacation."

"Vacation? He's been on vacation for two years."

As I make my way down an icy side street, trying not to fall on my ass, I spot a brown well-traveled Toyota Corolla at a stop sign. I sneak up behind it, crouch down, and grab the rear bumper. The car takes off, and I slide along on the icy road watching out for dry patches of pavement that might mess me up. The car takes a left and goes down Main Street as several people point at me and laugh. When the car nears the Strike and Spare, I let go of the bumper and slide to a stop. I brush the snow off my clothes and hustle inside, ten minutes late for work.

It's the usual Friday night crowd and the place is packed with once-a-month bowlers who are looking for a place to hang out and have a good time. I focus on my work, trying to keep a low profile, so's people don't think I'm a simp for picking up garbage and cleaning toilets.

By the time the alley empties out, it's after midnight. I don't make it home till after midnight and there's nothing worth eating, so I go straight to bed.

I'm in the middle of a sexy dream, when I hear the doorbell ring. I open my eyes and think, *What the hell? It's Saturday. Leave me alone.* I trudge my way to the door anyway, open it a smidge, and see three bearded men in matching blue coats and fur-lined caps with flaps. I open the door wider, look past them, and see a truck with *Ralph's Moving and Storage* on the side. The oldest dude hands me some kind of official letter as the two younger guys head back to the truck. I read it over and complain, "I don't understand any of this shit."

As the old guy joins his buddies, I hear him say, "Not my problem. All I know is it gives me the right to empty your house." The younger guys hurry inside with dollies, slide past me, and hustle into the kitchen like they're going to get a bite to eat. The tall one growls, "Ya want anything in this fridge, ya better get it now."

I grab the last piece of pizza from my date with Claudia and what's left of a carton of chocolate milk as the men make two trips and roll the fridge and stove out the door.

Totally bummed, I slump down on the floor and eat pizza and drink milk as the old dude sizes up my living room. When the young guys come back, I watch as they carry off all our beds, the sofa, two armchairs, and the dining room table.

Looking for a distraction, I click on the TV, but before I can change channels, the old duffer takes the remote from my hand, while the other fellas remove the flat screen from the wall. I just sit where I'm at and groan, "Come on, not the TV too."

The old timer shakes his noggin. "Sorry, kid. It's on the list."

The house is pretty much empty now, and I'm asleep on the floor in my room under my mom's favorite quilt, surrounded by piles of my clothes. The doorbell rings, so I sit up and yell, "Go away! There's no one here!" It rings again, so I trudge my way to the front door thinking what now and open it.

This time it's a black-suited man with a serious voice, who looks me over and says, "You must be AJ. Is your uncle here?"

"No…he's on vacation."

He gives me this 'I don't believe you' look and introduces himself all prim and proper-like. "My name's Vince Anderson, and I'm a loan officer at Greenvale Savings and Loan."

I turn back and eye my empty living room and grumble, "Sorry, I got nothing left."

Standing next to him is this sheriff's deputy, who hands me what I'm about to find out is an eviction notice. I read it over and the banker says, "You have two days to vacate. The house is being foreclosed on."

I get kind of pissy. "I don't care what this says, I'm not

leaving. This is my parent's house…my house."

The Barney Fife look alike raises his shoulders. "If you refuse to vacate, I'll be taking you to jail."

The banker tries to explain. "Since you weren't twenty-one when your parents died, the loan was put in your uncle's name and he hasn't made a payment since your folks died."

"Why not?"

"You need to ask him that question."

"Can you give me a little more time?"

"I gave Julius a thirty-day notice last month. It's too late to do anything about it now." The banker starts to say something else, but he stops himself. "Again, you have two days to vacate."

I look down at the deputy's feet and change the subject. "Hey, ya got a flat tire."

The deputy with a silver star on his chest, spins around and looks back at his car. "What the hell are you talking about?"

I point at his loose shoelace. He gives me a 'you're a smartass' look, but bends down and ties his shoe anyway. I read the notice again as the banker and lawman walk away. Still pissed, I yell out. "Where am I gonna go?"

The banker shrugs. "Not my problem."

After a sleepless night, I'm sitting on the curb out in front of what used to be my house. I'm feeling like a real ham and egger as I eat stale potato chips. Next to me are all my earthly possessions, three large black plastic bags filled with my clothes, a cardboard box with some family pictures, a dozen of my bowling trophies, and other crap.

A tan Dodge minivan drives up, and Coach Dwyer gets out and helps me put my bags in the back. After I climb inside, I sit brooding for a while until she breaks the ice. "You all right?"

I pout. "I'm sorry. I didn't know who else to call."

"It's okay. We'll figure something out."

When we get to her house, she helps me carry all my stuff inside. She takes me to this real swanky bedroom with pink lace curtains and a frilly bedspread. She notices me gawking at the bed and pats me on the shoulder. "I'll change that out. Make yourself at home. We'll have lunch in a few minutes."

Before she leaves, I bounce my butt on the bed and say, "You sure Mr. Dwyer won't mind me staying here?"

"I don't think so. He's been gone two years."

"Sorry, but you still call yourself Mrs. Dwyer?"

"That's to keep all the sniffin' men away." I like living alone."

"So, it's just the two of us?"

"That's right."

"You're not gonna Mrs. Robinson me are you, Coach?"

"Mrs. Robinson?"

"You know, Anne Bancroft in the movie, *The Graduate*."

"Afraid I missed that one."

I get right to it. "How much you gonna charge me for rent, Mrs. D?"

"Let's not worry about that right now, but if you stay long enough to draw social security, I'll need half."

WHEN I LEAVE Mrs. D's house the next morning, I'm already late for work. There's no chance to hook a car, because most of the snow has melted off the streets. I'm not much of a runner, but I race off hoping someone might stop and give me a lift. When I reach Main Street, I spot our replacement Ford Escort go by, so I haul ass after it. I'm about ready to give up the chase when the driver pulls up in front of the *Rexall* drugstore.

The long-haired thirty-something in a black leather jacket exits the Escort just as I show up all out of breath. I drop to one knee and puff, "Hey, man. Where'd ya get this car?"

The hippy type slides his fingers through his long hair. "Guy named Julius sold it to me."

"Are you kidding me? The insurance company gave my uncle and me the money to buy this car after my parents died in a car accident six months ago. Sure, you didn't steal it?"

The man opens the car door, reaches in the glove box, and pulls out a piece of paper. "Sorry about your folks, but I've got a bill of sale right here." He hands it to me and snorts, "I'll sell it back to you if you want. It's a piece of junk."

I study the evidence and hand it back to him. "Nah, I'm plowing for pennies. Sorry to bother you."

The latent hippy disappears into the drugstore as I take one last look at our old Escort and spout, "Shit, Uncle Julius. What's going on?"

IT'S A HOT Texas day, and Julius is stopped on the El Paso side of the border waiting to cross into Juarez. The officer in charge gives him the go-ahead, so he drives his nephew's Pinto slowly into Mexico. Five seconds later, the car backfires, and the officer squats down and covers his military-style cap. He looks around to make sure everything is clear and duck-walks his way inside the border patrol building.

As Julius speeds off, smoke bellows from the Pinto's tailpipe and the sounds of a mariachi band blare from the radio.

Chapter 11

Trailer Trash

I'M TRYING TO SLEEP, BUT THE MOON is shining so bright through my trailer trash bedroom window that it's keeping me awake. When I finally crawl out of bed to shut the curtain, my stomach starts to growl, so I head for the kitchen to see if the refrigerator has anything but beer in it.

When I pass through the living room, I see Troy laying on the couch watching TV as usual. Mom is working the late shift and Troy is drunk, of course, evidenced by the usual beer cans around him. I try to slip past, but he sees me. "Hey, Sweetie. Bring me another beer, will ya?"

I don't know why, but I grab a beer out of the fridge, a couple of Fig Newtons off the kitchen counter for myself, and walk back in the living room. I hand Troy his beer and snark, "Call me Sweetie again, and I'll shave your eyebrows off with a potato peeler while you're sleeping, which is pretty much all the time."

Troy grabs my arm and before I can pull away, he grumbles, "Sounds to me like Possum could use a cuddle. The old lady won't be home for a couple of hours. I ain't so bad."

I yank my arm free. "Keep your hands off me, skunk ass!" As I storm off to my room, I hear Troy chuckle and the familiar swoosh of an aluminum can opening.

I'm starting to drift off when I hear a loud belch coming

from the living room. Awake now, I listen as Troy wobbles down the hallway toward my room. I roll out of bed and lock my door. I remove my bowling ball from its bag and put it in the bed next to me. A few seconds later, I hear Troy tapping on my door. "Hey, it's me, 'skunkass.' Let me in."

I grip my ball and yell, "Go away!"

Troy chortles. "Little pig…little pig… if you don't unlock this door, I'm gonna huff and puff and blow it down."

"Leave me alone, you sicko!" Before I can move, Troy busts his way through my door and stumbles inside. I instantly rear back and throw my ten-pounder at Troy's ugly skull, but he raises up and it hits him in the chest.

He gasps for air as he sinks to the floor and groaning, "What the hell! You little bitch!" Troy gathers himself, struggles to his feet, and flips on the bedroom light. I hop out of bed and try to slip past him. I am halfway out my door when he grabs me by the arm and throws me back onto my bed. I don't know why, but I reach over and unplug my bedside lamp. I lift it up and use it to shield myself, because I assume the asshole is going to try and rape me. As Troy rubs his chest, he straightens up and glares. "You could have killed me." He picks up my bowling ball and squeezes his fingers into it. "Ya wanna rough, do ya?"

"Leave me alone, fungus breath!"

Troy bellows, "Awwh!" as he swings my bowling ball. He misses once, but with his second swing, he smashes the lamp into the side of my face. I cover my head with both my hands, fall back, and begin to cry. I hear a loud thud as he drops my ten-pounder on the floor. Then he flips off my bedroom light and stomps off, as I bury my bloody face in my pillow.

Two hours later, my mom makes her way to my room, where she finds my broken door. She pokes her head inside, where she sees my shattered lamp on the floor, and me lying in bed with a bloody towel covering my face. She snarls, "What the hell! What happened to your room?"

"Go ask Troy... Mr. all I got?"

"He's not here. What'd you do?"

"What did I do? Your man-child busted my door down. He was gonna rape me, Mom."

"I don't believe you."

Mom creeps down the hallway like Troy might still be in the trailer, checks the bathroom, and groans when she looks back at the broken bedroom door. I meet her in the hallway and remove the towel, revealing my bloody face and damaged eye.

She puts her hand to her mouth. "Oh, my God! What did you do to yourself?"

"Mom, your so-called boyfriend clobbered me with my own bowling ball."

My mom walks off mumbling, "You probably had it coming. You'd better hope Troy comes back."

I scream at the top of my lungs, "You can't be serious!"

The next day, my mom gets to feeling all guilty, so she takes me to see the doctor. I'm wearing a towel over my noggin as people gawk at me in the waiting room. Finally, some nurse herds me into the examination room and puts me on this tissue-papered metal table. She makes me get undressed, so I'm cold as hell, cuz I'm wearing nothing but an ass-revealing ugly robe that's been worn by God knows how many other people.

Finally, this white-coated doctor walks in and introduces himself like he's God's gift to the world. "Hello, I'm Dr. Hanson."

I nod. "You an eye doctor?"

"Ophthalmologist."

"Impressive."

I lower the towel and the doctor checks my eye over with this instrument he calls an ophthalmoscope, a fancy name for a magnifying glass. Anyway, he finishes up and gives me this phony all worried look. "How did this happen?"

"I got into an argument with a bowling ball."

"Did someone hit you with it?"

I hesitate. "I promised my mom I wouldn't say…."

"Did she do it?"

"No."

"Was it your father?"

"Nope. He's been gone for fourteen years."

"Well, you need to tell the authorities who did this. It's a serious injury that suggests you have been assaulted by someone."

I don't know why, but I lie. "I have an appointment to see someone tomorrow…or maybe I should say talk to someone." I quickly change the subject. "So how long until it heals?"

"Young lady, your eye has undergone ocular trauma, caused by a blunt force to your eye socket. At least it's not a globe rupture. But you're not going to be able to see anything out of your left eye for a while, and you're probably going to need surgery. If left untreated, there could be permanent damage…maybe even blindness."

"My mother doesn't have medical insurance. How much is something like that gonna cost?"

"Let's not talk money right now. The good news is your eye is stabilized and shouldn't get any worse for a while. The bad news is you're going to have limited vision until you have the surgery...plus your eye doesn't look so good."

Without permission, I jump to my feet and check myself out in the mirror on the wall. "I can't walk around looking like this."

I sit back on the table as the doctor reaches into a glass-doored cabinet. He opens a drawer, removes a black eye patch, and hands it to me. "For now."

For some reason all I can think about is Oedipus Rex and how he poked his eyes out and married his mother. Other characters come to mind, like the cyclops Ulysses blinded, Moshe Dayan, the one-eyed military leader from Israel, and Rooster Cogburn, the John Wayne character. Curious, I walk back over to the mirror, hold the patch up to my bad eye, and look sideways at the doctor with my good eye. "This is gonna do wonders for my self-esteem."

Chapter 12

Revenge

POSSUM WALKS DOWN THE HALLWAY on her way to her AP Calculus class, when two freshmen boys stop and stare at her. The taller of the two boys nudges his red-headed friend and closes his left eye. "Aargh...matey!"

His buddy laughs and they break out in song, "Yo, ho, yo, ho… a pirate's life for me."

Possum rolls her good eye. "You've got your entire lives to be idiots; why don't you take the day off." The boys high-five one another and disappear around the corner.

After a long day at school, Possum stands in front of the bathroom mirror studying her reflection. Frustrated, she picks up a pair of scissors and cuts her hair off in huge chunks.

When she exits her bedroom a few minutes later, she is carrying her backpack and bowling bag. As she walks past Troy, who is laying on the couch as usual, he notices her short hair and eye patch. He laughs and signals her to come closer. She gives him the finger, walks out the front door, slams it behind her, and screams loud enough for the neighbors to hear, "Asshole!"

Possum enters the Strike and Spare, where she finds AJ, Sam, and Buster eating pizza and bowling. Out of the corner of his eye, AJ spots her approaching and does a double-take when he realizes she's wearing a black eyepatch. Then he sees that her hair is short and she's wearing a backward ball cap. Sam and Buster notice her change in appearance as well and take turns staring at her.

After she opens her ball bag, she gives the three of them a sarcastic smile. "Go on, say it...'You're a pirate, a one-eyed Jack, Mike Wazowski'."

"Okay, I'll bite." AJ steps forward. "What happened to your eye?"

"Mom's wacko boyfriend was all set to rape me, but instead he clobbered me with my own Brunswick."

"Oh, my God. I hope you called the cops."

"No one saw him do it, and my old lady claims I did it to myself…made the whole thing up to get attention."

AJ adjusts his bowling glove. "You think she really believes that?"

"Who knows? She's crazy."

Sam chortles, "Why would anyone Oedipus wreck themself with a bowling ball?" AJ and Buster stare at him, and he adds, "Get it?…blind man, wreck, Oedipus Rex?"

AJ confronts his friend. "Not funny, Sam. That idiot could have killed Possum."

Possum grabs the ball from her bag and threatens Sam with it. He throws up his hands and backs away. "Well, excuse me for trying to lighten the mood with an original literary delusion."

She lowers her ball. "The word is allusion doofus…and practice on someone else."

Sam shifts gears, takes a big bite of pizza, and puckers his lips. "Wowser!"

Buster raises one eyebrow. "You like it or not? I had them put anchovies on it."

"Smells like lutefisk, but it does speak to me." Sam licks his lips and wrinkles his forehead like he has a migraine.

"Focus, you two," AJ scowls. "Possum's been abused. We can't let that jerk get away with this. Come on, let's go to the cop shop, so Possum can file a complaint."

"No, I wanna inflict more pain on Troy than the police ever would, and you guys are gonna help me." Possum fits her ball and with limited vision throws it straight into the gutter. Even more pissed, she yells, "Asshole!"

As her friends check out her new look again, she notices and growls, "Why do you keep gawking? This is the new me. Get used to it!" Possum lifts the patch and Sam tries his best to sneak a peek. She throws a second time, knocks down all the pins, flips the patch down, and plops down in a chair. She puts her ball away, wipes a tear from her good eye, and grumbles, "I'm moving out."

AJ pats her on the back. "Where you gonna go?"

"The Y.M.C.A. until I run out of money."

Sam chirps, "Don't do it. Heard their beds have cooties."

Buster adds, "What I heard is people run around all night naked."

B and S start singing, "Y, M, C, A! …Y, M, C, A!"

AJ clears his throat, rolls his eyes, and his two Yahoo friends swallow the next line of the song. After studying all three of their faces, Possum says, "I'm open to suggestions."

Buster sighs, "I got nothing. My mom's trying to get me to move out."

"You don't wanna camp at my place," Sam says. "My mom's weird as shit."

Buster's face lights up. "She doesn't look that weird to me."

"No, she's batshit weird."

"It's not weird to be weird. I'm weird myself. But it's only a matter of time until I find someone who likes my weirdness."

"I have to say, I don't agree with what you're saying, but I do like your self-defecating sense of humor."

Possum glowers. "Oh my God, Sam…self-deprecating."

"No, I meant to say defecating."

AJ interrupts. "Enough already. We're trying to help Possum find a place to live."

Possum squirms. "Don't worry about it. I'll be okay. Listen, I can't concentrate. I'm going to leave."

AJ perks up. "I might have an idea…Come on let's all go."

As they put away their bowling balls, Sam turns to Buster. "What you gonna do this summer?"

"Got me a job right here."

AJ does a double-take. "Here? The bowling alley?"

Buster points back at the Big Cheese pizzeria sign. "I'm a pizza man. I start Monday."

AJ turns to Possum and Sam. "What about you two? Any job prospects?"

In unison: "Nope."

As they exit the bowling alley and go their separate ways, Buster calls out to AJ. "Hey. You and Claudia a thing now?"

"Friends is all."

Sam asks, "What's the difference between being a thing and being friends?"

Buster wrinkles his nose. "Well, a thing is more hands-on, like maybe she lets you cop a feel or sneak a peek at her panties, but not all the time. Being friends means hanging out together…like with Possum…no sex."

Sam stares at Possum. "I think I'd like to try the hands-on part. Now I just need to find a willing participant."

Possum punches Sam. "Why you google eyeing me?"

AJ moves over and tries to settle things. "Claudia doesn't

wanna get sexual with anyone until after college."

"Yeah, right, until she gets horny," Buster argues.

Sam adds his thoughts. "She's blue balling you, AJ."

Possum moves over to AJ and throws up her hand. "Don't listen to these idiots; they know nothing about women. Enough talk, I'm ready."

"Ready for what?" AJ asks.

"Revenge. You said you'd help."

"Now?"

"Yeah, now. You got something better to do?"

AJ signals Buster and Sam to join him. "All right, boys. What we waiting for? It's time to rock and roll."

Possum takes the lead, and they march off like out-of-step tin soldiers.

An hour later, Troy Hanky steps out of the Jones' mobile home. He stops in his tracks when he sees several people gathered around his pickup. Some of them are snickering while others are taking pictures with their cell phones.

In the bed of his truck is a snow dick, shaped to look like a tiny snow-sculptured penis and two snowballs. Troy checks his truck further and sees that all four of his tires are flat. His voice deepens as he hollers, "Possum! You son of a bitch!"

The next day, Possum and her posse peek around the corner of her mom's trailer and watch as the front door opens and Troy struts out. Possum immediately yanks on a rope and a bucket of watery slush positioned on the edge of the roof falls on their victim's head. The gang flees the scene as a water-logged Troy Hanky runs around looking the trailer court for the perpetrators. Out of breath, he screams, "You little bitch! I know it was you!"

AJ AND POSSUM climb out of Coach Dwyer's van, and AJ

grabs a large plastic garbage bag filled with Possum's possessions. Both he and Possum follow their coach to the front door of her house as her new housemate says, "Mrs. D this is so rad. You don't know how much I appreciate this."

"It's okay. I've got a third bedroom with your name on it. 'Sides, I don't want the neighbors thinking it's just AJ and me living together."

"Thanks a lot, but just so you know, AJ and I are planning to get our own place as soon as we can afford it."

Mrs. D bristles. "You're not a couple, are you? There can't be any hanky-panky in my house."

"Oh no, ma'am. We're only friends. Right AJ?"

"Fer sure...with no benefits."

The bowling coach/history teacher whispers in Possum's ear, loud enough for AJ to hear. "Watch yourself. Boys are like dogs. They'll hump anything that moves."

Possum smirks. "I'll make sure my door is shut."

"Have you found a summer job yet, dear?"

Possum points to her eye patch. "No, but if I don't find something soon, I'm thinking about buying one of those metal detectors, so I can search for buried treasure."

"That's funny, but how about if you work for me around the house until after graduation? I'll pay you."

"When do I start?"

AJ pipes up. "You can clean my room." Possum punches him in the arm and follows Mrs. D to the third bedroom.

IT'S GRADUATION DAY and several seniors, led by AJ, Possum, Sam, and Troy, run out the front door of G.H.S. throwing their caps high in the air. AJ spots Claudia with who he assumes are her parents. He takes a step to join them, but when he waves at Claudia, she turns away. He watches a moment and strolls over to a group of friends. When he turns back, Claudia and her parents are gone.

A week later, on a warm early summer day, AJ is on his way to work when he spots Claudia in front of a downtown clothing store window. She notices his reflection behind her and spins around. "AJ, it's you?"

"Thought maybe you forgot who I am. You mad at me or something?"

"No, why would I be angry with you?"

"After graduation, you kind of ignored me. Were you embarrassed for me to meet your parents?"

"Yeah, I kind of was. They've been acting strange lately."

"Getting a divorce will do that to you. We're okay then?"

"Yeah, sure."

"You don't sound that sure."

"I'm sorry for ghosting you. I should have called."

AJ straightens his shoulders. "Let's start over. You wanna hang out this summer or not?"

Claudia smiles. "That's what friends do, right?"

"Okay. So I'll see you around. Gotta get to work."

"Where you working?"

"I told you, the Strike and Spare."

"Oh, yeah. That's right. I forgot." AJ starts to leave, but Claudia grabs his arm and shakes his hand. "AJ, you're the best."

Chapter 13

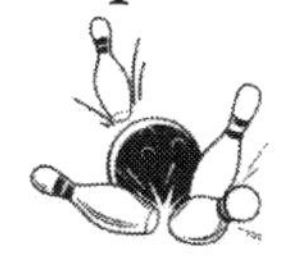

Goodbye Claudia

ON A SUNNY July afternoon, AJ and Claudia stroll through a quiet neighborhood not far from her house. Dressed in a white tank top and black shorts, Claudia says, "So after your uncle took off, you moved in with Mrs. D?"

AJ, dressed in a short-sleeved blue T-shirt and loose-fitting jeans, hops over a crack in the sidewalk. "I didn't have many options. He sees a pop can and begins to kick it down the sidewalk. "I'm just lucky Julius didn't sell all my clothes."

"Is he hooked on drugs or something?"

"No, Texas Hold'em."

"He's a gambler?"

"It appears he was…or is. I guy at the bank told me he wasn't very lucky and burned through a whole lot of money. That's why we lost the house and everything in it. Then he sold the car he just bought with the insurance money…and if that wasn't enough, he drove off in the middle of the night in my Pinto."

"Oh, my God….well, it's awfully nice of Mrs. D to let you stay at her house."

"I didn't have many options. Sam and Buster keep teasing me about her wanting to jump my bones since I'm not paying any rent."

"But you would never let her do that, right?"

"Nah. She's nice, but she's not Mrs. Robinson nice."

"Mrs. Robinson?"

"You know, the movie "*The Graduate*.""

"Never watched it." She stops. "Hey, this is my house."

"Yeah, so Saturday…you got anything going?"

"My parents are taking me to dinner. I think they wanna talk to me about them getting a divorce. I just wish they'd get it over with. It's so awkward, and I'm always in the middle."

AJ softens. "I miss having dinner with my folks."

"Sorry. I didn't mean to..."

"No worries." AJ notices Claudia's Tudor-style house. "Nice."

Claudia frowns. "Not that nice inside."

AJ raises his hand for a high five, and she leaves him hanging. Claudia changes her mind, slaps his hand, and chuckles. "To friends...with no benefits."

"Being with you is benefit enough for me. That was kind of sappy, huh?"

She snickers. "No, I like it. You came up with that yourself?"

"Yeah, kind of a random thought, but I guess it worked. See you later." AJ jogs off as Claudia tops the steps leading to her front door.

STANDING AT THE kitchen sink, Mrs. D washes dishes as AJ dries. She hands him a plate and studies his face. "AJ, it's not easy to stay friends with an attractive and intelligent girl."

"She says she only wants to be friends."

"Well, you know, she might be going through a lot if her parents are getting a divorce."

"The thing is, I don't wanna waste my time if she's not that into me."

Mrs. D hands him a clean fork. "You have a lot of time, so

try to be patient. I hate to use a bowling analogy, but the more you practice, the better chance you have upping your score with her. Stop thinking about knocking down her pins and have some fun. I know a lot of guys just want to have sex, but some girls are more interested in experiencing the mystery, excitement, and the remoteness of everyday life with a guy. It's called dating."

The next afternoon in Greenvale's only city park, AJ and Claudia are tossing bread crumbs in a small pond as several ducks paddle their way to the food. AJ's hand accidentally touches Claudia's arm, and she pulls away. AJ apologizes with his eyes and turns away. In the distance, he sees a swing set occupied by a teenage boy. The boy bails, so AJ points and Claudia race to see who can occupy the open seat first. AJ lets her win and she plops down on the wooden slat. She signals and AJ begins to push her.

It's Friday night at the Strike and Spare *and e*very lane is taken as AJ shows Claudia how to grip a house bowling ball. Full of confidence, she steps back and throws the ball as hard as she can. The ball veers right, skips the gutter, and ends up rolling down the lane next to them. Somehow, the ball manages to reach the pocket at the end of the lane and knocks down several pins. Claudia celebrates as AJ apologizes to the people next to them.

Minutes later they are seated inside the Big Cheese waiting for their food. Buster shows up and serves them their pizza. He waits for them to take a bite and AJ gives him a thumbs-up.

In the basement family room of Claudia's house, AJ and Claudia are watching *The Graduate*. When they get to the scene where Mrs. Robinson tries to seduce Benjamin Braddock, they stuff popcorn in their mouths and take turns drinking from a large cup filled with soda.

The movie ends and AJ follows Claudia upstairs, out the front door, and onto the front steps of her house. They stand awkwardly for a moment until Claudia reaches out her hand for AJ to shake it. "It's been a nice evening. Thank you."

AJ ignores her hand. "You know, sometimes friends kiss."

Claudia gives him a reluctant smile. "Summer's almost over. We've been so good."

"Well, maybe it's time for us to be bad."

"I had a serious boyfriend in the 10th grade. We started kissing and almost went too far. It destroyed our relationship."

AJ shrugs. "How about if I promise to keep my tongue in my mouth?"

"You're missing the point."

"So, you've never…"

"I'm a virgin, AJ."

"Yeah, well, technically, I am too."

"Technically?"

"Well, my hands got kind of busy once...."

Claudia puts her index finger on AJ's lips. "TMI…okay, so why don't we make a pact."

"What kind of pact?"

"No sex until after we graduate."

"From college? I don't even know if I'm going to college."

"Well, I am."

"How 'bout we take another vote the next time we see each other?"

Claudia frowns. "No, but after four years we can decide if we want to be more than friends."

"What are you, some kind of Buddhist monk? I don't think I can last four months. I've been awful horny lately."

"Horny for me?"

"No, the mailman. Who do you think?"

"Well, you know...you can always...you know. That would be all right."

"Wait. Did you just give me permission to jerk off?"

"AJ, you're embarrassing me."

"You think you might graduate early?"

Claudia holds up her pinky finger. "Come on, let's promise one another."

"Wait, we're still negotiating. How about if you at least let me on third base once-in-a-while?"

"I don't know what that means. I don't play baseball."

AJ sighs. "You're not gonna tell anyone about this, are you?"

"It'll be our little secret."

AJ tries again. "So, how about if we take this baseball theme a little further? Fingers and tongues get to do whatever they want, but no home runs?"

Claudia frowns and lowers her lip, so AJ wraps his pinky finger around hers. "You do realize these are our primo years for having sex?"

"I know. I have to wait, too."

"And you're sure about this?"

"A hundred percent."

"No fingers or tongues?"

"Stop. On three, say, 'I promise.' Ready? One, two, three..."

In unison, they say, "I promise."

Claudia snickers. "Now shake on it."

AJ shakes her hand. "I've never shook a girl's hand so much in my life." Claudia goes into the house as AJ stares at the door a moment. He mutters, "Shit. Four years."

TROY EXITS THE Jones' mobile home, checking for any sign of a possible prank. Not seeing anything, he climbs into his pickup, and tries to start the engine, but it won't turn over. He lifts the hood of his truck and discovers a fan belt that has been cut in half. He finds a note and reads it out loud. "I wanted to cut something else of yours off, but my friends convinced me what I'd have to look at would ruin the pleasure." Troy slams the hood down on his truck and throws the fan belt as far as he can.

SUMMER IS OVER as AJ helps Claudia carry the last of her belongings from her house to her father's five-year-old Volvo. AJ squeezes one last bag in the already full trunk, scans the car, and gives Claudia a sad face. There's an awkward silence, so he steps back and matter-of-factly says, "Well, good luck."

"Yeah. It's been an awesome summer."

"Four years, huh?"

Claudia laughs. "Yeah, I'll be back once in a while to visit my dad and, when my folks are officially divorced, I'll need to go to Milwaukee to see Mom."

"Don't forget I'll be here."

"Silly. You're my rock. Are you still thinking about going to junior college?"

"Maybe, but it's hard to save money working at a bowling alley."

Claudia lowers her lip and pouts. "Well, I guess this is goodbye." Sensing she might be feeling a little frisky, AJ moves in for a first kiss. Claudia steps back, lifts her index finger, and says, "How about a hug?" AJ bear hugs Claudia, until he gets a little too carried away and grabs her butt. She gently pushes him away and slides into the Volvo.

As she drives off, AJ yells, "Watch out for deer!"

IN THE KITCHEN of the Big Cheese, Buster furiously folds pizza boxes as AJ does a countdown. "Ten, nine, eight, seven, six, five, four, three, two, one…stop!"

Buster throws up his hands. "Twelve. Twelve boxes in one minute. That's a new record."

"But better yet, how long does it take you to make a pizza?"

Buster raises up. "Good idea!" He grabs a glob of dough and waits for AJ's signal.

AJ stares at his watch and yells, "Go!"

Buster quickly rolls out the dough and furiously scatters ingredients on the misshapen sphere as AJ studies his watch. A minute passes, and Buster throws up his hands for a second time. AJ leans over and studies the finished product. "Minute and ten seconds, but it looks like a giant taco. Keep practicing."

Buster tosses his apron aside, and they exit the Big Cheese, where they join their other two friends on lane number seven. Possum is wearing a T-shirt that reads, 'You don't have to stare, I know I'm a shortie.' Still wearing her cap on backward, she lifts her patch, winds up, and throws a strike.

Sam hollers, "Turkey!"

Possum sits down next to AJ and watches as her secret crush looks down at the floor. "What's the matter with you? You look like a sack of shit."

Buster stands up and grabs a house ball from the rack. "That's cuz he's a lovesick puppy."

Sam adds. "Forget her, dude. There's more than one gal in the woodpile."

Possum groans. "Sam, I'm not even gonna pretend to know what that means."

AJ smooths his hair. "I haven't talked to her in two weeks and she doesn't reply to my text messages."

Buster throws a seven-ten split and groans, "Crapola!" He wags his finger at AJ. "Here's a truth fart, buddy. She's gaslighting you for a reason."

Sam quips, "Yeah, your balls are gonna get so blue, they'll

probably spring a leak."

Possum shakes her finger at B and S. "Shut up, you bus stops." She scoots closer to AJ. "Go see her. Maybe she's just waiting to see if her macho man will pursue her."

"I'm trying not to be desperate."

"Too late for that. Don't be such a catastrophist."

"A what?"

Possum ignores his question. "Surprise her. Girls like her love surprises."

Buster throws his second ball, but he only knocks down the seven-pin. He slides over to AJ. "You can snag my van for a couple of days if ya gas it up when you get back."

AJ sticks out his chest. "I'm not gonna do it." He takes two steps and swings back around. "Okay, I'm gonna do it.

The next morning, headed down Highway 30 in Buster's rusted-out white Ford van, AJ cranks the volume up on the radio when he hears the song *Alley Oop* by the Hollywood Argyles. Fully engaged, he taps his fingers on the steering wheel and sings along. "Ally-oop, oop, oop, oop-oop."

An hour later and twenty miles west of Madison, AJ turns the radio off and the windshield wipers start flapping. Frustrated, he switches the radio back on and the wipers stop.

ON THE CAMPUS of the University of Wisconsin, students hurry past AJ as he takes in the stately brick and Tudor-style buildings, the beautifully manicured grass, and the multi-colored flower gardens around him. Not sure where he's going, he stops a young coed and asks for directions. She points at a five-story building in the distance and he hustles off.

AJ enters the girl's dormitory and approaches a girl in horn-rimmed glasses seated behind a cluttered reception desk. She lays her geography book down, and her eyes light up when she sees AJ's h. "Hi."

AJ grins. "You have a Claudia Giovanni living here?"

"Room fourteen, second floor."

"So, what do I do?"

"Knock on her door."

"That's it?"

"Yeah, visiting hours are from eight in the morning until midnight. Need to leave your driver's license here though."

He removes his wallet, takes out his license, and hands it to her. She studies it and beams, "Cute."

AJ hurries down the second-floor dorm hallway until he finds room fourteen. He freezes when he hears someone in her room crying for help. "Oh, my God! Oh, my God!"

AJ taps on the door, doesn't wait, and cracks it open a few inches. He peeks inside and sees a twin-sized bed surrounded by a half dozen beer cans. "Claudia? You, okay?" His lower jaw drops when he sees what appears to be his "special" friend under a sheet with her knees spread wide. He looks harder and sees the shape of another person under the sheet between her legs.

Startled by AJ's voice, Claudia instantly pulls the sheet up to her neck, and exposes her sex partner's naked body. The dirty-blond frat boy, with rock star features, glares. "Hey, man. We're kind of busy here."

AJ stares at the young man, trying not to stare at his junk. The wind outside the open window picks up and the curtains move. When the breeze reaches the bed, the young man's long blond hair flutters, making him appear to be some kind of Greek god. At a loss for words, AJ spins around and hustles down the hallway.

Claudia jumps out of bed and rushes to the door. With the bedsheet wrapped around her, she yells, "He's just a friend!"

Realizing he's been a frog in boiling water, AJ barks, "Yeah, I noticed he was shaking your hand."

Claudia tightens the sheet and walks back into her room, where her sex buddy is standing proud with a hand towel in front of his private parts. "Who the hell was that?"

"AJ Bowers...a friend from high school."

The young man tosses the small towel, pokes his head into the hallway, and hollers. "Hey, AJ! Your friend gives great BJ's."

"Don't be a jerk!" Claudia tries to slap him but misses. He laughs and gently ushers her back into the room.

AJ hurries to the front desk and holds out his hand. The receptionist gives him his license and snickers. "That was quick."

"Yeah, she was busy."

"Oh, I bet she was with Bruce?" As AJ storms off, she shouts, "Hey, I get off at five!"

STANDING OUTSIDE AJ'S bedroom door, Possum knocks. "Come on. You need to eat."

Mrs. Dwyer joins her. "We're worried about you. Come out right now or I'll...I don't know. I'll do something."

The door opens, and a disheveled AJ peeks out. He's wearing a tattered robe, his hair is a mess, and he's unshaven. Mrs. D takes him by the arm and ushers him to the dining room table. "We're having meatloaf and cornbread…your favorite."

Mrs. D and Possum take turns watching AJ pick at his meal. Demoralized, his voice deepens as he says, "My soul is on fire."

Mrs. D sighs, "Maybe Claudia isn't the girl you thought she was. Sometimes we don't get what we want for a reason."

AJ stabs his cornbread with his fork. "Have you ever wanted to die for someone and kill them at the same time?" Mrs. D and Possum look at each other as AJ tosses his fork on the table. "You know what? I'm done with women."

Mrs. D states the obvious. "You do realize you're talking about half the world's population?"

Possum adjusts her eye patch and adds, "And two-thirds of the people in this house."

Chapter 14

Buster's Special Delivery

"BUSTER, DUSTIN HAD TO GO HOME EARLY," my boss, Barney Franco growls. "I need you to deliver this ASAP." I stop rolling the dough out for tomorrow's pizza, and he lays an extra-large house special on the counter.

"Mr. Franco, I'm off in five minutes."

"Good. You can drop it off on your way home. 'Sides, it goes to the Hill house. Sam Hill is a friend of yours, right?"

I wanted to quote Sammy and say, "If a tree falls in the woods, why do I have to catch it?" I don't wanna be a smartass, so I chuck my apron, grab the pizza, and head out.

On the regular, I jump in my van, start it up, and stare at the gas gauge. Par for the course, that so-called friend of mine, AJ Bowers, returned my van empty, a real Minnesota move.

Anyway, I drive off and get about a block from the gas station, when my engine sputters and dies. I hustle three boys I half know, who are walking by, and they push me to *Steve's Gas Mart* on the next block. I toss them each a dollar and put five bucks worth of gas in my tank.

When I pass my favorite taco/weed truck famous for selling devil's lettuce and toilet wine out their back door, I think about stopping but keep moving cuz Sam gets real pissy when his pizza's cold.

When I pull up to Sam's place, I honk and wait for him to

come and fetch his damn pizza. I wait in my van a couple of minutes, because I'm not some lame delivery boy who goes to the door begging for tips. I'm an indoor man, who gets an extra dollar twenty-five an hour. Not to mention, Sam wouldn't tip me anyway.

The front door finally swings open, and my mouth starts to dry up when I see Sam's mother, Vanessa Hill. As she comes my way, I notice she's wearing a pink skimpy see-through nightgown under a half-open frilly white shawl…a real tease for sure. Anyway, she taps on my driver's side window, so I roll it down, and she coos, "Finally, my pizza."

I don't know what to say as I try not to stare at her cold weather nips. Finally, I stutter, "Ten dollars… and twenty-five cents… not including the tip."

She gives me this toothy grin and purrs like my Aunt Minnie's oatmeal-colored cat. "You're one of Sam's friends, aren't you?"

I don't say anything as she sizes me up and says, "Silly me. I forgot my money. Come inside while I get it for you."

"I don't know. Maybe I should wait here."

"Come on. I don't bite."

I fantasize about her biting my neck as I get out of my van and follow her to the front door. I feel like some kind of bloodhound who just picked up the scent as we approach the front steps. I picture myself being kidnapped and getting that Stockholm Syndrome that Patty Hearst came down with. When I get to the front steps, I get all jittery and say, "I'll wait right here."

"You'll do no such thing. It's cold. Get yourself in here."

My mind goes blank as she pulls me inside and I offer up the pizza. "Here you go, ma'am."

She doesn't take it and says, "Ma'am. Listen to you. All gentleman-like."

"Hey, is Sam here? Maybe I should say hi."

"He's visiting his father in Milwaukee."

"You ordered this extra-large pizza just for yourself?"

"Oh, I have a ferocious appetite, but why don't you stay and share it with me."

"We're really not supposed to eat pizza with our customers."

"You're funny. What's your name?"

"Buster."

"Is that your real name?"

I think to myself, why should I tell her my real name? Then I figure, *what the hell.* "Promise you won't tell Sam?"

"Girl Scout's honor."

I couldn't picture her as a girl scout, but I told her my name anyway. "Kumar. My dad named me. He immigrated from India."

"So exotic. Is your mother from India, too?"

"No, she's Italian and something else. They met in Chicago."

"I'll bet they are a lovely couple."

"Not really, they got a divorce when I was four."

"Not that it's any of my business, but what happened?"

"My mom started eating meat. Then she stopped being a Hindu altogether and joined a Baptist church. That was the end. My dad moved to Toronto, Ontario, and I haven't seen him since. After that, my Mom let me pick out my own name and I chose Buster."

"Well, that was nice of her but I like Kumar. And now I think it's time for us to break a few pizza rules, Kumar."

I look around to make sure I'm not being pranked and say, "Maybe one slice."

Sam's mother pulls me a little further inside the house all sexy-like. Next, she gently removes my stocking cap, the one my grandmother knitted me for my 18th birthday. I get sort of aroused and almost drop the pizza as I watch her carefully place my cap on a side table. Next, she gives me this cheerleader smile and says, "There, now it will be right there when you need it." She takes three steps up the stairs, and purrs again, "Follow me, Kumar."

"Wait. You wanna eat upstairs?"

"Of course, silly boy. Everything is much more comfortable up there."

She grabs my arm and I say, "Oh, I don't know..."

Not letting up, she reaches out and taps my stomach. "I'll bet you have a real six-pack under that shirt."

I don't know why, but I lift it up. She stares at my stomach, and I joke. "Yeah, I think there's room for a couple of six-packs in here." She laughs and finally, I get it. This woman wants my bod. She's probably one of those MILFs you see on those porn channels I don't watch. All nervous, I look around again, to make sure I'm not already in some kind of movie. Cuz, I've heard about people showing up naked on cable and never getting paid.

Halfway up the stairs, Sam's mom turns back. "You coming or not?"

I try to reason with her. "You sure you don't wanna eat in the kitchen?"

"No. Don't be shy. You're eighteen, right?

I panic a second and say, "Barely." All the blood in my brain goes south as I watch Sam's mom sashay up to the top of the stairs. As I follow her, balancing the pizza in one hand, I whisper to myself, "Pizza man."

Chapter 15

Temptation

There's a cold bite in the October air as AJ meanders down Greenvale's Main Street. He stops and gazes at his reflection in the store window, the one where he made his virginity promise to Claudia two months earlier. He moves a little further down the street where he sees a middle-aged homeless man sitting on the curb in front of the Greenvale City Liquor Store. The tattered man's hair is matted and dirty, his beard is unkempt, and he's drinking whiskey from a pint-sized bottle that's inside a paper bag. AJ sits down next to him and stares at the man's yellow and black flannel shirt. "Where'd you get the shirt?"

The intoxicated vagabond grins, "Buy all my clothes at the finest men's stores."

AJ leans back when he gets a whiff of the loner's breath. "The Salvation Army?"

"You shop there, too?"

"No, but I think that used to be my uncle's shirt."

"Huh. Tell him thanks for breaking it in for me." The man takes another drink from his bottle and extends his hand. "Name's Axel."

AJ pauses and offers the man a high-five instead. "I'm AJ." Axel acquiesces, laughs, and slaps his new friend's hand. When the drunk reaches back for his bottle, AJ wipes his hand on his pants and asks, "Is that shit any good?"

"You old enough to drink?"

"You want me to lie?"

The vagrant studies AJ's profile and hands him the bag. AJ removes the bottle and stares at it until Axel says, "Go on. I ain't got no cooties."

AJ wipes off the lip of the container with his shirt sleeve, takes a sip, coughs, and hands it back. "Thanks. Never seen you before. You live around here?"

"I live anywhere I want but this is my favorite spot." Axel stares at AJ. "Woman problems?"

"Yeah, how'd you know?"

"Had the same look on my face when I started living here."

As his new acquaintance drains the rest of the bottle, AJ pulls out his wallet. "Wanna share another one of those?"

Axel reaches out his hand and AJ hands him a twenty. The drunk struggles to his feet and slurs, "Be right back."

Buster drives by in his white van and notices AJ sitting alone on the curb. He stops and rolls down his window. "Dude, you look like shit. Ya still moping about Claudia?"

"Yeah, kind of. What are you doing?"

"Chillin' like a villain…. Hey, I got my cucumber pickled."

"What? You did? Who?"

Buster ignores his question. "Need a ride to work?"

"Nah, I'm taking a couple of days off."

Buster shrugs and drives off as Axel exits the liquor store. AJ swings around as his new friend squats. "You buy the good stuff?"

"Not a whole lot of difference between the good and the bad. 'Sides, ya don't drink this shit for the taste." Axel opens the bottle and takes a long drink. AJ wipes off the bottle again, takes a swig, and coughs.

IT'S MIDNIGHT AND raining hard when AJ arrives back at Mrs. Dwyer's house. He wobbles up the porch steps, pauses to get his balance, and fits a key. He manages to unlock the door and walks inside, where he finds Mrs. D and Possum seated on the couch watching TV.

They glare at him as AJ avoids eye contact. When he reaches the door to his room, he stumbles over a throw rug and mumbles, "Sorry. Sorry."

After he enters his room, he turns back, smiles at Mrs. D, and shuts his door. Mrs. D immediately stands up, goes to his door, and knocks loudly. AJ opens it a crack and covers his mouth. Barb Dwyer glowers. "You've been drinking."

AJ frowns. "Yes, I have."

"I will not have any drunks in this house. Next time it happens, you're out of here. Do you understand?"

"Yes, ma'am." AJ avoids eye contact and whispers, "It won't happen again."

Barb returns to the couch and gazes blankly at the TV screen. Possum finally says, "I think he's having a psychic breakdown."

"Yeah, well. I'm not going to put up with that shit in my house anymore."

"Anymore?"

"My husband turned this place into his own personal bar and I'm not going to let it happen again. This is my house. No drunks allowed."

A WEEK LATER, Sam arrives home carrying a suitcase. He lays it down when he sees Buster's van parked in the driveway. He enters the house expecting to see Buster, but the living room and the entire lower level of the house is empty. Finally, he yells.

"Mom? Buster?" He checks the stairway leading to his mother's bedroom door and hears someone laugh. He tries again. "Mom! You up there?"

From inside her room, he hears her say, "Yes, sweetie. Give me a sec. I'll be right there."

"Buster's van is outside. Is he here?"

Vanessa's door opens, and she makes her way downstairs dressed in a fuchsia-colored bathrobe. "Sammy, I thought you were staying at your dad's place until Monday."

"He had to work, so I'm home early."

"How was the bus ride home?"

Sam ignores his mom and scans the living room. "Where's Buster? Vanessa turns her back on him and her son lowers his voice. "Please don't tell me…"

Sam starts up the stairs, but she blocks his way. "Don't go up there, honey."

Buster exits Vanessa's bedroom with a shit-eating grin on his face. When he sees Sam, he freezes and whispers, "Hey, Samo. What's up?"

"You gotta be frickin' kidding me… You and my mother…?"

Buster takes a step down the stairs and stops when he sees his friend's twisted face. "Come on, man. I'm sorry. You know I have a hard time saying no… to girls… to women."

"Get the hell out of my house, you bastard! I have a gun and when I come back I'm gonna pepper your ass." Sam runs off as Buster speeds down the stairs and out the front door. "Bye, Mrs. Hill!"

Sam flies out of his room carrying a pellet gun and bolts out the front door. Standing on the front steps, he aims his pistol and fires away. Despite the chaos, Buster manages to make it to his van. He peels rubber as he backs out of the driveway and speeds off as pellets destroy his back window.

Having emptied his gun, Sam stomps back in the house. Vanessa, who is at the foot of the stairs, tries to grab her son's arm as he hurries past. Sam stops in his tracks and points his finger at her. "Now you're screwing my friends. What kind of mother are you?"

Not waiting for an answer, Sam storms back to his room. Vanessa raps on his door and pleads, "I'm sorry. I was really lonely. Come out here, so I can explain."

An hour later, Sam emerges from his room in camo pants, a camo shirt, and a camo ball cap. He's carrying a large duffel bag over his shoulder as he heads for the door. Vanessa jumps out of her living room chair and cuts him off. "Where do you think you're going, young man?"

"San Diego."

"San Diego? No, you're not."

"I'm of age. I can go wherever I want."

"Sammy, I'm sorry about Buster."

"Doesn't matter. I'm joining the Marines."

"You're doing no such thing."

"Actually, I already did…on my 18th birthday. Semper Fi!"

His mother's eyes widen. "Oh my God… how will I know if you're okay?"

"I'll send you a postcard." Sam pushes his mother aside and slides out the door as she stomps her feet and starts to cry.

Chapter 16

Jarhead

AS THE YELLOW SCHOOL BUS I'M ON nears Camp Pendleton, I sit all wrathy trying not to think about my loser ex-friend Buster and my whore of a mother. I try not to, but I picture them humping each other, and my stomach starts to gurgle. That passes, and I start to wonder if I made the right decision by joining the Marines. *Yeah, I did. There's only so much Wisconsin shit a guy can shovel.*

As I continue to stew in my own gravy, I see thirty, maybe thirty-five other recruits as scared as I am scrunched down in their seats. Most of them are probably older than me, but it's kinda hard to tell cuz a lot of the guys have different shades of skin and are dressed like where they came from. None of them have blond hair or Scandinavian skin, like I got from my mother's side of the family, though. As I look around and listen to them talk, I realize I might be a minority for the first time in my life.

Sitting next me is this Mexican guy, who appears to be my age, so I get all friendly and say, "Hey, I'm Sam Hill. Where you from?" He doesn't answer, so I look out the window and pretend like I didn't say a gosh damn thing.

A few seconds later, the guy adjusts his blue doo rag and sneers, revealing his silver-grilled teeth. He lifts his chin and mumbles, "South LA."

"Yeah, the city of angels. I got a cousin who lives there. Maybe you know her…Susan Hill?"

I laugh at my own joke, but he doesn't seem to get it, so I keep going. "I'm from Wisconsin." Still nothing. "Greenvale…it's a town full of bowlers, not far from Milwaukee. I guess that's why I'm so good at striking up a conversation; get it, striking?" I get nothing from LA, so I move on. "I'm a pretty good bowler myself. You bowl?"

Finally, his grill opens for business and he snarls, "Shit, bowling's for losers."

I let it go and throw him another question. "Yeah, so what do you do for fun in L.A.?"

He snorts, "I do drive-bys, sell drugs, and cut people."

"Really?"

He gives me this high-pitched dolphin giggle, so I figure that's his way of telling me he's only kidding. A few seconds go by, and he gets kind of chatty. "I worked at a hair salon and tattoo parlor."

I notice two yellow-eyed monkey tattoos, one on each arm, and I nod, "I like your monkeys."

He checks his own arm. "Shit, man. These are gorillas."

"Sorry, did you etch them yourself?"

"Hell, I'm the hair guy. Traded some cuts for these tats."

He gets quiet again, so I say, "So why'd you enlist?"

"Either that or some lame-ass detention center."

"Wow. I didn't know they still do that…I mean give people a choice…jail or the Marines."

"Well, I'm special. What's your soap opera?"

Happy to share, I say, "I enlisted a month ago when I turned eighteen."

"And you're on this bus already?"

"Yeah, it wasn't supposed to happen for three months, but I

called my recruiter and he had an early spot, so he swore me in right away."

"You Pokemon some girl or somethin'?"

"Pokemon?"

"Knock her up…make a baby."

"Nah." I grin. "My gramps was a Marine, so I thought I'd try it out."

Miguel gives me a 'what the hell?' look and says, "Try it out? This ain't no summer camp, homey. You can't go home in two weeks."

I shift directions. "I don't think I got your name."

He takes a moment, "Miguel…Miguel Louis Flores. My homies call me Maniac."

I think about fist-bumping him, but I slap the bus seat instead. "All right, Maniac. I like that."

He slows me down. "I'm not your friend yet, Uncle Sam."

Before I can respond, the bus slows down. When it comes to a stop, we wait for a couple of minutes and stare out the windows at acres of asphalt and a dozen or more ugly gray buildings. Finally, the front door flies open. A Black muscle-bound gunnery sergeant wearing a tan shirt and pants and a campaign hat climbs on board and screams at the top of his voice, "Get the hell off my bus, you shit for brains worms

We grab our shit and fall over each other as we scramble our way to the front of the bus. As we squeeze our way out through the narrow door, a slender Hispanic staff sergeant stands waiting for us at the bottom of the bus steps. Then he yells at the slow movers. "Let's go ladies! We don't have all day! Move it! Move it!"

The sergeants line us all up a foot apart, call us a few disgusting names, and claim we're the ugliest recruits they have ever seen. The Black sergeant walks past me and abruptly does an about-face. "You the Pillsbury Doughboy?"

I figure he's used that line a few times, so I say, "I'm Sam Hill."

He turns to the other drill instructor and snickers, "Hey, doesn't this nobody look like one of them biscuits that pops out of a can?" Some mouth-breathing idiot behind me chuckles, and, sure enough, we all end up doing a hell of a lot of push-ups.

They keep pestering us as we stand at attention trying to look invisible. The California sun starts to get to me, but thank God the big cheeses tell us to stand at ease. Next, they tell us that we're lucky bastards to be in the 4th platoon and part of C company. Then they get all formal-like and introduce themselves as Gunnery Sergeant Wilson and Staff Sergeant Gomez. I take note because I don't wanna screw up their names and do any more push-ups than I have to. All at once, I have this random thought about my grandfather, who warned me about all the Marine shit language. Now that I think about it, I've heard the F-bomb more in the last few minutes than I usually hear in a month.

Further down the line, Sergeant Gomez spots a tall lanky fella and eyeballs him, cuz he's wearing blue jeans, western-style boots, a pearl-buttoned shirt, and a dirt-stained Stetson. "Take that shitty hat off, cowboy!" The poor guy looks around like he's trying to find a hat rack. Out of options, he leans over, and carefully places it on the ground. Pretending not to see it, the sergeant takes a step, plants his foot, and smashes the crown of the Stetson into the ground. "Sorry, cowboy. There's no littering on our parade deck."

Sergeant Wilson steps up and takes his turn. "Your mother dress you like that, Tex?"

"I'm from Kentucky, sir."

The sergeant's eyes light up, and he goes ballistic. "Don't call me sir, ya cherry-ass hillbilly! I work for a living. Drop and give me twenty."

The guy must be in pretty good shape, cuz he whips off the push-ups like nothin' and jumps to his feet. The sergeant doesn't let up. "Kentucky? Your parents related to each other?"

The hillbilly thinks about the question all nervous-like and finally says, "Not that I'm aware of, sir." He realizes his mistake, drops to the ground, and does twenty more push-ups.

Sergeant Wilson chuckles and moves over to Miguel. "Now what do we have here?" My almost-friend doesn't wait and swipes the doo rag off his head, stuffs it in his pocket, and gives the sergeant a tinsel-toothed grin.

"Why you smiling at me, El Crapo? You think you're some kind of gangster?"

Miguel sneers. "Black guerillas twenty-two."

Sergeant Wilson gets in Miguel's face. "Hear that? We got us a real live hip-hop gangster here, Sergeant Gomez."

"Better send in your letter of resignation, Crapo," Sergeant Gomez scoffs. "You're in our gang now."

Wilson lets out a horse laugh and snarls. "And you'd better get rid of those metal teeth or you're gonna get a visit from our very own dentist in the middle of the night." Not finished, Wilson turns to Sergeant Gomez and says, "He still has Parkinson's, right?"

"Yep, shakes like hell when he uses them rusty wire cutters."

The drill sergeants finally stop badgering us and march us over to this gray building, where three lance corporals give us two sets of fatigues, fit us for boots, and hand us each a chrome dome. In case you are wondering, a chrome dome is the Marine Corps' name for the silver-painted insert inside an actual metal combat helmet. Guess we'll get the metal part later when the bullets start to fly.

After we change out of our civilian clothes and climb into our Marine Corps fatigues, we march around the parade ground until a couple of the bigger guys drop out of formation and fall to the ground exhausted.

The yelling starts again and our sergeants march us six at a time into some sort of military-style barbershop. I wait my turn and watch as the half-dozen recruits before me get scalped in a minute each.

I'm next, so I drop down onto a padded folding chair in front of the sheep shearer corporal and try to lighten the moment. "A little off the top please." The corporal turned barber ignores my joke and gives me this sinister look when he spots my ponytail. He instantly grabs a large pair of scissors and hedge-clips it off, kinda like he's removing a dead limb from a tree. I gaze down at the floor at what has been a part of my life for three years and kind of tear up. Then I get this hair-brained idea, eye the corporal again, and say, "Can I take that with me?" The sadistic son of a bitch chuckles and removes the rest of my hair with five quick passes of his oversized electric razor. He chortles, "There ya go, hippie boy. You're a real jarhead now."

Next, the sergeants march us to our barracks and give us military green bedding and old-school foot lockers. Somehow Miguel and I get assigned to the same bunk, and he claims the top and I take the bottom. For some reason, they have us practice making our beds over and over again. They even time us to see how fast we can get in and out of our racks, like maybe one day the barracks might catch fire.

So this is how it goes. Sergeant Wilson yells, "Prepare to mount!" We stand at attention for twenty seconds or more and he hollers, "Mount your racks!" Then we jump in our beds like some goalie trying to cover a hockey puck. After about twenty minutes of that horseshit, both sergeants turn out the lights and we lay in the dark at attention. Once we hear them walk away, we fart and play with our balls until we fall asleep.

Funny thing is, every morning for the next two weeks I always wake up early cuz I have the same crap dream with Buster and my mom being naked in bed together. I almost always hear Buster roar, "*Extra cheese! Extra cheese!*" and my mom scream, "*Extra pepperoni!*" Then I wake up all embarrassed cuz I have a semi.

Unlike Wisconsin, every day at Camp Pendleton is sunny, except for an occasional afternoon downpour. As you might imagine, chow time is my favorite fifteen minutes of the day. They don't let us talk, but we get a chance to relax for a while. The food isn't that great, but there's a lot of it. I am what the Marines call a double rat, cuz I'm underweight. From day one, the sergeants nagged me to eat extra, so's I would fatten up. I think it might it might be working, because my pants are starting to squeeze my balls. "Oorah!"

A couple of weeks crawl by and I manage to keep my nose clean. I even start to feel pretty good about myself cuz now I know how to clean an M-16, march in a straight line, and bounce a quarter off the blanket that covers my rack.

Miguel and I talk quite a bit now, and he's not so cocky anymore. I think everything changed when they cut off all his hair and he was forced to vacate his metal teeth. He lets me call him Maniac now, but only when we're alone.

One night, I even pulled a prank on him when I swiped his grill that he always hides under his pillow at night. I even left a quarter, like I was some kind of tooth fairy or something. Next morning, he was all pissed, until I handed his grill and let him in on the joke. After I explained what a tooth fairy was, he thought it was pretty funny.

Four weeks in, we both get assigned KP duty. We report to the mess hall and this bald-headed cook, Staff Sergeant Lester

O'Reilly, hands us two buckets of potatoes to skin. He rolls away, gives us a belly laugh, and grunts, "Two more buckets after you're done with them." *Right, I know. Classic kitchen duty right out of some Beetle Bailey comic strip.*

I start kinda slow but pick up the pace when I see Maniac double timing me with his peeler, like he's some sort of spud master. I kick his pail. "Slow down. Making me look bad."

"I'm from the hood. I'm good with a knife."

I grin. "You ever peel anyone?" I laugh at my own joke as usual, but Maniac doesn't even smile.

We are finishing our second round of potatoes when the Sergeant Snorkle look-alike waddles over to us. "I need one of you guys to help me put the stew together. I'm short-handed." Before I can answer, Miguel trots off leaving me the cook's assistant.

O'Reilly takes me in the kitchen and puts me in charge of boiling the taters Miguel and I peeled. I finish up and pour them into two huge metal pots that the sergeant had filled with mixed vegetables and overcooked stew meat. Curious, the staff sergeant dips a wooden spoon into one of the pots, takes a taste, and grumbles, "Nah. Needs a little more flavor. Go in the back and get me two more cans of tomato sauce. Should be on the top shelf next to the window."

When I get to the storage room, I see cans everywhere. I check the shelf above the window, but those cans are labeled beans and corn. I search everywhere for the damn sauce, and I'm about ready to go back to tell Sarge I can't find them, when I see some big ass cans sitting over in the corner by the back door. I check them out and they're just what I'm looking for…t-sauce. The cans look kind of strange, you know like bulging out on both sides, but I figure that's just the way it is. I check a little closer and see that the dates on the lids are 1944. Wow vintage. I guess the

Marines don't like to throw anything away.

When I get back to the kitchen, O'Reilly is nowhere to be seen, so I take matters into my own hands and open the cans of sauce myself. I hear a kind of a "swoosh" both times, but figure that's just the way it is. Anyway, I empty the sauce equally in both pots, and just like in the Army, I try to be the best I can be and toss the cans in the dumpster in the alley.

Once I get back, I have this urge to cook, so I grab O'Reilly's wooden spoon and stir one pot and then the other. The Sarge finally waltzes in and yells, "What the hell? Where's my sauce?"

All proud, I say, "Took care of it; put a can in each pot."

O'Reilly grabs the spoon from my hand like I'm trying to steal his job and begins to stir his stew. He growls, "Get you a hair net. You need to help me serve. Doors open in five minutes."

Now wearing matching blue hairnets, Sarge and I hotpad the stew into the serving area. For a peaceful moment, I stand behind the counter stirring, waiting for the doors to open. We finally hear a whistle, and a hundred-plus men stampede through the door like they're looking for gold. I stand there smiling and all I can think about is how proud I am for making this meal happen.

An hour later, when I get back to the barracks, it has already started: a real diarrhea and pukefest. Men are fighting each other to get to the half-dozen toilets in the head. Some of them are shitting in the shower room and latrine sinks. Others don't make it that far and crap in their pants, or worse yet they squat in the dark corners of the barracks. Since I didn't eat any of the stew myself, I stand and watch, trying to stay out of the way. When the men in my platoon run out of toilet paper, some of them start using their own shirts to clean themselves, while others run outside and hide behind trees and bushes.

After a couple of minutes, the whole place starts to smell like one of those livestock barns at the Wisconsin State Fair. Not sure what to do, I try being some sort of hero by gathering up as much ass-wiping junk as I can find: newspapers, magazines, pillowcases, and even old socks I pull out of the lost and found box. If ever there was a shit storm, this has to be one of the biggest.

It wasn't long before the top brass claimed we had poisoned an entire company of men, some who ended up in the infirmary, and others who shit themselves until they were totally exhausted.

When all was said and done, the medics figured out that the cook and I had botulated one hundred-plus Marines with tainted tomato sauce. Later, I found out O'Reilly had put the bad tomato sauce cans in what he thought was a safe place, so's to get rid of them when he had time.

O'Reilly got busted down to corporal and they put him in charge of the laundry room. Since I was just following orders and not even a private yet, they put me on permanent latrine duty. That kept me busier than a one-armed drummer, cuz the fellas made sure to leave a shitty mess for what I did to them. Like I told Miguel this morning, sometimes you get the bear and sometimes the bear shits on you.

One day while I was cleaning my toilets, Sergeant Wilson walks in still holding a grudge and points at me. "Hill, I want those toilet seats clean enough so I can make sandwiches on them."

I try to lighten the mood by saying, "You want tomato soup with those sandwiches?" He didn't think that was so funny and made me scrub the entire floor of the barracks with a bucket of water and a sponge. So let that be a lesson to me. Don't say anything unless your sergeant asks you a question.

A couple of days later, I shot Sergeant Wilson in the ass and my time in the Marine Corps was over.

Chapter 17

Beer, Beer, Beer, Beer, Beer

TROY STANDS IN THE DRIVEWAY of the Jones' mobile home admiring his newly-painted bright blue Ford pickup. Next to him is forty-year-old Lance Munson, an oversized man wearing bib overalls, a button-down denim shirt, and high-top leather work boots. Troy slaps the hood of his truck, gulps down the last of his beer, tosses the can over his shoulder, and belches. "Lance my man, you done good."

"Two thousand dollars' worth of good. Where's my money?"

Troy squirms, "Ya know, I lost my job, right?"

"Yeah, I heard they canned your ass for all the time showing up drunk."

"Shit, I got more work done drunk than those other bastards combined."

"Well, until I get the money you owe me, I'm taking back this car I sold you."

"You can't do that. That's my old lady's ride."

"Not my problem. I'll give it back when I get paid."

Troy hesitates and then hands Lance the keys to the Honda. "When I get my unemployment check Friday morning, I'll settle up with ya."

"All right, I'll be back here Friday afternoon. Don't try and dodge me, or me and my crew will destroy your ass and bury you in the pet cemetery on the edge of town."

"Shit, Lance. Your friends are my friends."

"I wouldn't be so sure about that."

Troy raps the fender of his newly painted truck. "Hey, anyone see you do this work?"

"No, why?"

"Just wonderin'."

"Friday." Lance walks over to his old Honda and tries to start it, but the engine coughs and dies.

Troy circles the car, finds a bowling pin stuck in the tailpipe, and pulls it out. "Now try it." The car's engine finally turns over and Troy mutters, "Damn midget!"

As Lance drives off, he reaches out his side window and gives Troy the finger. Troy reciprocates by yanking on his crotch with his left hand and pointing at the Honda with his right. "Back at you, asshole."

THE WATERING HOLE is packed, as a blond barmaid, Judith Miller, squeezes past several people in order to reach AJ and Axel's table. AJ, who stares a little too long at her breast-revealing top, manages to say, "Two beers."

Aware of what he's looking at, she leans back and smirks. "You're not twenty-one. You need a legal guardian to even be in here."

AJ scoots his chair back. "How do you know how old I am? I could be twenty-one."

"Let me guess. You left your driver's license at home."

AJ pouts and the barmaid smiles. "My sister and you were born on the same day. Her birthday is June 12th and she'll be 19.

"Betsy Miller?"

"That's right."

"Wow, the joy of living in a small town." AJ thinks a

moment. "That's why I brought Uncle Axel here with me. He's my legal guardian. Give him my beer…and when you're not looking..."

"I thought your Uncle Julius was your legal guardian."

"Boy, you've got some memory. UJ left town a couple of months ago; UA's my uncle now."

"Your uncle now? You can't just name someone your uncle."

Axel finally speaks up. "Come on. Give him a break. His parents were killed in a car accident a few months ago."

The barmaid softens. "I know and I'm really sorry about that."

AJ tries again. "Sorry enough to bring us two beers? I won't tell."

Judith tightens her lips. "You know, I could get fired for this." She starts to leave but turns back to Axel. "No offense, but I think I've seen you digging in the trash out back and sleeping in the alley."

Axel doesn't skip a beat. "I collect bottles. It's hard work. Sometimes I have to take a nap."

Judith walks off, and when she returns she leaves two glasses of beer on their table. She checks to see if anyone is watching and sneaks away as AJ takes a sip and says, "Kinda hoppy, but I like it."

"Not the kick you get from whiskey for sure." Axel peers into AJ's eyes. "Just the same, it can sneak up on you and give you the same buzz."

They clink their beer mugs together and AJ chants, "Beer, beer, beer, beer, beer!" AJ gulps down half of his beer and leans over to his drinking buddy. "Do me a solid and stop me before I get too drunk, or I'll be in deep doo-doo with Mrs. Dwyer."

Axel sits up. "Mrs. who?"

"Mrs. Dwyer, the lady I live with."

Two hours later, AJ staggers out of The Watering Hole and into the cool night air. He trips over a crack in the sidewalk and cackles, "I think I'm drunk."

Axel grunts, "I think you are."

"I thought I asked you to stop me."

"That's like asking a drowning man for a life raft." AJ waves him off and goes his own way as Axel shuffles off to the back alley of The Watering Hole.

When AJ reaches Mrs. Dwyer's place, he circles to the back of the house and tries to open his bedroom window. It won't budge, so he stumbles around to the front door. He tries the door and is surprised to see it open. Once inside, he loses his balance and trips over the throw rug in the middle of the living room, crushing Mrs. D's coffee table. When he sits up, the living room lights come on, and he shields his eyes.

AJ exits Mrs. D's house carrying two large black plastic garbage bags and a box of his prized possessions. When he arrives back at The Watering Hole, he toddles behind the building and finds Axel sleeping under some dirty clothes and bar rags. Next to the full-time drunk, is his own portable bar with two half-empty whiskey bottles propped up on a cardboard box. AJ kicks several empties out of the way, lays his box down, uses one of his bags for a pillow, and puts the other bag on top of him as a makeshift blanket.

AJ STANDS BEHIND the counter of the Strike and Spare spraying disinfectant in bowling shoes as his boss approaches. Monty studies AJ's clothes and holds his nose. AJ tries to explain. "I had a rough night…and I'm not feeling so good."

"Well, you look like shit and smell like a wet chicken."

AJ lifts his arm and sniffs. "I don't smell anything."

"That's cuz you've got odor fatigue. Take a shower for God's sake."

"Just so you, I am feeling better."

"Yeah, well, I'm not an idiot. I know a bad case of the bottle flu when I see one. Clean the bathrooms and go home. If this ever happens again, I'll fire your ass."

Monty slips away as Possum enters the bowling alley. She spots AJ at the desk, shuffles over, and squints at him with her one good eye. "You look like...."

"...I already know; I look like shit."

"Where'd you sleep last night?"

"Alley behind The Watering Hole. And don't be Jehovah witnessing me."

Possum taps her finger on the counter. "All I have to say is you'd better not blame Mrs. D for unhousing you, she warned you."

"I know. I've been depressed…haven't been thinking straight."

"You do know Mrs. D's husband turned into an alcoholic and she booted his ass?"

"I thought he was dead."

"Well, he's not…and I've got some other news." AJ questions her with his eyes, and she continues, "Sam joined the Marines."

"He did?"

"Yeah, he left a month ago."

"Damn. Guess that explains why I haven't seen him lately. Christ Almighty, he could have at least said goodbye… Why didn't anyone tell me?"

"Buster didn't want me saying anything, cuz he blames himself."

"What's he got to do with it?"

"Sam caught Buster was poking his mom."

AJ mutters. "Jesus, Buster."

Possum steps back from the counter. "AJ, I gotta go."

"Tell Mrs. D I'm sorry, will ya?"

Possum leans forward. "You need to tell her yourself."

AJ's mood swings, and he growls, "You know what? Tell that uppity bitch that thanks to her and her rules, I'm sleeping on the street now. Possum glowers as AJ continues his rant. "You know what, tell her I'm doing just fine without her help."

"You ungrateful bastard. She took us in after we had nowhere to go."

"Why you all high and mighty all of a sudden?"

"Cuz you're going to shit."

"You're one to talk. Stop trying to be someone you're not and take a break from feeling sorry for yourself? Ya got a bad eye; cry me a river. There are a lot of people worse off than you."

"Oh, you mean like you?"

"Yeah, like me."

"Get over yourself! Boo-hoo. You found out your so-called girlfriend is a slut." Possum starts to leave but changes her mind. "And for your information, this is who I am; I can't help it if I'm smarter than you. And by the way, jerk face, you're the reason God created the middle finger." Possum gives her a dirty look and rushes out of the bowling alley.

Still hung over, his hair a mess, and his shirt tail is hanging out, AJ reluctantly scrubs the floor in the women's bathroom. He takes a moment, leans the mop against a sink, and stares into the mirror. Without warning, Monty walks in and takes a long look at his disheveled hire. AJ grabs the mop and grins. "What's up, boss?"

"I've changed my mind. I'm firing you now."

"You are? Why?

"I told you everything needed to be clean around here."

"Yeah, I've been cleaning my ass off."

"Look in the mirror."

"I already did."

"Can't have you looking like that."

AJ checks his reflection in the mirror again and touches his face. "Yeah, I might be a little rough around the edges."

"You used to turn heads. Now they turn in the opposite direction. Come back when you're back to being yourself."

"You can't do this. I got nothing. No family, no girl, no friends, no place to live. Now, no job!" Monty holds out his hand for the mop. AJ scowls, "Screw you! Screw this whole frigging town." He tosses the mop and his ex-boss catches it in mid-air.

AJ exits bathroom as a young woman walks inside. She takes a step back when she sees Monty holding a mop. Flustered, Monty offers it to her. "Need a job?"

The woman cringes. "Uhh, I have a job. I work at the credit union." She hurries out of the bathroom and Monty looks at himself in the mirror and begins to mop.

Chapter 18

Taking The Lambeau Leap

IN THE ALLEY NEAR THE REAR ENTRANCE of The Watering Hole, AJ and Axel squat in front of a small fire sharing a bottle of whiskey. AJ toasts the street light as it comes on and takes a swallow. "This shit has been going down a lot easier lately."

Axel turns to AJ. "Means you're an official drunk like me."

"Nah, I'm not a drunk...yet."

"Look at you… me. We're the same."

AJ studies Axel's face and hands him the bottle. "Did I tell you I got fired today?"

"Now we really are the same...homeless and jobless."

"Least there's no one telling us what to do. No rent, no bills to pay."

Axel counters, "No food, no family, no friends."

AJ slurs his words. "You sound like a bottle-half-empty kind of guy. We're friends, aren't we?"

"Because I buy you booze. We'll find out what kind of friends we really are when you turn nineteen and can buy your own firewater." Axel hands him back the bottle. "Finish it off."

"Thanks." AJ finishes the bottle off. "Got family anywhere?"

Ignoring the question, Axel wobbles to his feet. "Come on, I know a place where we can get a hot meal."

"Nah, Go ahead. I can't eat right now. I'll get something

later."

"Suit yourself. I'm all about free food."

LANCE MUNSON, DRESSED in military green, waits impatiently on the porch of the Jones' trailer house. Suddenly angry, he pounds the door with his fist. "It's Friday, you bastard! Where's my money?" He kicks the door. "Don't screw with me, Troy! If you don't pay me, I ain't kiddin' about planting your ass in a pet cemetery." Lance throws up his hands, shuffles back to his truck, and drives off. Seconds later, inside the trailer, Troy parts a curtain and peeks out a kitchen window.

AXEL IS IN a serving line in the basement of a local church with several other down-on-their-luck men and women waiting to be fed. He sniffs the air and smells a strange blend of baked bread and body odor. On the other side of the counter are four volunteer servers, one of them Barb Dwyer.

As Axel nears the counter, he hangs his head as Barb ladles a large helping of hamburger and tater tot casserole and puts two homemade buns on his plate. He holds it out a little longer, and she gives him a second scoop of hotdish. Axel bears his teeth. "Thanks, Barb. It's been a while."

Barb looks up and takes a step back, surprised by Axel's rough exterior. He tries to explain. "I know. I could use a shower." Barb doesn't say anything, so Axel shuffles off as she busies herself with the next person in line.

A few minutes pass and Axel notices Barb going from table to table giving people more hotdish. When she reaches his table, he holds up his hand, suggesting he might want another helping. Barb frowns, "I already gave you extra."

"No, sit. Let's talk." Barb tries to walk away, but Axel takes her arm and gently pulls her down in the chair next to him. He gazes into her eyes and softens his voice. "It's been a long time.

How are you doing?"

"Really well…until now."

"I heard you gave my friend AJ the boot."

"Your friend?

"Yeah, he's a good kid."

"So that's why…? AJ's your drinking partner isn't he? Axel, you're such a jerk. He's just a kid."

Barb starts to stand, but Axel rests his hand on her shoulder until she relaxes. "Hear me out. I gave up booze and I'm gonna convince AJ to do the same. He needs to gets his shit together."

"Do you have your shit together?"

"Yeah, I'm on the wagon."

"What wagon? Who are you trying to fool? I smell booze on your breath."

"I know. I just stopped drinking… when I saw you."

"Just like that, you're finished?" Barb shakes her head. "Do you know how many times I've heard that?"

"Yeah, but this time it's different. I've had an epiphany."

"What kind of epiphany?"

"A plan. First, I'm going to start going to AA meetings. Then, I'm going to get myself a job and find a place to live. And after we get back together, we'll move to another town and start over."

"I'll believe it when I see it…the first part, not the part where we get back together and move."

"Come on. You still got the hots for me and you know it."

"Have you looked at yourself lately?"

Axel ignores his estranged wife's question. "Well, just so you know, I have a job interview tomorrow."

"What, with the sanitation department? Nobody's going to hire you looking like that."

"I'm gonna clean myself up. Get back to the real me. You

remember the sober me, right?"

"Barely."

Axel takes a deep breath. "Barb, we had a good marriage until I screwed it up and started paying more attention to the bottle than I did you."

"It's been two years, Axel. I'm doing fine without you."

"But you still love me."

"And how do you know that?"

"Because you haven't filed for divorce."

Barb stands up. "That's because I haven't gotten around to finding a good lawyer, but seeing how you've messed up AJ's life, I'll be seeing one next week."

"Barb, I'm serious. I stopped drinking."

"Yeah, an hour ago. A drunk pretending to be sober is still a drunk.

As Barb heads back to the kitchen, Axel raises his voice, "Ya gotta admit our sex life was awful good." People shift in their chairs and laugh as a red-faced Barb disappears into the kitchen.

AJ STUMBLES OUT of a local burger joint with a tray filled with cheeseburgers. A young female employee runs out of the place and yells, "Hey, you can't take that tray!" She takes two steps his way as AJ leans over, balances the tray, and barfs on it. Before AJ can say anything, the burger gal scrunches up her face and trots off. "Gross! Never mind. Keep it."

As the sun sinks below the Main Street buildings, Axel enters The Watering Hole back alley, where he finds AJ sound asleep. He sits beside him and clears his throat. AJ doesn't move, so Axel taps him on the shoulder. There's still no response, so he tickles his ribcage.

AJ giggles in his sleep until he opens his eyes and spots Axel.

"Oh my God. I had the weirdest dream. I was a little boy, and I was wrestling with my dad and Uncle Julius. We were talking about bowling, and, for some reason, Dad started tickling me and said if I didn't stop drinking he was never gonna show up in my dreams again. Weird huh?"

"Yeah, weird." Axel puts his hand on AJ's knee. "Maybe you should listen to your dad…maybe we both should."

"What?" AJ sits up straight. "You think my dream was some kind of sign or something?"

"I think it is." Axel grabs a half-full whiskey bottle and pours the contents on the ground.

"Wait!" AJ tries to grab the bottle out of Axel's hand, but it's too late. "What are you doing? That's all we got left. Yesterday I sold my coin collection. Once that money's gone. I'm broke."

"AJ, if nothing changes, nothing changes. Do you wanna live in this alley for the rest of your life? Winter's coming, and believe me, being homeless during a Wisconsin snowstorm is no fun."

"Why you all of a sudden making a quantum leap?"

"Cuz, I saw my wife and I want her back."

AJ stares at his friend. "Your wife? You're married?"

"Yeah, I've already lost two years of my life being stupid. I need to make my way back to the real world. You with me or not?"

AJ looks away and then turns back. "Probably should. This being free shit isn't all it's cracked up to be."

Axel yawns. "First thing in the morning, I'm gonna find me a job. I suggest you clean yourself up, go back to that bowling alley, and try and beg for your old job back." He yawns again. "Big day tomorrow." Axel lays down and quickly drifts off.

AJ takes in what they promised one another, reaches for the almost empty bottle, pours the last drop of whiskey in his mouth, and mumbles, "One last taste for the road."

SEATED ON THE living room couch, Mrs. D knits while Possum reads Agatha Christie's *ABC Murders*. There's a moment of silence until Mrs. D nods. "I saw my husband yesterday."

Possum puts her book aside. "How long has it been?"

Mrs. D checks the wall calendar. "Twenty-three months, but who's counting? He says he's stopped drinking… again."

"You believe him?"

"He had liquor on his breath. Any word on the library job?"

"I have an interview next week."

"That's wonderful." The house phone rings and Mrs. D lays her knitting down and picks up the receiver. She listens a moment and hands it to Possum. "It's for you."

Possum whispers, "Hello." She listens a moment and her eyes widen. "When?...She gonna be okay? Can I see her?" Possum hangs up the phone and whispers, "My mom's in the hospital."

"Oh, no. I'll take you there right away."

THE SNOW FLIES as Axel makes his way out of the alley wearing a clean white shirt and tan khaki pants he got from *The Salvation Army* store a block away. His hair is combed, he's shaved, and he looks like a new man.

Axel peers in The Watering Hole bar window at a "Help Wanted" sign and goes inside. The owner, Fritz Whiting, standing behind the bar counter, sees him and frowns. "You know you're not welcome in here. You've got a tab longer than my arm."

"I'm here to work it off…the tab, not your arm." Axel smiles and turns serious. "You've got a job, and I want one."

"Oh, really?

Yes, I assume you would prefer someone with experience. I used to bartend when I was in college."

"I would be like me hiring a fox to guard a hen house."

"I hear you, but I'm not drinking anymore and I know alcohol. If you don't like my work, you're no worse off than you are now."

Fritz squints. "You gave up drinking. When?"

"Yesterday at lunch. I'm done."

"Yesterday?" Fritz snickers. "I have to say, I've never hired a recovering alcoholic to work in my bar before, let alone one who is only a day sober." Axel pleads with his eyes and the bar owner bites his lower lip. "Well, I'm short-handed, and I'm all about second chances. One o'clock tomorrow work for you?"

"I'll be here at twelve-fifty."

ON THE OUTSKIRTS of Greenvale, *Mutt's Truck Stop* is surrounded by semis, motor homes, and other road vehicles. AJ exits the front door and covers his face, trying to shield himself from the large flakes of an early Wisconsin snowstorm. Like Axel, he's dressed in clean clothes, having taken a truckstop shower. However, he is only wearing a light jacket which is insufficient for the unforeseen winter weather.

By the time AJ reaches the business district of Greenvale, the streets are blanketed with ice and snow. As AJ trudges along, headed for the bowling alley, he struggles to stay on his feet. When he sees a blue pickup roll up to a stop sign in front of him, he does his usual thing and grabs hold of the back bumper.

The driver, Troy Hanky, who happens to check his rear-view mirror, spots AJ just as he crouches down out of sight. Troy cackles as he slowly drives away from the stop sign. When he reaches Main Street, he guns his engine and picks up speed.

AJ tightens his grip on the bumper and yells, "Hey, slow down!" Troy stomps on the gas pedal and AJ fights to hang on.

As the truck slides sideways, it throws the hitchhiker up onto the sidewalk. AJ slides on his back and comes to a sudden halt when he slams headfirst into a fire hydrant. Troy checks his driver's side mirror and growls, "Eat me!" before he speeds away.

The snow is coming down harder now and the wind has picked up as a police car arrives with flashing lights. The forty-five-year-old officer, Ryan Bybee, parks near several bystanders, who are staring down at the damaged eighteen-year-old. Sprawled up against a yellow fire hydrant, AJ is unresponsive. Finally, a red-bearded man drops to his knees, removes his parka, and covers AJ with it. Then he checks to see if the injured boy has a pulse. When the tall policeman arrives, he pushes his way through the circle of bystanders and turns to the bearded man. "He still breathing?"

"I was gonna give him mouth-to-mouth, but he smells like Everclear."

A twenty-something wearing a red stocking cap and a pillowed blue ski jacket pipes up. "Wisconsin SWI."

The policeman glares at the young man. "SWI?"

The young man's eyes twinkle. "Sliding while intoxicated."

The cop bristles. "Get the hell out of here!" The smart aleck slinks away as the cop puts his hands over AJ's mouth to make sure he's still breathing. Satisfied he's alive, he turns to the bystanders. "Ambulance is on the way. Anyone see what happened?"

The bearded man explains. "Blue pickup was speeding along with this young fella hanging on his back bumper. Truck swerved, and he went flying."

"See who was driving?"

"Nope."

The policeman kneels down and taps AJ on the shoulder. "Keep breathing, kid."

An ambulance pulls up and two paramedics rush to the

scene. They carefully load AJ onto the gurney just as Axel shows up. "Oh my god! What happened?"

The bearded man takes Axel aside. "He slid smack dab into that there fire hydrant. I think he might have been drunk…the slider, not the driver."

"Where's the driver?"

"I don't know. He didn't stick around."

THE GREENVALE HOSPITAL parking lot is filled with snow-covered cars and trucks. Still clean-shaven and smartly dressed, Axel walks in the hospital's door and double-times it to the Emergency Room front desk. The nurse is staring down at her ledger when Axel interrupts her. "You have an AJ Bowers here?"

The nurse studies her computer screen. "They took him to his room, but he's unconscious. No visitors allowed. You a relative?"

"Uncle."

"You can wait if you want."

Axel moves to the waiting area, sits, and picks up a magazine. When he looks up, he sees Barb across from him staring his way.

She scowls. "Really, Axel? His uncle?"

"Honorary uncle. What are you doing here?"

"AJ's friend Possum, the girl who's been living with me… well her mother, Amber Jones, is in intensive care. I happened to be here when they brought AJ in." Axel picks up a magazine and thumbs through it. There's a moment of silence until Barb says, "You look… a lot better."

"You always look good. Hey, I got the job I interviewed for."

"Really? Where you working?"

"The Watering Hole. I'm their new bartender."

"Isn't that kind of like hiring a lifeguard who can't swim?"

"Guy who hired me pretty much said the same thing."

They sit quietly until Barb finally says, "Do you know what actually happened to AJ?"

"Apparently he took the Lambeau leap into a fire hydrant."

Barb squints. "He must have been hooking cars again."

Axel checks the clock and jumps to his feet. "Damn! I'm going to be late for my AA meeting." As he trots off, he glances back at Barb. "Check on him for me, will you?"

Barb waits for Axel to leave and whispers to herself, "No, but I'll check on him for myself!"

Chapter 19

Waiting

POSSUM STANDS NEXT TO HER MOTHER'S hospital bed staring at her swollen eyes and bandaged face. The battered woman has several tubes attached to her arm and a heart monitor beeps at a slow rhythmic pace. A nurse shows Barb Dwyer into the room, and she sidles up to Possum. "How's she doing?"

"She's sleeping a lot, has a concussion, lots of bruises, but no broken bones. The doctor says she's gonna be all right."

"Do you know what happened?"

"The *Reader's Digest* version is that she let Troy in the trailer…a big mistake…and he beat the hell out of her because she wouldn't give him a beer."

"Troy? The same jerk who damaged your eye?"

"Yeah, her so-called boyfriend."

"Did the police arrest him?"

"They can't find him."

"Possum, AJ's in the hospital too."

"What?"

"He slid headfirst into a fire hydrant."

Seated in AJ's room only a few doors down from Amber Jones' room, Barb, Possum, and Axel wait for AJ to come out of his coma. Like Possum's mother, he is hooked up to several tubes, but he's wearing an oxygen mask. A middle-aged white-coated doctor enters the room and shines an ophthalmoscope in both of AJ's eyes.

Axel stands. "How's he doing, Doc?"

The doctor gently pulls AJ's eyelids up as he answers Axel's question. "Not bad for someone with five broken ribs and a severe concussion. But he's not out of the woods yet."

Axel follows up. "Does the CT scan show any signs of a brain hemorrhage, contusions, or other abnormalities?"

"Swelling of the brain, some internal bleeding, but nothing I haven't seen before."

"Once the brain swelling subsides, I'm sure you'll have a better idea as to his chances for a full recovery."

"Yes, just waiting for him to regain consciousness. You a physician?"

"Gave up my practice a few years ago."

The next morning, Ryan Bybee, the handsome and recently divorced policeman who was at the scene of AJ's accident, stands at Amber's bed taking notes. She is conscious now but appears lethargic as the officer converses with Possum. "When she gets better, we're going to need her to come down to the station to file an official complaint. Right now, we have a warrant out for Troy Hankin's arrest. You see him, call 911 right away." The cop pockets his notepad and exits the room.

Still half asleep, Amber takes her daughter's arm. "Where is Troy going?"

THREE DAYS HAVE passed and AJ is still lying in bed, dead to the world. Sitting across from him are Possum and Buster, who exchange magazines, and flip through the pages. Possum checks the clock, lays her magazine down and stands up. "Gotta go. You're in charge."

Buster sits up straight. "Where you going?"

"It's ten o'clock. Mom is getting discharged now. Make sure you call me if he wakes up."

Possum exits AJ's room and walks down the hall as a female orderly enters Amber Jones' room pushing a wheelchair. Possum remains in the hallway reluctant to go inside. She begins to cry but quickly dries her eyes when two nurses walk past.

When she finally enters her mother's room, Amber Jones is sitting in a chair dressed to go home. Possum helps the orderly lift Amber up and into the chair as the exhausted woman takes her daughter's hand and squeezes it. "Honey, you're coming home with me, right?"

"Sorry, Mom. I can't right now."

"But I need you."

"I know, but I need me too. Maybe we can meet up sometime."

"How am I gonna get home?"

"I called you a cab. The driver is going to meet you at the hospital entrance in ten minutes."

"Where are you going?"

"I need to check on AJ. He's only a few rooms down from here."

"You love AJ more than you love me"

Possum ignores what she just said and rotates her mom's wheelchair so it faces the door. "You be safe. Call me when you get home." The orderly rolls Amber away as Possum rubs away a tear.

Still waiting for AJ to regain consciousness, Possum and Buster sit staring at a muted soap opera on the TV above them. Possum breaks the silence. "So are you still seeing Sam's mother?"

Buster shrugs his left shoulder. "How'd you hear about

that?"

"Sam told me before he left for San Diego. You remember Sam, your best friend?"

"I can't believe he ran off and joined the frickin' Marines."

"It's something he's been planning for a while. So answer my question."

"After Sam blew a gasket and Swiss-cheesed my car, I never went back. That woman's batshit crazy."

"And you're profoundly stupid."

"On the surface, I might appear to be stupid but..."

"No, you're stupid under the surface too. Sam is holding you culpable for what you did to…with his mother."

"Gimme a break. I told him I was sorry. He wouldn't listen."

"I wonder why. You were porking his mother."

IN THE BASEMENT of the Presbyterian church, Axel is enjoying another free meal. He sees Barb approaching with a platter of chicken and nudges the man seated next to him to slide over. The man grumbles something and moves to the end of the table. Barb hesitates, sits down, and offers Axel another helping. "More chicken?"

"No, I'm good, but I'm happy to see you."

"Wish I could say the same. You been up to see AJ lately?"

"I was up this morning; no change."

Barb softens her voice. "I probably shouldn't have kicked him out of the house."

"You know, sometimes a fella has to learn the hard way."

"And what have you learned, Axel?"

"You really wanna know?"

"No, but I've got another question. Are you still living on the street?"

"I'll have you know; I have a suite at the YMCA."

"But you still can't afford to feed yourself?" Barb rethinks her comment and apologizes with her eyes. "Sorry, that wasn't nice."

Axel lets it go. "I've been paying off my bar tab with my tips, but I get paid again on Friday. What do you say we have dinner Saturday night?"

"I have other plans."

"That's right; first Saturday of the month. Bunco night."

"I'm surprised you remember that."

"I remember a lot of things, Barb."

She takes a moment and whispers. "You were such a good doctor, Axel."

"Yeah, until I showed up for surgery drunk. I could have killed that man."

Barb stands up. "Don't take this the wrong way, but you need to forgive yourself even if I can't forgive you." As Barb hurries away, Axel tosses his fork in the air and catches it.

POSSUM SITS ALONE in AJ's hospital room reading yet another Agatha Christie novel, *Death on the Nile*. The door opens and in walks Sam Hill. His hair is military short, but he's wearing civilian clothes. Possum squeals, "Sam, you're back!" She races over, hugs him, and steps back. "Wow, Samson, the Marines really rocked your bod." She notices a tattoo of a bowling ball and pin on his arm and adds, "That's real gangster, but where's your uniform?"

"I'm out."

"Out? Do you mean out, out?"

"Yeah, I'm on permanent leave."

"But it's only been a few weeks. How'd you manage that?

Sam ignores her question and edges closer to AJ's bed. "Heard what happened. How's he doing? Not brain dead, is he?"

"He's always been a little brain dead." Sam stares at Possum and she repents. "Sorry, totally inappropriate." She tries again. "Doctor says it's too early to know if there will be any permanent damage, but I wish he'd wake up, so I can worry about something else."

"So what's next?"

"We wait."

They take a seat and sit silently until Sam's stomach begins to grumble. He jumps to his feet. "It's chow time at Camp Pendleton."

"The food here stinks. Wanna order pizza?"

"Our drill sergeants always told us pizza is for the weak. But what the hell! I'm not a Marine anymore." They high-five, and Possum walks over to the phone and picks up the receiver.

An hour later, Buster enters the hospital room carrying a large pizza. Possum looks up from her book and smiles. "Pizza man at your service!" Sam, who is looking out the window, turns when he hears a familiar voice. Buster shifts his eyes to Sam and drops the pizza box on the floor. "Shit."

Instantly angry, Sam stares daggers at Possum. "Son of a bitch! Did you set this up, Possum?"

"Time to settle this. You two have been friends too long."

Buster picks up the pizza as Sam turns his back and grumbles, "Too long is right. I've moved on."

Possum shoves Buster. "Tell him you're sorry."

"Already did. Sent him a postcard. He never wrote back."

Not letting up, she eyes Sam, who raises one eyebrow and grunts, "After I didn't read it, I gave it to my bunkmate, so he could wipe his ass."

Buster lifts his chin. "With a postcard?"

Sam turns back around. "You're missing the point."

Possum tries again. "Sam, lower the arrogance and tell Buster you forgive him."

Sam squares his jaw. "You still seeing my mom, you mother-sucking mother?"

Possum taps the ex-jarhead on the shoulder. "Watch the vocab, Marine."

Buster tiptoes back into the conversation. "I haven't seen her since the day you left."

"You saw my mother naked. I've never seen her naked."

Possum squirms. "Do you wanna see your mother naked?"

"Now you're missing the point."

Buster gripes. "Come on, man. We were consenting adults."

"You're eighteen; my mother's forty-two."

"Still…consenting adults."

"You didn't have my consent. Friends don't screw each other's mothers."

Possum keeps trying. "Okay, we know the problem. So how we gonna fix it? Buster?"

"Okay, I shouldn't have slam-dunked his mother. I'm sorry…it was all on the card I sent you."

"Sam, it's your turn." She waits for him to say something, but when he doesn't, she threatens to hit him.

Sam steps back. "I wish I would've had a bigger gun to shoot him with."

Possum frowns. "Come on."

Sam's voice fades away as he tries again. "I wish my mom wasn't so all the time horny and you weren't such a shithead to take the bait."

"There. Now, shake hands."

Sam balks. "Not yet. He still owes me."

"Owes you what?"

"Ten Hail Marys and twenty push-ups."

Buster wrinkles his nose. "What?"

Possum groans, "Do it, Buster."

He drops to the floor, starts doing push-ups, and mutters, "Hail Mary, full of grace…something, something… Hail Mary, full of grace…something, something." Out of breath, he continues to do push-ups, while chanting his own version of the prayer.

Possum shifts her attention back to Sam. "I didn't know you were Catholic?"

"Yeah, I'm all about practicing the pillows of Islam."

"Yeah, I'm pretty sure you meant to say pillars…and you've got the wrong religion."

"Whatever."

Buster finishes his last push-up, struggles to his feet, and dusts himself off. Possum grabs them by the arms, pushes them together, and forces them to shake hands. As Buster's breathing slows, he addresses Sam. "Why aren't you in some desert blowing things up?"

Possum tries to help. "The Marines didn't work out, so Sam resigned, right Sam?"

"No, I got my ass kicked out cuz I poisoned a hundred men with tomato sauce. A few days later when I was cleaning my M-16, it went off and the bullet grazed my drill sergeant in the butt cheek. A lot of blood. Our Company Captain claimed I was a danger to the Marine Corps and sent me packing."

Buster pats Sam on the back. "I saw *Full Metal Jacket.* He probably deserved it. So you're home for good then?"

"Yeah, got me a bad conduct discharge."

"Are you back living at home?"

"Yeah, but you better not be delivering pizza there."

Possum steps over. "You l haven't forgiven Buster have you?"

"Almost, but not quite."

Possum glares at Sam. "I think it's time we settle this thing with a Bowl Off."

Sam squints. "Are you kidding me? That's AJ's thing."

"I'm sure if he were awake, he would approve." Possum surveys the room. "Now to find a couple of bowling balls."

Buster nods. "Mine's in my van...in fact, I've got two."

"Perfect. Sam, you get to choose which one of Buster's balls you wanna use."

"I don't wanna touch any of his balls."

Possum says, "Funny. You two meet me in the parking lot in twenty minutes."

In the hospital parking lot surrounded by mounds of snow, Sam and Buster shiver as they hold their twelve-pound balls close to their chests. Sixty feet away are two bowling pin formations comprised of ten quart-sized water bottles. Possum checks the bottles one last time and walks over to Sam and Buster. "Same deal as always. We're going to settle this disagreement once and for all. As you know, bowling rules apply. Both of you get a chance to knock down as many water bottles as you can. Two throws each. "Sam, if Buster wins, you have to forgive him for humping your mother. Buster, if Sam knocks down more pins than you, you have to supply him with one free pizza a week for six months.

Sam adds, "Pepperoni, double cheese, and I pick them up."

Possum turns to Buster. "He wants to pick them up himself."

"I heard him."

Sam blows on his hands, preparing to throw first. He takes his time, rears back, tosses his ball, and knocks down six bottles. "Shit!" He tries again and eliminates three of the four remaining bottles. "Double shit!"

Buster grins and rolls his ball. All ten bottles of water scatter in every direction. Sam throws up his arms in frustration. "Not fair! Haven't bowled in six weeks…and I didn't get to use my own ball."

Possum points. "It's over Sam. Don't be a sore loser."

Sam turns to Buster, rolls his eyes, and says, "Forgiven." As they walk away, Buster puts his hand on Sam's back, but Sam removes it and mutters, "You still owe me a pizza."

BARB DWYER WALKS in AJ's hospital room, followed by Axel, who can't stop smiling at her. Barb does a double take when she sees her former bowling team members standing next to AJ's bed. "Everyone, this is Axel, my…AJ's friend. Axel, this is Possum, Buster…and Sam. Anyway, along with AJ here, they're four of the best bowlers I've ever coached.

Axel smiles. "Nice to meet you."

Barb scoots over next to Sam. "I hardly recognized you. You're back from the Marines? You on leave or something?"

"Yeah, mostly something."

"You look so… so strong."

"Yeah, I don't know if it's better to be strong and look weak or be weak and look strong."

Barb squints, "Ahh. Good old Sam-speak."

Axel shifts to AJ's bed and studies his profile as everyone else watches his bedside manner. "Listen, AJ is still comatose, but you guys can help. His brain is functioning at its lowest stage of alertness. It needs to be stimulated."

Sam steps back. "I'm not stimulating him."

"No, listen. You guys need to talk to him, sing his favorite songs, read, call him by name, and maybe talk about bowling."

Buster knits his brows. "You some kind of doctor or

something?"

Axel responds, "As of right now, I'm just something."

Barb moves to Axel's side. "This man used to be one of the finest neurological surgeons in the state of Wisconsin."

Axel races to the door. "This used-to-be needs to get to work."

Barb follows him out the door. "I'll give you a ride."

AJ's three friends stand at the foot of his bed softly chanting. "AJ! AJ! AJ! AJ! AJ!"

They finally give up and Sam tries telling a joke. "Here's one for you. There's these two Minnesotans, Ole and Lars, and they decide to go ice fishing. When they get home that night, Ole's wife, Lena, says, 'Where's all the fish?' Ole, he says, 'By the time we dug a hole big enough for our boat, it was time to go home.'"

Buster tries. "How about this one? Why don't mushrooms get invited to parties?" Sam grows impatient as he waits for the answer. Finally, Buster delivers the punch line. "Cuz they're fun guys."

Possum prunes her face. "Oh my god dot com."

Not giving up, Sam walks over and grabs a tambourine while Buster picks up a bongo. Possum joins them, and the guys play their instruments and sing *Blue Moon,* by the Marcels. Next, they sing several lines from Barney's theme song: "I love you, you love me, we're a happy family." They finally end with AJ's favorite oldie, *Alley Oop*. Possum and Buster are pitch-perfect, but Sam's monotone voice is a half beat behind. When they get to the refrain of *Alley Oop*, they punch the "alley-oops" and throw up their hands. AJ's eyes start to flutter, but none of his friends notice.

Discouraged, Buster and Sam lay down their instruments and Buster starts to reminisce. "Remember when we waxed the Lake Superior Demons, and you almost rolled a 300? Think I bowled a

220 that day. Good times. Good times." There's still no reaction from AJ, so Buster takes a seat.

A few minutes later, Possum reads a passage from *A Midsummer Night's Dream,* while Buster and Sam check their cell phones. "'I had a dream, past the wit of man to say what dream it was...The eye of man hath not heard, the ear of man hath not seen, man's hand is not able to taste, his tongue to conceive, nor his heart to report, what my dream was.'"

Frustrated, Possum points at Sam and Buster, and the three of them chant, "AJ! AJ! AJ! AJ!

AJ's eyes start to twitch and Possum notices. "Oh, my god! I think he hears us." They rush to his bed. Nothing more happens until AJ's plastic urine bag starts to fill. They watch for a few seconds, shuffle back to their chairs, and start checking their cell phones again

AJ's Dream

So, I'm in the middle of this sweet dream when I hear someone chanting my name: "AJ, AJ, AJ, AJ, AJ." A few seconds later, I hear someone singing one of my favorite songs, "Blue Moon," and sure enough I see a blue moon shining over the top of a frozen lake that looks like Lake Winnebago, where Mom, Dad, and Uncle Julius used to take me fishing for walleye.

Anyway, I spot these two fur-coated fishermen in the middle of the lake drilling a giant hole in the ice. I slide over to ask what the hell they're doing as they fit their rowboat into the hole.

Then I hear a familiar voice coming from the trees near the lake: "I had a dream, past the wit of man to say." The gal's voice trails off and out of the trees runs this purple dinosaur Barney-type singing, "I love you, you love me, we're a happy family." A few seconds later, I see this caveman dressed in leopard skins and carrying a big club, chasing after Barney and screaming,

"Alley, oop, oop! Alley, oop, oop" The cave dweller, who's carrying a basket of mushrooms, tosses them at the big reptile, and they run off all helter-skelter-like back into the trees.

Finally, someone yells my name again, "AJ! AJ! AJ! AJ! AJ! For some reason, the sound of my name makes me wanna take a leak. There's no bathroom anywhere, so I pee in the hole the fishermen made earlier. When I finish, I pivot, and there stands Claudia with a fitted sheet covering most of her naked body. When I lean in for a kiss, she lets the sheet drop to the ice, and I squeeze her left butt cheek.

As the gang gathers their belongings and starts for the door, Possum hears AJ moan. "Wait." She speeds over to AJ's bed, takes his hand, and whispers, "Are you there?"

AJ puckers his lips, squeezes Possum's hand, and slowly opens his eyes. He sits up, checks out the tubes attached to his body, and reaches out to Sam and Buster standing frozen in the doorway. "Where you two going?" Buster and Sam rush to his bedside, high-five each other, and do their best to group hug their wide-eyed friend. AJ gently pushes them aside, and checks himself over. "What's going on? Why am I in this bed?"

Buster eyes AJ. "You don't remember what happened?"

"All I remember is a lake, some fishermen singing my fav music, a caveman chasing a dinosaur, and copping a feel of Claudia…. Oh, and there was a blue pickup and a fire hydrant."

Buster gives his friend a thumbs up. "That's a start."

AJ holds out his hand. "I need a drink." Possum pours him a glass of water and AJ smirks. "Got anything stronger?"

Possum wags her finger. "That's as strong as you get."

Chapter 20

Back In The Real World

A MALE ORDERLY PUSHES AJ'S wheelchair towards the front door of the hospital as Axel and Barb meet him in the entryway. AJ, who is wearing the same clothes he had on when he checked in, looks at his tattered sleeve and tries to smooth it out. He gives up and snickers at Axel when he sees that he's dressed in a new garb. "You're looking awful fancy."

Axel grins. "Forgot to tell you. I got a job bartending at The Watering Hole."

"Are you shitting me? I thought you… I thought we gave up drinking."

Barb nods. "Exactly my point."

Axel gets right to the grit. "Well, you know what they say, 'Keep your friends close and your enemies even closer.'"

"You two know each other?" AJ studies Axel's face. "Are you dating my teacher?"

Before he can answer, Barb says, "He's my husband, AJ."

"Oh my God. You two are full of secrets. Buster looked your name up and says you used to be some kind of fancy brain surgeon."

"It's been a while."

"AJ stares. "What's with all the *Wizard of Oz* crap?"

"You mean like *Wizard of Oz*, the movie?"

"Yeah, I clobber my head like some Dorothy, and I'm

dreaming all kinds of crazy shit. I wake up and find out the bum I've been sharing a back alley with is not only a brain surgeon but he's married to my bowling coach."

Barb tries to help. "We're the same people. Our lives are just a little bit more complicated than maybe you thought they were."

They finally arrive at the front door. The orderly pushes AJ outside and looks around. "You three together or is someone picking you up?"

AJ turns to Mrs. D. "Would you mind dropping me off at The Watering Hole?" Barb rolls her eyes but doesn't say anything as she heads for her van. AJ looks at Axel. "Maybe that was a yes, maybe it was a no. I guess I can always hook a car."

"Don't even think about it."

"Okay, maybe I'll just call for a cab. Can I borrow ten bucks?"

Axel furrows his brow. "You're not going back to living behind that bar. You need to stay away from there. The bottle cost me my medical career and a beautiful wife."

"Well, I have no career and no woman to lose."

"You're a bowler. What does a bowler do after he throws a gutter ball?"

"I don't think I've thrown a gutter ball in my life...Well, maybe a couple of times when I was a kid."

"Listen, son. You're missing the point. You've got another roll left, so go for the spare."

"That's easy to say, but I have nowhere to go." Barb drives up and interrupts their conversation.

Axel helps AJ out of his wheelchair, and they climb in the back of the van. "Barb, would you please drop AJ and me off at the Y?"

"No, you're both coming home with me. Axel, you can share AJ's room, but my house rules are the same."

Axel is the first to respond. "No drinking."

Barb faces the front of her van and snorts. "And we need to get you some new clothes, AJ."

TROY AND HIS blue pickup pull up to the Jones' mobile home. Troy honks his horn, rolls down his window, and yells, "Amber! Come out here and check my new paint job! I'll take you for a ride!"

Inside the trailer, Amber stands with her back against the front door afraid to move. She hears Troy yell again. "Sorry about last week! Won't happen again!… Come on! I know you're in there! I've got beer!" There's still no answer, so Troy screams, "Bitch!" He lays on the horn, slams both fists on the steering wheel, and glares at Amber's trailer.

DRESSED IN THE new clothes Mrs. D just bought him, AJ sits at the dining room table across from Possum eating lasagna. He takes a small bite and lowers his fork. "Thanks for taking me back, Mrs. D."

Barb walks over and hands him a basket filled with buns. He takes one, and she sits next to him. "Well, I'm happy you're feeling better."

"When does Mr. D get off work?"

"Bar closes at one. He should be home by two."

"You gonna wait up for him?"

"No, but I'll be wide awake until he gets home."

AJ changes the subject. "How's the bowling team doing this year?"

"I don't know. I'm not coaching anymore."

"Really?"

She chuckles. "I have all the bowlers I need at home." The phone rings, and Barb reaches over picks up the receiver.

"Hello… Yes, hold on. Possum, it's for you."

Barb hands Possum her phone. She listens for a few seconds and interrupts. "I'll call 911…. Lock yourself in the bathroom." Possum listens again and says, "I don't care. Do what I say. I'll be right over." She hands the phone back to Mrs. D and says, "Troy is parked in front of Mom's trailer, and she's convinced he's going to try and break in. I need to go."

Barb reacts. "You told her you'd call 911."

"Oh yeah, I forgot; could you do that? I need to get over there right away."

"I don't know if that's a good idea…"

AJ interrupts. "I'll go with you."

Possum puts on her coat. "You need to rest."

AJ grabs his coat. "No, I'm good." They start for the door, but AJ stops. "Wait, are we gonna take a taxi?"

Barb grabs her keys and tosses them to Possum. "Take my van."

Possum drives slowly, while AJ fidgets in his seat. Finally, he says, "This Troy is some grade-A asshole."

"Double A."

AJ has another thought. "You know, you might wanna pick up the pace, given the sitch."

"I only have a learner's permit."

Before AJ can respond, a blue pickup truck speeds past them.

AJ sits up straight and points. "That's the truck that chucked me into the fire hydrant."

"You sure?"

"Hundred percent."

"That's Troy's truck."

"Damn! At least he's not with your mom. You'd think the

dipshit would go off the grid with the police looking for him."

"You don't know Troy."

Possum carefully parks across the street from her mom's trailer, as the Honda Civic her mom used to drive pulls up in the driveway. They watch as Lance Munson gets out of the car and makes his way to Amber Jones' door.

AJ furrows his eyebrows. "Who's that?"

"I have no idea, but that's my mom's old car." They exit Mrs. D's van as a police car displaying red lights arrives.

AJ chuckles, "Now we got us a party."

Gun drawn, the police officer, Ryan Bybee, approaches Lance as if he might be a perpetrator. "Freeze, asshole!" Now on the porch steps, Lance raises his arms in the air, pivots on his heels, and faces the policeman.

AJ and Possum approach from behind, and the startled policeman whips around. He points his gun at them and yells, "What the hell? Get back."

"My mom's inside and that's not Troy Hanky."

Officer Bybee shifts his gun back to Lance. "Okay, everyone relax." He grits his teeth. "Now, who the hell are you?"

Lance looks shaken. "Lance…Lance Munson."

"You sure you're not Troy Hanky… the asshole who put this young lady's mother in the hospital?"

Possum interrupts. "That's not Troy."

Lance complains, "That bastard Troy owes me three thousand dollars. I'm here to collect."

Possum studies Lance. "I don't know this guy, but he's driving my mom's old car. It's right there."

The officer nods at Lance. "You steal that car?"

"I repossessed it when Troy didn't pay me."

AJ adds. "Officer, we passed Troy in his blue pickup, the one he tried to kill me with."

Lance adds. "The one I fixed up."

Officer Bybee holsters his weapon. "Okay, okay. Let's all take a deep breath. Too many names and not enough plot. We need to start by seeing if your mother is all right."

Possum leads the way to the door and knocks. "Mom, it's me." The door slowly opens, and Possum leads everyone inside.

Officer Bybee is seated across the kitchen table from Amber, Possum, AJ, and Lance. He finishes writing and glances down at his notepad. "Okay, so this is what I heard. This Hanky fella tried to break in here an hour ago, the same guy who put you, Amber Jones, in the hospital with multiple bruises and abrasions…and who a couple of months prior, abused you, Natalie "Possum" Jones, by damaging your eye with a bowling ball (not reported). Troy also ran you, AJ Bowers, into a fire hydrant and owes you, Lance Munson, $3,000.00 for repairing his truck, and said perpetrator drives a blue Ford pickup…."

Possum adds, "And said perpetrator is an asshole."

Ryan shakes his pen at Possum for cussing and addresses Lance with a firm voice. "This truck you repaired? Was there anything unusual about it?"

"Not really. I replaced a panel on the driver's side and painted the whole thing blue. He said he hit a deer."

"Wait. You painted the truck blue? What color was it before?"

"Red."

AJ interrupts. "Did the panel have any white paint on it?"

Lance nods, "Matter of fact it did."

"Did you ask Troy how it got there?"

Officer Bybee raises his hand like a school boy. "Hold on, Sherlock. I'll ask the questions if you don't mind. Did he tell you how the white paint got there?"

"Told me he was driving drunk and scraped a guard rail."

"You still have the side panel?"

"Yeah, it's in my garage somewhere."

AJ, whose face has turned pale, eyes the policeman for some kind of explanation. Instead, the police officer says, "All of your stories have one thing in common…Troy Hanky. So, I'm going back to the station to file this report. I'm also gonna put out an APB for a blue Ford pickup. Amber… Mrs. Jones, do you have any idea where Troy might be?"

Visibly upset, Amber checks the calendar on the wall. "He got his unemployment check this morning, so I'd check out the bars and liquor stores."

"Good to know. Okay, so all of you need to lay low and let me do my job." The handsome cop gazes at Amber. "Ma'am, if you see him, call the police department and ask for Officer Bybee." The policeman turns to AJ and stares. Finally, he says, "Snowball."

AJ looks befuddled. "Snowball?"

"Yeah, you're the kid that threw a snowball… at my truck."

"That was a long time ago. Isn't there a statute of limitations on something like that?"

There's a moment of silence, then Officer Bybee turns to the rest of the group and adds, "And nobody, I mean nobody, should approach this Troy. Understand?"

Amber breaks the silence. "We understand, officer."

The policeman makes his way to the door. "I'll stop by and check on you later, Amber."

Officer Bybee leaves, and Possum teases. "Ooh, la, la."

Amber jabs her daughter in the arm. "Stop."

AJ eyes Amber. "May I use your phone?"

The owner of The Watering Hole, Fritz Whiting, watches from the corner of the bar as Axel mixes drinks, collects money, and manages the till. Proud of himself, Axel grins at Fritz, who has been watching him from across the room. The phone rings and his boss says, "Go ahead. Answer it."

Axel puts the phone to his ear and says, "The Watering Hole." He listens for a moment and nods at his boss. "It's an old friend. I'll keep it short." Fritz walks off as Axel tightens his grip on the phone and lowers his voice. "AJ, you wanna get me fired? I just started working here. What do you need?"

Chapter 21

Finding Troy

AJ AND FRIENDS STRUT DOWN THE STREET carrying bowling ball bags. AJ comes to a stop in front of The Watering Hole, and lays out his plan to his friends. "Everyone has a cell phone, right?" Possum, Sam, and Buster hold up their phones, and AJ says, "Okay, you check out the other bars while I cover the two liquor stores. Text or call if ya see Troy or his blue truck. We'll meet inside in thirty minutes or less."

Sam asks, "You safe being in a liquor store?"

AJ scoffs. "Yeah, yeah, yeah."

An hour later, the posse minus AJ, is seated at a table in The Watering Hole. The place is empty, and they look nonplussed as AJ rolls through the door. Possum slaps her hand on the table. "Anything?"

"Nope. You guys?"

Sam chuckles, "Got attacked by a rapid squirrel."

Possum grimaces. "The word is rabid."

"No, he was really fast."

AJ takes a seat and watches as Axel wipes off the bar counter. The new bartender is wearing a black polo shirt with the bar's name written above a small pocket. He points at AJ. "That Troy fellow you wanted me to keep an eye out for hasn't been in yet."

"Would you know him if you saw him?"

"No, but Fritz would. He says he's a real loser."

From the table, Sam studies Axel's face. "Hey, you're AJ's wizard friend who told us how to wake him from the dead?"

"That's right. Truth is, we've both come back from the dead… looking for a new start…freshwater. Aren't we buddy?"

AJ grins as Buster nods. "How do you two know each other?"

"We were alley mates and now we're roommates at Mrs. D's house."

Sam leans back and whispers. "Don't wanna pigeonhole you in a box AJ, but are you two a couple?"

AJ shakes his head. "That's kind of a Carl Lewis long jump there, Sam. It's only temporary." AJ catches Axel's eye. "A round of cokes, please."

Axel grins. "Good choice."

Buster chortles. "Diddly damn. That new friend of yours is a real stud meister…I mean for an older man."

Sam stares at Buster and back at AJ, "What? Now you're both interested in men?"

AJ closes his left eye. "Did you not hear what just I told you?"

"Yeah, something about some guy named Carl."

Exhausted by Sam's dip shittery, AJ says, "Axel's married…to Mrs. D, and I'm not gay. But If I decide I wanna be gay, I'll be sure and let you know."

Buster raises up. "Wait. Mrs. D is married to that Axel guy? You have to be kidding me."

AJ nods and Sam tries again. "So, if Axel is married to Mrs. D and you're sharing a room with him…?"

"We'll talk later."

Possum raises her eyebrows. "Sam, you need to stop painting everyone with a broad brush. You sound like a homophobe."

Sam blushes. "I'm no homophobe; I love women...It's just with what's happened with my dad, I wanna know the score."

Possum wags her head, "The score is three to zero…and you're the zero."

Axel arrives with four Cokes, and Buster grabs one as Axel disappears. Buster takes a big gulp, belches, and spouts, "Didn't Mrs. D tell us her old man was dead?"

"Maybe, or maybe she said she wished he was dead." The Hollywood Argyles' song, *Alley Oop,* comes on over the barroom sound system and AJ raises his hand. "Okay, this is my song!" When they get to the tune's refrain, they all scream the alley-oops in unison. When the song ends, AJ's face lights up. "That's it."

Sam says, "What's it?"

"We need to get back together and bowl as a team. It's been too long. We'll can call ourselves the Alley Oops." AJ takes the lead and they all sing, "Alley oop, oop,… oop… oop, oop."

When the song ends, Possum lifts her glass and finishes off the last of her Coke. When she looks up, she sees Troy walk through the back entrance of the building and take a seat at the bar counter. She scoots her stool back and hides behind Buster. AJ notices and says, "What's going on?"

Possum whispers, "That's him; that's Troy."

The temperature in the bar changes as AJ holds up his hand. "Our target has landed."

Sam and Buster sneak a peek as Sam whispers, "When Mohammed doesn't come to the mountain, the mountain comes to the bar."

AJ taps the table. "Okay, everyone, keep it neat." Sam and Buster down their Cokes.

At the bar, Axel looks over at AJ as if to say, 'Is this the guy?' AJ gives a thumbs up and Axel slides over, shifts his attention to Troy, and politely asks, "What'll it be, young man?"

"Straight whiskey…old man; no ice."

Back at the table, Possum, still hiding behind Buster, peeks over at Troy and whispers, "Now what do we do?"

AJ stands. "I'm gonna get us some more Cokes."

Buster belches again. "I'm Coked out. Get me one of those Shirley Temples. Make sure it has a cherry...and one of those umbrellas."

AJ moseys over to the bar and sits down next to Troy. Axel serves the fugitive his drink, turns back, and begins to organize the whiskey bottles on the shelf. AJ smirks at his roommate. "You're so organized."

"That's because I'm too lazy to look for things."

AJ grins. "How long we been on the wagon now?"

"Almost three weeks."

"Give me three rum and cokes, hold the rum…and one Shirley Temple…extra cherry."

Troy hears the order and chuckles. AJ scoots his bar stool over. "Remember me?"

"I ain't good with faces, especially ugly ones."

"You drive a blue Ford pickup, right?

"Yeah, what's it to you?"

I hooked a ride on the back of your bumper a few weeks ago and you tried to kill me."

Troy's face darkens and he begins to squirm on his stool as Axel makes AJ's drink order. Troy downs his shot of whiskey and stands up. "That was your dumbass fault."

AJ doesn't let up. "That truck of yours used to be red, right?"

"Why do you think that?"

"Your friend Lance told me."

"Asshole."

AJ takes a breath. "Highway Patrol said a red vehicle clipped the side of my parent's car, causing it to leave the road and crash."

"I don't know what the hell you're talking about."

"Over there is my friend Possum. You know, the one you hit with a bowling ball… and beat up her mom so bad she ended up in the hospital" Troy looks over at the table, spots Possum, but he doesn't say anything. AJ continues, "Let's see, that's two counts of assault and battery and one count of vehicular homicide. Axel, would you please call the police department? We got a wanted man here." AJ waves his friends over. "Look what I found." They hurry over and surround Troy.

Troy jumps to his feet, grabs a beer bottle, busts the end of it off on the edge of the bar, and thrusts it several times at his young adversaries. Possum, Sam, and Buster step back, as AJ lowers his shoulders and charges Troy like a Spanish bull. The villainous toreador steps aside, and AJ crashes into a barstool. Seeing his chance to escape, Troy hightails it for the door as AJ's friends help him to his feet.

Troy stumbles out of the bar growling, "Don't mess with me you little pricks. I got nothin' to lose."

As the lawbreaker staggers down the street, inside the bar AJ gathers himself and yells, "Okay, grab yer balls; it's time for an old-fashioned ass-whooping."

As AJ and company hurry out the door, Axel picks up the Buster's Shirley Temple, stirs it with the umbrella, and takes a sip. He grimaces, removes the cherry, and pops it in his mouth.

Chapter 22

Best Plan Is No Plan At All

AJ AND COMPANY BUST OUT OF The Watering Hole carrying their bowling ball bags. At the end of the block, they spot Troy race-walking.

Possum asks, "We got a plan?"

AJ puffs out his cheeks. "Best plan is no plan at all."

Now two blocks away, Troy stumbles and falls. He picks himself up, rounds a corner, and staggers down a dark alley. AJ sees him disappear and yells, "Let's go!"

The foursome takes off running and when they reach the edge of the city laundromat next to the alley, they peek around the corner. They watch quietly as Buster removes a camouflage cover from his blue pickup and throws it into the bed.

AJ takes the lead as they step into the alley. Troy sees them and backs up against his truck. "What the hell? Why you ass wipes following me?"

Possum points. "I don't know, maybe because you're a shameless SOB who doesn't care about anyone but himself. Did you forget you destroyed my eye and almost killed my mother?"

AJ steps forward. "And by the way, your friend Lance is down at the police department describing how he painted your truck blue. Oh, and he still has the side panel he replaced… the one that is evidence you killed my parents."

"Nobody seen me kill anybody. What are you little pukes gonna do about it anyway?"

Buster eyes Sam. "I don't know, vigilantes usually like to hang people…but maybe that's too easy…I say we stone him and draw and quarter his ass."

Sam offers up his idea. "How about we Rasputin him? You know, shoot him, poison him, and throw him off a bridge."

Buster clarifies the sitch. "We don't have a gun or any poison, and this town doesn't have any bridges."

Sam growls, "Okay, let's set him on fire."

Having heard enough, Troy reaches through the passenger side window and removes a handgun from the glovebox. AJ and company step back, remove their bowling balls from their bags, and raise them in unison. Troy laughs as he points his gun. "What ya weenies gonna do, bowl me to death?"

AJ yells, "Bowl on!" and he lofts his ball high in the air. It lands dead center on the windshield of Troy's pickup. The enraged culprit looks at truck, grits his teeth, and screams, "Shit!...Shit!" He swings back around and fires a round that hits Sam's ball.

Sam checks the extra hole in his ball and screams, "This is my favorite ball, anus breath!"

Possum taps Buster's shoulder. "Ready?"

They both holler, "Bowl on!" and toss their balls. The black and blue spheres speed down the alley and knock Troy off his feet. Rattled by what just happened, Troy sits up and watches as Sam rolls his ball and hits him dead center in the gonads. Holding his crotch, Troy stumbles to his feet, climbs in his pickup, and starts the engine. He burns rubber as he backs out of the alley as AJ and friends tumble out and try to avoid being hit.

When the pickup reaches the street, Troy slows long enough, so that AJ is able to grab hold of the vehicle's back bumper.

Possum sees what's happening and screams, "No! What are you doing?"

AJ hunkers down and yells back, "I have no idea!"

As the truck takes off, Possum yells, "Buster! Call 911!"

Troy, who is unaware that AJ is attached to his truck's bumper, slows down and drives at a moderate speed down Main Street. Several people see AJ attached to the pickup and wave. Troy thinks they are being annoyingly friendly and gives them the finger. Not wanting to attract any attention, he drives slowly down the street, making it easier for AJ to hang on.

Suddenly, two police cars, lights flashing, speed past Troy's truck, responding to Buster's 911 call. Troy checks his rearview mirror and watches as the cop cars skid to a stop in front of the laundromat. He panics, picks up speed, and heads for the edge of town.

On the outskirts of Greenvale, Troy slows down and merges onto a county road. AJ seizes the opportunity and pulls himself up and into the truck bed. He crawls carefully over to the rear cargo window and looks at Troy, who is focused on the road ahead. As the sound of sirens grows louder, Troy adjusts his mirror to see how close the police cars are, but instead, he spots AJ smiling at him like a lunatic.

When Troy turns back to the front of his vehicle, he sees Lance's Honda coming his way at breakneck speed. As the police cars continue to close in on Troy's truck, AJ sizes up the situation and grabs the vehicle cover flapping in the wind.

Back inside the vehicle, Troy tightens his grip on the steering wheel and watches as Lance takes the center of the road, suggesting he wants to play chicken. From inside the cab, AJ hears Troy scream, "Holy shit!"

Somehow, AJ manages to throw the tarp over the cab of Troy's truck and onto the windshield, just as Lance steers his

Honda into a ditch to avoid hitting Troy's pickup.

Unable to see through his front window, Troy stomps on the brake and his vehicle slides sideways. AJ hangs on for dear life until the truck comes to rest in the middle of the road. He checks his body for any injuries as the police cars skid to a sudden stop behind him. AJ gives a thumbs-up as three police officers, including Ryan Bybee, jump out of their vehicles and circle the truck with their guns drawn.

Troy's truck, now sandwiched between the squad cars and Lance's Honda is still covered with the tarp. Troy doesn't wait, squeezes his way out of the truck, and crawls out from under the tarp. Gun in hand, he jumps to his feet and fires away. The policemen don't hesitate and Bonnie and Clyde Troy's ass, bullets riddling his entire body.

Thirty minutes later, the police cars, a tow truck pulling Buster's pickup, and a red and white ambulance drive away with sirens blaring. Still standing on the road, AJ and Lance survey the scene. AJ finally says, "Think maybe I could catch a ride back to town with you?"

Lance opens his car door. "Yeah…wanna ride inside or hitch onto my back bumper?"

Chapter 23

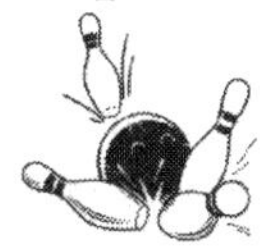

A Change Is As Good As A Rest

IT'S ALMOST CHRISTMAS, and my friends and I are in the Strike and Spare as usual. Finding a job proved to be a real Easter egg hunt, so after I cleaned myself up and changed my ways, I'm back working at the bowling alley again.

It's my day off, and we're pretty much waxing the other team, while Barb and Axel sit at the table watching the computer tally our scores. I gotta say we look pretty fancy in the bowling shirts the Dwyers bought us. We even have our team's name, *Alley Oops*, printed on the back.

I watch as Buster rolls a seven-ten split, and it's the same old thing as Possum and Sam yell, "Split happens!"

I take a seat next to Axel, and he gets all serious. "Found out that Troy fella was wanted in Minnesota for armed robbery and four counts of DUI."

I wanna smile, but instead I say, "Why doesn't that surprise me?" The truth is I've tried to get Troy's face out of my head, but I kind of wish I had gotten the chance to hear the judge sentence him to life in prison for killing my folks. Oh well, I guess him being shot by three Greenvale policemen is justice enough.

I look over and Axel holds up his can of coke. "To the better things in life...and eight weeks sober."

He offers me one, so I grab it, pop it open, and say, "I like free things." We toast each other as Troy throws his second ball and leaves the ten-pin standing.

Sam scoffs, "Come on, man…open frame."

Buster brags, "Check out my score, doofus. I'm up twenty points on both you and Possum."

"There's no I in team, Buster," Possum scolds.

Sam adds, "There's no I in karaoke either." Possum stares hard at Sam and he mumbles, "Why you mall gawking at me?

"Cuz you're such an idiot."

I laugh as Sam gives Possum the finger and scoots off to the bathroom. For some reason, I start thinking about how far Axel and I have come since our back-alley days and get kind of misty-eyed. In case you're wondering, Axel moved out of the room we shared and in with Mrs. D a few weeks ago. Possum and I even stood up for them when they renewed their vows in the backyard. It got kind of weird after that, and Possum and I got the go fever.

We had managed to save up some money and moved into a one-bedroom apartment. Trying to be a gentleman, I sleep on the floor in the living room on a blow-up mattress, so Possum can have the bedroom. Our place is pretty much empty, but we do have some garage sale crap, a used TV, and two beanbag chairs Mrs. D gave us. We're saving up for a Walmart microwave and maybe even a DVD player. We split all the expenses and even though our meals aren't Mrs. D-like, I always say, enough is as good as a feast.

Okay, that's all that. So, I stop daydreaming and watch as Buster gawks at two perky blondes two lanes over. It's my turn to bowl, but I listen in as Buster continues to check them out. Sam comes back from the can and busies himself putting away his shit as Buster snarks, "The tall one is a real looker."

Possum grimaces and says, "The tall one is Jennifer Hill, Sam's sister? She's here visiting him from Milwaukee."

Buster's ears perk up. "Sister? Wowser. Think Sam would mind me asking her out?"

"I don't know, but his mother might."

"Yeah, well, I don't want anything to do with that woman. The cheese slid off her cracker a long time ago."

As Sam's sister and her friend walk past Buster, Jennifer winks at him and wiggles her butt. His face lights up, and he turns to Possum. "You see that?" He checks with AJ. "You saw that, right?"

I shake my head and walk back to the scoring table in time to hear Mrs. D say, "I'm proud of you Axel."

I trampoline on what she said. "What's he up to now?"

She hesitates and says, "It's our little secret. Tell you later."

Axel pulls out a chair. "Speaking of secrets. Sit down AJ." I sit, and he winks at his wife. "Did you know these four have an interview with the United States Bowling Corporation next week?"

My old coach's eyes light up. "USBC, the bowling company?"

"Yep."

Mrs. D leans forward. "I'm not trying to be funny, but that place is right up your alley, AJ."

"It's up all four of our alleys."

We finish up our game, high-five one another, including Mr. and Mrs. D, and break into our favorite song, *Alley Oop.*

A FEW DAYS later, I get a frog up my butt and decide I wanna set a world record for the longest strike in bowling history. I figure it might help with my upcoming job interview, so I convinced what I hope will soon be my ex-boss, Monty Owens, to make a few calls. Sure enough, the Guinness World Record people sent this suit-wearing geek to Greenvale for my lame-brained attempt to get myself some bowling cred.

It's Monday morning, and our gang and some nosy people are gathered on Main Street in front of the Strike and Spare getting ready for my attempt to make some weird shit history. Luckily, the streets are clear thanks to some overnight warm wind that came all the way from the West Coast and melted everything.

Next to me stands the *Guinness World Records* adjudicator from New York City, Stanley Penski, who's holding a clipboard all official-like. The world record man appears to be in his fifties, is tall and lean, and has his hair slicked back like a Leonardo Di Caprio lookalike.

Anyway, I shrug my shoulders, make a phony warm-up move, and raise my ball. Several people start honking, "Bowl on! Bowl on! Bowl on!" I give the dirty geese the evil eye for making me nervous and they slow their vibe.

Stanley gets all official-like, adjusts his tie, and says, "I checked, and the street gradient is to your advantage, but I see no reason for this not to be a record."

I rub my throwing arm and say, "Good to know."

Stanley, who seems to be enjoying all the attention, clears his throat and addresses everyone like he's a high school principal making the morning announcements. "All right, Mr. Bowers, everything is in order for your attempt at the world record for the longest strike in bowling history."

I wanna put on a show but not overdo it, so I swing my ball a few times. Now I'm so stoked, I think I'm gonna pee my pants, but quickly realize the time for that has passed. I nod at Stan my man, rear back, and throw my fourteen-pound ball as hard as I can down Main Street.

Right away, I jet off, trying to keep up with my ball. Several people trail behind as Stanley, Buster, Sam, and Possum jump in Buster's van.

A few seconds later, Buster and company drive past as I try not to lose sight of the ball. I watch as it takes a straight path and picks up speed. Two blocks later, the ball slides around a banked corner that Sam and I built out of two-by-fours last night. Just like we planned, it rolls straight for the ten bowling pins Buster and I set up earlier this morning.

I struggle to keep up as Buster's van pulls up next to me and Stanley points his camera out the window. Out of gas, I lean over and try to catch my breath. When I look up, I see the ball hit the head pin and nine pins fall down. I start to panic, but a garbage truck drives past, vibrates the pavement, and the final pin tips over.

Buster, Sam, and Possum run over and high-five me as Stanley snaps a picture, calmly records what happened on his clipboard, and hands me an official world record certificate.

A few days later, USBC, where my parents and UJ worked most of their lives, hired Buster, Sam, Possum and me, like we came in a four-pack. They put us in the warehouse, where we started loading bowling equipment, balls, and pins into trucks all day long. I even get a chance to drive a forklift when the old-timers take a day off.

To tell you the truth, the job is pretty rigid…sort of like we're in Hitler's Germany and we're trains that always having to be on time, Monday through Friday, eight to five, and back at it again the next week.

As for the Dwyers, their little secret was that they were moving to Pojaque, New Mexico, where Axel got his medical license back and is a small-town doctor. Never thought about it before, but I guess a brain surgeon has to know all the parts of the body too. Barb, she went back to teaching and even started another bowling team. I miss the D's every day, but I'm happy they were around to help me get my act together. Okay, lunch is over; I gotta get back to work.

PART TWO

Ten Years Later

"In bowling and in life, if a person made the spares, the strikes would take care of themselves." Stephen King

Chapter 24

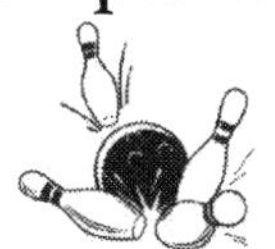

The More Things Change The More They Remain The Same

ICE AND SNOW COVER THE CITY'S MAJOR thoroughfares as AJ Bowers, now a full-bodied and handsome twenty-eight-year-old millennial, strides down Greenvale's Main Street. He's toting his tattered leather bowling bag, the one his parents gave him on his seventeenth birthday. And despite his heavy parka and large Bernie Sanders wool mittens, AJ still has a good-natured slacker charm that makes him a hit with all the ladies.

As the setting sun shines in several store windows, AJ stops in front of a sporting goods store. He looks through the display window and sees bowling trophies, plaques, and fancy-colored ribbons. He moves on to a corner clothing store and peers at two male and female mannequins dressed in bowling shirts and pants. In front of their shoes are ten bowling pins in V formation, a twelve-pound black ball, and two red leather bowling ball bags.

Behind him, a white Chevy pickup pulls up to a stop sign. AJ trots over, crouches down, attaches his bag to the hitching ball, and grabs the back bumper. The truck takes off and AJ slides along the icy road hopping over mogul-sized speed bumps that weren't there when he was a kid.

As the truck travels down Main Street, several people point at AJ and laugh. A young man, dressed in a Green Bay Packers jersey, yells, "Hey! When ya get your license back?"

AJ yells, "Next week!" As the truck nears the Strike and Spare bowling alley, AJ removes his bowling bag from the hitch, releases the bumper, and slides to a stop not far from the fire hydrant that almost ended his life ten years earlier. He brushes the snow off his clothes, crosses the street, and weaves his way through the bowling alley parking lot. The pot-holed blacktop is packed with working-class cars with frost-covered windows and rusted-out fenders. He is dwarfed by mounds of recently plowed snow. When he passes the largest snow pile, he stops and reads the sign: NAME THE DAY AND HOUR THIS SNOWPILE MELTS AND WIN FREE BOWLING FOR A YEAR. SIGN UP INSIDE. AJ hurries to the front door of the bowling alley just in time to open it for a gaggle of middle-aged moms dressed in puffy, hooded parkas, talking about their favorite TV shows.

"Hey ladies, how you doing?"

Three of the women smile and chirp in unison, "AJ!"

He's about to step inside when an eighty-five-year-old woman reaches her cane into the doorway blocking his way. AJ chortles and says, "Mrs. Jollymore. Nice to see you."

She offers AJ her arm, and he takes it. "You're such a gentleman."

As he escorts the slow-moving woman towards her vehicle, he tightens his grip on her arm and steadies her. "Gotta be careful, ma'am. This parking lot is pretty slippery."

When they reach her oversized late-model Ford pickup, she unlocks it, and he helps her up into the driver's seat. Before he can react, she reaches down and pinches his cheek. "What is it my granddaughter says? Oh, yeah…you're real eye candy, AJ. If only I was 40 years younger..."

"Now, now, what would Mr. Jollymore have to say about that?"

"Shit. The last time Clarence got excited was when our neighbor lady forgot to shut her bathroom blinds."

She giggles, revs the truck's super-duty engine, and fishtails out of the parking lot, leaving AJ spitting snow.

He laughs, wipes the snow off his clothes, and starts back to the entrance of the bowling alley. When he passes the bowling sign, he watches as two neon bulbs flicker and die, changing the name of the place to the Strike and Spa.

Chapter 25

The Alley Oops

WHEN I GET INSIDE, I SPOT some of my halfway bowler friends headed home after five o'clock league play. For some reason, I stop and take everything in: the lanes full and bustling, people laughing and carrying on, drinking their favorite brews, and of course, the sound of balls smacking the pins.

Something comes over me, and I look around the place and picture how much of my life I've spent here. Reality sets in and I realize I'm going nowhere fast and my inspiration train only takes me to this bowling alley….it's kind of like I've been swimming upstream in the same water all my life.

After my fire hydrant accident ten years ago, I took some time off from drinking. I'm back at it again, but this time it's only beer. I hit the suds too hard six months ago and ended up driving Buster's moped into Lake Evinrude. Just my luck a cop who was patrolling the area gave me a DUI. I don't wanna end up back in the alley behind The Watering Hole, so I've been taking it easy.

I look over and see Buster, Sam, and Possum warming up, so I wave and they wave back. Before I head their way, I see a kid slamming his fist on the alley's one and only old-school arcade console as Ms. Pac-Man gives up the ghost. Doing my second good deed for the day, I trot over, pop a quarter in the machine, and he says, "Thanks, AJ!"

For some reason, I keep a distance from my teammates and plop down on a plastic bowling alley chair. As I lace up my shoes, I think about the last decade I've spent working at USBC. Kinda hard to believe, but the four of us got our ten-year pins last week.

Anyway, here's the *Reader's Digest* version of everything and nothing that has happened with the rest of my life. Not a lot has changed since high school, except I have a real job now and live alone. Possum and I shared a place for a while, but things got kind of weird after I walked in on her and saw her buck-naked. I still have the occasional flashback, when she gives me a surprised look like the one she gave me in the bathroom.

Not long after that, we began to act like a married couple, always fussing, her telling me I was an asshole, and me calling her a bitch. It may seem kind of weird, but the reason I moved out was because she accused me of using her toothbrush. Truth is, I did use it, but I don't want someone busting my balls over some damn toothbrush. We're still good friends; forgive and forget I always say. Now that I think about it, I guess I really haven't forgotten all our shit, but I'm not one to hold a grudge…at least not for very long.

Speaking of grudges, Claudia Giovanni, the girl who said we should save ourselves until we were a serious couple? Well, she's back in town. After I caught her screwing that blond-haired frat boy in her dorm room her first month of college, we lost touch. I'm sure there were plenty of other guys after that, but who's counting? 'Sides,…I had my share of one-nighters after that.

Anyway, Claudia moved back to Greenvale two years ago. She had just finished law school and landed a junior lawyer position at Jones, Sherwin, and Williams. I remember her arrival well because it was a week after the USBC breakroom fire, which I promise to tell you about later. Anyway, I waited a couple of weeks for her to settle in and asked her out. I don't know if she felt guilty for destroying me or what, but she said yes, and we've been together ever since.

We went at it like rabbits for a couple of months, but our sex life has slowed down to a crawl. Now, the stars have to be lined up just right for me to get lucky.

I've never told anyone, but Claudia is my first serious episode with a woman. Why I'm so stuck on her, I don't have a clue. I know things are different because I get kind of jealous when she starts putting all sorts of kinky moves on me….like I know she didn't come up with those positions all by herself. Her losing the key to the handcuffs was the worst part…cuz we had to go to the hardware store for a hacksaw all stuck together. Anyway, we've been talking about a future together…okay, I've been doing most of the talking.

My daydream ends, and I have this random thought about Axel and Barb Dwyer. Possum and I used to get a postcard and an occasional call from New Mexico, but that only lasted a couple of years…then nothing. It's been eight years with no contact, so I don't know if Axel fell off the wagon, or if they just got tired of us not calling them back. I did try to call them a couple of months ago, but I got a message saying the number was no longer in service.

Before I make my way over to my team, I slip on my *Alley Oops* team shirt that has the caveman Alley Oop himself on the front. On the back is our sponsor's name, The Watering Hole. Anyway, I slide over to lane seven, high-five the gang, and take a few warm-up tosses. On the lane to the left of us, I watch as pins fly and balls roll in a chaotic, beautiful ballet. Right as I'm ready to lay down my first roll, I sniff the ball and make a prayer-like challenge to myself. "Roll a strike, strike it rich." Kind of ridiculous I know, but a guy's gotta have his own unique routine and that's mine for now. Anyway, I focus on the head pin and let it rip. I watch as my gleaming red-marbled globe glides down the aisle and my fourteen-pounder sends all ten pins flying.

Buster pats me on the back as I return to the ball rack to retrieve my ball. In the distance, I see Claudia approaching. As usual, she looks stunning but out of place in her matching black jacket, pants, and high heels...a real platinum package. When I reach her, I give her a hug. It's a little too much public affection for her taste, so she pushes me away and sits down away from the action.

I smile anyway. "Glad you could make it, Claud. I'm on fire!"

"I thought you were done."

"No, you're just in time to see us bury Fred's Funeral Home. If we win our last couple of games, we'll be playing for the league championship against Jones, Sherwin, and Williams. So, you're gonna have a tough choice to make. Root for your office team, or root for the *Alley Oops*. I'm pretty sure I know who you're gonna pick."

Claudia's eyes flicker. "I'm leaving in thirty minutes with or without you."

"Come on, you can't go. You're my good luck charm, my ace in the hole, my muse!"

I notice my shoe is untied and bend down to tie it as Claudia mutters, "You know I hate this game."

My shoelace breaks and I sputter, "Well shit."

Claudia gives me a 'will you please hurry up' look and says, "There's something important I want to talk to you about."

"I get it. I'll roll fast. God, how'd I get so lucky?" I kiss her on the cheek and jet over to the front desk where Dale is staring at his cell phone. Dale is a freckle-faced twenty-two-year-old Howdy Doody-looking guy who is pretty much doing the job I did ten years ago. "Hey, man, you got a spare shoelace?" Without looking up, he grabs one out of a drawer and hands it to me. As I cut away,

I punch him in the arm. "Thanks, man. When I buy my own alley, I'm gonna hire you and give you a raise."

The scrawny kid yawns and says, "Good, I could use a little extra money, I'm getting married soon."

I turn back and smile. "Wow. Good for you."

I go over to our team's lane and find Possum, who is getting ready to roll. She's still shorter than hell and has gained a little weight over the years, but it's mostly all curvy and in the right places. Her hair is longer, but she still wears it pulled back and buried under a Brewers cap. Her being a tomboy has never been a problem for me. In fact, I kind of like it. Her feisty attitude hasn't changed much. She still has the same bizarre knack for cutting through any shit anyone throws at her. If that's not enough, she holds her own on our team with a one-ninety-plus average. Possum's a real jewel for sure. Oh, and I almost forgot. Her mom started dating Officer Bybee after Troy Hanky got himself whacked by three-quarters of the Greenvale police department. Anyway, they got married, sold Amber Hill's trailer, and moved to California. Kind of strange with Bybee helping to kill Troy and then marrying the idiot's ex…but Possum didn't have a problem with it for sure.

All of us guys have put on twenty pounds of beer weight since high school and Buster and Sam are the same dopes they've always been, only Buster has a goatee that looks like it's been drawn on with a black magic marker.

Sam, he's got his own look. His hair is thinning, and he has this comb-over thing going on. In the back, he has a man bun like he's trying to make up for what's not going on up front. It looks ridiculous, but Buster and I don't say anything cuz we're glad it's not happening to us.

Okay, back to the bowling; I watch as Possum adjusts the black patch she still wears over her right eye, grips her ball, and focuses on the pins sixty feet away.

Dave Franklin, the director of Fred's Funeral Home, and their team's best player goads her on. "C'mon, Helen Keller. We don't got all day."

I manage to control my temper as Buster tries to boost Possum's ego. "You's got it. Smooth like peanut butter."

Concentration blown, she lowers her ball and rants, "First off, shut the hell up…second, go fetch me a beer."

He hops up and says, "Fer sure. Was about to get myself one."

Possum rolls a straight ball and knocks down nine pins. Pissed off, she lifts her eye patch, rolls her second ball, and picks up a spare. She lowers her patch before anyone can see what's behind it as Sam and I high-five each other.

Next up, our arch-enemy Dave from Fred's, knocks down nine pins, leaving the seven-pin mother-in-law wobbling. Sam, our team's best annoyer, yells, "Stand up and fight, ya bastard!" The pin stays up and Sam takes another jab. "Don't you hate it when that happens?" Hoping for a spare, Dave throws a nothing ball, missing the lone pin by a foot. We all chuckle as the loser slinks back to his chair.

Buster returns with two beers as I grip my ball and step up to the line. From behind me, I hear Sam holler, "Come on, AJ. Down the toilet."

Possum puts her hand over her patch and says, "Wait! The eye speaks! One roll, ten pins, no survivors."

I nod, refocus, and throw a strike. When I step back to join my friends, I happen to see a worn-out old timer perched in a chair at the far end of the alley. I look closer and see he's wearing a woven Mexican poncho, a cowboy hat, and sunglasses. Next to him is this gimongous golden retriever. The old man catches me looking his way, so I turn away. I can't help myself and gawk at him again as he pets his dog. The way I figure it, he might be a seeing-eye dog, cuz of the way the animal is tethered to the belt around his waist.

It's the last frame, and my final throw will seal the deal, but instead of concentrating on the task at hand, I sneak another peek to see if the old man is still there. He's gone, so I eye the pins and snarl, "Hello, my name is Inigo Montoya. You killed my father. Prepare to die."

I knock down all ten maples, and Sam yells, "Can opener! Take that to the bank and smoke it, casket boys." I wink at Claudia, fake a mic drop, and the four of us raise our beer bottles and sing our *Alley Oop* team song, annoying everyone around us as usual.

Still celebrating our win, Sam moves over to Claudia and offers her a high-five. She rolls her eyes and stares at me like I'm the one responsible for him being a doofus. She leaves him hanging, so he high-fives himself. Embarrassed, he shuffles over and squats down next to me. He cups his hand and whispers, "Got yourself a real King Kong ball buster there…"

I whisper back, "If that makes me Fay Wray, I don't mind, cuz I'm sharing a bed with her tonight."

Gil Williams, a tall lawyer in his early 40's, who is Claudia's boss, struts over like he owns the place. I don't like him, because he always has a twinkle in his eye when he sees her. Plus, when the jerk found out I was dating her, he let me know that he was the creep who stole my entire inheritance from Uncle Julius in a poker game ten years ago. I'm never gonna like the cocky bastard, but I don't say anything cuz Claudia has to work with him. Anyway, the asshole winks at Claudia and smirks at me. "You know, Bowers, I wouldn't bother showing up to the championship. We're going to cream you like we did last year."

Sam and Buster stand up in my defense as the rest of Gil's team from Jones, Sherwin, and Williams join him. Sam sputters, "Says who? We got a lot more cream than you do, and we're not afraid to use it."

Gil's three teammates burst out laughing, and then the fancy lawyer winks at Claudia again and waddles off like some constipated goose. I even catch Claudia smiling at his funky-looking ass. Before I can say anything, the team we throttled from Fred's Funeral Home walks past, and Sam hollers, "Dead men walking!"

Possum joins in, "Put another nail in the coffin!"

I can't help myself, and I take my own jab. "Have Fred send us some 'stiffer' competition next time."

Not to be outdone, Sam says, "Don't let the horse ya rode in on kick your asses on your way out, boys."

Dave flips all of us the bird, and Sam tries again. "Hey, Carly Simon, are you so vain you think we're talking about you?"

Possum grins. "Wow, that's one of your better ones, Sameo."

Buster drops to the bench and puts on his street shoes. "Guys, if I die, don't take me to Fred's. Who knows what those bastards would do to my nuts when no one's around."

Sam reshapes his comb-over. "Ya, mean like play tic tac toe on your ass with a scalpel?"

Buster stands up. "Or tie my willie in a knot."

"Or maybe before they close the coffin lids, they would cover your dead body with Cheese Whiz and put rats inside your coffin."

Possum mutters, "Okay, enough already. I think we can all do without the visuals."

Meanwhile, Buster puffs out his chest, clinches his butt cheeks, and gawks at a young lady two lanes over. "Talk about a visual. Ooo-wee!"

I'm embarrassed to say it, but I check out the attractive blond and her two brunette friends myself. The blond throws a gutter ball and Buster whispers to Sam, "Hold my beer."

Buster starts over to her, but Sam grabs his arm. "I'll handle this. A girl like that isn't going to hang out with an ignorant lowlife like you."

Buster pushes Sam's hand away. "Hey! I might be ignorant, but I'm no lowlife."

Sam blocks his way. "Ya drink like a chimney, smoke like a fish, and you're no smarter than a bowling pin. If that ain't a lowlife, I'll eat this ball."

Sam lifts his bowling bag, and Buster reacts. "Be happy to help you with that."

They begin to slap-fight, and I step in. "Hey! Keep it down, would ya? You guys are acting like a couple of…"

Behind me, I hear Possum say, "Lowlifes."

I glance back at Claudia and give her my 'it's not my fault' grin.

She shuts me down by putting on her coat and raising her voice loud enough for everyone to hear. "I'll meet you at the car."

The four of us watch as she wiggles her butt all the way to the door. I give Buster and Sam the business for chasing off my woman and drooling over her. "What's with you two?"

Feeling no shame, Buster tries to bust my balls, "How's come you're only embarrassed by us when Claudia's around?"

Sam adds, "Yeah, we's your friends. And friends are friends… are friends."

Possum groans, "Wow, Sam, that's deep."

Buster defends Sam. "He's right. AJ, yer ol' ball and chain should accept us for who we are."

I get all defensive and try to support Claudia the best I can.

"She does accept you, only in her own way."

Sam argues. "Please. That woman wouldn't give us the time of day even if she had a watch."

I get all emotional and hold out my arms. "Isn't it enough that I love you guys? Hold me." I attempt a group hug, but Buster pulls away and hollers, "Get off me, ya perv. To The Watering Hole!"

Buster and Sam break into a chant. "Beer! Beer! Beer! Beer! Beer!"

As the three of them walk off, I yell, "You guys go ahead. Claudia's got something special planned."

Kinda pissed, Sam hollers, "For cripes sake, AJ! Are you so pussy whipped, you can't have a beer when you want?"

Buster adds his three cents. "Come on. King Kong is ditching us for some sexy time with his own personal ball buster."

Irritated, I tap back into the conversation. "I heard that."

Buster growls. "Yeah, you were supposed to hear it."

An attractive couple walks past, and Buster eyes the young blond. He starts to whistle, but Possum slaps his arm. "Back off, Boogaloo. That's Jennifer…Sam's sister."

"Wow, it's been ten years. She's aged really well."

The young man with Jennifer tips his cap at Possum. "Nice to see you again, Natalie."

I take a closer look and realize Jen's date is none other than Theodore Ennis, who has grown six inches and put on forty pounds. Dressed in a Canadian tuxedo (jeans and a denim shirt), our old classmate has shed his horn-rimmed glasses, grown out his hair, and turned into a Matthew McConaughey look-alike. Possum sizes up the situation and removes her cap. "Theodore, is that you?"

"Yes. It's been a long time."

"Ten years." Possum grows silent, so I take over. "What

have you been up to, Theo?"

"Four years at the U of W, where Jennifer and I started dating my senior year, three years at Harvard Medical School, and I just finished my residency in Chicago. I'm opening my own practice in Milwaukee in a few months."

"You're moving back to Wisconsin? Why?"

Theodore squeezes Jennifer's arm. "I have my reasons…and you know what they say: 'There's no place like home.'"

"How's your bowling?"

"About the same as it was ten years ago."

I watch Possum's eyes narrow as Theodore puts his arm around Sam's sister. "Jennifer, this is my old crush, Natalie…Possum. I was besotted with her in high school. Unfortunately, my infatuation was unrequited, and we had a tumultuous relationship. "Possum, this is my fiancée, Jennifer Hill."

Jennifer grins and offers her hand. "You're so cute."

Possum ignores Jennifer as she looks the unlikely couple over and grunts, "Congrats." She stares at Theodore a little longer and adds, "Hey, sorry about the whole high school thing. I treated you like…."

"Like shit…Thanks, Natalie. That means a lot." Theodore smiles at Jennifer. "Possum tended to marginalize me a lot, but as we both know, I have an indomitable spirit for proving people wrong."

Possum fumes as she puts her cap back on. "Now there's the Theodore I remember…still a pompous dweeb."

Theodore grins, "And the Possum I remember who never minces words."

We watch as Theodore and Jennifer walk off holding hands, while Buster makes an ass of himself by gawking at Jennifer's butt.

Possum snarks, "Buster, take a cold shower." She turns to

Sam. "Why didn't you tell us Theodore was dating your sister and is about to be your brother-in-law?"

"Thought I did. Or maybe I thought I did. Don't know, but that's not the worst of it. My mom's getting married too."

Buster's eyes widen. "Really? Who's she marrying?"

"Some jerk she found online. I've never met him, and I don't plan to either."

Possum tries to help. "Don't be a moron, Sam. You're going to have to meet him sometime. He's going to be your stepfather."

"Well, I'm sure as hell not changing my last name."

"You don't have to; you're twenty-eight years old. What's his last name?"

"Samuels."

I remember Claudia is waiting and hightail it for the door.

Chapter 26

Something Important Indeed

CLAUDIA AND AJ ARE SEATED IN THE FRONT of her late model BMW in the Strike and Spare parking lot. AJ's face droops as he peers out the passenger side window staring at the moon. He turns to Claudia and pouts, "You're right; this is important. So, let me get this straight; you wanna break up with me because you don't respect my job, cuz you hate my friends, cuz you don't think I have a career plan, and because our relationship is dysfunctional? Come on! That's a whole lot of labeling. And as far as my job, I'm working my way up the ladder. I just need a little more time."

"Well, I need to be with someone who's not stuck on the bottom rung of the ladder, someone I respect. You've been loading bowling balls onto a truck ten years for God's sake."

"Hey! I'm good at loading balls. You should watch me load balls. My ball-loading skills would blow your mind."

"Do you hear yourself?"

"What? I was named loader of the year for the past two years."

"You sound like that's a real accomplishment. You know what? It's really not. You're a ridiculous man-child and I'm sick of it. Don't you think it's time to grow up, AJ?"

"Wow. That's harsh, Claudia."

"Break-ups tend to be that way. We had our fun; now it's

time for us to go our separate ways."

"…So, basically, you used me for sex."

"That's it. Out of my car."

AJ doesn't budge. "All these years, and I've never even met your parents."

"And now it doesn't matter."

AJ takes in what Claudia said and changes the subject. "All right, I was going to tell you, but I'm thinking about moving to Milwaukee and buying a bowling alley. Once I get settled, I thought maybe you could join me."

"A bowling alley…in Milwaukee? You're still serving out a DUI. How you going to get there, walk?"

"Be nice…I thought maybe you could drive me there."

"Here's another thing, AJ. I don't want to be in a relationship with some alcoholic who has delusions of grandeur and doesn't even have a driver's license."

"I'm no alcoholic. I only drink beer now."

"Yeah, a lot of beer…and who gets a DUI driving a moped?"

"Hey, I almost drowned…and I've changed my ways. Last month, I promised myself I wouldn't have more than three beers a night. So far, so good."

"That's what alcoholics do; they promise."

"You'll see. I get my license back next week. I've been secretly working on the business plan for three months. I think I might be able to convince Buster, Sam, and Possum to work for me."

"I have a question."

AJ sits up. "Shoot."

"Where do you plan to get the money necessary to buy a bowling alley?"

"I'm gonna borrow it."

"Do you know how much a Milwaukee bowling alley is going to cost? Nobody's going to loan you that kind of money. You have no collateral…you have nothing."

AJ blinks twice. "I'll figure it out. It's all part of the plan."

"And another thing, buying your own bowling alley so you can hire all your lowlife friends…their words, not mine…who drink more beer than you do is a terrible idea."

"This is Wisconsin! What else are we gonna do? 'Sides, my friends are a lot of fun when you get to know them."

"I've tried, and I'm embarrassed to be around them."

"And, now you're embarrassed to be with me."

"Last night I watched a video of you coming out of an office naked."

"Who sent that to you?"

"I don't know. Someone emailed me a link."

"Shit…Sam!"

"It really doesn't matter because we're finished."

"That whole thing happened before we got together."

"I don't want to hear about it."

"Come on, let me explain." Claudia doesn't say anything, so AJ keeps talking. "It was a Saturday night and Lacey, my boss's daughter, stole her dad's key to USBC; you know, cuz we needed a place to go. So, we were clowning around in the breakroom and the power went out."

"Clowning around?"

"Yeah, so anyway, the electricity goes off and the security system locks the door, and we couldn't get out. The heat shut down and we got so cold…we had to burn all kinds of shit. We were stranded there until Monday morning. Sam showed up for work early, thought it was funny, and filmed us being rescued. The jerk promised he'd never show it to anyone."

"I'm curious. What happened to your clothes?"

"Yeah, we got busy and left them in the hallway before we went into the breakroom."

"I don't want to hear anymore. I saw the whole thing and it was disgusting. That's the kind of behavior that tells me we shouldn't be together.

AJ turns away, and Claudia softens. "We had our fun, but I've got my law career going now and I'm…"

"I love you….and I wanna take care of you."

"AJ, I don't need anyone to take care of me. You can't even take care of yourself."

"So, you never want to see me again?"

"Only from a distance."

"C'mon, Claud, long-distance relationships never work out, you know that." Claudia fails to hold back a giggle, so AJ sees an opportunity and tries again. "See, I make you laugh."

"Yes, you do. You did."

"And I'm a damn good kisser….or did you forget?" He moves in for a smooch, but she leans back. He tries again. "Come on. One for the road."

Claudia gives in and they kiss sweetly. It starts to get heated, so she pushes him away. "Enough! You have to leave. And, take those lips with you."

"Fine. But my lips will be at The Watering Hole, if you wanna…"

"How many times do I have to tell you? We're done!"

"All right, already!" AJ vacates the BMW and slams the door. Claudia speeds off, leaving him alone in the parking lot.

THE WATERING HOLE is lit by a street lamp and a neon sign in the bar window. Inside, TVs are tuned to a variety of games, and the place is hopping with bowlers in team attire and locals wearing Brewers, Bucks, and Packers jerseys.

AJ and company sit at a table, slightly intoxicated. Buster downs the last of his beer and signals the barmaid for another. Then he holds his empty mug up to AJ and says, "To Claudia. May we be so lucky as to never see her again!"

Sam salutes AJ. "And may Claudia eat bad sushi and die a slow and painful death! Like I always say, you can't trust a woman who hates your friends."

Possum squints with her good eye. "You've never said that in your life."

Buster adds, "Don't know what you saw in her anyway."

"She did make me feel like I was crazy…but kind of in a good way."

Buster assumes the role of a psychiatrist as he battles AJ's ego. "She was a gaslighter ten years ago, and she's still a gaslighter. You don't need any more of her psychodrama."

"Yeah, there's that, but I've seen you guys checking out her ass every time she leaves."

Sam straightens up. "That's because she has a stick up her butt, and she wants to put one up yours, too."

Buster piles on. "I thought I saw her whittling something."

"Least I tried. When have you two ever been in a relationship?"

Sam and Buster don't answer, so AJ changes the subject. "Sam, did you send out that video of me and Lacey being naked?"

"Might have sent it to a few people."

AJ leans in. "Was one of those people Claudia?"

"Yeah, so? I thought she'd get a kick out of it."

"You promised me you wouldn't show it to anyone."

"I blurred out your private parts."

"I don't want anyone else seeing that, you hear me?"

"It's too late. I posted it on YouTube last week."

"Take it down, you hear me?"

Sam beams. "It's quality, man…alarms going off, firemen with axes and hoses, smoke everywhere, you and Lacey naked. I couldn't keep something like that to myself any longer. You know, statue of limitations."

Buster chimes in, "Still can't believe you hooked up with Frank's daughter…and he didn't fire your ass."

Possum adds, "Takes a lot of balls breaking into USBC just to get a little nookie."

Sam sticks out his chest. "That video has ten thousand hits and I'm about to make some serious money."

"Well, if you don't take it down, I'm taking you down."

"Why? It's hilarious. And why do you give a gosh damn what Claudia thinks now anyway?"

AJ threatens to slap Sam. "Because, it's my willie, and I should get a say as to who sees it."

"I told you. I took care of it."

AJ takes a big gulp from his beer mug. "Let's change the subject. You're driving me down an emotional cul-de-sac."

Possum pats AJ on the shoulder. "'At least now you can move to Milwaukee if you want."

Sam sneers at Possum. "What are you doing? Quit putting ideas in his noggin!"

"Been wanting to go there for five years, but it doesn't matter now. Claudia's right. I'm a loser. I'm all the time broke. Can't save any money."

Possum adjusts her cap. "Enough excuses. Make an existential decision and leave."

Sam scoots forward, "Don't listen to her. You belong here with us."

"Let's not have a hissy fit; I'm here for now…and don't say anything about me wanting to leave; USBC is talking about laying people off."

Sam salutes AJ again. "Loose lips sink fish."

Buster points. "If you do leave, you have to pay me back for drowning my moped."

Possum raises her beer mug. "I say we celebrate. To the end of the longest two years of AJ's life."

Buster adds, "Ours too."

AJ fires back, "Come on, guys. Wish me luck. I'm looking for freshwater, so I can start over."

They clink their mugs in unison and Possum yells, "Here's to starting over!" They all finish their drinks, except for Sam, who nurses his beer.

A bouncy barmaid appears. "Another round, gentlemen?"

Possum stares at the blond, who is dressed in a short skirt and V-neck sweater, and lowers her voice an octave. "I'm not a man, sweetie, and I'm certainly not gentle."

The young girl realizes her mistake and lowers her head. "I'm sorry, I didn't mean anything."

"Don't worry about it. It happens all the time."

The barmaid tries again. "Would anyone like another beer?"

AJ waves her off. "Not for me, three's my limit." He rethinks his decision. "Ahh, hell. Bring me another one."

She gives the table a "don't forget to tip me" grin and turns to Sam. "How about you, sir? Another beer?"

Sam smiles. "Sir, I like that." He downs what's left of his beer and tries to turn on the charm. "Does the pope shit in the woods?"

The barmaid gives him a strange look, and Buster tries to explain. "Don't mind him. His brain doesn't know what his mouth is saying half the time." Sam slugs Buster in the arm, which sets off a furious but wimpy slap fight over the top of Possum, who covers her head trying to protect herself.

"Quit it, ya morons. Use your words!" Possum shoves both

of them, and they settle down.

The beer continues to flow as AJ turns maudlin. "Hey guys, I've been thinking."

Possum grumbles, "Oh, god. Here we go."

"I'm gonna try to get her back. Every couple breaks up a few times before they make it work."

Buster raises his eyebrows and snorts. "That's movie shit, AJ."

Now half-baked, Sam adds fuel to the fire. "You can't chase that gal no more; she'll whip that stick out of her butt and beat you to death with it. She ain't worth it."

"But what if she is?"

Buster and Possum harmonize. "She's not!"

AJ stumbles to his feet and heads for the door. "You guys suck."

Sam jumps up, cuts AJ off, and yells loud enough for everyone in the bar to hear. "Only one way to settle this!"

A guy sitting alone at the bar counter raises his arms in the air and screams, "Bowl Off!"

Everyone in The Watering Hole gets the message and they begin to chant, "Bowl Off! Bowl Off! Bowl Off!

People laugh as AJ steps around his friend and runs for the door. Sam stumbles after him and hollers, "Somebody stop that man!"

Two burly bouncers reach over and grab AJ. They restrain him while Buster stands on a chair, cups his hand, and announces, "Here's the sitch, folks. Earlier tonight, our friend AJ got dumped by his uppity-assed girlfriend."

Several people let out "oohs" and "awws" until Buster raises his hand and quiets them. "No, no, don't feel sorry for him. She's a real witch. Wait, did I say witch? I think y'all know what I meant to say." Several men raise their arms in the air and grunt as Buster raises his hand to silence them again. "Now that she's given him the gift of freedom, he's acting like some deer trying to cross the highway. And so you see, over the horizon, there's his used-to-be-girlfriend in an SUV waiting for the chance to crush our Bambi here and take herself home some roadkill."

People boo loudly, and Buster raises his voice. "But why in the world would he wanna stand on the highway and let her flatten his ass? We say he shouldn't, but he can't decide. All he can see are the headlights…what say you?"

The crowd chants again, "Bowl Off! Bowl Off! Bowl Off!"

Sam waits for them to quiet down and barks, "Gather your empties folks. It's on!" Everyone in the bar, including bartenders and barmaids, slip on their parkas and hurry to the door.

On the street in front of The Watering Hole, Buster and Possum gather twenty empty beer bottles and line them up in two pin formations sixty feet away.

As people compete for a good place to see, Buster explains the rules. "AJ, you bowl for team 'Beg-Claudia-to-Take-Ya-Back-Even-Though-She-Doesn't-Want-Ya,' and Sam, your team is 'Listen-To-Your-Friends-AJ-We-Got-Your-Back-You-Moron.' You each get two throws. Once the bottles have spoken, it's binding!"

Sam removes the ball from his bag. Possum tries to hand AJ his ball, but he steps back. Enjoying all the attention, Sam softens his voice and pleads, "Come on, AJ, it's the Alley Oop way."

AJ finally takes his ball from Possum and frowns. "Fine. But I'm gonna crush you."

Sam steps up to an imaginary scratch line, rears back, and throws his ball down the sidewalk. He shatters nine of the ten bottles, but his ball keeps going and ends up in a snow pile. The crowd cheers as a drunken bystander scoops the ball out of the snow bank and rolls it back to Sam. Sam wipes it off, lines up his second shot, lets it fly, and smashes the final bottle to smithereens.

The crowd goes nuts as Buster assesses the situation. "Helluva roll, Sam I am! Only way AJ can beat you is with a strike. You got one shot, buddy boy."

AJ blows on his hands, raises his ball, steps up, and launches his ball with all his might. The sphere careens down the street and obliterates every bottle. The crowd cheers as the ball picks up speed, jumps the snow pile, ricochets off a light pole, and crashes through the windshield of a vintage Maserati. Sam's eyes widen and he screams, "Haul ass!" Everyone scatters as the car's alarm blares.

Minutes later, AJ slides to a stop in the Strike and Spare parking lot. He bends over as he tries to catch his breath. Satisfied he's far enough away from the crime scene to not get caught, he climbs the snow pile contest hill and sits his butt down. He looks up at a full moon and howls. "Howoooh! Howoooh!"

The old timer that AJ saw in the bowling alley earlier in the evening steps out of the shadows with his dog and grumbles, "Hey, what's going on?"

AJ's skeleton jumps out of his exoskeleton when he sees the oddly dressed man he saw earlier in the bowling alley. Still wearing a poncho and sunglasses, the old-timer chuckles. "Didn't mean to interrupt…whatever it is you're doing."

AJ tries to stand up, but loses his balance and slides down the hill on his butt. He jumps up, dusts the snow off his pants and snickers, "You scared the shit out of me, mister." AJ studies the man's profile. "Do I know you?"

The old-duffer steps forward and smirks. "It's me."

AJ's eyes light up. "Uncle Julius?"

"Yeah, kiddo. How ya been?"

AJ attacks his uncle with a vicious hug. "Oh my God. It's really you."

"Yeah, it's really me."

AJ studies his uncle's face and his dog. "Wait. Are you blind?"

Julius removes his sunglasses, revealing his battered face. "Doc says I'll be back to normal in no time."

"What happened to your face?"

"It's a long story. Can I tell you later?"

"Am I gonna have to wait ten years?"

"Yeah, about that…"

AJ interrupts. "What's your dog's name?"

"Rufus."

"Well, then…" AJ picks up some snow, makes a large snowball, packs it tight, and smashes it into his uncle's face.

Julius clears his eyes and tightens his lips. "Okay, I guess I had that coming."

"Mom and Dad die, and you up and leave me? No explanation, no phone call."

"Keep it down, will ya?" Julius scopes out the parking lot, all nervous. "What I did, I had to do...to protect you."

"Protect me from what? Whatever it was, it didn't work. They took my house, everything in it…and you stole my Pinto."

"Maybe I can make it up to you. I want to give you something." Julius pulls a baseball from under his shawl and hands it to his nephew. "I'm sorry. I should have been there for you. I was hoping maybe you'd let me...pick up the spare."

AJ examines the ball and says, "Ten years and you give me a baseball?"

"Look who signed it."

"Yeah, Hank Aaron. He's probably signed thousands of balls."

Julius smiles. "Check the date on it. He wrote it himself."

AJ eyes the ball again. "April 13, 1954."

"I had him sign it the first day he played in the majors…when he was a rookie with the Braves. He went 0 for 5, and the Braves lost to Cincinnati, 9 to 8. He's still the greatest Brewer-Brave of all time. Boy, he could really knock the cover off the ball, couldn't he?"

"I don't want this." AJ tosses the ball to his uncle.

Julius throws it back. "No, I want you to have it. It's special. One of a kind. Take care of it better than I took care of you."

"You can't just fix things with a ball."

"I understand. I ran away from my life; I abandoned you. I didn't realize everything I needed was right under my nose."

"So, where the hell have you been?"

"It's complicated."

"Could you at least give me a hint?"

"I'm not trying to be mysterious, but there are some things you're better off not knowing."

Headlights pass by, and Julius ducks down behind the snow hill. "Gotta go. What do you say we meet up and talk about ol' Hammerin' Hank sometime?"

AJ nods. "Fine. *Carl's Diner*. Monday night at six. I'm busy this weekend."

Julius puts his sunglasses back on. "Boy, he could knock the cover off the ball, couldn't he?"

"Yeah, you already said that."

"That's what makes the ball so valuable. Hold on to it, ya hear? Maybe one day it'll bring you pleasure, too."

"Yeah, sure."

As Julius walks away, he says, "You gonna catch hell for wrecking that car?"

"I'll be all right. Million bowling balls in this town, and I doubt anyone is gonna squeal on me. Hey, you didn't tell me what happened to your face."

"Hit and run."

"Any idea who it was?"

"Yeah, I've gotta a pretty good idea who it is."

AJ waits for a name, but Julius slips away and disappears around the corner. In the distance, he hears his uncle yell, "See you Monday night!"

Chapter 27

Secrets Revealed

AJ OPERATES A FORKLIFT as Buster, Sam, and Possum finish loading boxes of bowling balls and pins into a USBC truck. Dressed in a blue suit coat and tan jeans, warehouse supervisor Frank Kilroy holds a clipboard close to his chest as he oversees the operation. The tight-lipped boss with loose jowls lifts his hand and yells, “All right, that’s it. Another truck will be here in a few minutes. Take five.”

As Frank walks off, AJ joins his friends and they sit on a stack of wooden pallets. Possum parks herself next to AJ and says, “Did you get your ball back?”

“Naw, but I got three more like it at home.”

“You do know that was Frank’s Maserati you destroyed?”

“What? You gotta be shitting me.”

Possum curls her lip. “Debated whether I should tell you.”

Buster leans over. “Relax. No one’s gonna tell on you.”

AJ panics. “Oh my God! I just remembered something. That ball has my initials on it…AJB.” Everyone laughs except for AJ. “It's not funny you guys. Frank already hates me for what I did with Lacey.”

OUTSIDE A WHITE brick building with red shuttered windows, a sign reads: LAW FIRM OF JONES, SHERWIN, and WILLIAMS.

Inside, standing at Claudia Giovanni's desk, are two legal assistants putting the finishing touches on a contract. The phone rings and Claudia clears her throat. "Yes sir. We have it right here. Yes, I'll bring it right in." Claudia hangs up the phone and straightens her black blazer. "Excuse me. Mr. Williams needs this."

The assistants smirk as Claudia picks up the document and walks away. When she reaches Gil William's office door, she raps once and waits. Finally, Gil chirps, "Come in, Miss Giovanni."

She pauses a moment, peeks at the legal assistants who are gawking behind her, and slips inside. Dressed in a tailored three-piece gray suit, Gil is seated behind a massive mahogany desk in his well-appointed office. Claudia hands him the folder, and he motions her to sit down. "So, how'd he take it?"

"Not very well, I'm afraid." Claudia's phone buzzes and she reads the text message.

Gil's eyes darken. "It's him, isn't it? Let me see."

"Maybe."

"Come on. Let me see."

Claudia reluctantly hands her cell phone to Gil, and he reads the message with a high-pitched voice. "I'm a mess without you. Please give us another chance. You're still my Pooh Bear." He hands the phone back and sneers, "Pooh Bear? Give me a break…wah, wah, wah. How pathetic is that?"

"Don't be mean. He's hurting."

"You're out of his league, and he knows it. You're gorgeous. Come over here."

Claudia slides over to Gil. He taps his knee. She sits on his lap and stares into his eyes. "Okay, I kept my end of the bargain. How are you doing on your end?"

Gil kisses her on the cheek. "I told you. I'm waiting for the right moment. Vicki needs to think it's her idea or she'll take me to the cleaners. Can you imagine how embarrassing that would be?"

"But it's not embarrassing having an affair with the only junior lawyer in the office? Which, by the way, everyone has pretty much figured out by now?"

"So, what if they know. Why do you care? It comes with the territory."

Claudia slides of Gil's lap and steps back. "What's that supposed to mean? What am I some kind of law firm bonus?"

"That's not what I meant."

"Gil, I'm not interested in being an office cliché."

Gil tries to lighten the mood. "Aren't we feisty this morning?"

"I'm serious. I thought we felt something for each other."

"Come on, sweetie, we do."

"How's this for sweet? I'm not sleeping with you again until you're out of that house."

"Chill out."

"I mean it. I went through a brutal breakup, and you're still living with your wife…probably still screwing her for all I know!" Claudia begins to cry, so Gil hands her a box of Kleenex and she covers her face. "Did I make the biggest friggin' mistake of my life?"

"Of course not. You're amazing, and you're on your way to being a great lawyer."

Claudia lowers the tissue, sniffs, and says, "Do you really believe that?"

"Of course. And think about the opportunity you have here. You are learning from one of the best legal minds in the state." Gil chuckles. "Guess that makes you my legal lover."

"More like illegal lover if you ask me."

"Hey, we could role-play *Pretty Woman*. Me, a powerful business mogul who needs a no-strings-attached date. You, the helpless and sexy down-on-her-luck street hooker."

"Really, Gil? I'm feeling awfully vulnerable right now. Did you just say 'no strings attached'?"

"You're right; bad choice of words. But you're so damn hot. I can't help myself. Listen, I'm going to get out. Just give me a little more time."

Claudia blows her nose. "Promise?"

"Promise. Now come back over here." Claudia moves over, Gil lifts her chin, kisses her hard, and places his other hand on her butt.

Claudia whispers in his ear, "Maybe in a couple of days after you move out, we'll see about that *Pretty Woman* thing." She removes his hand, slowly pulls away, and walks out the door.

IN A GATED community, Gil Williams' six-thousand square foot custom-built two-story house dwarfs the neighbors' homes, with its enormous yard and well-manicured lawn.

Inside her personal gym, Vicki Williams, who is wearing a skin-tight pair of black pants and a matching shirt, is lying on a mat lifting two barbells. The room has an in-the-wall stereo system, and she's surrounded by an arsenal of gym equipment, including free weights, a stationary bicycle, and two treadmills. Her sculpted body glistens as her tight workout clothes reveal her bulging muscles. Exhausted, she lays the barbells aside, sits up, and listens to the music for a while.

A song she doesn't like comes on, so she grabs a remote and clicks it off. Then she jumps to her feet, walks over to the corner of the room and finds her black Rottweiler, Goliath, waiting patiently. She guides him over to the smaller of the two treadmills, while she hops on the larger one. The dog and his master run side- by-side in perfect rhythm as Goliath occasionally barks. Vicki's face reddens, her prominent jaw juts out, and her black-haired ponytail swings from side to side as she picks up the pace.

Ten minutes pass and Vicki slows both treadmills to a stop. She lifts her water bottle to drink, but it's empty. "More water!"

In the living room, sitting in a large high-backed leather armchair, Gil is hidden behind his newspaper. When he hears Vicki yell for water, he reluctantly lays the paper down, revealing his black linen pajamas.

He walks into the kitchen, takes an aluminum water bottle out of a cream-colored custom cabinet, and fills it with the European packaged water in the refrigerator. Next, he reaches under the sink and pulls out a jug of clear liquid ammonia. He stares at the lethal concoction a moment, considers adding the substance to Vicki's drink, but he puts it back under the sink. He picks a bowl off the floor and adds the purified water to it as well.

Almost done, he goes to the refrigerator and takes out four ice cubes. He places two in the water bottle and two in the dog bowl. He carefully carries the two containers into the workout room, where he finds Vicki and Goliath still taking a break. Vicki gives Gil a hostile stare and grumbles, "You sure took your sweet time."

Gil hands his wife the bottle and places the dog dish next to Goliath's treadmill. He turns to leave and the dog growls. Vicki frowns and lifts her chin. "Forgetting something?" Gil walks over to Vicki and kisses her on the cheek. Goliath growls again; this time showing his teeth. "Don't be jealous, Goliath. Daddy loves you, too."

"Vicki, I need to run over to the office to check on that contract I've been working on."

Vicki grins. "You're not meeting up with one of those young gals from the office, are you?"

"Come on. Look at you. Who else do I need?"

He starts to leave again, but Vicki motions him back. "Aren't you forgetting something else?"

Gil pivots back. "What?"

"You promised you'd take Goliath in for his annual physical this morning."

"I did?"

"Yes, you did, Poopsie. His appointment is at nine. And you need to pick him up afterward at eleven. Don't be late; Goliath gets all stressed out. That gives you two hours to check on your contract and do whatever else naughty men do."

Goliath is seated in the back of a black E-Class Mercedes Benz with a seat belt wrapped around his chest. Gil checks his rear-view mirror and the dog growls, so Gil growls back. Goliath whimpers and lies back down on his custom-made doggy bed.

ON THE WESTERN edge of Greenvale, the morning sun lights up a middle-class neighborhood. A residential street remains quiet as a seventy-five-year-old man exits his modest house and fishes his newspaper out of a rosebush next to the front steps. He pricks his finger on a thorn and yelps, "Damn it." As he sucks his index finger, he hears a dog barking loudly inside the exceptionally run-down two-bedroom house next door.

He stares at the eyesore a moment until he hears the dog howl. He shuffles over and sees the uncut grass and two newspapers lying on the sidewalk. He grumbles, "White trash, lowlife." After he makes his way up the steps, he rings the doorbell. No one answers, so he knocks…still nothing.

The old man descends the steps, waddles over to the front window, and peers inside. Suddenly, his neighbor's large golden retriever appears in the window and barks. The old man hollers, "Whoa!" and stumbles backward, falling square on his butt. He gathers himself, struggles to his feet, and makes his way back to the window. There he finds the dog staring at him with an empty food bowl in his mouth.

Thirty minutes later, the old man and four other neighbors watch as two paramedics navigate a shrouded body on a gurney through the front door of the ill-kept house and into an ambulance. Police officer, Tyler Becker exits soon after, with the golden retriever on a leash. The neighbors gawk as he loads the animal in the backseat of his squad car and drives off.

AJ, WHO IS wearing red boxer shorts, is sprawled out in his only chair watching *Pretty Woman*. He hears a gentle knock, so he puts on his robe, which has an obscene image of a bowling pin hanging down from two bowling balls. When he opens his front door, he sees Claudia with a smug look on her face. Happy to see her, he lets his robe fall open.

Claudia covers her eyes. "Oh my God!"

"Oops." AJ closes his robe and grins. "Old habits die hard. What are you doing here?"

"I came to give you a heads-up."

"What kind of heads-up?"

"Our firm represents USBC, which includes your boss, Frank Kilroy. Frank found your ball in the front seat of his car and he came to us wanting to sue you."

"Wait? It was only his windshield. Doesn't he have car insurance?"

"He wanted to sue you for his emotional stress."

"Well, as my friend Sam would say, "You can't squeeze orange juice out of a turnip."

Claudia ups the vibe. "So, I should win an ex-girlfriend achievement award. I convinced him...well, Gil and I convinced him that suing your ass was a waste of time."

"Thanks…where's the ball?"

"Frank still has it."

"Shit. He's gonna fire me."

"I mean...yeah, probably. He's not really your best friend right now."

"Wow, I can't believe you stood up for me." AJ reaches out to Claudia and his robe falls open again.

Claudia grimaces. "Seriously!"

"Jeez. Sorry." He covers up.

Claudia takes a step back. "Anyway, I should go. I hope you

still have a job."

"Wait. Let me ask you something. If I got another job, one with more of a future, would you consider getting back together?"

"I'm afraid it's the whole package I'm after, but you showing a little initiative would certainly help."

"Really?"

"Listen, I never said I would take…"

"…Done! I start my job search tomorrow. You wait and see. I'm gonna make myself a better man."

"AJ, it's not a question as to whether you are good enough for me to take you back. You're just not me material."

"You just said you want the whole package. Just so you know, I'm going to turn myself into a package a UPS driver will want to keep for himself. Wait, that didn't come out the way I meant it to."

"Whatever. Just don't quit your job until you find a better one." She hesitates, kisses him with passion, and steps back. "Damn, those lips of yours."

"Why you keep kissing me if you wanna break up?"

"We're already broken up, but giving up those lips is taking a little longer than I expected."

"They kinda come with that package we've been talking about, ya know?"

Claudia slaps her own face. "Stop it, Claudia! You're being ridiculous!" As she rushes off, she yells, "No more kissing."

AJ leans back in his doorway and spews, "You didn't seem to mind it that much! Just you wait.! In no time, I'm gonna be a new man!" Feeling hopeful, he goes back inside, hoists his ball, and rolls it down his hallway.

In the apartment below, Helga Clodfelter is in her kitchen frying bratwurst and boiling sauerkraut, when she hears a loud thump and the sound of a ball rolling above her. The resident landlady, dressed in a pink muumuu, ducks down, glares up at the ceiling, and scowls.

EVENING COMES AND Claudia is parked in her BMW six blocks from AJ's apartment. Next to her car is a large sign that reads, *ROYAL MOTEL SEVEN.* Gil rolls up in his Mercedes and parks next to her. They exit their vehicles at the same time, and Gil chuckles. Claudia stares at him as they head for the motel's office door. She tugs on his jacket sleeve and says, "I have no idea why I keep doing this."

Gil grins. "Oh, I think you do."

Inside their sparsely lit room, accentuated by shag green carpet and brightly painted red walls, Claudia and Gil lay naked in a queen-sized bed. Gil is sound asleep and Claudia is staring at a large water stain on the ceiling. Her cell phone vibrates and she covers it with a pillow, so as not to wake Gil. She waits a moment, uncovers her phone, checks the screen, and sees that it's AJ calling again. She lets it buzz a couple more times and buries it back under the pillow.

Chapter 28

Losing What You Thought You'd Already Lost

"YOU'RE ALL FIRED!" Frank tightens his grip on a bowling ball as he faces AJ and his three friends, who are standing next to the forklift and a pallet filled with boxes containing company bowling balls, pins, and other supplies.

Sam steps up to Frank. "You can't do that. We've been here ten years."

"Watch me…I found this ball in the front seat of my Maserati that I parked down the street from The Watering Hole. Does anyone know who it belongs to?"

Buster snickers, "I got all my balls."

Sam tries to reason with his boss. "Why would we know? We might not have been at The Watering Hole when whatever happened…happened."

Frank glares and Sam laments. "Okay, we were there, but that could be anybody's ball. This town's full of balls."

Frank points at AJ's initials on the ball and Buster, Sam, and Possum sneak a peek at their friend. Frank continues. "Okay, all of you report to HR. You're done."

As Frank starts off, AJ calls out, "Okay, it's mine. I rolled it. Those are my initials. You know that. I know that. What's with all the drama?"

Frank circles back. "I wanted to see if you'd admit it."

"Yeah, I did it. You happy now? I broke some glass."

Frank growls, "You're lucky I'm not pressing charges."

"I heard you wanted to sue my ass. Why didn't you?"

"I would if you had anything worth taking." Frank points. "Bowers, you need to gather up your shit and leave." Frank tosses the ball to AJ, who nearly drops it.

Possum steps up. "Mr. Kilroy with all due respect, you can't fire AJ for something that isn't work-related. It was an off-site accident."

Sam joins Possum. "Yeah, what happens at The Watering Hole stays at The Watering Hole!"

"Okay, USBC is making budget cuts. I need to let one of you go. AJ, you were the last one hired."

Possum tries again. "We were all hired the same day."

"I checked. AJ was the last to hand in his paperwork. You three get back to work."

AJ sticks out his chin. "This is about me and your daughter Lacey, isn't it?"

Frank doesn't respond as he struts away with a satisfied look on his face.

AJ mutters, "Well, shit."

Inside the USBC headquarters administrative suite, sit three businessmen from Texas. They are dressed in expensive black suits and wearing silver bolo ties and matching white cowboy hats. As they wait to see Jim Jeffries, the president and owner of USBC, they take turns ogling Mildred Pearson, an attractive administrative assistant, who pretends not to notice. She smiles politely, picks up her phone, pokes a number, and waits. "The three gentlemen from Dallas have arrived." She listens for a response and then makes eye contact with the Texans. "Mr. Jeffries is ready to see you." The men stand up, straighten their suit jackets, and move toward the office door. It swings open and Jim Jeffries almost collides with them. The Texans give Mr. Jeffries a boisterous laugh and he ushers them into his office.

Inside his office, Jeffries and his guests join Gil Williams, Frank Kilroy, and Antonio Giovanni, who take turns shaking the Texans' hands. The out-of-towners take a seat as Gil reviews the contract he has prepared for the sale of USBC. He gloats, "Mr. Jeffries, it's a great offer."

Jeffries scoots forward in his chair and stares at Gil. "I hate to admit it, but I'm having second thoughts. Selling and moving the company to Texas…I don't know. What if we cut our expenses some more? We're already laying off people in the warehouse, right Frank?"

Frank nods. "Got rid of AJ Bowers today."

Gil grins as Antonio taps his pen on the table and says, "We still need an infusion of cash, Mr. Jeffries. So, unless we can find an investor real soon…"

Mr. Jeffries stares at the Texans, slightly embarrassed. "Sorry for waffling at the last-minute gentlemen, but a lot of our locals depend on this place."

The Texans gawk at Gil, who raises his eyebrows and argues his point. "These men have come in good faith. Let's not blow it. These gentlemen have made us a generous offer and they are ready to sign the contract."

Jeffries' face turns pale as he avoids eye contact with Gil and the Texans. "This is not an easy decision. I don't want to have seller's remorse."

The oldest of the three Texans stands up. "We came here because we thought we had a deal."

Gil clears his throat. "I'm sorry. I thought we did too. I think Mr. Jeffries just needs a little more time."

The other two Texans stand and join their colleague as he makes his farewell statement. "We'll sign the contract before we leave. We're not flying back to this cold country again. Mr. Jeffries, have your lawyer here fax us a notarized copy in the next two weeks or the deal's off."

AJ ENTERS HIS three-story apartment building and trudges his way up to his second-floor door carrying his bowling ball in one hand and a lunch bucket in the other. His sixty-year-old landlady intercepts him as he puts a key in his door. Helga Clodfelter's eyes are accentuated by thick, uneven black mascara-drawn eyebrows. She is wearing a flower-patterned blue muumuu and carrying a bag of garbage. She slaps the bag across AJ's butt and admonishes him with a heavy German accent, "Rent money. Mach schnell! Two weeks late. Thin ice, you! Friday you pay or kaput."

AJ spins around and drops his ball. He picks up the fourteen-pounder and apologizes with his eyes.

Helga growls, "You no drop balls in mein building again."

AJ scoots back against his door. "Sorry about that, Ms. C. Hey, about the rent, I need a bit more time, my...succulent landlady.'"

"I no suck."

"Oh, no, succulent means...well, something good. Here, let me take that out for you."

AJ tries to grab the garbage bag from her, but she doesn't let go. "Rent money or erection!"

He laughs. "I think you mean...eviction?"

"I throw ass out!" Helga grabs the garbage bag, tosses it over her shoulder, and storms off.

Chapter 29

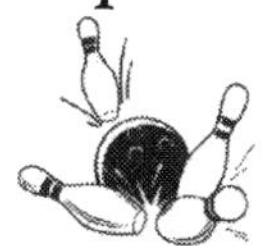

Waiting For Uncle Julius

IT'S SIX O'CLOCK IN THE PM when I walk into *Carl's Diner*, Greenvale's very own stuck-in-the-60's eatery. The first thing I hear is this sixty-year-old busty waitress scream into the kitchen. "Two hockey pucks, on the fly, drag 'em through the garden and Wisconsin, with frog sticks in the alley and extra sea dust!...Oh, and I almost forgot…a cup of mud." As she pours the coffee, I can't help but notice her old-school beehive hairdo that's Lucille Ball red.

She walks off and the boss man, Carl Labrowsky, points at the counter. "You can park there if you want." The chunky man with an obvious comb-over scoots off as I plop down on a stool facing the order window. When the well-seasoned waitress gives me a flirty smile, I notice the letters DNR embroidered on her uniform, but I don't say anything cuz who knows what that could mean. From the kitchen, I hear some cook or dishwasher type singing *Oh What a Beautiful Morning* from the musical *Oklahoma.* Carl walks over to the window and hollers, "Shut the hell up, Leroy! You're annoying the customers."

As the owner walks off, I hear Leroy yell, "You're an asshole, Carl!"

I laugh as this pretty-faced waitress about my age, limps over with a pot of coffee and stutters, "Would you…would you, like some…coffee?" I nod and the short-haired gal pours me a cup. A bell dings, she spins around, picks up an order, and hurries off. I nurse my coffee for a few minutes, and she shows up again. "C…Can I…warm you…up?"

"Warm…me up?"

"Your cof…fee."

"Sure, why not. You stutter."

She glares at me, like WTF, and I feel like a loser for what I said and roll my eyes. "Lady, I'm sorry. I don't know why I said that."

She tops my cup off and gives me a dish of her own dirt. "Did you notice I limp, too?"

I gulp. "I'm sorry, that was totally...Well, I'm pretty much a…."

"A dumb...a dumb shit?"

"I was gonna a doofus, but that works." Things get quiet again until she says, "You waiting for someone?"

"Yeah, my uncle."

"Anything else I can get you until he gets here?"

"New job? New girlfriend? Rent money?"

"You sound like a country song." She stutters again, "Now you need… a mangy dog and you'll… be all set."

I grin. "Things can only get better."

"Rough week, huh?"

"Dreams dying all over the place." I'm kind of liking this gal, so I get kind of flirty. "You new?"

"Been working here…two years."

"Wow, I guess I haven't been in for a while."

"I'm Zooey…Bingham, by the way." She holds out her clenched hand, and we fist bump.

"AJ Bowers."

"You know, Mr. Bowers, dreams…never really die. They only get…rerouted…sometimes. Zooey grabs a sweet roll from the display case and plops it down in front of me. "On the house."

She goes into the kitchen, and I look down at the sweet roll, fighting off tears. The front door opens and in walks a cop I know, Tyler Becker. All I can think is, *Oh, shit; I'm about to be arrested.* I hop up, lean over, cover my face, and attempt to sneak past him. He's too quick for me and blocks the door. I notice he has a dog tied to a leash next to him, one that looks like Uncle Julius' dog.

Becker lowers his voice and grumbles. "Where you think you're going, Bowers?"

Feeling a lot of angst, I retreat and sit back down. "Officer Becker! If'n it ain't my favorite law enforcement official."

Becker turns serious. "We need to chat."

"It was an accident…honest."

"An accident? How do you know that?"

"Cuz I'm the one that rolled the ball."

"I don't know what you're talking about. I'm here to give you some bad news and make a delivery. Meet Rufus. He's yours now."

"Mine? He belongs to my Uncle Julius. Why?...Oh, shit."

"Yeah, afraid we found him dead yesterday morning."

My stomach cramps, and I choke out, "How'd he die?"

"Fellas at the morgue are checking that out right now."

Becker pats me on the back and all random-like I say, "There weren't any bullet holes in him, were there?"

"All I know is he stopped breathing." Becker looks me over. "You know something?"

"Nah. I hadn't seen Julius for ten years and for some reason he showed up a couple of days ago. We were supposed to meet here at six."

"I'm sorry, kid. He, uh...Well, these are for you. We found them stuck to this dog's fur."

Becker hands me two oversized sticky notes and I read the first one out loud: "AJ, *Carl's Diner*, 6 p.m." Then I read the second one which has a notary stamp on it. "I leave all my earthly treasures to AJ Bowers, my nephew."

Becker pats me on the back again. "Like I said, nobody knows what happened. Most likely natural causes, but you never know."

"What else could it be?"

"Well…I probably shouldn't say, but your uncle was into some shady dealings; God rest his soul. Wanted in four states and Mexico. Can't rule out foul play. State's paying for an autopsy. Should have the results soon."

Becker hands me the leash, another piece of paper, and a

key. "Like I said, he left you a h

ouse and some other...'treasure.' That's the address."

"Wait, a house?"

"Yeah, lucky you. It's a real mess. You'll have to see a lawyer to get it deeded over to you. Oh, and stay away from Maseratis."

Becker leaves and Rufus barks. Then the dog jumps up and puts his paws up on my chest like he wants to dance. I push him down as Zooey shows up. "Hey! You got your dog, country boy."

The next morning, I'm feeling all bummed out about UJ dying, so I decide to walk to the other side of town with Rufus to scope out the house he left me. When we get there, Rufus starts yanking on his leash, excited to be home. I stand there a moment, staring at the crappiest yard and the shittiest house I've ever seen. I nod at Rufus. "Muchas grassy ass, Uncle Julius."

I'm hesitant to go inside, but when I do, I discover Becker was right. The house is filled with crap: old newspapers and magazines, plastic bags full of dirty clothes, boxes of old books, coolers with nothing in them, two laundry baskets full of hotel toiletries, old calendars, and too much other shit to even mention.

Julius was obviously a hoarder. I keep moving and see at least a hundred yellow sticky notes all over the living room walls. I read some of them and realize that most of the post-its are reminders of things Julius didn't wanna forget, like the combination to some padlock that is nowhere to be found, dates relating to who knows what, and the names of some random towns in Mexico.

I keep checking out the house as Rufus trails close behind me. Then I start to wonder how long UJ lived in this dump. A year? Five years? How did he stay hidden from me all this time? And why didn't he bother to contact me? I pat Rufus on the head and mutter. "Jules sure had a shitload of shit, didn't he, boy?"

Rufus barks in agreement and takes off down a hallway, leading me into the bathroom. I'm instantly overwhelmed by a god- awful smell, so I pinch my nostrils and holler, "Holy crap!" All excited, Rufus barks again and I grimace. "You probably like this. It smells like an indoor outhouse."

DEPRESSED BY THE triple combo of my uncle dying, losing Claudia, and inheriting a crap house full of shit that I don't know what to do with, I hole up in my apartment for two days eating the cold pizza Buster dropped off, munching on stale Cheetos, and drinking fizzed-out Dr. Pepper. I did scrape up enough money to buy Rufus a bag of dog chow, but he's more interested in my pizza than any dry dog food.

Every once in a while, I text Claudia, but I get nothing cuz she's still ghosting me. A few times, I hear someone knock on the door, but I ignore it. I figure it's probably Old Lady Clodfelter wanting her rent money. My cell phone rings every now and then, but I ignore it cuz it's all the time someone trying to sell me something. Then I get to thinking it might be Claudia calling, so I wait for my phone to ring again like I'm some codependent fool you read about in a dentist's office magazine.

An hour goes by and my cell phone rings again. I almost pee my pants, but I wait three rings cuz I don't want her thinking I'm desperate. I check the screen, and it's not her number. I answer it anyway, cuz I'm kinda lonely. All macho-like, I say, "Hey."

I listen as this fella with a Norwegian accent states his business. "Yah, so this is Sven Olafson, the business manager from Greenvale Hospital. Is this AJ Bowers?"

"Yeah, what's up?"

Sorry for your loss, but we got this uncle of yours, Julius Bowers here, and we wanna know if you want us to ship him over to Fred's Funeral Home."

"I don't know how that works

"You're his nearest relative, so that's why I'm calling you."

"Yeah, I don't have a vehicle, so just send him over." I say my goodbyes, click off my phone, and it rings again. This time it's some Greenvale lawyer, who tells me what I already know: UJ's dead, and he left me his house and all his earthly possessions. What I didn't wanna hear was that I have to sell his place right away. Back to his old tricks, UJ had mortgaged the house up the ying-yang, not to mention there are a shitload of taxes he didn't bother to pay. I know, right? Déjà vu all over again.

Anyway, the legal eagle said the house was a wash and made me promise to pay all of Julius' funeral expenses and clean out the house. The way I figure it, if I can sell some UJ's shit, I might have enough money left over to buy an old truck and move to Milwaukee. Wait. Then I remember I still owe Old Lady Clodfelter rent money. Could things get any worse?

Chapter 30

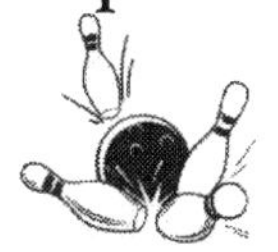

Things Do Get Worse

CLAUDIA EXITS THE LAW FIRM of Jones, Sherwin, and Williams carrying a ton of work. AJ appears out of nowhere and surprises her as she unlocks her BMW. Claudia shrieks and drops her load. "Sorry, I didn't mean to scare you."

As they both bend down to pick up several manila folders, Claudia says, "What are you doing here?"

"I've been texting you, but you never text me back."

Claudia notices that AJ is wearing a white shirt and tie, a black suit jacket, and a tan pair of dockers. "Why are you dressed like that?"

"Goin' to a funeral. Could use a friend even if we're not getting back together."

"Whose funeral is it?"

"Remember my Uncle Julius?"

"The one that took off after your parents' accident?"

"Yeah, well, he showed up the other night, looking old as Morgan Freeman. We were supposed to meet up and talk, but he up and died."

"Oh…I'm sorry."

Gil steps out of the law firm building, hurries over, and sidles up to Claudia. "This guy bothering you?"

"It's OK, Gil."

Gil frowns at AJ. "I know you're upset; I get it. But I have to protect my staff, so don't do anything you'll regret."

AJ snarls, "Like what?"

Gil gets in AJ's face. "Like stalking Claudia at her job. She doesn't wanna talk to you anymore."

"What are you, her guardian devil or something? She can speak for herself." AJ's tone of voice changes as he turns to his ex. "Wait. You're with this jerk?! Really, Claud?"

"I was gonna...I'm sorry you had to find out like this."

AJ points at Gi. "You suck!" Then he points to Claudia. "And so do you!'

Gil baits AJ. "We'll see who sucks Friday night, won't we?"

"Yeah, we's gonna kick your asses."

"In your dreams, loser. You come near Claudia again and I'll write up a restraining order and serve it to you myself."

AJ tries to speak, but he's got nothing. Instead, he slips past Gil, and tries to give him a shoulder bump. He misses and almost falls down. Gil laughs as AJ huffs off, gritting his teeth.

AJ trudges up a sidewalk leading to a chintzy white plastered building, and a sign reading: FRED'S FUNERAL HOME / LEAVE THE REST TO US. Once inside, AJ wanders down the hallway until he finally finds the entrance to the chapel. He comes to a stop when he sees a wooden music stand with angel wings and a small whiteboard dangling from it with his uncle's name printed in black marker ink: JULIUS BOWERS. He opens the door of the empty chapel, moves to the front row, and sits down on an orange plastic folding chair. From there, he stares at his uncle's body, propped up in an open casket.

On the other side of the funeral home, Buster's van pulls up. P,S, and B pile out and start looking for an entrance. Buster takes the lead and signals Sam and Possum to follow him. They stop in their tracks when they reach a metal side door. Buster throws up his hands. "I don't think this is where we go."

Sam scoots past and opens the door. "Come on; all roads lead where we're going." Sam squeezes through the door and Buster and Possum reluctantly follow him.

Inside the funeral home embalming room, Buster and Sam stare at each other and Buster says, "What the hell?" Possum gets a whiff of formaldehyde and pinches her nostrils. "Come on guys, let's get out of here."

Sam spots a shroud-covered body on a metal gurney in the middle of the room and holds up his hand. "Wait."

The fluorescent-lit room has an eerie feel to it as Buster watches Sam approach the gurney like he's about to disarm a bomb. Possum whispers, "Come on, dude. You're freaking me out."

Sam carefully takes hold of the corner of the sheet and lifts it up, revealing the naked body of an elderly woman. He pokes the woman's arm as Possum and Buster back away. "Holy shit!; I think this is our first-grade teacher...Mrs. Service."

Suddenly interested, Buster rejoins Sam and says, "My God. You're right. It is her."

They stare at her corpse as Possum backs up to the door. "Come on, you perverts."

Sam continues to stare at his old teacher and says, "You go ahead, Possum. We'll meet you outside."

Still the only one in the funeral chapel, AJ stands in front of his uncle's coffin staring at his bruised face. Behind him, the door swings open and Possum, Buster, and Sam tiptoe in and sit in the back row. AJ still thinks he's alone as he addresses his uncle's corpse. "Not sure what to say here, Julius. Could've used your help, growing up and all." He notices a pair of sunglasses in his uncle's front pocket, so he removes them, cleans the lenses with his shirt tail, and fits the glasses on his uncle's face. He takes a moment and attempts to mold a smile on Julius' face.

Buster pops up from his seat. "Hey, buddy. This is kind of a looky, no touchy situation."

AJ swings around and spots his friends. "Hey, thanks for coming." He waves and pivots back to the coffin. "Jules looks so damn grim. I just want him to be happy wherever he's going."

Sam jokes. "Well, he's dead now, so let sleeping dogs sleep."

"Yeah, thanks for that, Sam."

Buster adds, "Told ya not to bring him to Fred's. Bet he don't even have pants on."

Possum pulls Buster down into the chair next to hers. "Really?"

"This is the only place in town," AJ explains. "What was I supposed to do? Bury him myself?"

Sam plops himself down and eyes Buster. "Holy Walleye. Can you believe we saw Mrs. S naked?"

Buster changes the subject and hollers at AJ. "What do you say we hit The Watering Hole and toast your uncle's life? I'm bone dry."

"Go ahead. I'll meet you there in a few minutes." AJ takes a moment, frisks his uncle's suit, and removes the sunglasses from his uncle's face. "No sense letting them go to waste." He checks to see if anyone is looking and puts the glasses in his shirt pocket.

As his friends exit the chapel, they pass a strong-jawed fifty-year-old big-bosomed Hispanic woman. A step behind her is her forty-year-old Italian male friend, who is built like a brick wall…a real Lenny Small look alike straight out of Steinbeck's *Of Mice and Men*. Both of them are dressed in black suit coats and have matching gray felt fedoras, but the woman has a slim unlit cigar clenched between her teeth.

The couple tiptoe up the aisle toward the casket trying to keep a low profile. When they get to the front of the chapel, the woman removes her hat and pockets her stogie. The big man, who is staring at the casket, whispers, "This asshole ain't running no more."

The woman slaps the hat off her partner's head, adjusts her boobs, and scowls, "The man's dead. Don't be disrespectful!"

AJ hears what they just said and gives them a half-smile. "Did you know my uncle?"

The woman ignores his question. "Dios mio! You look just like him." She throws her comforting arms around AJ and squeezes tightly. "It's all right, Papi. I know. Que triste."

AJ awkwardly returns the hug. "Do I know you?"

"I'm Auntie Tina…and you must be my beloved nephew, AJ?"

The big man steps up and muscles his way into the conversation. "I'm Tiny, Tina's boy…man friend."

Tina gently moves Tiny out of her way. "Your uncle never stopped talking about you. Every day I told him, Jules, you go find that boy. He needs you. But he never could face what he did. Leaving you to fend for yourself after your parents..." She chokes up, pulls herself together, and pats AJ's face. "But you grew up fine on your own, didn't you?"

"Not really. Hey, so were you and UJ married?"

Tiny chuckles and Tina whacks Tiny on the back of his head. "Well, we never set a date. Jules and I didn't exactly end on the best of terms, pero que pasión. Lot of good memories, though."

Tiny elbows her from behind and laughs. She swats him again and grins at AJ. "Speaking of memories, I..." She chokes up.

AJ notices and asks, "What is it?"

"It's just...well, did he leave me anything?"

"He didn't mention you."

"Of course not. I told Jules everything should go to you. But there were a few sentimental items, nothing of value, mind you; I just thought he might have...left me something special?"

AJ shrugs, and Tina throws her arms around him again and offers him a copious blessing. "Hizo que los santos contigo, mi nino. May the saints be with you, my boy."

As she releases AJ from her bear hug, Dave Franklin, from the funeral home and bowling team, appears and hands AJ an envelope. "This is for you."

AJ opens the envelope, reads what's inside and his jaw drops. "This is a big number. I could have cremated him for sixty dollars' worth of lighter fluid." Tiny laughs, and Tina gives the big man a shove.

The funeral director scowls. "Yeah, too late for that now. You need to pay it by the end of the month."

Dave pivots to leave, but AJ calls him back. "Hey, he has pants on, right?"

"Yeah, sure. Why wouldn't he?" Dave struts off with a twinkle in his eye.

AJ looks at his uncle a little longer and steps back. "Well, Auntie Tina, Tiny. Nice to meet you, but it's time for me to get really drunk." He starts for the door as Tina gazes tenderly down at Julius. A few seconds later, Tina's face darkens as she grips both sides of the casket. In a rage, she shakes the wooden box.

"Where is it, you effing traitor?"

AJ turns back as Tina continues to rattle the coffin. Tiny takes her arm and tries to calm her down. "Easy, babe, we'll find it." After witnessing the attack on poor ol' Julius, AJ hustles off not sure what to think.

A few minutes pass, and Dave Franklin enters the embalming room dressed in a pair of black coveralls, a red flannel shirt, and yellow rubber gloves. He quickly notices a foggy mist coming out of two of the refrigerated storage cabinets that are open. He surveys the room and walks over and snaps both doors shut. Next, he rolls his embalming machine over to the waiting corpse and removes the white sheet. He jumps back when he sees that Mrs. Service's false teeth are resting on her naked chest.

Chapter 31

Finding A Job

AJ SLIPS INTO *THE WATERING HOLE,* where he finds his friends on their way to Drunksville. Seated at their usual table, they jointly look up and smile. Buster instantly flags the barmaid and points at his buddy. "Four beers! He's buying."

AJ waves her off. "Ignore him, I'm broke."

Buster grumbles, "What about your inheritance?"

"I got shit."

Agitated, Buster mutters to the barmaid, "All right, I got it." He shifts in his chair and glares at AJ. "Was dining on the thought that you was rich now with your uncle's house and all his shit."

"Your approximater is off-kilter. House is the bank's, and I'm gonna have to sell it…and all of UJ's crap in order to pay his back taxes and funeral expenses."

Sam stares at his beer. "Bummer."

"Yeah, but I think he might have been hiding something, some kind of treasure."

Possum gives her eye patch a gentle tug. "What? Like he was some kind of pirate?"

Sam chimes in, "Argh, me matey!"

Possum continues to probe, "I thought you said his house was a shit pit."

"It is, but here's the facts...A: There's the sticky note about treasure. B: Officer Becker told me he might have been part of some shady dealings. Third, when I was leaving the funeral home, that Tina woman shook UJ's coffin so hard, I thought he was gonna fall out." AJ whispers, "Then she said, 'where is it you effing traitor?'"

Sam lowers his jaw. "He didn't answer, did he?"

Possum shoves Sam. "Shut up."

The beer arrives and Buster hands everyone a mug. "Hmm. Your dead uncle didn't look like the treasure-hiding type."

Possum takes a big gulp and says, "I'm with Buster on that."

"What the hell? You guys don't know what a treasure hider looks like. What if he was one?"

AJ's friends consider what he just said and down their beers. Buster hands the barmaid a twenty and whispers, "We're going on a treasure hunt. Wanna come?"

The barmaid smiles. "Sorry, Hun. I have to work."

The four amigos bolt for the door and head into the dark of the night like bats out of hell.

AN HOUR LATER, AJ, Buster, Sam, and Possum sit on the living room floor of AJ's new old house, lit by two flashlights. As they open boxes, empty drawers, and flip over cushions, there's an occasional "yuk" when someone finds something rotten or disgusting. The treasure hunt free-for-all continues in silence until Possum voices what they've all been thinking. "Been nice if your uncle would have paid his electric bill."

Sam jumps up and waddles toward the bathroom. "I gotta take a leak." Rufus whines and follows him.

AJ taps Possum on the knee. "Wait for it."

From the bathroom, they hear Sam scream, "Holy Shit!" AJ laughs as Sam retreats from the god-awful smell holding his nose and snorting, "I can hold it."

Rufus stays in the bathroom whining, so AJ covers his face, hurries down the hallway, battles the smell, and wrestles his dog into the living room.

On the front steps, lit by the moon, the exhausted and grime-covered friends crack open cans of beer. Possum adjusts her cap. "You inheriting this place is worse than him leaving you nothing. What are you gonna do with all of this shit ?"

"Get my license back on Friday, so I'm planning to rent a U-

Haul and move it back to my place. Gonna Craigslist it all."

Buster straightens up. "How you paying for a truck? Thought you were broke?"

"Get my last USBC check tomorrow."

Sam scratches Rufus's head. "Least ya gotta dog out of the deal." Rufus waddles over to AJ, who pets him fervently.

They take turns scratching Rufus as Sam looks at the door. "Place wouldn't be so bad, if you was to clean it up. Get you a flat screen, and it could be Brewers, brats, and beer all summer long."

"You ever listen to anything I say? It ain't mine for reals…just the crap in it. Bank's foreclosing on the house next week."

"Well, shit."

"Doesn't matter. I'm planning on watching the games from the third base bleachers this summer."

Sam crushes his beer can. "Don't start that big city Milwaukee shit again." He gives Possum the evil eye. "This is your fault."

"Cool your jets. He's not going anywhere."

"Think I won't? What's stopping me? Don't have a job anymore."

Possum runs her fingers through the fur on Rufus' neck and says, "C'mon, AJ. You've been talking about running off since high school. If you really wanted to go, you'd be gone by now."

"Shows how much you know." AJ jumps to his feet, Rufus in tow. "Gotta get home and figure this all out."

Buster stands up. "Night's not even middle-aged yet."

"Not gonna end up like my uncle…crappy house, no family, broke, and...dead." Rufus punctuates what AJ said with a bark and B, S, and P head for the van as well. AJ looks back at the house. "Step one, get me another job, so I can save enough to leave this dump." They hop in the van, Buster takes the wheel, and they drive off singing the *Alley Oop* song.

BACK IN HIS apartment, AJ is sound asleep on an Army cot, while Rufus lies at his feet. There are several beer cans on the floor next to him, and there's a half-empty bag of Cheetos on his stomach. AJ's lips are covered with orange Cheeto dust as his eyes flutter and he snores.

In his dream, AJ is dressed in a bright pink onesie at the Strike and Spare. As he readies to throw his neon lime-green 16-pounder down the eighth lane, a bright circular light shines on him. Several people in the gallery begin to cheer, including Claudia, who is dressed in a bright pink sweater that matches AJ's outfit. Her breasts appear to be larger than usual, and the initials "AJ" are prominently displayed on the front of it. She reaches down and holds up a sign that reads, "AJ Bowls Me Over." Two women standing next to Claudia see the sign, grab their chests, and drop to the floor.

Not far away, Sam, Buster, and Possum are dressed in matching outfits as well, but their onesies are bright orange. Possum polishes AJ's ball with a white towel and then carefully hands it to him. He kisses the ball, lifts it in the air, and all the people in the gallery let out a collective gasp. As he wipes his brow, the back of his shirt reveals ten multi-colored bowling pins that twinkle on and off. AJ wiggles his butt, and a teenage girl screams and joins the other two women on the floor. Claudia gives the fainting women a look of disgust as AJ continues to ham it up for his fans.

Everyone begins to chant…AJ! AJ! AJ! He smiles and goes into a series of wind-ups. Several ladies hold their breath every time he brings the ball back into position. Finally, he rolls the ball and it hits the head pin. All the pins fall except for one, which wobbles back and forth. AJ winks at his fans, glares at the wobbling pin, and blows at it. The final pin falls and the crowd goes wild. Lights flash and the volume of music increases as people mob him. A group of out-of-control women knocks him to the ground and pile on top of him. Slowly, the ladies peel off, leaving AJ lying lifeless on the bowling alley floor.

Claudia rushes to his side, lifts him up into her arms, and the crowd cries in unison: "Mouth to mouth! Mouth to mouth! Mouth to mouth!" Claudia leans down and gives AJ mouth-to-mouth resuscitation as the crowd cheers.

AJ wakes from his dream with a blank look on his face. He stares at Rufus and realizes the dog has been licking the Cheeto dust off his face. He wipes off his mouth and glances at a picture of Claudia that is still sitting on the plywood coffee table he made in middle school shop class. He picks up his cell phone, clicks Claudia's contact number, and the phone rings four times. AJ listens to her new message: "If this is someone I want to talk to, please leave a short message and I will get back to you, but if this is AJ Bowers, stop wasting your time calling me and find a job!"

"Job!" AJ checks the time on his cell phone. "Shit! Shit! Shit! I'm late." He peels off his clothes and rushes for the bathroom.

The middle-aged owner of A.G. Real Estate sits at his desk studying AJ's two-page resume. He looks up and smiles at AJ, who is sitting across from him and wearing the same white shirt and tie he wore to his uncle's memorial service.

"Thanks for coming in today, Mr. Bowers."

"Sorry, I was late, sir. I picked a bad day to have a flat tire."

"Fat Tire. That's one of my favorite beers.

"What? No, not Fat Tire. Flat tire. Flat, flat, flat."

"Relax, that was my attempt at a little humor."

"Oh yeah, Fat Tire the beer. Guess I'm not quite awake yet."

"I see here you graduated from Harvard with a B.S. in corporate law, an M.B.A. from the University of Wisconsin, and had an internship at a law firm in London called, *Hill, Jones, and Shetty*. Very impressive, Mr. Bowers."

"Yeah, I've been busy."

"Before we go any further, I have some bad news."

"Bad news? Already?"

"First, let me say that a person with your credentials is overqualified to work at my real estate agency."

"Oh, I'm willing to dumb myself down if that helps."

"That's all right, Mr. Bowers. I think you're already dumb enough. You see, I mentioned your name to my daughter, and she said you two went to high school together."

"Well now, I wasn't much of a high school student. You know boys mature a lot slower than girls."

"Mr. Bowers you need to stop bullshitting me. I did some checking of my own and I know you just got fired from USBC…and the truth is, you couldn't get a job scrubbing toilets at Harvard let alone graduate from there." AJ squirms in his seat as the owner continues to challenge his credibility. "I also know you didn't even go to college."

AJ takes a deep breath. "I did take an online accounting course at Avis Community College…but I had to drop it."

"And the law firm in London? Is there even such a place?"

AJ sags in his chair. "My friends' last names."

"And the real reason you were late?"

"I overslept."

"Because?"

"Too many Old Milwaukees."

"Yeah, I smelled beer on your breath when we shook hands."

"Sorry, sir. I've kind of hit a rough patch in my life. My uncle died, my girlfriend left me, and, like you said, I got fired."

"My father used to say a person's mental side and physical side cross over at age thirty and everything goes downhill from there. "How old are you, AJ?"

"I turned twenty-eight last month."

The manager laughs. "Maybe you're an early bloomer."

AJ grins. "That wouldn't surprise me."

"Actually, what my father told me is pretty much bullshit. Ambition and perseverance have no age limit. So, here's a little advice. You seem to be a bright enough young man, but in case I'm wrong, I'll dumb it down for you. First, find a job, any job, and do it well. It doesn't matter if you have to clean toilets or scrub floors, clean them better than anyone else has ever cleaned them. You don't have to join the Army, to be all that you can be."

"Cleaning toilets and floors at the bowling alley was my first job ten years ago."

"And how did that go?"

"I got shit-canned for being a drunk."

AJ listens intently as the real estate executive continues. "And USBC…why did they fire you?"

"BWI."

"BWI?"

"Bowling while intoxicated. I accidentally put a ball through the windshield of my boss' Maserati."

"Frank Kilroy's car?"

"You know him?"

"Yeah, but let's get back to the subject at hand. It appears drinking too much might be an issue for you."

"I've been pretty good for ten years, but what I did was a mistake. It was all part of a perfect storm. My girlfriend dumped me, I had one too many beers, and we decided to have a Bowl Off."

"I'm sorry. Did you say bowl off?"

"Yeah, it's a goofy contest I came up with a few years ago to settle disagreements. Anyway, my ball went cattywampus and it ended up in the front seat of Frank's car…The thing is, I have a dream to own a bowling alley, but nobody thinks I can do it. I wanna prove them wrong, but I need a job."

"You do need a job, but it's not going to be selling real estate. The truth is, you may have to go back to cleaning floors and bathrooms until the right opportunity comes along."

"Yeah, my dad used to say, 'How you do anything is how you should do everything.'"

"Wise man, your dad. Don't give up on your dream, just because other people think you can't do something. I always wanted to sell real estate, but my folks thought I should be a lawyer. Despite their objections, I dropped out of law school and began to sell houses. Best decision I ever made."

"Good advice, sir. I'm sorry, I don't even know your name."

"You really want to know?"

"Yeah, sure. Why not?"

Antonio removes his nameplate from his desk drawer and places it on his desk. AJ reads the name aloud. "Antonio…Antonio Giovanni…Claudia?"

"Yeah, my daughter."

AJ gives Antonio a 'What the hell?' look.

"Claudia knows nothing about this interview. I do, however, know you two were dating She refused to let us meet you. Not a good sign. Anyway, she has her own set of problems. The real estate agent stands up, signaling the interview is over. As he shows AJ to the door, he says, "Something else. Before you broke up,

Claudia referred to your friends as lowlifes. She's wrong; a man can never have too many friends, even if other people think they're lowlifes."

"This has been heavy, sir. It's gonna take me a while to wring out my sponge, but I think I can do it. Thanks." AJ shakes Antonio's hand and leaves.

An hour later, AJ is still wearing his white shirt and tie and sitting across from a bank officer. He watches as the blue-suited woman reads his new half-page handwritten resume. She flips it over, hoping to find more. Finally, she hands it back and shakes her head no. AJ reaches out to shake her hand, but she picks up her cup of coffee and ushers him to the door.

The next day, AJ is wearing a white polo shirt and faded blue jeans. He stands outside of Wong's Chinese Buffet staring at a "Helped Wanted" sign. He walks inside and looks for the owner.

Outside the restaurant, a young couple checks out the menu posted in the front window. Trying to decide if they should go in, they stare through the window and see AJ hand an Asian-American owner his resume. The elderly woman and AJ talk for a while, but, for some reason, AJ bows. The owner crumples his resume, hurls it at him, and AJ hightails it out of the restaurant. AJ hurries past the young couple waiting outside. They look at one another and walk off in search of another eatery.

Inside a video arcade at the Greenvale shopping mall, AJ stands across from the store manager as he checks his application form. Satisfied, the white-haired man shakes AJ's hand and gives his new security guard a red vest and cap. AJ puts them on, and his new boss pins a badge on his vest, like he's awarding him the Silver Star.

Not far away, two teenage bullies torment a younger boy at the POP-A-SHOT basketball game. Distracted by what's going on behind him, AJ watches one of the older boys dump a red slushy on the younger boy's head. As the delinquents walk away laughing, AJ hustles over to a basketball game console and puts two quarters in the coin slot. Basketballs pop out of the machine and AJ grabs three of them.

Eager to show off his security skills, AJ throws a ball at the tallest juvie. He hits him square in the back, and the kid yells, "Ohh!" Not satisfied, AJ clutches the other two balls and chases the boys out of the arcade. As the teens run off, he rolls the two remaining balls at the same time and knocks the legs out from under both teens. Defeated, the troublemakers stumble to the floor, pick themselves up, and hurry for the nearest mall exit.

Several customers who followed AJ out of the arcade cheer. AJ bows as the manager arrives. He turns to his new boss and smiles, but the man holds out his hand. AJ hands him his vest and cap and walks away as the bystanders boo the manager.

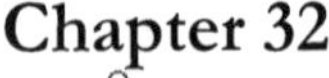

Chapter 32

Moving On

MOVING SLOW, AJ CARRIES A BOX of worthless crap out of his uncle's house and places it in the back of a small U-Haul truck. Rufus, seated in the cab with the window down, whimpers, so AJ pats his head. "Okay, come on boy." He opens the truck door and Rufus hops out and follows AJ as far as the For Sale sign on the lawn. The dog stops, sniffs the sign, lifts his leg, and pees on it. AJ chuckles, "I know. I feel the same way."

AJ wanders through the house with Rufus at his side. He removes several sticky notes that are still stuck to the walls and reads them to Rufus. "'Make it up to AJ.' 'I had to run.' 'Your past follows you, friends don't.' 'The best treasure is right under your nose.' 'Follow your nose, it always knows.'"

AJ peers down at Rufus. "Your owner, UJ ,was one bizarre, dude." The golden retriever wags his tail and *barks*."

AJ finds a couple more notes on the kitchen counter and reads them aloud. "'Dump the treasure.' 'Treasure dump.'" Frustrated, AJ kicks a chair. "What treasure? There's no treasure here, Julius! This place is a hell hole!" Finally, he sees another Post-it note stuck to Rufus's tail and monotone reads yet another message. "'I'm a treasure dumper.'" He spots a cigar box on the floor, removes all the remaining notes from the walls, and tosses them in the box.

He puts the box on top of the refrigerator and Rufus barks. AJ groans, "Yeah, I know. He was certifiable." Frustrated, AJ starts opening kitchen cabinets and drawers. He stops when he finds a stack of newspaper clippings. On top is a weathered cutout with a headline reading: "Local Couple Killed in Car Accident."

He takes a seat, starts to read the article, and reminisces.

AJ's nine-year-old self is standing in the backyard of his home watching his father, Augie, and his Uncle Julius rake leaves. Augie playfully tosses a handful at his brother while AJ's mother, who is washing dishes, watches from the kitchen window. Both AJ and his mother's eyes light up as they witness the men drop to the grass and begin to wrestle each other.

The brothers grunt and groan and try their hardest to flip each other over. The competition is fierce, but neither man can get an advantage, because they are equal in strength. Finally, Julius manages to turn his brother over and starts to tickle him. They laugh uncontrollably as Augie fends Julius off by smashing leaves in his face. Without warning, AJ jumps on his uncle's back trying to rescue his father. Julius rolls to the ground, taking AJ with him, and the three of them lie in the grass and giggle.

AJ's daydream ends when he hears a noise outside the house. He folds the clipping and puts it in his shirt pocket, still lost in memory. When he looks up, he sees Tina Suarez and Tiny Riley walk through the front door. Tina walks straight over to AJ and looks around. "Place looks like shit, but it's kinda homey."

AJ hops to his feet. "You scared the hell out of me. What are you guys doing here?"

Tina ignores AJ's question as she adjusts her bra and says, "What ya gonna do with all this crap?

"Sell it, if I can. See something you want, let me know. Pretty much everything I want is in the truck."

"Tiny, go check out the truck." The big fella doesn't move, so Tina raises her voice, "I said go!" Tiny slinks out the door as Tina moves squarely in front of AJ. "You're cute in the way he was. Boyish face…manly body." She reaches around his waist and squeezes his butt cheek a little too hard.

AJ pulls back and massages his ass. "Thanks…I guess."

"No more beating around the bush. Julius owes me money. A lot of goddamn money…and we're here to collect. Understand?"

"Okay."

"Good. Cuz if we don't find it, we're coming after you."

"Me? He...I...didn't find any money. All's I got is his crap, and I don't even want most of it. The bank is making me clean this shit up, so they can sell the house."

"He put Post-it notes everywhere. Did you see any?"

"Yeah, I did, but they didn't say anything about any money…so, I got rid of them."

"Where are they?"

AJ hesitates and says, "I burned them in effigy."

"You what?"

"Yeah, kind of like a celebration of UJ's crazy life…you know like the burning man thing they do in Nevada every year."

"I hope you're telling the truth, cuz if I find out you're holding out on me...the consequences won't be pleasant." She pats AJ on the shoulder, and Rufus growls at her. Tina shows her teeth again. "Shut up, you mangy mutt! I never did like you!" She shuffles off for the door and mutters, "I'm going to check on Tiny."

Tina leaves and AJ grabs the cigar box from the top of the fridge. Not sure where to hide it, he grabs one of UJ's old jackets off the floor and puts it on. He quickly puts the box inside it and zips the jacket closed.

He waits a few seconds, tethers Rufus to his belt, and quietly walks out the back door. When he peeks around the side of the house expecting to see Tina and Tiny, there's no one there. He hurries to the front of the house and watches as T and T drive off in their black Oldsmobile. Half a block away, they slide to a stop at a yield sign as a black cat crosses the road in front of them.

Tina rolls down her window and yells, "Shithead!"

AJ steers the U-Haul in the direction of his apartment. Almost home, he watches as Tina and Tiny's Oldsmobile speeds past him back to Uncle Julius' house. AJ shrugs and moments later arrives at his apartment complex parking lot.

Three teenage boys stand waiting for him to get out of the truck. He opens the back of the U-Haul and the boys survey all the stuff they've been hired to carry up to AJ's apartment. The smallest boy assesses the workload and runs off, while the other two start unloading.

Exhausted, AJ is seated on the edge of his old army cot while Rufus lies on the floor next to him. There are beer cans, empty chip bags, and other debris scattered on the floor as usual. But now AJ's apartment is filled with cardboard boxes, old furniture (including a green, flower-patterned sofa), piles of dirty clothes, small kitchen appliances, and plastic tubs filled with dishes. There are also bowling balls lying in various corners of the apartment, including several he inherited from Uncle Julius.

He reaches over to his handmade coffee table and grabs the Hank Aaron signed baseball. He looks it over, rolls it across the table, checks his watch, and picks up the remote control. He turns on the TV and switches channels until he finds the reality show *Vigilante Judge.* AJ lays back on his cot and stares at the screen. He drifts off as Rufus unties one of his shoes.

IN HIS DREAM, AJ is seated in the front of a courtroom across from Claudia as a bailiff calls out, "All rise!" He and Claudia stand along with two dozen courtroom observers behind them.

Ambrose "Tex" Collins, enters the courtroom. The white-bearded judge is a modern-day version of Roy Bean out of Langtry, Texas, the hanging judge (circa the late 1800's). Even though Tex has a reputation for being a "hanging judge" himself, it's strictly metaphorical. However, if he could, he'd probably sentence the occasional criminal to the gallows, if Texas law would permit it.

Tex is wearing a traditional black robe, but a not-so-traditional white cowboy hat, accented by lizard-skinned boots. After he shuffles into the courtroom and sags into his chair, the bailiff hollers, "Everyone have a seat!"

AJ stands behind a small table in dirty jeans and a rock star t-shirt. As they take their seats, AJ gawks at Claudia, who is wearing a black dress suit and carrying a matching black leather bag. Behind them in the front row of the gallery are Possum, Sam, and Buster. They smile proudly at one another, happy to be anywhere but work.

Theme music plays and fades out as an announcer's mellow voice introduces the show. "This is the courtroom of Judge Ambrose Collins, where the cases are real, but the verdict is seldom what you expect."

The bailiff notices Sam, Possum, and Buster still upright, so he waves at them and yells, "I said sit down!"

S and P sit, but Buster, who has been making eye contact with a pretty woman across the way, remains on his feet. Possum yanks him into his chair as AJ nervously rocks back and forth. The judge, who speaks with a Lone Star drawl, has an expression on his face that suggests he's not happy with the way AJ is dressed. "Did ya forget you were coming to court today, young man?

"No, I remembered."

People laugh as AJ sways back and forth in his chair again. "And stop fidgeting! You're making me dizzy."

"Sorry, sir. I'm a little nervous."

"Well, get un-nervous." The judge studies the document in front of him and raises his eyebrows. "According to your petition, Mr. Bowers, you're suing Ms. Giovanni here for the emotional damages you've suffered as a result of her 'dumping you.' Your words, not mine."

"Yes, Your Honor. It's been rough."

"What do you do for a living, Mr. Bowers?"

"Uh..."

"Uh is not an answer. Do you or do you not have a job?"

"Not right now."

"Get one! So, what kind of emotional damage are we talking about here?"

"A lot of pain and suffering, your honor."

"Yours or hers?"

"Mine."

The judge addresses Claudia. "Ms. Giovanni, for the record, please tell the court why you dumped this moron who dares to show up in my court looking like he fell off a freight train?"

Claudia glances at AJ. "Well, Your Honor, he can't keep a job, his apartment's a mess, and he hangs out with a bunch of lowlifes."

Buster and Sam jump to their feet. They stare at the judge, and Buster yells, "We object Your Honor!"

The judge grimaces. "Wally, remove those idiots from my courtroom." The bailiff signals two security guards, and they quickly start to usher Sam and Buster out of the room. Embarrassed, Possum trails behind with her head between her hands.

The courtroom quiets down as the judge winks at Claudia. "Continue, honey…Miss Giovanni."

"Your Honor, his dream is to own a bowling alley."

AJ turns to Claudia and interrupts, "There's nothing wrong with me wanting to own a bowling alley.Damn it! It ain't your turn to talk, so shut the hell up. I don't find you nearly as charming as this gal might have mistaken you to be at one time!" Realizing his mistake, the judge looks to the back of the room. "You can edit that out, right, Darren?" People laugh, so the judge raps his gavel again. "All right, it's not like some of you haven't used the f-bomb."

People settle as the judge waits for AJ to speak. Finally, AJ stutters, "I want… I just want…"

"I really don't care what you want. This isn't "Who Wants to Be a Millionaire' and I ain't no goddamn Regis Philbin." People groan, so the judge eyes the bailiff. "What did I say?...Goddamn? Shit. I'm sorry."

Wally whispers, "No, it's just that Regis died not that long ago."

"So?"

"People really liked him."

The judge eyeballs the back of the room again and Darren yells, "Keep going; I got it."

The bailiff sits down as Tex smiles at Claudia. "What else you got young lady?"

"Well, I recently found out that AJ set fire to his company's breakroom. And when they opened the door, they found him naked and hungover with his boss' daughter."

"Do you have any evidence to support this claim?"

"I do, Your Honor. If you will allow me…Exhibit A." AJ is surprised as Claudia hands a disc to Wally. The bailiff puts it in a DVD player, switches off the lights, and a screen drops down from the ceiling.

The video plays, showing Buster holding a fire extinguisher and Frank Kilroy wielding an ax. They are standing outside the USBC breakroom door as the camera reveals AJ and Lacey's clothes scattered in the hallway. Smoke seeps out from under the door as Frank raises his ax and destroys it. Frank's blond-haired daughter immediately scampers out wearing a red thong and holding a paper towel over her breasts. A few seconds later, AJ rushes out, his manhood hidden by a superimposed red rose. Lacy apologizes with her eyes and lowers her head. The twenty-five-year-old woman disappears as a dumbfounded AJ makes a one-eighty, revealing yet another superimposed rose covering his butt.

The lights come back on and the judge snarks at AJ, "I know I'm going to be sorry for asking, but why did you and that young lady choose to have sex in a company breakroom?"

"We couldn't afford a motel room, so Lacey borrowed her father's keys to the building."

The judge reveals his poker face. "Do you come from a family of idiots Mr. Bowers, or are you the only one?"

"It really wasn't as bad as it looks, Your Honor."

"Was that you in that video?"

"Yes."

"Then it's as bad as it looks."

"But I can explain…"

"Young man, don't piss on my leg and tell me it's raining."

Claudia speaks up. "Your Honor, I'm an up-and-coming lawyer at a reputable law firm. I can't afford to be associated with this man-child any longer."

AJ tries again, "Your Honor, I think…"

The judge raises his hand. "I don't care what you think. Pardon the cliché, but this isn't my first rodeo. I eat morons like you for lunch. If I could get away with it, I'd sentence you to be hanged, but the state of Texas won't let me. My ruling is for the defendant; you should have dumped this lowlife a long time ago. Goodbye and have a happy life."

As Judge Collins walks out of the courtroom, the announcer says, "That concludes our featured case for today. What we've seen in this courtroom today is one step forward for womankind and two steps back for the lowlife men of the world."

AJ's dream ends when he hears someone knocking at his door. He jumps to his feet, and his shoe falls off. He hops over, opens the door a crack, and sees two prospective buyers.

WITH A FIFTY-DOLLAR bill in hand, AJ watches as two well-dressed men maneuver a table out of his apartment. They bump into the door frame and AJ says, "Hey, come on; easy does it."

Out of nowhere, Helga Clodfelter appears wearing a yellow muumuu and peers into the apartment and complains, "All dese noises you make. I don't like." Helga sees the fifty-dollar bill AJ is holding and grabs it.

AJ tries to get it back. "Hey, I need that."

Helga tucks the bill between her large breasts and grumbles, "You pay rest; Mach schnell!"

"I'm trying to get rid of this mess as fast as I can."

"You sell mess?"

AJ eyes his apartment. "Yeah, as fast as I can."

"You sell those men mess?"

"Some of it. Trouble is, I'm running out of the good shit."

Helga gives her hapless renter the evil eye, and dawdles off. AJ shuts his door, wanders into his kitchen, finds a sharp knife, and walks back in the living room. There he finds a large cardboard box. "Okay, boy, it's time for you to have your own place."

A few minutes later, AJ is sitting on the floor putting the final touches on a cardboard doghouse. His creation has a cutout window, a mailbox slot that says "mail," and a front door that opens and closes. He writes Rufus at the top of the doorway with a large black marker as the dog wags his tail and walks in the front door of his new house. AJ stands, reaches in his pocket, and pulls out a doggy treat. He drops the treat through the mail slot and Rufus gobbles it up.

AJ admires his work as he scratches his dog's back. "What do you think, fella? State-of-the-art or what?" Rufus barks and walks over and pees on the side of his new home. AJ throws up his hands, "Shit, man!"

AJ trudges down the hall to his bathroom, opens the medicine cabinet, and stares at the numerous med bottles as if he's contemplating suicide. He picks up a bottle of sleeping pills, removes the lid, and shakes out a handful. He stares at them a moment until Rufus barks loudly. Startled, he drops the pills in the sink and they disappear down the drain. He looks in the mirror and mutters to himself, "I can't do anything right, Rufie."

AJ reaches back in the cabinet, grabs a bottle of Flintstone vitamins, shakes out a handful, and swallows them.

LIT BY TWO kerosene lamps, Tina and Tiny smash the walls and floors of UJ's house with a hammer and axe. Tina nods at Tiny. "Check the bathroom."

Covered in drywall dust, the bulky man lays his hammer down. He goes to the bathroom, but the smell stops him in his tracks outside the door. Tiny retreats to the front room, where he finds Tina staring at the wall. She turns around and says, "Anything?"

"Nothing. Sorry, babe."

Tina tosses her hammer in frustration, and it lodges itself in the wall. "It's time for us to find that dirtbag AJ and squeeze the truth out of him."

Chapter 33

Baseball And More

As I work my way down the hallway carrying another overgrown box of my uncle's shit and two sofa cushions, I trip over my own shoe and almost fall on my ass. I look down and sure as hell, my right tire is untied again…third time this week. Anyway, I loosen Rufus from the rope I have fastened to my belt, unlock the front door, and soft-kick him inside.

When I pick up the last of UJ's so-called treasures, Old Lady Clodfelter rounds the corner and spots me trying to balance my load. I manage to squeeze through the door just as she arrives. Before I can close the door, she pokes her head inside and checks out my junk-filled living room. When I drop the rest of UJ's crap on the floor, Helga pushes the door open, sniffs the air, and starts looking around like I'm hiding an elephant.

Luckily, I don't see Rufus anywhere, but she sidesteps me and walks in my kitchen. "Why all dis scheisse you still got now?"

"Told you, Ms. C, I'm getting rid of it as fast as I can, but I keep finding more. As soon as I sell it, I'll be paying my rent."

"You still sell mess?"

"As fast as I can. If want anything, just let me know."

Helga rolls her eyes, stomps down the hallway, and mumbles, "I call police now."

I yell after her. "Wait! I'll have your money in two days, max!"

Back inside, I find Rufus hiding in the bathroom, so I drop to my knees and look in his eyes. "What's with you and bathrooms?"

SEATED IN A booth at Carl's Diner with my Hank Aaron-signed baseball in front of me, I scroll through my phone checking for websites that might buy the one cool treasure UJ left me. My new friend, Zooey, strolls over with a coffee pot and smiles like she's happy to see me. "Figured out where your dreams are going to take you yet?"

"Thought it was Milwaukee, but I'm stuck here for now."

"Greenvale's not so bad."

"Yeah, but I'm looking for something more than "not so bad."

She pours me a cup of joe. "What's with the baseball?"

"Checking to see if it's worth anything. Signed by the greatest Brewer of all time."

"Paul Molitor?"

I roll my eyes. "What? No. Hank Aaron. We're talking the greatest no roids home run hitter ever."

"My son would disagree."

"Your son?"

"Zeke knows everything there is to know about base…"

"From the kitchen, we both hear dishes crash to the floor and Leroy scream. "Wash the goddamn dishes yourself, Carl! They're as clean as I can get them! You know what, screw you!"

I watch as Leroy storms out of the kitchen followed closely by Carl, who points his finger. "Get back here, so I can fire you!"

"You can shove those plates up your ass! They'd fit too, with room to spare."

Leroy huffs out the diner door, leaving the owner flabbergasted. He apologizes to an older couple seated at the counter. "Sorry, folks. Just cleaning out the kitchen."

An ambient bulb lights my brain, and I begin to marinate my thoughts. I finally figure out how the sausage is made and pop over to the counter where the older man and his wife are getting ready to leave. "You two all set here?" The old fart tips me four quarters, and I gather up their dirties and walk into the kitchen. After I scoot past Carl, I stop at the sink and start rinsing the dishes.

Carl, who followed me into the kitchen, growls, "What the

hell you think you're doing?"

I nod. "I need a job, and you need a dishwasher. Beats scrubbing toilets."

Carl gives me an up-and-down look and grunts, "All right…but no funny business, or I'll fire your butt so fast your head will spin…like that gal in that horror movie."

"Linda Blair…*The Exorcist*?"

"Yeah, that's her."

"Classic film." I give my new boss a thumbs up and scrub away.

Carl chuckles, "By the way, our toilets need cleaning twice a day." I roll my eyes as I hear Zooey and Beulah on the other side of the order window giggle.

BACK HOME, AFTER four hours of washing other people's dirty dishes, I help an old couple out the door with a box of odds and ends I don't want. I'm counting my money when Helga and Officer Becker show up. I try to bury the cash in my pocket before the old lady can see it, but it's too late. "Ach! See? Drug money. You throw in jail. Mach schnell!"

Becker steps forward. "AJ, your landlady here claims you're selling methamphetamines out of this place?"

"As in drugs?"

"He sell mess; no pay rent."

I wave Becker and Helga inside. "Come in. Does this place look like a meth lab to you?"

Becker and Helga check out my living room, still filled with a lot of Julius' junk. Helga starts down my hallway headed for the bathroom, so I lie and say, "I wouldn't go in there if I were you. I dropped a bomb just before you showed up."

I watch as Becker checks out my kitchen and Helga does a one-eighty and hurries back down the hallway to join him. "I don't see any signs of a meth lab, ma'am."

"You look more Officer. He one of those 'mess' lab druggists for sure."

"I am not!"

Becker blinks. "Ma'am, did you say meth or mess?"

"Yah, he tell me…he sell mess."

I lower my shoulders. "See there. Silly misunderstanding."

Becker raises his eyebrows. "The word is mess, Ms. Clodfelter, not meth. His place is a mess. Das Durcheinander."

Helga's eyes flutter. "I make mistake...maybe. But he no pay rent. You take him anyway."

"I've got most of the rent right here." I pull a wad of bills out of my pocket and count the rent money into Helga's outstretched hands. "Let's see, with that fifty I gave you already, we're almost even. Oh, and I got a new job today, so I can pay the rest at the end of the week."

Helga stuffs the cash between her breasts as usual. "I still say he make drug money."

"I told you. I got all that cash selling my uncle's crap. As soon as I get rid of some more shit, this place won't be such a mess…such a pigsty."

Becker takes a seat in UJ's wooden rocking chair, when I hear a bark in the bathroom. Helga hurries down the hallway holding her nose, and I yell, "Nothing to see in there."

Helga opens the bathroom door anyway and Rufus comes bounding out. When he reaches me, he sits, so I reach in my pocket and hand him a Cheeto.

Helga returns to the living room. "I hear dog many times. Now I see him. You pay pet deposit."

I reach in my other pocket, pull out my last twenty bucks, and hold it out. "That's all I've got. I was saving it to buy groceries."

Helga's face turns sad, and she waves me off. "Hmph." Helga starts to leave as Becker hangs back.

The policeman climbs out of the rocking chair and reaches for his wallet. "How much you want for this chair?"

"Take it. It's yours."

"You trying to bribe a police officer?"

"Okay, twenty dollars."

"How about ten?"

I hold out my hand and Becker hands me a ten spot. He picks up the chair and starts for the door as Helga grabs the

Alexander Hamilton out of my hand and pockets it.

In the hallway, Becker stumbles and almost falls on his loose shoelace as Rufus barks. Helga waits for the officer to tie his shoe and helps him to his feet. "In my country, a man in uniform is a very handsome man."

I turn to go back inside but remember something. "Hey, Becker, any word yet on how my uncle died?"

"Oh, yeah. Bad news...autopsy revealed he either killed himself or someone poisoned him. Found pepperoni pizza laced with arsenic in his stomach."

"Really? He hated pepperoni."

"You know anyone who might have wanted to kill him?"

"Saw him last week for the first time in ten years. Kinda wanted to kill him myself…but I didn't have any pepperoni with me." I roll my eyes. "Sorry. That wasn't funny." Then I look up at the ceiling and say, "Sorry UJ."

Becker ignores what I said and starts back down the hallway. Helga takes his arm, and he looks back at me and says, "I don't know why, but the captain thinks it might be drug-related. We were hoping you might shed some light on the subject. He have any suspicious friends, shady associates, or rogue girlfriends?"

"Maybe...nah, I got nothing."

"You come up with anything, give me a call."

"Sure. You bet." Becker and Helga disappear around the corner and I go back inside and remove the cigar box I hid under the couch. I dump the sticky notes on the couch as Rufus barks. "Look for clues, boy. We find that money, we're outta here."

ON THEIR LUNCH break, Possum, Sam, and Buster are seated on the warehouse loading dock sharing a meal. As they chomp down on leftover KFC chicken, cold French fries, and celery and carrot sticks, they intermittently drink from cans of soda that they purchased from a nearby vending machine. Possum smiles. "Good lunch, Sameo. You outdid yourself with the carrots and celery." She shifts over to Buster. "You're up next. What exquisite food can we expect for lunch tomorrow?"

Sam doesn't wait for Buster to answer and cries, "Pizza!"

The guys start to put their pop cans down next to Possum, but she holds up her hand. “Stop. That’s where AJ used to sit. Show some respect.”

Chapter 34

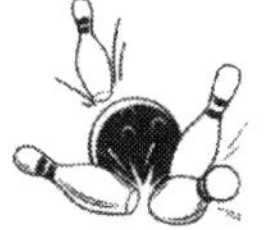

Dishes Ain't Washing Themselves

CARL'S DINER IS CRAZY BUSY as Zooey Bingham and Beulah Winslow hustle to keep up. AJ buses tables as Carl mans the grill. Zooey sticks her head through the serving hatch and yells at Carl, "Two Adam and Eve specials on a raft and one Noah's boy on the side. Drag the hashbrowns through Wisconsin. One bowl of elephant dandruff with baby juice, and two chicks, wreck 'em."

AJ starts for the kitchen loaded with dirty dishes, but he stops at the counter when Zooey turns his way. "Why don't you stutter when you deliver an order?"

Her stutter resumes. "I…I just…sometimes I…"

"It's okay. Just curious." AJ hustles into the kitchen.

Backpack on back, Zooey's ten-year-old son walks in the diner and sits down at the counter. "Mom." She doesn't respond, so he tries again. "Mom!"

She finally hears him. "Zeke? What are you doing here?"

"School burst a pipe in one of the bathrooms. It smelled like a dead squirrel's anus."

AJ makes his way back out of the kitchen carrying a stack of plates and eyeballs the young boy. "Hey there. You must be Zeke… baseball guru extraordinaire."

Zeke turns to his mom. "Who's this joker?"

Carl pokes his head out the window and yells, "Order up!"

Zooey grabs two cheese omelets and hurries off. "Zeke, find a booth in the back."

Her son grabs his backpack to leave and AJ steps up. "Hear you's quite the baseball fan."

"I'm more than a fan; I'm a fanatic."

"I like that. You play, too?"

"Pitcher. I'm 4-0. Prolly strike you out."

From the kitchen, Carl hollers, "Dishes ain't washing themselves!"

AJ points at Zeke. "I'm up to bat. When things slow down, I got something I wanna show you. It'll blow your mind."

In the kitchen, AJ washes dishes while Carl minds the grill. Out front, Zooey and Beulah wait on customers as Zeke sits in a corner booth doing his homework.

Carl finishes an order, plates it, and rings the bell. Then he shuffles over to AJ's stack of clean dishes. He picks up a plate like he might wanna buy it. "Gotta say, this might be cleaner than the day I bought it…and, just so you know, two of my regulars complimented me yesterday on how clean our bathrooms are."

"Sounds like a raise to me."

"Let's not get ahead of ourselves. You've only been here two weeks."

Beulah yells out another order. "Burn two strips of bacon, dry white toast, and two scrambled."

AJ steps over to the order window. "Hey, Beulah, I've been meaning to ask. What's the DNR on your uniform stand for?"

Behind him, Carl interrupts. "Do not resuscitate."

Beulah snickers. "That's right. I'm not interested in being a vegetable."

AJ grabs a stack of dirty dishes and smiles. "You got something against vegetables?"

"No, but I'm more of a meat eater." She barks like a toy poodle and winks at Carl, who tightens his teeth and growls.

Beulah disappears and AJ smirks at his boss. "You and Beulah got something going on, Carl?"

"A few years ago, but not anymore. Not easy to work with someone all day long and have a relationship."

"I think that's what they call marriage."

Carl chuckles, turns back to his grill, and cracks open two eggs.

It's almost closing time, and the place is nearly empty. Zeke and AJ are seated in a booth next to each other as the young boy rolls AJ's Hank Aaron baseball in his hand. AJ's eyes sparkle. "Best Brewer ever."

Zeke raises up. "No way…Paul Molitor."

"What do you mean? Aaron broke the Babe's home run record."

"Yeah, but he was playing for Atlanta when he did it."

"Huh…the pitcher?"

"Al Downing."

"Inning?"

"The 4th."

"Date?"

"April 8th, 1974."

"What'd he have for breakfast?" Zeke gives AJ a puzzled look, and AJ chuckles. "Kidding. Damn, kid. How'd you know all that?"

"Internet…and my dad."

"He must be one smart dude…your dad."

"He was. Knew more than the Internet."

"Oh. Is he…?"

"He died in a car accident. Mom was driving. That's why she stutters so much."

"Oh, shit. Shoot. I'm sorry. Not trying to one up you, but both my parents died in a car wreck ten years ago."

"No kiddin'? Who took care of you?"

"I was already eighteen, but I lived with my Uncle Julius for a while…'til he took off. Had a rough time…even ended up sleeping…well, you know, I was pretty messed up for awhile."

"You don't seem that messed up now."

"Behind this charming personality is an idiot ready to strike at a moment's notice."

Zeke laughs. "You's funny."

"I try."

The boy offers a fist bump, and AJ obliges. "Man, your hands are really wrinkly."

"Occupational hazard. I just hope it doesn't screw up my bowling grip."

"You bowl?"

"Hell, yeah! Soon as I can, I'm moving to Milwaukee and buying my own alley."

"Don't people bowl here?"

"Sure, everybody bowls here."

"So, why do you have to go to Milwaukee?"

"Cuz I don't wanna compete with the *Strike and Spare*. This town only needs one bowling alley."

"We used to bowl all the time before the accident. Mom got her picture on the wall for throwing a 250."

"Whoa."

Zeke sighs, a little sad. "When we moved from Iowa, I thought she'd take me bowling again, but we never…"

Now wearing a winter parka, Zooey interrupts. "Ready to go, son?"

Zeke fits his coat, and AJ helps him put on his backpack. The boy hops out of the booth, still holding the baseball and says, "Ready."

Zooey's stutter kicks in hard. "Thanks for keep…keeping an eye on Zeke."

"No problem. Smart kid."

"A little too smart sometimes."

Zeke fakes anger. "Hey!

AJ points his finger at Zooey. "Uh...bowling?"

"Excuse me?"

"I wanna take you guys bowling. Hear you used to be quite the roller."

Zooey eyes Zeke. "You little…you be quiet." She shifts her attention back to AJ. "I'm so…sorry, but I don't rea…really bowl anymore."

"Oh, come on. It'll be fun."

"Yeah, Mom. Cut AJ some slack. He's a nice guy."

As Zooey steers her son to the door, she turns back and grins. "We'll think about it."

AJ raises his voice. "Nice to meet you, Zeke."

The boy swings back around. "Almost forgot." He winds up like a major leaguer and hurls the baseball at AJ, who manages to snatch it out of the air before it hits the front window…smack.

AJ shakes his right hand and then rubs it on his leg. "Yowser! You got some heat, kid." He joins the young waitress and her son at the door, and they exit together.

On the sidewalk outside the diner, AJ stares at the night sky. "Getting kind of late. Need me to walk you two home?"

Zooey gives AJ a curious look. "No, I ha…have my car. Right over there. You…you need a ride?"

"Nah, I'm good. I'm only a few blocks away. Buying me a ride soon as I get paid."

As the Z's walk to their car, AJ adjusts his cap and gloves and turns for home. In the distance, he hears Zeke say, "You like him, don't you?"

"What? Shhh. No. He's… just…."

"Mom, you always stutter when you get nervous."

"That doesn't mean…get in the car, smarty pants." Zooey checks to see if AJ might have heard what Zeke said, but he is nowhere to be seen.

Chapter 35

Not Really A Date

I HEAR THE FAMILIAR CLATTER OF BALLS smacking the pines as I stride into the *Strike and Spare*. The place is hopping with regular bowling junkies and families just wanting to have a good time. When I reach lane sixteen, a real pie alley where our team always scores well, I see Possum, Sam, and Buster already lacing up their bowling shoes.

I park my butt and pull my shoes out of my bag as Possum gives her opinion. "Ya know, it's been proven that if your friends like your significant other, the relationship usually lasts."

"She's not significant. We work together."

Looking like he just woke up, Sam yawns. "But you did ask her out on a date?"

"Technically, but it's not a real date. Zooey has been super kind to me. Her kid wanted to bowl, so I thought I'd be a nice guy and invite them to join us."

"I get it. I'm kind of that way myself; you scratch my ass and I'll scratch yours."

Possum fits her ball and toes the line for a practice toss and says, "TMI, Sam." She goes into her wind-up, stops midway, and turns to AJ. "Her having a kid might take you down a road you've never been before."

I give Possum a look she's probably never seen from me before as I double-knot my shoes. "Guys, seriously, it's not a date. You think if it was, I'd bring her to meet you, lowlifes?"

Buster towels off his ball and adds his two cents. "Don't worry, we'll sniff her out for you."

I roll my eyes as I spot Zeke and Zooey coming our way.

"Here they come. Behave yourselves."

I head over, but not before I hear Sam whisper to Possum, "They're both wearing bowling shirts."

Possum whispers back. "He's a goner."

I zip over and greet the two Zs at the front desk. "Hey guys; glad you could make it." Not sure if I should go in for a hug, I hesitate and fist-bump them instead.

Dale, seated behind the counter, is texting on his phone. When he glances up, I take charge. "Dale, my man, two pairs of your best kicks."

Dale lays down his phone, studies Zooey and Zeke's feet, and grabs two pairs of shoes off the shelf for them. Zooey checks the shoes and says, "Wow…how did you know what size we wear?"

"Yeah, Dale really knows his shit…shoes."

"Now who's stuttering?"

I chuckle as I usher Zooey and Zeke over to our lane, where I introduce them to the gang. "Zooey and Zeke, these are my friends, Possum, Buster, and Sam." I warn them with my eyes to behave, and they get my drift. I'm up first, so I smell my ball and show off by offering up a prayer. "Roll a strike, strike it rich." I rear back, put a little extra mustard on my throw, and demolish the pins. When I turn back, Zooey has a sly look on her face, like the one I've seen her give me at the diner whenever I say something clever.

Sam is next. He rocks back, but when he lets his ball fly, he rips a loud fart that people two lanes over can hear. There is dead silence until Zeke giggles and yells, "Fart!".

Sam's face turns tomato sauce red, and Possum whispers, "Nice shot, but we could do without the sound effects."

Buster can't resist. "For your sake, I hope that was a fart and not a shart." Sam is about to give Buster the finger, but he changes his mind when he sees Zeke.

S and B pick up a couple of spares and Possum shuffles over to Zeke and pats him on the back. "Zeker! You're up." I smile and think to myself, 'That Possum she can be a real charmer when she wants to be.'

Anyway, I sit down next to Zooey, behind the scoring table as Zeke hops to his feet. Possum gives the Z boy a few pointers while I check in with Zooey. "I've been meaning to ask. The ZZ name thing, was that deliberate?"

"Zooey is really my mid…middle name. Zeke's father's name was Zach, so after a while, I …started going by Zooey. It's a dorky couple thing, I know. Then when Zeke came along…"

"Big ZZ Top fans were ya?"

"You'd think…think so, right? Go Zeke!"

We all watch Possum cheer Zeke on as he rolls a slow ball strike. All excited, Zeke runs over and I high-five him. He sits on the other side of his mom and beams. "How'd you like my ringer?"

"That was amazing, sweetie!"

I reach over and pat the boy wonder on the shoulder. "Way to go, Z."

He grins and whispers. "We're tied, AJ."

Possum comes over, fist-bumps Zeke and he says, "Thanks for the help, Possum."

Possum sits on the other side of the boy, and leans over. "Hey, you're the one that rolled it."

Zeke raises his eyebrows. "I have a question."

"Is it an open question, a rhetorical question, or a probing question?"

"I don't know. Just a question."

"I'm kidding…shoot."

"Why does everyone call you Possum?"

She leans in and whispers in his ear loud enough for Zooey and I to hear. "When I was a little girl, I used to pretend to be asleep in order to avoid trouble…and sometimes so I could hear other people's secrets."

"Did it work?"

"Every time."

"You got an eye under that patch?"

Zooey glares at her son. "Zeke!"

Possum winks with her good eye. "That's one of my secrets."

"Cooooool." Zeke studies Possum's body. "Hey, I'm almost

as tall as you."

"Yeah, you and all your other elementary school friends. I'm a miniature for sure."

I hear what Possum said and laugh. It's my turn, so I step up to the line, and throw another strike. When I turn back, I say, "Sam you're up and then Buster." I don't see them, so I look around. "Where are those posers?"

Possum clears her throat and points two lanes over, where Buster and Sam are flirting with a red-headed local. I stare at them for a few seconds and watch as the girl frowns and waves them away.

Possum puts her hand on Zeke's shoulder. "Let that be a lesson, young padawan, on how not to pick up chicks. The dork side is strong, but you must resist it."

I change the subject. "How's 'bout you show us some of your big game talent, Zooey?"

"Yeah, Mom. Kick some ass!"

"Zeke!...no, I'm just…just watching tonight."

"Come on!"

I pat Zooey on the shoulder. "Yeah, Mom, come on!"

Zeke and I plead together. "Pleeease."

Zooey takes a moment and stands up. "Fine...it's been a while. I'll probably throw a gutter ball."

I watch carefully as Zooey grabs a ball, eyes the pins like a pro, and moves into her release…BLAMO! STRIKE! We all go crazy! There are high-fives all around as Sam and Buster rejoin us for the celebration. Somehow, during the excitement, I end up giving Zooey an awkward hug.

I hold her in my arms a little too long until Zeke yells, "The three strikateers strike again!"

Zooey immediately pulls away from me and grabs her coat. "We gotta go."

Zeke stiffens his back. "Why?

On the verge of tears, Zooey grabs her son's arm and starts for the door. "I just...we're leaving. Right now."

Confused, I walk over and help Zooey on with her coat. "Hey, listen, I'm sorry if I said something to upset you."

Sam whispers in my ear. "Way to go, dingleberry."

As Zooey helps Zeke on with his coat, she begins to tear up. "No, it's not your fault. We never should have come here."

Zeke pulls his mother down to him. "Yes, we should have! Dad thinks so, too. He's probably up there high-fiving angels."

"Okay, that's enough!" She takes her son by the arm. He tries to pull away, but she holds on tight.

"I wanna keep bowling."

"I told you. We're going home."

"We never do anything fun! I wanna finish." Zeke breaks free, grabs me around the waist, and squeezes tight.

I pat Zeke on the head and say, "Hey…buddy, umm…"

Possum sees Zooey is having a meltdown so she kneels in front of Zeke. "Tell you what? If you go home now, I'll give you a peek at 'the eye.' What do you say?"

Zeke's mood shifts. "Is it gross?"

"You'll have to decide for yourself. You ready?" Zeke sits up and takes a deep breath. Sam, Buster, and I pretend not to watch, but our curiosity kicks in, and we inch forward in time to see Possum flip up her patch.

All at once, a golden light on the ceiling comes on and bathes Possum's face. Zeke gazes at Possum's damaged eye and his mouth opens wide. "Whoa!"

"I know. Right?"

Buster, Sam, and I lean over and shade our eyes in order to get a good look, but before we can see anything Possum refits her patch and grins. "Later, boys."

Zeke hugs Possum and joins his mom. As the Binghams walk off, Zeke pivots back. "Bye. Thanks for the best night ever."

They slip out the front door, and I eyeball Possum. "That was weird. Didn't you think that was weird?"

She taps me on the shoulder. "Don't worry about it, Romeo. She's a winner and the kid's adorable. You've got yourself a project…but at least they're not lowlifes."

I nod. "Like I said, it wasn't a real date."

Chapter 36

A Real Date

WHEN AJ ARRIVES BACK AT HIS APARTMENT, his door is wide open. He panics and hustles inside, where he finds Helga Clodfelter and Sgt. Becker in the living room gawking at Rufus, who is staring back at them through the window of his cardboard doghouse. Becker sees AJ and sighs, "There you are."

AJ scopes out his living room. "What's going on?"

"Your landlady here caught two people trying to break into your place."

"They run fast when I show them dis." Helga removes a German luger from her yellow polka-dotted muumuu and AJ steps back.

Becker gently pushes her gun down, and she puts it back in her pocket. "I checked. She does have a permit to carry a concealed weapon."

"Excuse me, but I am feeling kind of light-headed." AJ walks over and sits on his couch, grabs a loose cushion, and holds it close.

Helga taps Becker on the shoulder. "What'd I tell you about this one?"

Becker's eyes narrow as AJ carefully places the cushion back where it belongs and apologizes, "Sorry. It's a security blanket kinda thing."

The cop tries to be clever. "I don't think someone broke in here just to eat your porridge."

"Porridge?"

Becker keeps the whole three-bears thing going. "Yeah, you know like Goldilocks. You hiding something?"

Naw, look at this place. None of this shit is worth anything."

The sergeant shrugs. "I don't know. Maybe they got the wrong apartment."

AJ agrees. "That's probably it."

The policeman exits the apartment and Helga and AJ follow close behind. In the hallway, Helga pulls her gun again and points it at AJ, who is standing in the doorway. "My papa…he use in war. I not afraid to shoot. You pay rent."

The cop takes Helga's gun and ushers her away as AJ backs into his apartment and locks his door. From the hallway, he hears Becker say, "Ms. Clodfelter, we need to talk about gun safety."

CLAUDIA STROLLS INTO the law firm building wearing a long black trench coat. She walks directly to Gil Williams' door and knocks softly. While she waits, she turns back and sees three administrative assistants gawking at her. She knocks again. Still no answer, so she opens the door and slips inside.

Standing with his back to the door, Gil is reading a book that he just removed from his bookshelf. "Are you wearing the trench coat I told you to wear?"

"Yes."

Still not turning back, he whispers. "What's under it?"

"I'm under it. You going to put that book down, or am I going to have to take it from you?" Claudia hears Gil chuckle as she leans seductively on his desk. She sees a document, picks it up, and quickly reads what's written on the first page.

Gil shelves the law book, turns around, circles his desk, and gently loosens the belt on Claudia's coat as she continues to read the document. Gil slowly slips her trench coat off, revealing her racy red lingerie that is accentuated by high-heeled black leather boots. He grins and grips her butt with both hands. "Do you know how much I want you right now?"

Claudia pushes his hands away, steps back, and holds the doc up. "USBC is moving to Texas?"

Gil grabs it from her and lays it on his desk. "Yeah, it's a hell of a deal."

Claudia takes another step back. "That will ruin Greenvale.

Half the town works there."

"If you want to be successful, sometimes you have to do unpopular things. They'll find other jobs."

"Where?"

"I don't know. Wal-Mart. Not my problem. Come here." He pulls her close. "You should be happy for me. I'm about to make a shitload of money. Let's enjoy the ride."

THE NEXT MORNING, AJ and Zooey arrive at the diner at the same time. AJ holds the door open for her and they exchange awkward glances. He breaks the silence as they walk inside. "Another day, another sink full of dirty dishes."

Zooey raises her chin. "Listen, I'm real…really sorry about the other night."

"Nothing to apologize for. I'm worried about you is all; Zeke too. Everything all right?"

"We're fine. It's just...Well, when…whenever one of us would roll a strike, Ze…Zeke's father would always say, 'The three strikateers strike again.' So, when Ze…Zeke...when he said that, I guess I...I kind of felt guilty for..."

"For bowling with another man?"

"Not…not for bowling, but...Are you gonna make me say it?"

"Oh...you mean...for having feelings?"

Zooey wipes a tear away. "I don't know what I mean..."

"Listen, I'm not trying to complicate things. We can just…"

"No! Maybe thing…things should get com…complicated."

AJ takes a deep breath. "Oh. Okay. Well, then, why don't we go for the spare? That sounded wrong. I mean a do-over. An official date. Pizza. The three of us. No lowlifes."

"AJ, if your friends are lowlifes, so am I."

"How about the Big Cheese in the bowling alley? Tomorrow night at seven? I'll meet you there."

"Sure, why not. We love pizza."

They go their separate ways, AJ to the kitchen and Zooey behind the counter. Beulah hands her workmate an apron and winks. "Nice."

THE BIG CHEESE is packed. AJ and Zooey are seated together on one side of a corner booth while Zeke lies sound asleep across from them. With two half-eaten pizzas still on the table, AJ and Zooey appear to be having a serious conversation. "Zeke said you were the one driving."

"Zach al…almost always drove, but he was tired, so I said I'd dri…drive."

"And someone t-boned your car?"

"Yeah, but…but it was my fault. I wasn't pay…paying attention, didn't see a stop sign, and drove past it onto a busy highway. Semi smashed into Zach's door, and he died instantly."

"That's awful. What about you and Zeke?"

"Bro…broke my leg in three places and didn't talk for three days. When I finally began to speak again, I stuttered. Zeke never got a scratch. Fun…funny thing is he was in the back in his car seat. When the truck hit us, our car spun around three or four times and Zeke started to laugh." Zooey takes a deep breath. "Zeke said your folks died in a car crash too."

"Yeah, they were on their way to our state bowling championship in Milwaukee when their car went off the road and rolled twice. Highway Patrol thinks someone probably crossed the center line and clipped the side of their Taurus…hit and run."

"I'm sorry."

AJ changes the subject. "So, how did you like the pizza?"

"The pep… pepperoni was good…the Cheeto one not so much. I didn't even know Chee…Cheeto pizza was a thing."

"Yeah, Buster came up with it. It's a bestseller."

Zooey sits back. "That's right, he used to work here."

"Yeah, it seems like only five seconds ago."

There's a moment of silence as they look through the bay window facing the alley watching Sam, Buster, and Possum bowl. Zooey nods. "Do they come here every night?"

"Yeah, pretty much."

"And what about you?"

"Almost pretty much, but not as often as during my high flyer days?"

"High flyer days?"

"Y'know, when I was in high school, I practically lived here."

"Yeah, so after high school, you got the job at USBC?"

"Yep. Ten years and they fired my ass."

"Right, for the bowling ball incident?"

"Yeah, but Frank claimed he had to lay me off to save the company money."

"Well, if he wouldn't have, we might not have met. You're still waiting on that dream job, right?"

"Yeah, I wanna buy my own bowling alley."

"Wow. You would be great at that."

"You're a glass-half-full kind of gal; I like that. What about you? How'd you end up a waitress?"

"I enrolled in college and thought I wanted to be a nurse, but when I met Zach, I suddenly wanted to be a mom." Afraid she might be oversharing, Zooey hesitates…but keeps going. "Got married and nine months later I had my dream job."

"Zeke's a lucky boy."

"I'd like to think so, but it hasn't been easy."

Zooey and AJ continue to talk as Claudia walks into the pizzeria and over to the take-out counter. As she waits for her order, she hears a happy couple laughing across the room. When she glances over, she realizes it's AJ with another woman. Her face droops. The pizza arrives, and she scoops up the box and hurries out the door.

Back in the dining area, Zooey moves a little closer to AJ, who doesn't seem to notice. "So, what does AJ stand for?"

"Augustus Julius. Augustus after my dad and Julius after my uncle. For some reason, my family liked Roman emperors.

"Surprised you didn't order a Caesar Salad."

AJ laughs. "I see what you did there."

"It's okay, you don't have to laugh at my bad jokes."

"No, that was very clever…especially coming from a very special person like you." AJ takes a breath and leans in for a kiss.

Zooey moves away. "I should get pumpkin head home."

AJ recovers. "Right, yeah. Here, let me…" He stands, reaches down, carefully picks up Zeke, and cradles him in his arms.

"He's kind of a load. I should wake him up."

Trying to be a gentleman, AJ nods. "No, I got this."

As they prepare to leave, Zooey looks through the window again and watches as Sam and Buster celebrate wildly over Possum's latest strike. She smiles AJ and says, "I like your friends a lot, but do they ever leave here?"

"No, they pretty much close the place down."

Buster, Possum, and Sam see AJ exiting the Big Cheese and wave. AJ tries to wave back, but he can't because he's carrying Zeke. Celebrating his last strike, Buster hands Possum a beer. "No pins standing me up tonight."

Possum thin slices the moment. "Sam, it's your roll."

Sam's eyes open wide. "It is." He jumps to his feet, snags his ball, and moves to the foul line. "I get confused. It should be AJ's turn. Missing practice for a woman ain't cool. We got a championship comin' up."

Possum wipes her ball off with a towel. "You guys are the ones that need the practice. He's our best roller."

As Buster waits for his turn, he taps into the conversation. "He just broke up with that dirt Claud. Why's he gotta bring another hen into the chicken coop so soon?"

Possum slaps Buster's arm. "You should be happy. She's one more reason for him to stick around…and stop referring to women as chickens."

Sam is still standing frozen behind the line readying to bowl. He looks over at B and P and says, "What good is it if he ain't on the lanes with us?"

Buster sputters, "Throw the damn ball, Sam." Sam defies Buster, lowers his ball, and waits for Possum's perspective on AJ.

"Everyone's gotta grow up sooner or later, get married, have some babies, get a mortgage. Maybe AJ's finally getting around to it. Hell, maybe one day I will too."

Shaken by what she said, Sam rolls a gutter ball. Curious, Buster moves next to Possum and says, "Got some gal in mind?"

Possum narrows her eyes. "In mind for what?"

"You know, marrying and...whatnot."

"Why would I marry a girl?"

Sam walks over and studies Possum's face. "Cuz you's... ain't you gay?"

"Are you kiddin' me? I'm a jack-in-the-box waiting for the right guy to turn my crank so we can play *Pop Goes the Weasel.* You're up Buster."

Buster hurries over, rolls his ball, and throws a strike. He rushes back to his two friends and narrows his eyes at Possum. "We didn't know you were a straight shooter." Then Buster backs his Dodge all the way out of the garage, trying not to go down a rabbit hole, and says, "Possum, so I'm thinkin'...since you's not gay and all, maybe you and me could…"

"Don't say it," Possum grumbles. "Don't even think it."

Irritated, Sam comes in hot and heavy. "Yeah, don't even. You heard her; she wants to be with someone who wants a family…like I do."

Buster yells, "I want a family!"

People on the lanes next to them laugh and Possum steps back. "What are you two talking about? We're friends."

Sam stutters for the first time in his life. "Ya…ya know, ya just said one day you might wanna get married and have you some babies. So, I's just lettin' ya know, I'm loaded with babies…in case that 'one day' comes along and you wanna…"

Possum holds her hand up stopping Sam in his tracks. She sits down, leans over, and covers her face. "The idea of us having a child together scares the hell out of me."

Sam sits down next to Possum. "I just wanted to let you know your options is all."

Buster squeezes his butt down on the other side of Possum, creating an ice cream sandwich. "Hey, I got first dibs."

Sam jumps up. "Do not." Buster bounces over and gets in Sam's face. "Do too!"

They begin to slap-fight one another until Possum stands and separates them. "Shut up! Me and my eye are the only ones deciding anything around here. I have a proprietary right as to who I date or don't date. Now, go get me a beer!"

Buster complains. "I already got you one."

"So, get me another." Possum snickers as she watches Sam and Buster hustle to the beer counter to get her a beer.

In the *Strike and Spare* parking lot, AJ is still holding Zeke as Zooey opens her car door. She reaches to take her son from him, but when they're making the hand-off, their eyes lock. Zooey leans toward AJ, who takes the hint and they lock lips. As they extend their kiss a little longer, Zeke's eyes pop open and he hollers, "Busted!"

AJ puts him down and Zooey steps back. With no evidence of a stutter, she smirks. "I thought you were asleep, mister."

"I was playing possum. You guys gonna get married?"

Zooey wags her finger. "In the car now." She shoves him in the front seat and shuts the door. AJ waves at Zeke through the window and the smiling boy waves back.

Zooey beams. "Thanks for the pizza. Guess I'll see you tomorrow, Augustus Julius Bowers." She pecks him on the lips, walks around to the driver's side door, and climbs into her yellow Malibu.

Zooey drives off, but when her car is out of sight, AJ claps his hands together, stares at the full moon and hollers, "Wowser!"

Minutes later, AJ whistles a tune as he makes his way down his apartment hallway. When he reaches his door, he stops in his tracks when he sees it's open again. He peers into the living room and creeps inside. The place is absolutely torn apart. His crappy couch is ripped open, kitchen drawers have been emptied, several walls have holes in them, and his clothes are scattered everywhere.

He hears Rufus bark twice, followed by the sound of scratching coming from the bathroom. Before he can react, the apartment door closes behind him. He spins around and sees Tina and Tiny staring at him. He watches as the hefty man makes his way over to the kitchen fridge, opens it like he owns the place, and grabs a piece of cold pizza. When AJ turns to Tina for an explanation, she shuffles into the living room, kicks a can of green beans across the room, and grumbles, "Like how we redecorated the place?"

"You did this?"

"That's right, and now I need some answers."

AJ steps towards Tina as Tiny devours another piece of pizza. Angry, AJ snarls, "How many times do I have to tell you? I've got nothing."

Ignoring what AJ said, Tina backs him up against the door. "Where is it, pretty boy?"

"I told you. I don't know what the hell you're talking about."

She backhands AJ across the face as the sound of Rufus barking emanates from the bathroom. "The treasure, the pot of gold, the effing cash! I wanna know where you're hiding it."

"I don't know anything about any treasure." Tina backhands him again. "Owwww! That hurt."

"Know what people do when they're hiding something? They lie."

From the kitchen, Tiny growls. "When Tina gives me the okay, I'm gonna hit you so hard you're gonna shit your pants."

Tina gives the heavy hitter a shut-the-hell-up glare as AJ tries to reason with them both. "I'm telling you the truth; I didn't find anything worth anything."

Tina raises her hand as if to strike him again, but stops. "Either tell me where it is, or I'm gonna sic Tiny here on you."

AJ gives her a defiant shrug, so she points at her three-hundred-pound-plus partner, who now has tomato sauce on his face. Tiny swallows an Oreo cookie he found on the kitchen counter, lumbers over, and smashes AJ in the face. AJ stumbles back and grabs his nose, blood gushing out of both nostrils. Tina nods and Tiny punches him in the gut, followed by an uppercut that knocks him off his feet. The big fella straddles his helpless victim, bends over, and delivers three more blows to his head.

AJ struggles to remain conscious as Tina sneers at her "beloved" nephew. "Tiny's good at what he does, but you should see what he can do with tools!" Tiny laughs as Tina pushes the big lug out of the way. "Ya got twenty-four hours to cough up that money or next time Tiny won't be so nice."

Tina and Tiny exit the apartment and, from the hallway AJ hears the beefy man yell, "Twenty-four hours is one day!" As AJ lays on the floor weeping softly, there's a smack, followed closely by the squeal of Tiny's high-pitched voice, "Owwh…!"

INSIDE THE GREENVALE Police Station, Officer Becker is seated behind a desk across from AJ filling out a report. AJ's face is badly bruised and swollen, and he has tissue stuffed up both nostrils. Becker lays his pen down. "I'm gonna level with you. This sounds like something out of a movie. But it ain't like you've never cried wolf before."

"Why would I lie about something like this? Check out my face? It looks like a meat lover's pizza."

"Why didn't you tell me about these two thugs before? We might have prevented them from destroying your apartment…and your face."

"Well, to tell you the truth, I was sort of hoping I'd find the money they keep talking about and you know relocate to Milwaukee."

Becker furrows his brow. "If you find any money, you bring it here immediately. It's evidence."

"What about Tina and Tiny? They assaulted me."

"I'm gonna try and track them down. Gotta admit, I'm kind of stoked. Never had a case like this before."

"Becker, I don't wanna die. They told me I only have twenty-four hours."

"Ain't nobody dying on my watch." Becker laughs, pleased with himself. "I always wanted to say that."

"Glad I could be of service, Columbo."

A few blocks away, Gil and Claudia are seated in an upscale restaurant, having finished their dinner. Claudia picks up her oversized napkin, sniffles, and wipes the tears from her eyes. The waiter hands Gil the check, and Claudia starts for the door.

Across the street from the restaurant stands Gil's wife, Vicki, in a camo jogging suit. Goliath is on a leash next to her. When she sees Claudia approach the door, she lowers her binoculars, stares through the restaurant window one last time at Gil, and jogs off with Goliath.

An hour later, Vicki Williams is in the garage putting the finishing touches on a small-scale French guillotine. Goliath is at her side when she reaches over and pushes a tiny button on the mechanism. The blade drops down, slices the carrot, and half of it falls into a miniature wicker basket. Goliath growls.

From inside the house, Vicki hears the front door open and Gil yell, "Sorry I'm late. I had a busy day!"

She fits another carrot and says, "I'm busy. There's some leftover lasagna in the fridge! Help yourself."

"No, worries! I grabbed a bite to eat on the way home!"

Vicki pushes the button again and slices a second carrot.

Suddenly, the interior door of the attached garage opens and Gil freezes in the doorway. "Hey, honey. What's going on?"

Vicki quickly covers her guillotine with a blue plastic sheet. "Poopsie, you startled me."

"I see that. What are you working on?"

"It's a French food processor. It slices carrots and celery, …but I have to be careful because it can cut off other things too…you know that might be in the wrong place at the wrong time."

"You mean like a finger?"

"Yeah, a finger…but not always a finger."

"Interesting. Can I see it?"

"It was supposed to be a surprise gift, but now that you know about it, I guess I'll have to show it to you when I'm finished." Goliath growls and Gil exits the doorway and heads back in the house.

IN THE MIDDLE of the night, by the light of the moon, Buster shovels snow from the large hill in the *Strike and Spare* parking lot. Determined to win the snow-melting contest, he scoops snow into the back of his van.

Chapter 37

Now What Do I Do?

I CHARGE INTO THE DINER, ten minutes late for work, and Carl checks his watch. "It's about time." I turn his way and he gets a good look at my battered face. "Holy shit. What happened to you?"

He follows me into the kitchen, and I say, "You should see the other guy."

I walk over to my sink full of dishes, and Carl tosses me a clean apron. "I'm thinking not a scratch?"

"Good guess."

"Well, you're hands aren't damaged, so get to work."

Zooey walks in, and her jaw drops. "Oh, my God, AJ!"

I cover my face. "It's nothing. I just..."

"Did you get into a fight?"

"I think both parties have to participate in order for it to be a fight…but I'm pretty sure I hurt his knuckles."

Zooey smirks. "Do you need some ice?"

"No, I'm good."

Zooey walks into the dining area, and I follow close behind with a tray full of clean glasses. I hear a familiar giggle, so I check the entrance and watch as Gil and Claudia stroll into the diner. Quickly, I drop down behind the counter and duck walk back into the kitchen. Zooey follows me and gives me a 'what the hell are you doing?' look. So, I stand up, move to the window, and give her the lowdown. "It's Claudia, my old girlfriend, and her boss."

Zooey immediately pours two glasses of water, grabs a couple of menus, and crosses over to the booth where Claudia and Gil are already seated. I exit the kitchen, crouch back down behind the counter and prepare to eavesdrop on my ex and her asshole boss. I raise up and watch as Zooey places the glasses and menus in front of the lawyers. "Hi, I'm Zo…Zooey, I'll be your ser…server. Can I get you some…something else to drink?"

Gil doesn't bother to look up from his menu. "Two bottled waters. I don't drink tap water…especially when it's served in filthy glasses."

Sorry, we don't have any bottled water, but rest assured our g…glasses are the cleanest in town. I think you'll be very pleased."

Gil gives Zooey an evil stare. "I don't give a rat's ass what you think; I want bottled water."

Zooey stutters even more. "Si…sir, I told you we don't… don't have bo…bottled water."

Gil mocks Zooey. "Then give me a ca…can of co…coke…and move it. We're on the clock." Gil grabs both menus and tosses them to Zooey.

I'm burning hot now, as I hear Claudia say, "This water is fine for me." I continue to watch as my ex-girlfriend eyes Zooey and shifts nervously in her seat. "But, I'd like to see a menu again?"

Zooey tries to hand her one, but Gil intercepts it and gives it back to Zooey. "We know what we want. Blueberry pancakes for her, and I'll take the turkey dinner, no gravy on the potatoes, broccoli, uncooked, and a side of toast."

"Ohh…okay. Any…anything else?"

Gil snarls, "If I wanted something else, I would have said so."

Zooey leaves, and Claudia glares at Gil. He reacts by mimicking the waitress's stutter again. "And hu…hurry. I'm hun...hungry."

Zooey storms past me and disappears into the kitchen. I wait for my chance and join her at the window. She ignores me and barks Gil's order to Carl. "Blue plate special, no gravy, raw broccoli, side of toast. Second order… a stack of blueberry cakes smothered with blueberries."

Carl frowns. "We're running low on blueberries."

"Give her the rest of the blueberries. I'll explain later."

"Yes, ma'am."

Still fuming, Zooey rolls her eyes at me. "Your ex-girl…girlfriend's boss is a royal…."

"Asshole. I know. I heard the whole thing. You want me to give them the boot?"

"No, I can handle it." Zooey grabs a can of coke out of the fridge and hurries out the kitchen door.

Now, I'm pissed, so I put on my coat and stocking cap. I exit the kitchen, sneak over, and sit in the booth next to Gil and Claudia. As Zooey gives Gil his coke, she looks over at me all nervous-like, and gives me another 'What the hell are you doing?' stare…so I pick up a menu and act like I'm a paying customer. I keep my head buried in the menu and listen hard as Claudia gives her boss the business. "What the hell, Gil? Why are you being so rude?"

Gil chuckles. "C'mon, I'm just kidding around."

"I feel like I don't know you anymore…making fun of that waitress and ordering for me like I'm some little kid. Plus, I'm still angry with you for not telling me about selling USBC…."

"I'm making the deal for us."

"Who is us? You and your wife?"

"No, with that money I'll be able to afford a divorce. Listen, I'm sorry about the waitress thing. That was bad."

Claudia whispers. "Don't apologize to me."

I spend the next ten minutes hiding behind a menu until Zooey walks past me with Gil and Claudia's order. She stops dead in her tracks, starts to say something to me, but I hold up my finger to my lips and she continues over to their table. She carefully puts their plates in front of them, and Gil gives her a fake smile. "Hey, there she is! Waitress of the year. Listen, I'm sorry about what I said earlier. That was uncalled for..." He checks his plate and the tone of his voice changes. "What's this shit? I distinctly said no gravy."

Zooey instantly begins to stutter. "Oh, I'm, I'm so…sorry. Carl mus…must not have heard me."

I tighten my fists as Gil mocks her again. "We're in a hu...

hurry! I told you that!"

"I'm…I'm so…sorry, I…"

"Don't be sorry. Take this shit back and get me what I asked for."

I jump up and yell, "Hold on!" Gil and Claudia turn my way, but I'm off to the kitchen before they can identify me. When I get there, I toss my coat and cap and grab a pot of mashed potatoes. Carl follows me to the door as I stomp my way back to Gil's booth. I pick up his plate and pour the contents on his lap. Before he can react, I grab his spoon, scoop a huge clump of mashed potatoes from the pot, and smear it on his face. "There you go, mashed potatoes, no gravy!" Not satisfied, I scoop up another potato snowball with my hands and step back.

Claudia sees what I'm about to do, but all she can say is "AJ." I rear back, throw the spud ball, and hit Gil square in the face. Claudia gives me a look like she thinks she might be next and hides under the table.

As Gil wipes off his face a second time, he sputters, "You're going down, asshole!" He climbs to his feet and throws the weakest punch I've ever seen. I avoid it and step back as Zooey scampers off. I steal a hard roll from a neighboring table, chuck it, and it hits Gil on the forehead. Stunned, he picks up a ketchup bottle and squirts it at me. He retreats by hunkering down in his booth. I fire away with whatever food I can grab from other people's tables. When I run out of ammo, Gil sees his chance and hustles off to the bathroom.

As Carl makes his way over to the fracas to intervene, a young guy on the other side of the diner yells, "Food fight!" Right away someone throws a plate of food that hits Carl in the chest, and the owner drops to his knees. As he tries to recover, I step back and watch as everyone begins to weaponize the contents of their blue-plate specials. It's pure pandemonium as people scream, splat, and splash each other like a scene from some *Three Stooges* movie.

From my booth that I've turned into my own personal foxhole, I see Beulah enter the fray armed with a perfectly good banana cream pie. "AAAARRRRGGGG!" She hurls the gooey pastry and hits a handsome off-duty fireman in the crotch. The cinder monkey laughs, scoops a handful of the pie filling from his pants, and chases after Beulah. The waitress ducks down behind the counter, but he finds her.

The fireman is about to glop Beulah when Carl climbs to his feet, surveys the chaos, and yells, "What the hell!" Beulah peeks over the counter, sees Carl coming her way and grabs her chest. The seasoned waitress takes a deep breath, sinks to the floor, and her beehive wig falls off. Carl doesn't notice because now he's busy dodging hamburger buns and coleslaw. He spots me and trudges over as I'm cocking a pot pie. He grabs my arm, and my pie falls to the floor. "Stop it; damn it all!" There's a moment of silence until a generous helping of chocolate pudding hits Carl in the face, making him look like some kind of rabid raccoon. As he wipes the pudding off, he screams at the top of his lungs. "Stop it! Stop it now!" Everyone freezes as Gil exits the bathroom. The lawyer surveys the damage until the owner looks at Gil and snarls. "Who is responsible for this? I need names, people…or I'll kick each and every one of your asses!"

Dirtbag Gil slides over to Carl and points his finger at me. "That punk right there."

Carl waves me over, and I instantly know I'm toast. "Was it you?"

"Yeah, well, I guess…technically."

"What did I tell you, kid?" Carl holds out his hand, so I remove my apron.

Zooey steps over, reaches out her hand, and I take it. She gives me a half-smile and says, "You okay?"

"I'm fine." I toss my apron to Carl and start for the door. I stop at the counter when I see Beulah lying on the floor and watch as the handsome fireman performs mouth-to-mouth on her willing lips. "Is she gonna be alright?"

The young man takes a breath and shrugs his shoulders. "I think so, but she breathes for a little while and then stops."

Grey-haired Beulah finally opens her eyes and stares at the fireman, whose lips have been on her lips. She winks. "Mouth-to-mouth with the right person is a real turn-on."

I point at the DNR on Beulah's chest, and her rescuer rolls his eyes. "I didn't see that."

Beulah closes her eyes, "More air."

When the fireman doesn't respond, Beulah touches the crown of her head. She realizes her wig is missing, so she looks down at the floor, grabs it, hops to her feet, and runs into the kitchen.

Satisfied Beulah is all right, I call out Gil for being an asshole. "If you ever talk to Zooey like that again, you can sue me to death for what I'll do to you." As I make my way out the door, I hear the remaining customers in the diner clap and cheer.

I'm headed down Main Street, looking like a slob, when I get to The Watering Hole. I check my wallet, find my last twenty, and go inside. Four beers and two hours later I exit the bar still covered in food stains and head for home.

When I reach my apartment building, I stumble up the stairs to the second-floor hallway leading to my apartment. Outside my door, I see everything I own, including all of Julius' crap, piled up against the wall. Rufus, who is tethered to the door handle, barks like he's mad at me or something. "Hey, buddy. You okay?" Rufus starts licking my pants, feasting on the ketchup and mustard stains. "You should have been there…dog heaven."

I take a closer look at my door and find a piece of paper with bold letters written on it: NOTICE OF EVICTION. I look down at my dog and grumble, "Ain't this a pisser." I'm all set to go find my landlady when I hear footsteps.

When I look back expecting to see Helga, I see Claudia instead. She has a pathetic expression on her face as she slides over and invades my space. Looking a little tipsy, she looks at my crap and says, "Are you moving?"

"Apparently, I am."

"If you need a place to stay…"

"I'm good. Have you been drinking?"

"Yeah, a teensy, teensy bit. That girl Zooey…you were a real gentleman to come to her rescue like that."

Claudia scoots even closer and softly fingers my bruised face.

"Wish it had been for me." She brushes my lower lip with her index finger. "What does Zooey think of these lips?"

"I…she…"

"Does she know they're mine?"

"Come on Claud, you're with that lawyer prick."

"Does that make you jealous?"

"Well, it did." Before I can say anything else, Claudia pushes me up against my door and kisses me passionately. I respond to the kiss more out of familiarity than anything else.

Claudia pulls back and gives me her all-too-familiar sexy grin. "Thought you could use some comfort right now."

She dives in for another kiss when I hear Zeke yell, "AJ!"

I pull away and see the two Z's standing at the end of the hallway staring at us. "Hey, what are you guys…?"

Zooey's face hardens as she grabs her son by the arm and hurries off. As they round the corner, I hear her say, "Come…come on. We got…gotta go."

Claudia caresses my arm as I stand frozen, not sure what to do. Then I hear Zeke holler, "No, I wanna talk to AJ!"

I scream, hoping the Z's will hear me, "It's not what you think!" I gently push Claudia away and race down the hallway. Still buzzed, I stumble down the stairway and out the door. Somehow, I manage to catch up with Zooey and Zeke in the parking lot. Out of breath, I try to explain. "Hold on. She just showed up at my door. She came on to me."

"Zeke, get in the car!"

"She kissed me. I didn't…"

Zooey settles Zeke in and crosses over to the driver's side door. "What you do on your own time is your business."

"It wasn't me. It was her."

"Don't know who…who was doing what, but you bo…both seemed to be really enjoying yourselves."

"Sort of…but not really."

In the car, I see Zeke pressed against the window watching me, so I wave. He moves away from the window, and I don't see him again. I turn back to Zooey, and she closes her eyes and says, "You know what, it does…doesn't matter anyway. I made certain assum…assumptions that I never should have made."

She gets in the driver's seat and I grab the door. "Can we please talk?"

"No, AJ! I don't have time for...complicated. I have a son and you have...you have Claudia. So…let go of my door."

I instantly feel like some kind of stalker and step back. She slams her door, so I tap on her window and yell, "I really care about you, and I think…"

From inside her car, Zooey hollers, "I'm sorry. This was a mistake from the very beginning."

She starts her car, and I try one more time. "Zooey, hold on." This time I bang my hand on her window. "Wait!" Before I can say anything else, she fishtails her Malibu out of the parking lot, leaving me standing all alone.

Chapter 38

Leaving Town Is Not That Easy

LATER THAT EVENING, AJ ENTERS The Watering Hole, where he finds his friends at their usual table. They appear to be having a serious conversation as AJ takes a seat in time for him to hear Buster tell Possum, "I'm good Thursday."

Sam clears his throat. "Actually, could I have Thursday night, if I give you all day Saturday?"

Buster celebrates by slapping the table. "Weekend! Nice."

AJ scoots up his chair. "What the hell are you guys talking about?"

Possum yawns. "They're scheduling alone time with me. What happened to your face?"

Sam offers a suggestion. "Looks to me like Bambi got run over by that SUV we were talking about."

"No, but I got beat up, fired from the diner, and Zooey and Zeke saw me kissing Claudia."

Buster downs the rest of his beer and burps. "Sorry…grab a beer and give us the details."

AJ pulls a twenty out of his pocket and hands it to Buster.

Buster leans back. "What's this for?"

"For all the leftover pizza you used to give me. I got my first and last diner check this morning.

AJ signals a barmaid with shoulder-length brown hair and she skips over. AJ grins. "Give me two Belgian Reds."

"Just for you?'

"Yeah, for me. I don't like to wait."

"Sorry, I can only serve you one beer at a time."

"That's okay. Buster here is gonna own it until I finish my

first one."

The tall barmaid rolls her eyes. "Okay, if you say so."

She hurries off as Buster studies her butt. Possum slaps his arm, and he pivots back to her and says, "Okay, what we celebrating?"

AJ grabs Sam's empty beer mug and holds it in the air. "To Milwaukee! I'm leaving tomorrow."

Sam sits up. "Watchoo talkin' about, Willis?"

Possum and Buster roll their eyes, and AJ responds by pointing his finger at them. "I thought you guys would be happy for me."

Possum's eyes widen. "How you gonna get there…the bus?"

"I bought an old pickup for three hundred dollars. Got just enough money left for gas."

Possum continues. "What you going to do for money when you get there?"

"I don't know. Get a job I guess."

Possum holds up her hand. "You know what? Let's back this whole thing up a bit. First off, who rearranged your face?"

"Tiny, Tina's big ass boyfriend."

"Who are Tiny and Tina?" Possum says.

"They were at Uncle Julius' funeral."

Buster pipes up, "Oh, yeah. Strange looking couple."

"Anyway, they claim to be his friends and say I owe them."

Possum continues, "For what?"

"They think I found a shitload of money in UJ's house."

"Well, did you?"

"No, but I'm still looking."

Sam shakes his head. "We checked that dump over for your so-called treasure and there's nothing in there but shit."

Possum keeps pushing. "Okay, second question. How did you get fired from the diner already?"

"I started a food fight."

Buster laughs. "Nice!"

Possum shakes her head. "And why were you kissing Claudia in front of the two Z's? I thought you had something going there."

"Yeah, that's over. I managed to screw it up big time when Claudia showed up at my door all lovey-dovey and Zooey and Zeke got an eyeful."

Possum leans forward. "That doesn't make sense. Why would you do that? They both adore you."

"I really don't wanna talk about it right now."

Sam pokes AJ's arm. "Hold on, you can't go. We got the championship tomorrow night."

"I'm leaving right after."

"If we win, we gotta defend next year!"

"Sam, the universe has been screaming at me, but I ain't been listening. It's time to go. I got nothing here."

"What are we? Chopped kidney?"

"I'll be an hour away. You know the score. I'm tired of getting the shit kicked out of me. I'm sure that's why Uncle Julius left Greenvale back in the day."

Buster argues. "Yeah, and look what happened to him… dead and alone."

"Damn, dude, that's dark. Sometimes success only comes with a whole lotta risk. At least UJ tried. Now I need to seek my fortune."

Buster grumbles. "What are you, one of the three little pigs?"

Possum softens the tone. "I'm not sure you running off to Milwaukee is going to make you happy, AJ."

Sam tries again. "In my book, yer sticking your neck out on a damn limb!"

"Yeah, well, it's my neck."

Sam's face turns red. "I thought we were friends through thin and thick…family. Thought you knew that by now. So, here's my lesson, AJ…Up yours with a rubber rose!"

Sam storms off as AJ yells, "Come on, man! Don't be a dumb shit."

When Sam reaches the door, he yells, "Don't bother showing up tomorrow night! We'll find us a replacement!"

Sam leaves and Buster tries to soften the blow. "He doesn't mean that."

From the street, Sam screams, "Yes, I do! He opened the can

of worms. Now he's gotta lie in them!"

There's a moment of silence until Buster hops to his feet. "Well. I'd best be off, too."

Buster leaves and Possum puts her hand on AJ's arm. "Whatever happens, I'm proud of you. I only hope what's in Milwaukee is really what you've been searching for."

THE NEXT MORNING in the apartment parking lot, AJ and the two boys who helped him earlier, load a ripped-up couch into the back of his new-old Ford pickup, which is jam-packed with his belongings.

The truck is faded blue, has rusty fenders, bald tires, and two dented side panels. With no room left in the truck bed, AJ points and the boys throw the remaining crap into a nearby dumpster. Rufus barks, and AJ glares at his dog like he said something important. "That's right, boy. Good riddance." Ready to go, he hands the teens a twenty-dollar bill each, and they hustle off.

Out of nowhere, Zeke appears, wearing a ball glove and a Brewers cap. "Hey, AJ."

"Zeke! Hey. What are you doing here?"

"I don't know. Wanna play catch?"

On the front lawn of the apartment complex, AJ and Zeke throw a ball back and forth. Zeke makes a nice catch and yells, "Mom's real pissed, ya know."

"Gee, I wonder why?"

"Well, mostly cuz you was kissing that pretty woman."

"I know. It was a mistake."

"She's been crying a lot, too. Like after Dad died."

What the boy said hits AJ hard. "I'm really sorry about that, Zeke."

They trade a few more throws, until Zeke tosses a perfect strike with some heat on it. "Guess what? I changed my mind about who the greatest Brewer is."

AJ rubs his hand. "Oh, really."

"You're right. It's Hammerin' Hank… 755 home runs, no roids. He left for Atlanta, but he came back to Milwaukee."

AJ studies the grass-stained ball a moment and tosses it softly back to Zeke. Then he points at his truck. "You know what? I wanna give you something." AJ walks over and grabs his Hank Aaron-signed baseball out of the glove box. He hands it to Zeke like it's a bag of gold and grins. "Keep it somewhere safe."

Zeke hugs AJ. "Wow! Thanks a lot. I love you."

"Yeah...OK...I...Well, I figured it'd be a nice going away present."

The boy's expression changes. "What do you mean?"

"See my truck? I'm moving to Milwaukee. Gonna save up some money and buy me that bowling alley I've been dreaming about."

"Cool! Can we come?"

"Oh, I don't think so, Z. It's not really…"

"But…don't you love my mom?"

"We only just…"

"I saw you kiss her! And she doesn't stutter when she's around you. That means she loves you, too."

"Buddy, you's ten. You don't even…"

"I'm not stupid. You love that other woman, don't you?"

"No, it's just...complicated. I'll keep in touch. Promise."

Zeke pounds his fist into his glove. "Bullshit!" He pushes AJ with all his might and AJ stumbles backwards.

"Hey, language…and that's adult abuse."

Zeke backs away. "I don't have to listen to you. You're a nobody…You're just a...a big fat jerk off! Zeke winds up like a major leaguer and hurls the ball with all his might, hitting AJ flush on the nose. AJ falls to the ground hard and groans like a cat in heat, "Ooowwwwh!"

Zeke surveys what he's done and takes off running. AJ slowly climbs to his feet all woozy and waves. "Get back here right now, young man!" He holds his nose as blood flows out of it. "Come on. Again?" Zeke disappears as AJ picks up the ball and sees that the cover is coming off. "What the hell? It's damaged. Jeez, Uncle Julius. Thanks for nothing!"

He finally notices the edge of a sticky note poking out of the ball, so he removes it and reads it to Rufus: "AJ, I abandoned you when you needed me the most, and I'm sorry about that. Long story short is I pissed off some very bad people in Mexico and they are closing in on me. The house is a dump, but I hid something there for you that I hope will help make up for what I done. Sometimes everything you ever need is right under your nose…or at least under Rufus's nose. Love, UJ."

AJ stares at the note a little longer. "Well, I'll be a monkey's uncle." AJ pinches his nose to stem the bleeding and rushes over to his truck.

Chapter 39

Moving Day

AJ PARKS HIS PICKUP IN FRONT of his uncle's old house and makes his way to the front door with Rufus a step behind. Tissue stuffed up his nose again, he tries to open the door - locked. He empties his pockets searching for his key, but he can't find it. Frustrated, he pulls his sleeve over his fist and tries to break the small glass window at the top of the door. No dice. He looks down at Rufus. "It's always so easy on TV."

He looks up and down the street, makes sure no one is watching, and smashes his fist against the window several more times. Finally, crash! He carefully reaches through the broken glass, lowers his arm on the other side of the door, and manages to unlock it. As soon as they get inside, Rufus trots straight for the bathroom, barking. AJ follows close behind, but he stops in the doorway and plugs his nose. "Still got my sense of smell."

As Rufus sniffs around the bathroom, AJ notices a loose board next to the base of the toilet and yanks on it. He can't break it free, so he grabs the toilet bowl itself and moves it back and forth. The entire toilet finally separates from the rotting floor and water sprays everywhere. AJ quickly locates the water line and turns the valve off as Rufus barks. He stares into the hole, sees a black plastic bag, and removes it. He tears it open and finds bundles and bundles of cash. When he examines the hole again, he spots a second bag, equally filled with hundred-dollar bills and dozens of savings bonds. "Uncle J! You rascal! Treasure dump for damn sure!"

Soaking wet, AJ pulls the bags into the living room and

removes fistfuls of cash. As he counts the money, he takes a joyful whiff, but winces because the bags smell like shit.

Now standing in the bed of his truck, AJ pulls the stuffing out of his ripped-up couch and carefully places the cash and bonds inside two of the cushions. Like giant snowflakes, pieces of stuffing float into the air toward Uncle Julius's house. In the cab, Rufus barks at the sudden "snowfall."

After he zips the bulging green cushions closed, AJ jumps down from the pickup and puts the cushions in the cab next to Rufus. Just as he's about to start his truck, Tiny and Tina pull up in a black Oldsmobile and park behind him. When AJ realizes who it is, he hunkers down below the steering wheel next to Rufus and the cushions. As he tries to decide whether to make a run for it or stay put, Rufus begins to whine. AJ softly covers the dog's snout and whispers, "Shhh."

Tina, who has an unlit cigar in her mouth, climbs out of the Olds and adjusts her bosoms. She points to a spot in the yard and Tiny grabs a shovel out of the back seat. He immediately starts to dig up the lawn, looking for any sign of a hidden treasure. Tina approaches the pickup and sees all the crap piled in the back as several pieces of stuffing float past. Tiny leans on his shovel and smiles. "Hey, babe. Snow!"

Tina spits a piece of cotton out of her mouth and scowls at her man. "It's not snow, ya dumb ass." She points to the back of AJ's pickup. "That's Julius' shit. AJ must be here." Rufus barks, so she walks to the driver's side door of the pickup just as AJ pops up in his seat. Tina jumps back and the cigar falls out of her mouth. "Christ almighty! You scared the hell out of me, AJ!"

AJ cracks open his door but covers his face when his driver's side window explodes into pieces. When he lowers his hands, he sees Tiny peering through what's left of the glass, holding his shovel high in the air. "What the...?"

Tina jumps back in the Oldsmobile and begins to watch the action like she's at a drive-in movie theater as AJ slides across the seat past Rufus. He manages to escape out the passenger door just as Tiny circles the truck waving his shovel. "You're mine now, boy!" Tiny swings the shovel like a baseball bat, narrowly missing

AJ's head. AJ runs around the truck, but the big man cuts him off, swings again, and breaks the passenger side window. Tiny regroups, raises his weapon in the air, and growls, "Where is it? Don't make me dig a hole and put you in it!" AJ fakes one way and the other as Tiny stands frozen waiting for his target to stop moving. Finally, AJ bolts back to the passenger side door and squeezes through the broken window. A step behind him, Tiny screams, "Oh, no you don't." He grabs both of AJ's legs, but Rufus growls and bites the big man's arm. "OWWWH! You damn mutt!" Tiny releases AJ's legs, grabs Rufus' paw, and bites him back. Rufus whimpers and whines as Tiny spits fur from his mouth.

AJ gets back in his truck as Tiny repeatedly smashes the hood with the shovel. Before AJ can put the vehicle in gear, the giant bashes the windshield, and it spiders.

AJ starts the truck, puts it in reverse, and backs into the Oldsmobile… crunch…destroying the car's grill! Tina honks the horn as Tiny continues to bash away. AJ lurches backward and demolishes a mailbox. The big man circles around, takes one more swing, and breaks the pickup's left tail light. AJ burns rubber and roars off as a frustrated Tiny throws the shovel in the direction of the truck and hollers, "I will hunt you down, ya little shit!"

Still in the Oldsmobile, Tina leans out and fires two shots, shattering AJ's rear window. A block away, Rufus props himself up in the truck's now vacant window and growls.

AJ and Rufus howl with delight as they speed along in the dark of the night headed for the promised land. The interior of AJ's truck is covered with shards of glass. In fact, AJ has to move his head from side to side, so he can see through his shattered front windshield. "Woo-hoo! Nice work, boy. Milwaukee, here we come!" Rufus barks. "You're right, Rufie. Screw Milwaukee. Let's go to Jamaica. Buy every bowling alley on the island. Gotta be millions of dollars in those cushions." Rufus howls as AJ grabs his uncle's sunglasses from the dashboard and fits them on the dog's face. Rufus whines, and the expression on AJ's face changes.

"What are you talking about? I ain't giving the money to the police." Rufus whines again. "Why?... Cuz UJ left it for me… for us!" Another whimper. "What about Zooey? She doesn't want me back, and that suits me fine. It's you me and buddy." Rufus paws AJ's arm. "Well, yeah, Zeke's a great kid, but he'll be fine without me. I mean, I got along fine without my…" Rufus growls. "Well, maybe not, but…you know." The truth hits AJ like a ton of bricks. "Okay, okay! I need a little time to figure things out." Rufus wags his tail and barks. "What are you talking about? We're on our way." Intense growl. "What? The championship is the least of my concerns right now." Rufus howls. "I know, I know, I promised. But Sam said, they could find a sub."

"BARK!"

"Damn it, you're right! What if he's another Theodore?" AJ makes a sweeping U-turn in the middle of the empty highway and starts back to Greenvale.

AJ pulls into the *Strike and Spare* parking lot, where he finds an empty spot next to the almost melted snow pile. He exits his wreck carrying the two cushions, goes to the bed of his truck, and grabs his bowling ball bag. Before he can take another step, Claudia drives up. She rolls down her window and stares at AJ's beat-up truck and the cushions. "What's with the cushions?"

"Long story."

"I see. Well, can we talk?"

"Not now; I gotta go." With tissue still up his nose, AJ balances the cushions and his ball bag and takes a step toward the bowling alley. He changes his mind, shrugs his shoulders, and steps back to his ex's car. "Damn it, Claudia. I'm late. What do you want?"

"What happened to your nose?"

AJ pulls the tissue out of his nostrils and tosses it. "I'm fine. What's up?"

"I want to apologize…for everything. For hurting you and then trying to get you back…." She begins to cry. "I've been a mess for a while, and I shouldn't have taken it out on you."

"Yeah, it didn't feel so good, but I'm gonna make it."

"Did I ruin things with you and Zooey?"

"Oh, no…yeah, you pretty much did."

"God. I'm sorry. It's just, when I saw the three of you together, looking like a family, I got...what if I talked to her?"

"Let the pins fall, Claud."

"You can't give up. What is it you always say? 'When you miss a strike, go for the spare.'"

"First of all, I haven't given up. Second, if you're gonna compare my life to a bowling game, it was you and Gil who put me in the gutter."

He turns to leave, but Claudia reaches out and grabs his arm. "Just so you know, I'm breaking things off with Gil."

"Hey, what you two do is none of my business…"

Claudia takes a deep breath. "AJ, Gil is helping to sell USBC to a Texas corporation. They're going to ink the final deal any day now. Moving the whole operation to Fort Worth."

"Is that what you two were talking about in the diner?"

"Yeah. I should have told you."

Claudia hears someone tapping on her passenger side window. She turns and sees Gil. She rolls the window down and he pokes his head inside. "Is that Bozo bothering you again?"

"No. Leave us alone, Gil."

AJ rises up. "Yeah, why don't you go destroy some more orphans by stealing all their shit."

Gil scowls. "What the hell are you talking about…orphans?"

"You broke my Uncle Julius and the bank took our house."

"That was ten years ago, and your uncle was a shit poker player. Now why don't you keep your mouth shut, so the adults can talk."

AJ manages to carry his couch cushions and bowling bag around the car, lays them at his feet, and faces off with Gil. "How 'bout we settle this whole thing right now?"

Gil sees the cushions and laughs. "What in God's name? I can't believe you used to date this clown, Claudia."

AJ kicks one of the cushions aside and takes a boxing stance. "Come on, asshole."

Surprised by AJ's sudden aggressiveness, Gil steps back and

snarls. "Think I'll save it for the lanes. I'm going to own you tonight just like I'm about to own this town."

"Yeah, we'll see about that, ya Judas." AJ gathers his cushions and bag and lets Rufus out of his truck. Claudia rolls up her windows and watches the two men speed-walk their way to the front door of the bowling alley as Rufus trails behind barking.

Inside the Strike and Spare, AJ and Gil go their separate ways. AJ marches straight over to Dale, who is powdering shoes. "Hey, Dale. I'll give you a hundred bucks if you watch my dog and these cushions for me? I need to bowl." Dale gives AJ a strange look as he puts the cushions behind the counter and finds a spot for Rufus.

As AJ walks away, he spots Sam, Buster, and Possum in front of a pinball machine and makes his way over. "Why aren't you guys warming up?"

Sam doesn't bother to make eye contact as he mans the flippers. "Well, if it isn't Benedict Cucumberpatch."

Possum groans. "Least you got the Benedict right."

AJ growls, "I'm here, aren't I?"

Sam adjusts his crotch, avoiding eye contact with AJ. "You're out. Already found a sub."

Buster punches Sam as his last steel ball disappears. "We did not."

"Guys, I'm sorry I gave you a scare. You have every right to be pissed. I've been doing some soul-searching, and I had a *Wizard of Oz* moment. The truth is what I've been searching for has been in Greenvale the whole time. I'm an Alley Oop, and I want to be an Alley Oop for the rest of my life...that is, if you'll have me."

Possum and Buster stare blankly at each other until Sam has a change of heart and attacks AJ with a giant hug. Buster and Possum join in until AJ breaks free. "Enough already. Let's roll!" AJ starts singing "Alley-Oop" and his friends join in as they strut to their lane and the championship match with Jones, Sherwin, and Williams.

ACROSS TOWN HUNGRY people study their menus as

Claudia walks into Carl's Diner and parks herself in front of the counter. She waves Beulah over and the older waitress, who has removed the DNR from her uniform, holds up her notepad expecting a takeout order. "What can I get you, honey?"

"Is Zooey working tonight?"

Beulah's voice drops. "Oh, it's you. I don't think you should be here. She told us what happened."

Claudia steps towards the kitchen. "Is she back there?"

Beulah cuts her off. "Afraid that's as far as you go, doll."

"Okay. Fine." Claudia sidesteps Beulah and parks in front of the order window. "Zooey? If you can hear me, listen up. I need a plate of shame with a little guilt on the side. I've eighty-sixed my relationship with AJ. We're not together, nor are we getting back together. And, for dessert, Zooey, know that he's fallen for you. And he's got such a loving heart."

Through the order window, out of sight, Zooey stands frozen. Tears stream down her face as Claudia continues. "I know I'm dragging this thing through Wisconsin, but extra cheese never hurt anybody. I've already sampled a cup of his kisses, but his lips are yours now. Keep them warm like a cup of mud and they'll always be there for you. Trust me. And, if you're smart, like I wasn't, you'll take him right off the menu. You understand? He's a good man." She smacks the counter and steps back, only to discover that everyone in the diner has been listening to her.

Carl sticks his head through the order window as Claudia starts for the door. Before she exits, she addresses everyone in the diner. "I worked my way through law school as a waitress." A half-drunk older man sitting at the counter, puts down his coffee cup, and applauds. Claudia bows as Zooey exits the kitchen. From the doorway, the lawyer shouts some parting words at Zooey, "Now, get over yourself and call AJ!"

Chapter 40

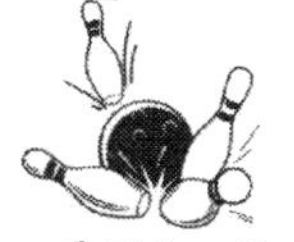

The Final Pin Standing

THE STRIKE AND SPARE IS TEEMING with bowling enthusiasts, and there's plenty of tension in the air. It's my Alley Oops team versus the law firm of Jones, Sherwin, and Williams for the league championship and all the marbles.

The way I see it, it's my chance to burn Gil for robbing UJ and me, stealing Claudia, and him trying to sell off the lifeblood of our town, USBC. Of course, I have mixed-up feelings going on in my brain, cuz I'm in love with Zooey and USBC fired my ass.

I won't bore you with some long-winded description of the whole championship game up to this point, but our team and JS&W have pretty much matched each other frame for frame like we're in some movie, like *Rocky* or *Hoosiers.*

Wouldn't you know it, the whole thing boils down to the score being tied and Gil and I are about to take our final rolls. Me and the other Oops watch as fancy lawyer, Gil, steps up and throws strikes in the 10th, 11th, and 12th frames. His team cheers him on like they won the lottery and high-five Gil. Egomaniac that he is, he cups his ear to the cheering crowd and yells, "That's how I roll!"

If I wasn't nervous before, I am now, as I fit my ball, and back away from the foul line. My hands are sweaty, so I reach over and wipe them off on my lucky towel.

Behind me, Possum whispers, "Come on AJ! You's done it before; you's can do it again."

The place gets all quiet as I sniff my ball and whisper, "Roll a strike, strike it rich." I rear back, release the ball, and it hits the head pin. Strike! One down and two to go.

My second roll is another strike, and Sam yells, "That's what I'm talking about!"

As I ready myself for my final attempt, my teammates stand up. Possum points at me. "Come on. One more strike to even things up, and we'll beat them in a tiebreak."

It's all quiet until I hear Gil shout, "Hey, AJ! I hear you're dating stutter girl! So…so…try not to throw a g… gutter ball."

Gil and his crew laugh as Possum tries to calm my nerves. "Ignore those idiots. You got this."

I stand frozen as Sam can't help but add his three cents. "Come on, AJ. The monkey's in your court."

Not to be outdone, Buster hollers, "Go get him, tiger!"

Concentration blown, I back up and stare at Buster and Sam. I lower my ball, walk over, and growl, "Will you two shut the hell up?" Sam adjusts his crotch, so I say, "Why are you always playing with your balls? It's rude."

I walk back to the line, regain my composure, and prepare to throw my final ball. Ruining my vibe, Sam whispers to Buster, "I can't help it if they itch."

Ignoring him, I step up, sniff my ball, and let it fly. My roll is sweet as my blue Brunswick hits the pocket…crash! The pins all scatter… except for the seven, which wobbles for a second and then stands straight up. I stare in disbelief, still expecting it to drop. Nothing. "Shit."

Gil's team goes nuts and Buster, Sam, and Possum collapse to the floor like they've been shot. Gil takes a step my way and gloats. "Good job, Bowers! You always find a way to lose."

I rush Gil like a Green Bay Packer linebacker, but Buster and Sam hop up from the floor and grab me. Possum tries to reason with me. "Relax. You're going to get yourself thrown in jail."

I push my teammates away and grab my ball. "Okay. Okay. I'm good." I start to calm down, but I can't leave well enough alone and throw a verbal jab at Gil as he's about to leave. "Hey, big shot! Everyone has a right to know, don't you think?" Gil turns to me with a defiant look on his face, and I nod. "You know, your big plan to destroy this town."

Gil gives me an 'I hate your guts' smirk and growls, "That gossiping bitch. You'd better not say a word, or I swear to God, I'll bury you!"

As Gil's teammates block his way, I hold up my hand like I'm some traffic cop and address several spectators who are still milling about. "I know a lot of you here work at USBC, so here's the scoop. Gil over there and his firm are trying to sell USBC to a group of money-hungry investors from Texas. So, that means all of you will have to relocate to the Lone Star State or find another job."

People murmur amongst themselves as Gil and his cronies walk away. At the door, Gil yells, "What a hero! Big man on campus. They're all going to find out in a few days anyway…and I'll be richer than I am now." Gil and his posse exit and the whole place goes quiet as everyone waits for more information.

People start to talk among themselves, so I raise my hand again and they turn silent. "Don't worry folks, I have a plan."

Sam yells, "What kind of plan?"

I hesitate and address the crowd again. "Sorry, I can't give you the details right now." Now in a pissy mood, most of the bowling enthusiasts disperse and start for home.

Possum breaks the silence. "Walmart here I come."

I try to ease my friends' pain. "Everything's gonna be okay. Let's hit The Watering Hole, and I'll tell you what's going on."

Possum grabs her bag. "I'm goin' home. Not in the mood."

As Sam helps Possum put her arm through her coat, he taps me on the shoulder and says, "Yeah, me neither."

Not to be outdone, Buster helps fit Possum's other arm in her coat. "Me three. Glad you're sticking around, buddy."

All at once, an older woman wearing a blue ski jacket covered with tournament bowling patches appears and steps up to Possum. "Sorry to bother you, Miss Jones, but can I speak with you a moment?"

Buster shrugs. "Go ahead. We're in no hurry."

We all watch as the silver-haired lady pulls Possum aside, and they talk for a good three minutes. Finally, they shake hands and the older woman ambles off. Possum rejoins us, and Buster's curiosity gets the best of him. "What's going on, babe?"

Possum smirks. "That was Mildred Goulet. She's a retired professional bowler. One of Wisconsin's best. She thinks I should go to the *Milwaukee Open* in two weeks. She's been watching me and is convinced I've got what it takes to make it on the PWBA circuit. Milwaukee's a qualifier, and she wants to sponsor me."

I high-five Possum. "Woah. What did you tell her?'

I said, "I think I'd like to do it."

Sam and Buster stare at one another. Finally, Buster yells, "Road trip!" With Possum sandwiched between them, Buster and Sam head for the door in a formation I've never seen before.

I stick around for a while all bummed about losing both Zooey and the championship. I have no place to go, so I start bowling again and keep at it until it's only Dale and me in the place. Finally, he strolls over with Rufus, lays the green cushions at my feet, and grumbles, "Hey, Dude. You need to leave. I gotta lock up."

I toss one last ball into the gutter, grab my cushions, and me and Rufus head for who knows where.

When I get to the parking lot, my cell phone rings, and it's Zooey. I take a deep breath and say, "Hey, it's you."

"Ze…Zeke tells me you're moving."

"Yeah, I was all set to go, but…. Can I come over?"

"AJ, I don't wa…wanna see you right now."

"I get that, but if you give me a chance to explain…"

She interrupts. "I don't wa…wanna see you tonight or to…tomorrow unless I'm gonna see you the next day, too. And all the days after that. Cuz, I got…I got a boy who can't sleep because he hasn't loved another man since his father died. And...and I love you, too. I was hoping that me and Zeke...well, that we could be your dream now. But I…I don't want no part of it unless you love us back."

"Well, I…"

She cuts me off again, as she stops stuttering. "So, this is how it's gonna work. You think long and hard about what I just said. Tomorrow, I'm gonna go about my day as usual. I get off work at ten. If you're outside the diner when I get off, we can talk about building some dreams. If not…Zeke and I will have to make do with some memories. That's it. Goodnight."

I pocket my phone all confused, but in a good way. Rufus and I hop in my truck. I put the couch cushions on the floor, start the engine, and a voice in my head nags me about what I already know I should do. I roll down my window to get some air, and two fancy-dressed gals walk past giggling.

The tall red-head snickers and says, "Nice ride."

A few minutes later, I pull up to Greendale's very own *Royal Motel 7* and park near a sign that reads: AS SEEN ON COPS." I grab my seat cushions, tether Rufus, and go inside to get myself a good night's sleep.

THE NEXT MORNING, I leave the motel, and drive my pickup full of shit down Main Street to Clyde's, a fancy men's clothing store. When I pull up to the curb, I roll my window halfway down, grab the cushions, step out of the truck, and leave Rufus to fend for himself.

An hour goes by, and I strut out of Clyde's wearing a black three-piece suit, the cushions tucked under each of my arms. I spot a flower shop across the street and waltz over there. This purple-haired lady behind the counter stares at me like I'm some kind of fancy-dressed burglar wanting to rob the place. She gives me another odd look and says, "The upholstery shop is at the end of the block."

"Nah, this is where I wanna be. I check out the glass-windowed refrigerator packed with flowers, grab the largest vase, filled with multi-colored roses, and waltz back over to her. I unzip one of my cushions, careful not to let her see how much money is in it. She watches me like a real snoop, so I do a one-eighty, remove a hundred-dollar bill, flip back, and hand it to her. She checks it out to make sure it's the real deal, grabs my change, and offers it to me. I see it's only seven dollars and wave her off. "Keep it. I don't do small bills anymore."

Chapter 41

Looking For Dollars

AJ PACES THE SIDEWALK IN FRONT of Carl's Diner armed with flowers and a box of candy. When he checks his phone, he sees it's 9:59 p.m. Suddenly, he hears the squeal of tires and Tina and Tiny's Oldsmobile with a damaged front end pulls up. Tina leans out the window driver's side window and hoots, "Ooh la, la, looking good."

AJ tosses the flowers, drops the box of chocolates, and takes off running. Tiny jumps out of the Olds and cuts him off…CRACK with a billy club. Down for the count, Tiny hoists AJ over his shoulder. He carries him to the car and puts him into the trunk that Tina has already opened. He hands Tina the flowers like he bought them for her, and keeps the candy for himself. T and T jump back in the car and roar off into the night.

Inside the diner, Zooey checks her phone: 10:00 p.m. "Goodnight, Carl. See you tomorrow." She steps out the front door and scans the street. Empty.

Minutes later, she paces the steps of the diner and checks her phone again: 10:05. As she descends the steps, a few flower petals blow past her feet, but she doesn't notice as she heads to her car.

ON THE OUTSKIRTS of Greenvale, in a deserted field, AJ is buried up to his neck in a vertical grave he dug himself minutes earlier. The Oldsmobile's headlights illuminate the scene as Tina and Tiny's bodies cast eerie shadows. Tiny pops the last piece of chocolate in his mouth and observes AJ, whose eyes are halfway shut. Tiny leans on his shovel and grins. "If you fall asleep, you might never wake up."

AJ tilts his head back. "I'm feeling claustrophobic…and my balls itch."

Tiny laughs and turns to Tina. "His balls itch."

She tries to slap the big oaf, but he ducks. "Shut the hell up!" She shuffles over, kicks dirt in AJ's face. Tina kneels in front of him and taps his head. "Tried being nice, but your auntie has run out of patience. Why you keep lying? You're a naughty, naughty boy."

Tiny grins. "Naughty."

Tina stands up, and the big man backs away. "What did I tell you?" Tina leans over. "We know you have the money."

AJ licks his lips. "I spent it all on an old truck, a dozen flowers, and the new suit I'm wearing…oh, and some candy."

Tiny dabs a bit of chocolate off the corner of his mouth and Tina growls at AJ. "Don't be so damn stubborn! You can't spend it if you're dead."

AJ doesn't respond, so Tina points at Tiny. The big man grabs a shovel, scoops some dirt, and throws it on their prisoner's head. AJ shakes the soil off his face, sputters, and spits. "I got nothing." Tina points and Tiny threatens to throw another shovelful. AJ's mouth is barely at ground level.

Tina tries again. "Whether you live or die is up to you. We made the mistake of letting Julius lie to us way too long. I loved him once and didn't want him to suffer, so we made the mistake of putting arsenic in a pizza he didn't like. So, then I had to have Tiny here hold him down, so we could pour the poison in his mouth. Not a pretty sight. So, no more slow deaths."

AJ spits. "You greedy bastards killed my uncle over some damn money?

"That's right…and you're next. Nobody's gonna find your ass if you don't come clean. Not a whole lot left of you to bury." Tina nods and Tiny scoops up some more dirt that happens to have a rock in it that falls out of the shovel directly on AJ's head.

AJ grimaces in pain. "Ooh! You son of a bitch, that hurt!"

"Last chance. Tell me where the money is, and Auntie Tina

will have Tiny pull ya right outta there."

AJ doesn't speak, so Tina gestures and Tiny scoops up a huge shovelful of dirt. AJ panics. "I told you. I don't have it!"

Tina puckers her lips. "More." The burly lug keeps tossing dirt until AJ's face is nearly covered. Tiny bends down and wipes off his victim's lips.

AJ sputters, "Okay, okay! It's in the bank!"

Tina roars. "You gotta be effin' kidding me!"

AJ licks his lips. "Two percent interest."

THE NEXT MORNING AJ is scrunched down in the back seat of the Olds next to Tiny, trying to clean his face off with some moist towelettes. His three-piece suit is covered in mud and dirt. Tina rolls up to the First National Bank and parks in front of one of Greenvale's oldest brick buildings. She shifts back to AJ and glares. "Any funny business and I'll shoot your ass."

Tiny adds, "And I'm gonna shoot your kneecaps." Tina reaches back to slap the big fella, but AJ is in her way, so she gives up and opens her car door.

The dirty-suited hostage enters the bank, followed closely by Tina and Tiny. There are a few customers inside, but no security guard. AJ swallows hard and whispers, "You guys sure you want me to take it all out?" Tina shifts the gun in her pocket so that AJ knows she means business. AJ steps up to one of the two tellers, while his kidnappers stand close enough to hear his every word. "I'd like to empty some money out of my account."

"How much would you like to withdraw, sir?"

AJ eyes Tina and then turns back to the female teller says, "All of it…please."

The long-haired blond with circular-framed glasses smiles. "Did you say you'd like to withdraw all of it, sir?"

Tina hears what's going on and interrupts. "Are you hard of hearing? He said all of it."

The teller's smile turns to a frown and then she notices AJ's dirt-caked suit. AJ tries to explain. "Yeah, I know. I just got off work…I'm a gravedigger." He chuckles at his own joke and whispers, "Yeah… I want all seven million." AJ smirks at Tina, and she scowls. Behind him and to his left, Helga Clodfelter approaches the other teller's window. The landlady spots AJ, but he doesn't notice her.

The teller leans forward. "Did you say seven million?"

AJ peeks at Tina and says, "Yeah. I'm good for it."

Tiny turns to Tina. "Seven million? I thought it was only three million? Are you holding out on me, babe?"

Tina and Tiny begin to fuss about how much money is at stake, so AJ sees his chance and whispers to the teller, "I've been kidnapped by those two killers standing right over there."

The teller doesn't hear him and leans forward. "I'm sorry, what's the name on the account?"

"AJ Bowers."

The teller types in his name. "Sir, there's only five dollars and twelve cents in your account."

This time, AJ whispers even louder. "I'm being held hostage by those two killers." AJ pivots his head to the left. "Right over there."

Tina and Tiny finish their argument and turn their attention back to AJ and the teller, whose face is drooping. "If you'll excuse me, I need to speak with my manager." AJ shrugs his shoulders at Tina, suggesting that everything is all right.

Not far away, the young teller whispers to the bank manager as AJ looks the lobby over for alternate exits. The thin-haired manager, wearing a pinstripe suit, studies the situation as he looks over at Tina and Tiny. Tina sees him staring her way, so she elbows Tiny in the ribs. The banker hesitates and pushes the alarm button under a counter. A red light above the teller windows starts to flash and a horn begins to blare.

AJ makes eye contact with Tina, whose face instantly turns white. She pulls a gun and Tiny follows suit. She points her .38 Special at AJ's chest. "You lying son of a bitch." Several bank customers see what's happening and either run out of the bank or duck for cover. Flustered, Tina and Tiny wave their guns at no one in particular. Tina yells, "Everyone, just stay calm!" She gathers her thoughts and aims her gun at the bank manager.

"You!"

The sixty-year-old man's eyes widen as he fingers his chest. "Me?"

"Yeah, you. Does this asshole have seven million dollars in this bank or not?"

The manager checks the screen again. "Five dollars and twelve cents."

AJ turns to Tina. "I really was gonna make a deposit yesterday, but I must have changed my mind. I'm a little confused right now….Oh, now I remember where I put it."

At the next window over, Helga removes the German luger from her purse, aims it at Tina and Tiny, and fires away. Two bullets hit the counter, so the bank manager and teller hunker down. Tina growls at Helga. "What the hell?"

Speaking with a heavy German accent, Helga squawks, "You thieving arschochs! You leave that boy alone…or I don't miss next time. I shoot you all dead." Tina raises her gun, so Helga fires her weapon again, still not hitting anyone. Tiny ducks down and covers his ears while Tina stands frozen in place. Helga's last bullet ricochets off the floor, and grazes Tina's left breast. The sad-faced woman watches her inflatable falsie hiss and slowly deflate.

Tiny panics, lowers his hands from his face, grabs AJ and Tina by their arms, and drags them out of the bank. When they reach the car, Tiny tosses AJ in the backseat like a twenty-pound bag of potatoes while Tina hops in the driver's seat and speeds off.

In the back seat, Tiny holds his gun to AJ's head and he whimpers, "Okay. I lied again. I was trying to buy some time. Can't blame a guy for trying." Tiny holds his gun to AJ's head. AJ holds up his hands, "The money's in the bowling alley. If it's not there, you can shoot me as many times as you want."

The black Olds speeds off as police sirens sound in the distance.

AJ, Tiny, and Tina enter the bowling alley and find Dale at the front desk studying his cell phone. Rufus is behind the counter eating a bologna sandwich. When AJ's dog sees his owner, he wags his tail and rushes over to him. AJ pushes Rufus away. "No, boy…now is not a good time." Rufus whines and lays on the floor.

Tina pokes her gun into AJ's rib cage and warns, "Last chance, Peter Pan. If I don't see any money, you're headed straight to Never-Never Land."

AJ reacts by rapping his knuckles on the counter. Dale pockets his phone and AJ gets right to the point. "Hey, Dale. How's it going, buddy? Can I get the key to the equipment room?"

Dale stares at AJ. "What the hell, AJ. I've been watching your dog for almost two days now. I had to take him home last night."

"We'll talk later. Now is not a good time."

Dale opens a drawer, pulls out a key, and hands it to AJ. The shoe man finally notices Tina's mismatched breasts. Tina sees him staring, so Dale grabs a shoe and wipes off a speck of dirt.

Tina and Tiny follow AJ as Dale hollers, "Hey! You serious about giving me a raise?"

Not turning back, AJ says, "You betcha. I'll get right on it."

Dale pats Rufus on the head as he watches the kidnappers and their hostage disappear into the equipment room leading to the pinsetter machines.

Possum arrives and taps on the counter just as Dale starts to text someone. When he sees her, he pockets his phone and she asks, "What's going on with AJ?"

"Don't know. He wanted the key to the equipment room."

"And you gave it to him?"

"Why not? He's the boss."

Possum gives Dale a 'what are you talking about look' and looks in the direction of the equipment room. "Was he alone?"

"No, he had a couple of weirdos in black suits with him."

"Call the police and have them send someone right away. Something's not right." Dale shrugs and pokes a number into his phone as Possum grabs a bowling ball and heads for the equipment room door. She tries to open it, but it won't budge.

"AJ!" She waves back at Dale and yells. "I think it's stuck."

In the equipment room leading to the pinsetter area, Tiny and Tina search for any sign of money. Seeing nothing, Tina raises her gun, and AJ points at his two sofa cushions in the corner. "It's in there."

Tina glowers at Tiny as she adjusts one of her fake eyelashes. "Don't stand there like an idiot. Check it out." Tiny pulls a pocket knife, opens a blade, and begins to shred the cushions. He finds a few stray bills and hands them to Tina. She counts the money. "Two hundred twenty dollars? Where's the rest of it, you pissant?"

Tiny quips, "Ants don't piss."

Tina ignores him, sticks her gun in AJ's face, and he backs away. "Whoa, whoa, whoa. Easy. That's all that's left. I spent the rest."

She growls, "You spent seven million dollars?"

AJ shrugs. "I've never been good with money." Tiny pulls his pistol from his front pocket, but he hears something and spins around.

Possum, who has finally managed to open the door, is standing only a few feet away and holding a bowling ball like she's ready to roll. "Hey, pal!" She tosses the ball at the big man and screams, "Catch!" The twelve-pounder hits Tiny in the stomach, and he doubles over and drops his gun. AJ sees his chance and bolts off as Possum retreats out the equipment room door.

Tina fires at AJ, and the sound echoes so loud that Tiny covers his ears. "Get him, you dumb shit!" Tiny hustles after AJ, who by now has managed to scramble through one of the pin decks. Three young boys who have been bowling on the lane, stare as AJ clears the pins out of his way, hops to his feet, and scoots down the oily, hardwood lane trying to stay upright. He takes a few more steps, slips, and falls into the gutter at the top of the seventh lane.

Meanwhile, Tiny has managed to crawl through the pin deck on the next lane over. On his knees, he spots AJ, holds his gun in the air, and fires a warning shot. A ceiling tile falls on the big man's head as everyone in the bowling alley freezes, including AJ, who is sitting in the gutter rubbing his ankle.

Tiny struggles to his feet and aims his gun at AJ as several people scream and run out of the bowling alley. "Tell me where the money is, or I'm gonna end you." Still sitting, AJ puts his hands in the air as the big man slips and slides over to him. Tiny continues to aim his gun at AJ, while a few lanes over, Buster and Sam quietly pick up two balls. Out of patience, the big man cocks his weapon and waves it. "Show me the money, Tom Cruise."

AJ grimaces but manages to stand up. "Okay, man. Take it easy, and I'll…." Tiny steps back to make room for AJ, but his feet slip. AJ seizes the opportunity, limps over, and throws his shoulder into Tiny. The big man falls on his butt and drops his gun. AJ dives to the floor, and they wrestle for control of the weapon as people step back and dial 911 on their cell phones, while others hold their phones up and film the action. Several shots go off: BOOM, BOOM, BOOM! and the bystanders duck for cover again.

Brandishing her own gun, Tina skates over and points her gun at the wrestlers. "Hold it right there!" AJ and Tiny freeze. "Get away from that gun." They both scoot away. Tina scowls at Tiny. "Not you, dumb ass!"

Tiny picks up his pistol, stands up, and dusts himself off. "Thanks, babe, but I had it under control."

Tina points her .38 at AJ. "Here's what's gonna happen. You're going to walk over here, real slow, and I'm going to shoot you…" CRACK! AJ looks over at Possum who is smiling, having just smacked the back of Tina's head with a bowling pin.

Two lanes over, Buster yells, "Now!" Perfectly synchronized, Buster and Sam roll their bowling balls at Tiny with all their might! Ball after ball hit him and the big man's legs go out from under him. Dale flips on the black lights and Bee Gees' disco music starts to play. On cue, the rest of the bowlers, including an enraged Mrs. Jollymore, launch their weapons, and a herd of balls thunder down the lane headed for Tiny!

Sam yells, "Run, AJ! Run like the breeze!" AJ limps for the front door as Tiny is pummeled by ball after ball. Somehow, Tiny manages to reach his gun and gets off one last shot - BOOM!

The bullet hits AJ in the ass. "Gah!" He takes a step, drops to his knees, and tips over like a fainting goat.

Pissed, Buster heaves another bowling ball like a shot put and hits the big man square in the forehead - CRUNCH. Tiny sags to the floor like a sack of potatoes and squeezes his skull as if it's ready to explode.

The front door opens and two police officers and four paramedics rush in. The policemen wrestle Tiny for a while, but finally manage to put both he and Tina in handcuffs. While the cops usher the hoodlums out of the alley, the paramedics load AJ onto a gurney.

Things start to settle down when Officer Becker busts through the front door, pistol drawn. "Freeze!" Everyone looks at him like he's arrived two hours late for his own birthday party and laughs.

As the paramedics roll AJ out of the building, the new millionaire grumbles sarcastically at Becker, "Nice work." Disappointed, the policeman scans the bowling alley. "Is it over?" Possum sneers at Becker. "Yeah, ya kinda missed it."

"Well, shit." Becker lowers his gun and holsters it.

Chapter 42

Big Changes

AJ'S HOSPITAL ROOM WALLS ARE INDUSTRIAL white but decorated with colorful flowers and balloons, many shaped like bowling balls and pins.

AJ is lying in bed stiff as a board, his lower body covered in bandages. Next to him is Officer Becker, who is holding a notepad.

"That delay tactic you pulled at the bank almost got you killed you know."

AJ clears his nose. "If they would've found out I already spent the money, they'd have killed me for sure."

"Okay for the record, how did you spend the money so fast?"

AJ clears his throat. "Well, yesterday, I bought a suit, some flowers, my uncle's old house, 51% of USBC's stock, and the bowling alley."

A Day Earlier

Dressed in his new three-piece suit, AJ hustles down Main Street carrying the flowers he bought, a box of chocolates, and his two couch cushions. An older gentleman passes him, raises his eyebrows, and chuckles.

AJ sits in Antonio Giovanni's real estate office clutching his cushions, one in his left hand and the other in his right. The secretary in the outer office leers at him until the phone rings. She lifts the receiver, listens a moment, and says, "Mr. Giovanni will see you now."

An hour later, AJ pulls the "For Sale" sign out of the lawn in front of UJ's old house.

That afternoon at the USBC headquarters, AJ is seated across from corporate president and owner, Jim Jeffries, warehouse manager, Frank Kilroy, and real estate agent, Antonio Giovanni. Antonio hands AJ three documents. "Half of USBC, one house, and one bowling alley…all in one day." AJ stands up and shakes Antonio's hand as Frank slips out the door.

Antonio exits Gil Williams's office and shuts the door behind him as Gil curses loudly. When Antonio walks past Claudia, he winks at his daughter who is cleaning out her desk. "Your new office building will be ready to move into in a few days. I'm even having a sign made: 'Law Office of Claudia Giovanni.'"

Later that night, before he's supposed to meet up with Zooey at the diner, AJ pulls up to the Strike and Spare, still dressed in his new suit. He grabs his cushions, tethers Rufus, and makes his way inside. After he enters, he hands Rufus to Dale and starts for the bowling alley equipment room still carrying his cushions.

Officer Becker finishes writing his report and scratches his head. "Quite the spending spree, son. I did tell you to bring the money to me. Evidence, ya know?"

AJ rolls over on his side. "The way I figured it, this town's future shouldn't be decided by some jackass lawyer, so I took matters into my own hands. If that makes me a criminal, better put the cuffs on me."

"Well, as much as I should probably do that, you and that money have done some real good for this town."

"Any idea where my uncle got it?"

"If I were to guess, I'd say your friends Tina and Tiny have connections to the Mexican cartel."

"Heroin, cocaine, marijuana?"

"No, more like avocados and limes."

"What?"

"The illegal importation of avocados and limes."

"You've gotta be frickin' kidding me."

"Funny, huh? Suddenly, the cartel is all about diversification."

AJ mumbles, "Avocados and limes."

"Yeah, I don't know where your uncle fit in, but the captain's guess is he ran off with the money you found and tried to hide out here in Greenvale. Not sure about the Tina and Tiny connection, but my guess is they were sent here to find him and the money."

"Damn, UJ; moving home wasn't very smart."

"I think he wanted you to have the money."

"He was here two years; why'd he wait so long to contact me?"

"You need to take that up with him; I mean, if you believe in the hereafter." Becker puts on his hat. "I'd better go."

"Avocado and limes…and I don't have to give the money back?"

"Seeing as how we'll probably never be able to trace where that cash came from for sure, the captain thinks we can sort things out in your favor. I guess when all is said and done, it will be Greenvale's little secret."

AJ flips onto his side. "I still got a pickup full of crap if the captain needs a bribe."

"Very funny. I'll see you at the alley."

"Yeah, maybe not for a while."

As Becker exits, Buster, Sam, and Possum pour into the room.

Buster moves to the edge of AJ's bed. "Can't believe all of us being in a shootout! What was it like, being plugged in the ass?

"For one thing, it hurt like hell."

Sam pipes up. "Ya get to keep the bullet?"

AJ holds up a plastic bottle with the slug inside. Sam grabs it and rattles the bottle.

Possum scolds, "What's wrong with you two? He could have died on us."

Sam hands the bottle back. "Hey, whatever doesn't kill ya, only makes you stranger."

Buster taps AJ's bed. "Least it's your butt cheek and not your bowling arm."

"Excuse these idiots." Possum moves over and squeezes AJ's hand. "I'm happy you're alive."

S and B look at one another, nod, and run over and dog pile on AJ, who grimaces in pain. "Oooh! Ouch. Hey, careful. Got a gaping hole in my ass."

As they unpile, Buster mutters, "Don't we all?"

Sam turns serious. "With all that money, I'm surprised you didn't take off for yellower pastures?"

"Hey, friends are friends are friends. Money is only important if you don't have it."

Sam spins around in order to hide a tear. "Yeah, so…do we work for you now?"

"Technically, I guess. But I promoted Frank Kilroy to oversee USBC, so's I can run the alley and take care of all us bowlers."

Buster raises up. "You promoted Kilroy? He fired your ass."

"Yeah, I know, but I pretty much deserved to be fired."

Sam pipes up. "What about us?"

"What about you?"

"We get new jobs, too?"

"Yeah, I'm working on that. How are you and Buster at cleaning toilets?"

Sam gives AJ the finger. "Funny man."

While Sam and AJ talk about other job opportunities, Buster takes Possum aside and whispers in her ear. She quickly eyes Sam. "No, he doesn't."

Sam peers at Possum. "No, I don't what?"

She gives him the stink eye. "Buster says you got herpes."

"Lying son of Seabiscuit! I do not. Why you telling her that?"

"Cuz you're always grabbing your balls."

"It's a rash. And why are you spying on my junk? 'Sides, I haven't even popped my cherry yet."

Possum grimaces. "Gross, you don't have a cherry to pop."

Buster keeps going. "Wait. You've never mustarded your hot dog with anyone?"

"Only the very tip, but that doesn't count, does it?"

Possum scrunches her face. "Oh, God, help me."

Buster keeps trying. "I still say you got herpes."

"Do not."

"Do too."

"Do not."

"Prove it. Drop your pants."

Sam considers Buster's suggestion, unbuckles his belt, but changes his mind and hurries out of the room.

Possum slaps Buster's shoulder. "Now see what you did."

"It's every man for himself…. So if you ever need a father for that child you might be wanting, I can put a baby in you whenever you're in the mood."

"Don't get ahead of yourself. My zygotes are off limits."

"You a commitment-phobe?"

"No, but I've never been in a relationship before, let alone with two yahoos at the same time."

Two hours later, Buster makes a casual observation to AJ. "Course, now the Alley Oops are gonna need us a fill-in. Your ass ain't in no condition to bowl right now."

Zooey, having overheard Buster, enters the room and hurries over to AJ. "Count me in."

AJ sits up. "Zooey! I'm so…" She interrupts him with a giant kiss.

"I'd kiss your owie, but…people might talk."

Possum rolls her eyes. "Jeez, guys. Get a room!"

AJ grins. "You're in my room."

Buster taps Possum on the shoulder. "He's got a point."

Zooey takes AJ's hand. "I'm so glad you're okay."

"Weren't my time. We got lots to do." They kiss again.

Possum groans. "Come on."

Sam shows up and gives Possum a piece of paper. "What's this?" She reads it and hands it over to Buster.

He scours the report. "So, I was wrong."

AJ nods. "What's that all about?"

Possum chuckles. "A note from Sam's doctor saying he has a grapefruit rash."

Sam puckers his lips. “I do eat a lot of grapefruit.”

“Wow, good to know.” AJ grabs the slug bottle. “Where’s Zeke? He’s gonna wanna see this bullet they dug out of my ass.”

Zooey hops up. “I almost forgot. I’ve gotta pick him up from school. Right now, in fact. He'll be…”

Possum interrupts. “You stay here and catch up with each other. I’ll get him and bring him back here for show and tell.”

“Are you sure?”

“Yeah, I got this.”

“Thanks, Possum.”

Possum starts for the door, but not before she eyes Buster and Sam. “Back in a jiffy.” Possum pecks Buster on the lips.

AJ snickers. “Hey! I didn’t know you two were a thing.”

Not skipping a beat, she leans over and kisses Sam as well.

AJ raises up. “Whoa.”

Possum puts her arms around Sam and Buster and beams. “Once the eye has spoken, there's no turning back. Gotta keep everything even, so's to decrease jealousy.”

Buster glows. “Being with you is like having the keys to Disneyland.”

She checks with Sam. “What say you?”

“Half a Possum is better than no Possum at all.”

AJ shakes his head. “I’m happy for the three of you…I think?”

Buster raises his arms in the air like someone who just scored a touchdown. “Listen up. I’ve got something I wanna tell you.”

Possum rocks back. “Wow, Buster, so dramatic. Did you win the Wisconsin Powerball?”

He takes a moment. “I want everyone to call me Kumar from now on. That’s my real name.”

Sam rolls his eyes, “Kumar?”

“As you all know, my dad is from India, and that’s what he chose to name me. Buster is not who I am any more. I’m Kumar.”

Possum gives Kumar a hug and steps back. “Not to steal your thunder…Kumar, but as long as we’re at it, I think everyone should call me Natalie.”

Sam wags his head. "I've got nothing; I'm still Sam."

The three of them immediately dive in for a three-way hug. AJ winks at Zooey. "Wow, 'times they are a changin'."

Natalie breaks away from the huddle. "Gotta go. I need to pick up Zeke. Why don't you two come with me and give these lovebirds some alone time." She hooks arms with Sam and Kumar, and they hustle out the door.

Zooey takes AJ's hand. "You're friends are really something."

From the hallway, Sam yells. "Don't we know it!"

Chapter 43

A To Z

It's been a real time-suck for the last six months, but I'm pretty much back to normal. After I became the major shareholder at USBC, I made sure everyone there got to keep their jobs if they wanted them. I know it's favoritism, but I did add a few new positions. Natalie is now the Assistant Human Resources Director and Sam and Kumar work in the new product design office. Like Sam always says, "You scratch my ass, and I'll scratch yours."

Even though I have a hitch in my giddy-up from being shot in the butt, I'm moving okay. I've had to adjust my game though, cuz my ball kept curving to the right. I throw an old-school straight ball now, but the good thing is, I'm back to knocking down the pins three or four times a week. And something else; After I got out of the hospital, I gave up beer altogether. I know it's Wisconsin, but it's one of the best decisions I've ever made. My three amigos even joined my abstinence in solidarity…but they only committed to two months. I still go to The Watering Hole with Zooey and the gang, but I only drink hop water…which makes Zooey happy.

Kumar, Natalie, and Sam moved in together. Matter of fact, I'm renting them Uncle Julius' old house. I don't charge them hardly anything, because they said they'd fix it up…which I know they won't. The neighbors talk a lot about them being a throuple, but they don't mind cuz they're happy.

Okay, so here's another update. Natalie finished fifth in the Milwaukee Open five months ago, so she's been competing in all kinds of PWBA tournaments…mostly in the Midwest. Go figure, USBC is sponsoring her.

Tina and Tiny's trial was last month. They were both convicted of killing Julius. The dumb shits left the arsenic bottle that killed him and a pizza box in the trunk of their car. UJ's spit was all over the lip of the bottle. The authorities never did find out for sure if those idiots were connected to UJ and his money but you've gotta know they were. Anyway, Tina got what she deserved…forty years in prison. Tiny, he only got thirty years. Something about his IQ being so low. No offense to dumb people, but sometimes it's good to be stupid. At least for now, I won't be looking over my shoulder for Tiny and his shovel.

In case you're wondering about me and Zooey, let me set the scene. Last week, we had the grand opening of my bowling alley, and there were scads of people in the parking lot waiting for my big reveal and, of course, they were shoveling in free pizza and pop. Anyway, me, Kumar, Sam, and Natalie, who is no longer wearing an eyepatch by the way, were all standing around trying to look important. That went on for a while until I scanned the crowd and saw Frank Kilroy. We made eye contact, and Frank came over to me like he was still my boss. I nodded and Frank gave me a grin I've never seen him give me before. "Thanks for saving USBC, AJ…and for not firing me…oh, and for the promotion."

"Water under the bridge, Frank. Tell Lacey I said hi." Happy to have buried the hatchet, I shuffled over to this canvas tarp covering the old Strike and Spare marquee as everyone watched me like they knew something was up.

Before I could say anything, Kumar, who I still once in a while to call Buster, picked up the snow contest sign and read the first part of it to the crowd: "Guess the day this snow pile completely melts..." Being the smartass he always is, he checked his phone and smiled ear to ear. "Hey, Mr. Owner, I guessed the right day! You gonna honor this?"

"What would be the point? You bowl for free anyway." Sam and Kumar high-fived one another and scampered off… but that wasn't the surprise.

What happened next was Zooey's car pulled up, and I ran over, and we x'ed and o'ed each other until the crowd started to boo. I waved them off and helped a blindfolded Zeke out of the car. The two of us guided him to the front of the building as he complained, "I don't wanna blind anymore. Can I take this off now?"

I patted Zeke on the head. "Not yet. Just a little bit longer."

Natalie, not exactly known for being a patient woman and having been half-blind herself for a long time scolded me. "Jeez loueez, let him see what's going on!"

Not wanting to drag the whole thing out, I guided Zeke to the front of the building. "All right, stand right here."

The time was right, so Zooey untied Zeke's blindfold and I signaled Kumar and Sam to do their job. They hammed it up like they were about to reveal the *Mona Lisa* and finally lowered the tarp. Everyone cheered when they saw the flashing neon sign, A to Z Bowling.

I looked over and watched as Zeke's eyes lit up. Then he turned to me and said, "Awesome! Are me and Mom the Z?"

"You know it. Like it?"

"I love it!"

Zooey joined us, and we hugged each other like a real family. When things calmed down, I pretended not to listen as Zeke pulled Zooey aside, leaned down, and whispered, "I'm gonna get my face on the wall like you did. Wait and see!"

Then I watched as Zeke finally noticed Natalie's missing eye patch and walked over to her. "Hey, what happened to your patch?"

With a sparkle in both her eyes, Natalie turned to me. "A good friend of mine paid to have it fixed."

"You's pretty, Pos…Natalie."

Together, Sam and Kumar repeated, "You's pretty Natalie."

Natalie instantly grabbed Sam and Kumar's hands and pulled them in for a three-way hug.

I pulled Zeke aside and pointed at the building. "The outside needs a paint job, so I'm thinking I'll let you and your mom decide on the color."

Zeke shot back like he'd already been thinking about it. "Brewer blue."

Then Zooey squinted her eyes and studied the building. "How about a nice rustic red?"

"Red's boring, Mom."

"What makes blue so much better?"

Seizing the opportunity for a little fun, Kumar grinned at Sam and me and said, "You thinking what I'm thinking?"

In unison, Sam and Kumar yelled, "Bowl Off!"

Everyone around us jumped on the bandwagon and screamed back, "Bowl Off!"

Confused, Zeke's eyes lit up again. "What's a bowl off?"

Not bothering to explain, Sam and Natalie started to gather beer bottles from garbage cans, while I ran into my bowling alley and fetched a couple of light-weight balls.

Sam helped me place twenty bottles in two bowling pin formations as I listened in as Natalie gave Zeke some advice. "You must learn these ways, young Padawan."

Kumar, who quickly appointed himself as emcee, jumped up on a box, and hollered, "Zeke, you bowl for team 'Brewer Blue,' and Zooey, you're team 'Rustic Red.' Two throws each. Once the bottles have spoken, it's binding!"

Zeke gave me this puzzled look and said, "I don't get it."

I tried to simplify it. "You knock more bottles down than your mom, and we paint A to Z Bowling Brewer blue."

Before I could say another word, Zeke gave me a high-five and yelled, "Cool!"

Everyone started to gather around as Kumar stepped up, handed the eleven-year-old boy a ball, and yelled, "Give it all you got, Zeker."

I watched as Zeke took aim and let his eight-pounder fly. People cheered as his ball rolled across the parking lot and smashed all ten bottles. There were high-fives all around as the four of us began to sing *Alley-Oop* and everyone joined in.

Seconds later, I watched as Zooey prepared to roll, the A to Z sign glowing behind her. When she released her ball, I reached in my pocket and squeezed the diamond ring I had hidden there.

THE END

AFTERWORD

HELGA CLODFELTER, WHO looks out of place in the Greenvale policemen's shooting gallery, stands next to Sergeant Becker. She's wearing protective eyewear and is dressed in a bright purple muumuu. She raises her German Luger, takes aim, and fires six successive shots that hit the target dead center. Becker pats Helga on the back, and she surprises him by kissing him on the cheek.

A HALF-NAKED MAN, lying face down on his bed, is being massaged by two large hands. As the giant masseuse works his way down the man's back, he gets a little too close to his cellmate's rear end. The smaller inmate sits up, slaps the big man across the face, and pushes him away. Tiny Riley, dressed in an orange jump-suit, shuffles over to his cell door, grabs the bars, and stares at the courtyard below.

VICKI WILLIAMS IS standing outside her bedroom cradling her recently completed miniature guillotine. She cracks the door open and peeks inside at her snoring husband, Gil. She tiptoes inside, closes the door quietly behind her, and a few seconds later, there's a horrible scream.

THEODORE ENNIS, DRESSED in a black tuxedo, steps out of a Las Vegas wedding chapel, making sure it's safe to exit. A moment later, his bride Jennifer-Hill-Ennis emerges wearing a white sequined wedding dress. She tosses her bouquet in the air and the happy couple runs off hand in hand. The door swings open again, and Dale Samuels from the Strike and Spare bursts out carrying Sam and Jennifer's mother, Vanessa Hill.

FACTS ABOUT BOWLING

*The earliest evidence of any form of bowling dates to 3200 BC and ancient Egypt.
*King Henry XIII loved to bowl and was said to have used cannonballs to knock down pins. He's also known for banning the lower class from playing the game.
*Built in 1840, New York, "Knickerbockers" was the first indoor bowling alley.
*People viewed the first bowling game on television in 1950.
*The American Bowling Congress deemed bowling a gentlemen's sport and women were not allowed to bowl until 1917, when the Women's Bowling Association was formed.
*The heaviest legal weight of a bowling ball is 16 pounds, but they have been known to weigh as much as 24 pounds.
*Most bowling balls have 3 holes, but they can be customized to have as many as 12.
*In 4th century Germany, churches held bowling rituals as a way for people to cleanse their sins. Monks would set up pins called kegels and throw stones at them, thus conquering sin.
*Nine-pin bowling at one time was considered a dangerous sport and banned by the government, so people got around the law by using ten pins.
*Bowling balls have specially shaped cores and fillings that improve the balance and hook.

Some of the above information was taken from the *US Bowling Corporation Website* (February 14th, 2021) *murreybowling.com*

ABOUT THE AUTHOR

Daniel Landes retired from South Dakota State University in 2011, where he served as an Assistant Dean of Arts and Sciences and as a professor of English.

Originally from Williston, North Dakota, Dan grew up in Great Falls, Montana, where he graduated from C.M. Russell High School. He went on to earn a Bachelor of Science degree in History at Minot State University, a Master of Science degree in English at Bemidji State University, and a Ph.D. in English from the University of North Dakota. He and his wife Martha live in Rio Rancho, New Mexico, where Dan continues to pursue his love of writing, film production, bicycling, and distance running.